THE CALL OF THE RIFT
FLIGHT

JAE WALLER

Published by ECW Press
665 Gerrard Street East
Toronto, Ontario, Canada M4M 1Y2
416-694-3348 / info@ecwpress.com

MIX
Paper from
responsible sources
FSC® C016245
www.fsc.org

This is a work of fiction. Names, characters,
places, and incidents either are the product
of the author's imagination or are used
fictitiously, and any resemblance to
actual persons, living or dead, business
establishments, events, or locales is entirely
coincidental.

LIBRARY AND ARCHIVES CANADA
CATALOGUING IN PUBLICATION

Waller, Jae, author
The call of the rift : flight / Jae Waller.

Issued in print and electronic formats.
ISBN 978-1-77041-354-2 (hardcover).
ALSO ISSUED AS: 978-1-77305-156-7 (PDF),
978-1-77305-155-0 (EPUB)

I. TITLE.

PS8645.A4679C35 2018   C813'.6
C2017-906217-4   C2017-906218-2

Editor: Susan Renouf
Cover design: Erik Mohr (Made By Emblem)
Cover illustration: © Simon Carr/
www.scarrindustries.com
Maps: Tiffany Munro/
www.feedthemultiverse.com

The publication of *The Call of the Rift: Flight* has been generously supported by the Canada
Council for the Arts which last year invested $153 million to bring the arts to Canadians
throughout the country, and by the Government of Canada through the Canada Book Fund.
*Nous remercions le Conseil des arts du Canada de son soutien. L'an dernier, le Conseil a investi 153
millions de dollars pour mettre de l'art dans la vie des Canadiennes et des Canadiens de tout le pays.
Ce livre est financé en partie par le gouvernement du Canada.* We also acknowledge the Ontario
Arts Council (OAC), an agency of the Government of Ontario, and the contribution of the
Government of Ontario through the Ontario Book Publishing Tax Credit and the Ontario
Media Development Corporation.

ONTARIO ARTS COUNCIL
CONSEIL DES ARTS DE L'ONTARIO
an Ontario government agency
un organisme du gouvernement de l'Ontario

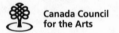

Canada Council
for the Arts

Conseil des Arts
du Canada

Canada

PRINTED AND BOUND IN CANADA   PRINTING: FRIESENS   5   4   3   2   1

For Rob, my one and always

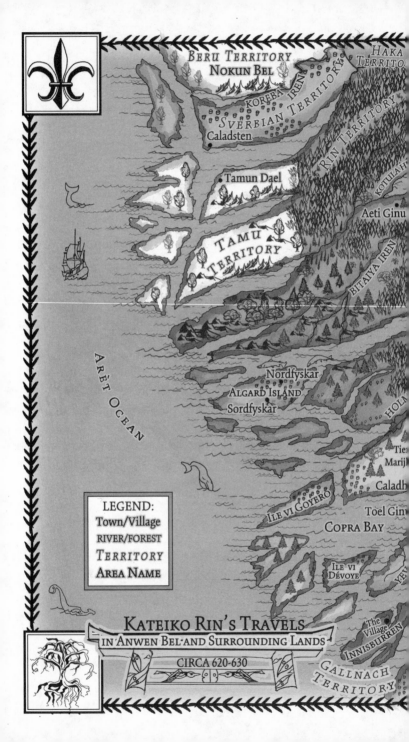

KOTULA IREN

•Vunfjel

TURQUOISE MOUNTAINS

NYHEMUR

NWEN BEL

VASTELAND

OBERU IREN

Sky Bridge•

Se Ji Ainu•

Dúnravn Pass

IYUN BEL

TØMMBRIND CREEK

•Crieknaast

ROANNVELDT

IYO TERRITORY

STENGAR

IYUN BEL

Rutnaast•

•Ingdanrad

N

IRREN INLET

EREMUR

E TERRITORY

YULA TERRITORY

Laca vi Miero•

UKAN BEL HÁRENGAR

0   30   60KM

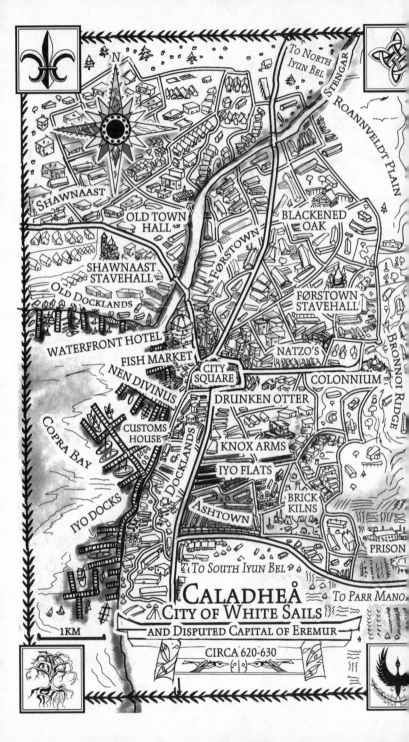

1.

AELDU-YAN

"Ouch!" I cursed under my breath and sucked on the line of blood that appeared across my thumb.

"You're doing it wrong." Fendul took my hunting knife and peeled a curl of dark wood from the palm-sized figurine. "Hold it like this. You'll stab yourself in the gut otherwise."

"Nei. It doesn't work that way." I yanked it back from him.

We sat cross-legged on the rocky beach of Kotula Huin, a still, glacial lake. Drifts of fog surrounded us. Colossal hills loomed over the valley, its dense layer of trees barely visible against the dark sky. A dull pink glow silhouetted the jagged peaks to our right. Behind us, the forest dripped. My fingers were too damp to grip the rawhide cord wrapped around my bone knife.

Voices drifted down the shoreline. "Don't you have somewhere to be?" I asked.

Fendul shrugged. "Not until the ceremony starts."

"So you're up this early for the fun of it." I rolled my eyes. I'd been awake for an hour already drying wood for a bonfire, along with my aunt Isu and three others who'd spent years learning to call water. Our skills weren't usually required so early in the morning, otherwise I might've been more reluctant to learn. Not that I had much choice. As the eldest — and only — child of an antayul, I was bound by custom to become one as well.

I bent my head over the driftwood. In my peripheral vision, I saw Fendul tossing a stone from hand to hand.

"Can you stop that?"

The stone fell with a clatter. "Concentration conquers distraction."

"Don't underestimate yourself," I muttered.

"Ever consider I'm not the problem?"

"Ever consider shutting up?" I tossed my knife away and flopped backward, piling my hair into a pillow.

Fendul's face appeared in my field of vision. We shared the same dark eyes, sharp features, and wiry build. Even after a summer apart, our skin had tanned to the same warm, muted shade — but while my light brown hair spilled past my waist, his hair was charcoal black and cropped short. We didn't have much choice in that either. He couldn't grow his long until he married. I'd never been allowed to cut my hair and never would be.

His amulet swung back and forth as he leaned over me. I reached up as if to touch the crow, carved from a black shark tooth, then pushed on Fendul's bare chest. "You're blocking my view."

"Of what? It's barely light."

"Of the clouds, bludgehead."

"Come on. Try again." He grabbed my hand and pulled me upright. I sighed and picked up the knife, letting him place my hands in what he insisted was the right position.

"What is that? A fox?" he asked.

"Nei." I could hear the pressure to elaborate. "It's a wolf."

"That's not the colour used for wolves. Lighter wood is more suited to . . ."

I stared at him. He trailed off. Without breaking eye contact, I flipped the figurine over my shoulder. It rustled through some bushes and thumped to the ground. He muttered something that sounded like "immature."

The clouds were brightening, turning pale pink and white like the smooth rocks I used to collect from creeks. The lake was turning turquoise. I stood up and sheathed the knife at my back next to my throwing dagger. "I'm going to find Nili."

I wandered down the shore. The beach would only exist for a few more days now that the autumn rains had started. Kotula Huin sat in the eastern reaches of Anwen Bel, a rainforest where everything was wet, covered in moss, or covered in wet moss.

Dozens of canoes made from hollowed tree trunks had been pulled up past flood level. My father had carved our family's canoe. A thin-billed kinaru with its long slender neck rose from the prow, its wings flowing down the sides. Supposedly our ancestors came from a kinaru egg laid on this very spot. Our tribe's name, the Rin-jouyen, was an ancient term for *people of the lakeshore*.

These days I shared our canoe with Isu, my mother's sister. We'd just returned from the east where we traded every summer with itherans, the foreigners who settled around our lands. My hair still smelled like goat from their alpine pastures. The remaining Rin had trickled in last night, exhausted after canoeing the lakes and rivers of Anwen Bel on their own trading trips.

Past the canoes, at the tip of a small peninsula, stood a pyramid of stacked driftwood. Drummers, carrying their hide drums on straps around their hips, stood angled toward it. Dancers faced them from the far side, their embroidered shawls making surreal silhouettes in the dawn light. I barely had time to notice Nili's absence before she dashed out of the forest, clouds of dark brown hair flying, her shawl streaming behind her.

"Help." She thrust out a handful of tangled black ribbon and a thin polished stick.

I gathered her hair into a tail and tied it with a ribbon. "Every year, Nili." I wouldn't have done it for anyone else. Hair was as sacred as the heart or blood and was bound by even more taboos, but Nili and I were long past the point where that mattered.

She half-turned, her round cheeks wide with a grin. "Isu said the firewood was done a while ago. What've you been doing?"

"Wasting my time." I slid the stick into Nili's hair and tied ribbons to each end so they hung down to her shoulders. "Fen thinks he can teach me to carve."

"Fendul couldn't teach a fish to swim. Don't let it get to you, ai?"

"Yeah. Whatever." I knotted her shawl laces around her wrists. "There. Get in place."

"I'll find you later." Nili waved and stepped into the dancers' line.

Fendul now stood on the opposite side of the bonfire from his father, Behadul. Both held lit torches. As sunrise crept closer, the rest of the Rin assembled on the shore, leaving gaps for those we'd lost. The dead took up more space than the living. We were a small jouyen now, just over a hundred people left. The elders said we once had thirteen thousand.

Among the gathered Rin, Isu turned, looking for me. I retreated under cover of the trees. Antayul were expected to watch and sing along. Not talk, not move, not be disturbed that six years ago I found my cousin, Isu's elder son, washed ashore here — months *after* we buried him. Storms had uprooted his grave and dumped his body in the lake. We could only tell it was him from his tattoos.

The elders said it was a blessing he returned to our sacred place of origin. Every autumn ceremony since then, I'd stood at Isu's side twisting snare wire around my hands until they bled, watching the lake, wondering which of my eight dead cousins would turn up next. This year I'd had enough.

A drum boomed as the sun burst over the mountains. Behadul and Fendul lowered their torches to the tinder. Flames licked up the pyramid. They retreated to the base of the peninsula, their torches forming a triangle with the bonfire. Drummers filed into a half-circle around the fire, swaying and stamping their feet as they pounded drum skins with leather mallets.

Dancers whirled and moved their arms like birds soaring across the sky and diving to earth. Their shawls — black outside and white inside, like kinaru wings — billowed out behind them. Clusters of crow feathers in their hands sliced the air. The dancers seemed to float above the earth, a second away from taking flight into an invisible world just out of reach.

Drumbeats echoed off the slopes. Behadul's voice resonated in a chant. The others joined until the entire jouyen called out to the lake valley. Legend said that the drums were loud enough to be heard in Aeldu-yan, the spirit world of our ancestral dead, and the echoes were the spirits' reply. The ceremony announced our return home from our summer travels.

Or, in my cousin's case, from his grave.

The music compelled me to move. No one would notice me back here. The spiritual stuff was bearshit, as far as I could tell. Dancing just kept me from thinking. Looking. Remembering.

I spun in a circle, eyes shut tight. I felt the familiar tingle in my fingers as I called water to me, and tendrils flowed out from my fingertips and snapped through the air. Then, everything changed. The tingle crept up through my chest and into the back of my skull. I opened my eyes.

Maybe it was the dawn light, fog in the valley, or smoke from the bonfire, but suddenly the world opened up, and I could see through to the other side — to Aeldu-yan.

My heart thudded. I didn't want to see my cousin's mottled, bloated face again.

Dizziness rolled over me. My water whips dissipated as I stumbled and fell to my knees. I blinked until my eyes focused on an immense rioden tree on the near shore. Its branches sprawled green and lush. I leaned sideways until my hair brushed the ground and I nearly tipped over — and the smudges of green vanished from the rioden, and it was once again black and bare, as it had been for the six years since lightning had struck it.

Rin elders said that the spirit world, Aeldu-yan, was a quiet forest that never changed. I always wondered how they knew. Curiosity battled with fear. I stretched out my arm, but the void drifted beyond reach.

*

An odd feeling lingered after the dance ended and the bonfire was extinguished, when the drums were just an echo in my head. I waited until the others dispersed before I drifted down to the lakeshore. Water lapped at the toes of my boots. The air smelled of fish and woodsmoke.

Nili appeared at my side. "What're you looking at?"

"I . . . don't know." I turned away from the lake and looked down at her bright eyes.

Nili was two years older but half a head shorter than me. She had a feather tattooed on each forearm that marked her as a dancer. Sweat gleamed over the kinaru inked on her upper left arm, its wings spread and long neck held straight — the same crest all Rin had.

"Do you ever . . . see anything weird when you're dancing?" I asked.

"Hmm." She bounced on the balls of her feet, ribbons swaying. "Sometimes it's like I can see the earth from above. Why?"

I had no idea what that meant. "Never mind."

"Let's go then. I'm starving." Nili ran back up the beach ahead of me.

I followed her into the forest. Auburn rioden swelled above me, their crowns a green blur in the fog. I shoved aside prickly branches that sprang back into place and flicked dew into the air. Evergreen needles carpeted the dirt. The damp was smothering after dawn in the open valley.

We emerged into a cluster of tents. They were more of a formality than proper shelter, just thin canvas panels roped to branches and staked into the ground. Nili left to find her mother and brother while I went to the tent I shared with Isu.

"Kateiko," Isu said. "Where did you run off to this morning?"

"I was with Fendul."

Isu skewered a fish and set it on the fire. She was lean and had calloused hands and greying hair. "You've been spending a lot of time with him since we got back."

"Only because boys keep hanging around Nili. It's like they forgot what she looks like over summer. Even Fendul's less annoying."

Isu huffed. As she turned away, she might've smiled. Maybe that'd distract her from asking where I went during the ceremony.

Breakfast was hurried, followed by stripping the camp. I half-listened to Nili's chatter as we set off in a winding column of people, wicker carryframes on our backs. Anwen Bel looked the same as always, glowing with yellow and white mushrooms, orange lichen, and a thousand shades of green — but something breathed under the surface. Some world I'd never believed in.

"I wish I attuned to a bird," Nili said hours later as we climbed Aeti Ginu on wooden steps half-hidden under clumps of feathery ferns and roots thicker than a man's waist. "Imagine if we could fly up this mountain."

"You wouldn't be able to fly with a carryframe," I said.

"Then I'd be a giant bird. Maybe a kinaru. Yeah, a kinaru would be good—"

"Kinaru don't exist," her younger brother, Yironem, said in front of us. "Mudskull."

Nili threw a scaly hemlock cone at him. It bounced off his head. She dropped her carryframe and ran laughing into the trees, skidding down the slope as he pelted her with cones. I rolled my eyes. A brawny drummer lingered by her carryframe as the rest of us went on.

The steps were almost vertical in places and I was out of breath by the time I reached the top — home. Aeti Ginu's plateau, mostly grass with clusters of berry-laden bushes, was the highest point within a day's hike. To the west, the wooded slopes were teal from haze. The eastern range was white with snow.

People trickled between narrow plank houses that stood like scattered sentinels, sod roofs covered with fuzzy moss. Aeti Ginu always looked bleak when we returned in autumn. Fishing nets gone from the walls, wooden racks for fur tanning packed away. When I shouldered open the door to my house, a flock of squawking birds retreated to the roof.

Isu put me to work immediately. I dragged mattresses outside and dumped reeking straw down the mountain. I scrubbed the canvas and gathered fresh grass to stuff inside. As I drew the last bit of moisture out of the blades, the tingling I'd felt at the lake crept into my chest like an itch that couldn't be scratched away.

Behadul and Fendul were at the far end of our plank house

when I went back in. I watched them talk as I arranged the mattresses on low dirt platforms. They stood straight-backed, hands on their sword hilts. They both wore breeches laced at the knees above their boots, their arms and chests bare. I wondered if Fendul would look like his father in thirty years. I pictured him with a long grey braid and stifled a laugh.

I flumped back onto my bed and stared at the vaulted ceiling. The house was too big. Too empty. Its one room could fit eight, maybe ten families, who would gather around the fire in winter to share food and stories under the gaze of wooden figurines on the mantelpiece. But it was just the four of us and the row of carved birds and bears and wolves.

Sometimes, during windstorms, it sounded like the figurines were howling. Isu said it was the voices of people who used to live in our plank house. I said they should find someone else to bother. They made it impossible to sleep.

Fendul interrupted my thoughts. "We should keep busy. There's a lot to do before dark."

I sat up and looked for Behadul, but he was gone. "It's barely afternoon."

"If we finish early, maybe we can go set some snares."

An opportunity to escape Isu. I ducked my head so he wouldn't see the smile that tugged at my lips. A thought surfaced that I'd rolled around until it was worn smooth. I hadn't planned to bring it up yet, but I couldn't wait any longer. "Fen, I need your help."

"With what?" He sank to the ground, sitting cross-legged with his elbows on his knees.

I dug my fingernails into the packed dirt. "I want to visit the Iyo-jouyen."

"You can't. You know the route to their territory is ruined."

"The storms were six years ago. It can't be that bad."

Fendul studied me, his dark brows drawn together. "Who's going with you?"

"Nili. Her mother already agreed. And . . . Isu said I can go if you come with us."

"Kako, you don't know what you're asking." He pinched his temples with a thumb and a forefinger. "What do you want? To see the ocean? You always complained your parents never took you."

I flicked dirt out of my nails. "It's not about that. I haven't seen Dunehein, my own cousin — my *last* cousin — since he married into the Iyo. Don't you want to see all the Rin who left?"

"It doesn't matter what I want."

"Then do it for us. You're the okoreni, the future leader of the Rin-jouyen. You're supposed to help with this stuff."

My gaze brushed over Fendul's tattoos. The kinaru on his left arm was wreathed by black huckleberries from his mother's crest. One day, the interlocking lines around his upper right arm, a finger-width shy of a circle, would be joined just like his father's.

Fendul hadn't been first in line for okoreni. His parents had two daughters before him. Neither girl reached a year — some foreign illness from itherans. Fendul, the third and last child, lived. He was eight when his father became okorebai and he became okoreni. He hadn't even been initiated into adulthood yet.

Growing up, I admired one thing about Fendul. Alongside me, he learned to trap game and tan furs, alongside Nili, to sew and weave, plus he helped the woodcarvers, herbalists, leatherworkers — all so he'd understand the work of the people he was bound by blood to lead. That hadn't stopped ten-year-old me from rubbing itchbine leaves in his gloves after he reset my snares the "proper" way. Or thirteen-year-old me from filling his bed with ice after he told Isu I snuck off to meet a canoe carver's apprentice among the huckleberry bushes.

He shifted his hand over his okoreni tattoo. "We can't go south, Kako."

"I need to get out of here, Fen. Something happened this morning. I saw the sacred rioden whole again. There's only one place dead things come back to life."

"Aeldu-yan." He was silent while it sank in. "We should feel fortunate to see it."

I snorted. "To glimpse a sliver of something, not enough to know if it's real? That's how people go insane."

"Then we'll find a way to prove it's real."

"I don't *want* it to be. Aeldu-yan never changes, but what about the aeldu? Burying my parents and cousins was bad enough. I don't want to see them after they've been dead for six years, wounds, rot, and all. I want to see my living family again."

He chopped a hand through the air. "No. My father will never agree."

"Fine," I snapped. "I'll figure out some other way so you don't have to get involved." I brushed chaff off my legs and stalked off.

✳

"I don't know what this is, but it's mine now." Nili collapsed next to me with a dramatic puff of breath. She bit off a piece of something pale yellow and leathery and spoke between chews. "Huh. Some dried itheran fruit. Not sure it was worth the fight."

"He let you win and you know it," I said.

Nili stuck her tongue out at me. "What's with you tonight?"

We were gathered around a firepit with other Rin our age, too old to be with the children, too young to have our own. Everyone we were permitted to marry was here. Which would mean coming right back here, every year, to houses full of the dead. Marrying a Rin was like choosing to only eat liver for the rest of my life.

People passed around a bottle of clear rye alcohol someone had bartered. Itherans called it *brännvin*, their word for "burn-wine." Yironem and his best friend looked scrawny amid a cluster of older boys playing dice. Yironem used to sit with Nili and me, until this spring when he turned thirteen and decided he didn't want a sister.

The brawny drummer that Nili had just fought a tug-of-war with stared at her from across the fire. Nili's ex-lover Orelein, twenty-one and thin as a javelin, stared at the drummer. The arrow Orelein was whittling snapped in his hands. He'd also sat with us until this spring when Nili decided she didn't want a lover — or at least, not him.

"Ore was like this all summer," Nili grumbled. "Talk about a mood-killer. I can't stay here and watch him sulk all winter, too."

"You might have to." I watched Fendul pass the brännvin on without taking a drink. "Fen won't do it. I asked earlier."

"Ass." Nili waved her half-eaten fruit around. "So, what now?"

"I don't know." I ran a finger over grass forcing its way up between two flagstones. "Let's go to the shrine. The star rain should start soon."

We looped around a few buildings to get out of sight. There was just enough moonlight to see by as we kicked our way through tall grass. Nili hummed to herself, occasionally spinning in circles like a spectral vestige of the lake dance.

The tiered shrine was the tallest building on Aeti Ginu, built at the edge of the western cliff. A towering gateway marked the entrance. Its posts were thick rioden logs with carvings of birds and twisting vines. The lintel displayed a row of kinaru, wings folded as if diving through the air. We were halfway up the dirt stairs when I heard footsteps.

"Unless you changed your mind, piss off," I said.

Fendul hesitated under the gate. "Kako, it's not up to me."

I ignored him and headed to the strip of ground behind the shrine. I lit a stone lantern as tall as my chest and replaced the latticed cover. The fish oil in the lantern well reeked from sitting out all summer. Light danced across the earth, cutting off where the cliff dropped away into darkness. The lantern was meant to signal the aeldu. If I was stuck here, maybe it was worth proving Aeldu-yan didn't exist. That my vision was just a fluke hallucination.

Narrow balconies wrapped around each of the shrine's three storeys. I climbed up their railings and gutters and pulled myself onto the rough shingles of the roof, my flail clanking at my side. I rarely took my weapons off except to sleep. Their weight on my belt was as familiar as a pair of worn boots.

Fendul shifted from foot to foot as if the aeldu were going to rise out of the earth. "We shouldn't be here. And you *really* shouldn't be on the roof."

"Ooh, the okoreni is mad. We're in for it now." Nili scrambled onto the shingles next to me.

He crossed his arms over his chest. "This is sacred ground."

"So sacred we stuck a building on it." I held out my arms as I walked along the slanted roof. Firelight glowed back by the plank houses. The mountains of Anwen Bel sprawled out in the distance.

"Ai! I saw the first one!" Nili cried.

"Shit." I flipped her an iron coin. Most of our trade was for food, tools, or cloth, but Nili and I kept a few itheran coins for betting. "I was sure I'd get it this year."

"You're breaking this many laws just to bet on falling stars?" Fendul asked in disbelief.

Nili's laugh exploded through the night. "Y'have to come up here for the best view!"

"Don't encourage him," I muttered.

Fendul's head appeared at the edge of the roof, followed by his body. "Do you two come to the shrine during every star rain?"

"Yeah. I imagine a star barrelling into you." I sat down and beamed at him. "Maybe this year. Punishment for violating sacred ground with us."

"I need to pee," Nili announced. She slid off the roof and disappeared.

Fendul fiddled with his crow amulet. "Can we talk about—"

"Nei."

"Kateiko." The exasperation in his voice was clear. "Why are you mad at me?"

"Because you're an ass."

"Kako?" Nili called, more tentative than I'd ever heard. "There's something down here."

"Ai?" I leaned over the edge. "Probably bats. The lantern might've disturbed them."

"I don't think so." Nili stared into the grass.

"Well, come back up, and—" I paused when I saw large amber eyes glint in the firelight.

A knee-high cat slunk forward on paws the size of my hands. Sharp tufted ears, mottled fur, knob tail. It yowled, revealing thick fangs.

"What *is* it?" Nili backed away, trapped between the shrine and the cliff.

"Snowcat." Fendul jumped down and drew his sword. I was right behind him.

The cat held its ground. I held its gaze, barely daring to breathe. A scar crossed its left eye. Every story I'd heard about snowcats ran through my head. They could swim rushing rivers, walk on snow without sinking, tear apart full-grown elk.

Fendul leapt forward. He cut a swath through grass as the cat shied away. He lunged again and opened a gash in its side. Blood spattered the ground.

"Don't kill it!" I cried — and I wasn't sure why, but I grabbed Fendul's arm and pulled him back. He stumbled into the lantern. It tipped, the stone cover rolling away.

"What's wrong with you?" he yelled.

"It's not attacking! Look!" I flung my hand out. The cat hissed.

"Idiot!" Fendul pushed me toward Nili without taking his eyes off the cat — but there was another problem. Burning grass rippled around the lantern, spitting out sparks.

"*Kaid*," I swore and lifted my arms. A wave of water rose from the earth and crashed onto the flames. I called up another wave—

—and the world split again. There was Aeldu-yan, its wooded mountains shimmering. Smoke and steam poured into the air and stopped at the cliff edge, swirling back like a diverted creek. I staggered toward the shrine. The railing collided with my ribs.

"Kako!" Nili pulled my arm over her shoulder and began to drag me away.

"Wait," I tried to say, but I could only gasp for breath. I looked up to get Nili's attention and instead found the last person I wanted to see.

Behadul stood at the corner of the shrine. I whirled, hearing his javelin cut the air, and saw the iron head sink into the snowcat's chest.

The animal shrieked. It reeled backward and tumbled over the cliff — and then there was silence. A single star streaked across the sky and winked out.

❋

"Explain," Behadul said to Fendul. He had dismissed the rest of the jouyen with a sweep of his arm. They scattered, shutting doors and windows behind them. The last person I saw was the eldest of the elders, her wrinkled face fixed on me with loathing.

We stood by the firepits, facing Behadul, Isu, and Nili's mother, Hiyua. Nili gripped my hand. It felt like a river shark had its teeth in my stomach. I silently begged Fendul to lie. *Say we lit the lantern to scare the cat off. Leave out the roof.*

Fendul took a deep breath. "I followed Kateiko and Nisali to the shrine. The snowcat was hiding in the grass. We didn't notice at first because we — we were on the roof."

I felt like he'd backhanded me with the flat of his blade. Nili wilted beside me.

His knuckles were tight on the hilt of his sword. "The cat went after Nisali. I tried to kill it, but Kateiko stopped me."

"It didn't attack!" I said, louder than intended.

"It would've bitten Nili's leg off!" Fendul snapped.

"Kateiko, once again you endanger yourself and others." Isu's face was drawn as tight as her grey-streaked braid. "What compelled you to go off alone at night, dragging Nisali along?"

"I chose to go," Nili said indignantly at the same time Hiyua said in a cool voice, "I'll ask you not to speak for my daughter."

Behadul held up a hand. His voice rumbled through the night. "No one may enter shrine grounds until the autumn equinox. Kateiko, Nisali, you know this."

"Fendul was there, too!" Nili said.

"Only because he went after you two, which the aeldu will understand. Our ancestors will be less forgiving of people traipsing around on their sacred home as if it were a fishing dock."

"Are we ignoring that you killed the first snowcat in Anwen Bel?" I demanded. "What if that was an attuned person?"

16

The wrinkles on his face betrayed no emotion. "Death is a fitting penalty for anyone who enters another jouyen's sacred ground."

A chill spread across my skin. "That's barbaric."

"We owe respect and protection to the aeldu—"

"That's all that matters to you!" I shouted. "You sent the Rin to war just to protect some stupid spirits! The Dona-jouyen was our *family* once! You don't care that we butchered them!"

Isu seized me by the back of the neck. Her voice was so low that only I could hear. "Inside. Now." She pushed me toward our plank house and pointed me in. "We'll talk in the morning." She shut the door very quietly.

When I was sure she wasn't coming back, I went out the far door. Grass rustled around my legs as I crept toward Nili's house, guided by light that spilled out around the shutters. I went in without knocking. Vellum lanterns painted with branches and flowers formed pools of yellow light in the long building. Nili and Hiyua got up. Yironem waved from where he sat with his friend. The other families ignored me.

Nili cast me a weak smile. "I didn't think Isu would let you out tonight. Or ever."

"She said inside. She didn't say where." I rubbed my eyes. "Can I sleep here tonight?"

"Of course." Hiyua wrapped her arms around me. I buried my face in her shoulder and inhaled the scent of fish oil, the same way my mother used to smell.

2.

ANWEN BEL

By morning I'd made up my mind. I refused to live here and go crazy from visions of the dead. I also refused to *die* here. That left one option.

"I know the route, roughly," I told Nili as we washed dishes outside. She scrubbed wooden bowls with lye soap while I rinsed them with a stream of water I called from the air. "Dunehein described it before he left. If we hike southeast, we'll get around the tip of that ocean inlet that comes in from the west. Then south to the Iyo border crossing, and then southwest to their settlement at Toel Ginu. Ten days max if nothing goes wrong."

"You sure it's not easier to row?" she asked.

"The rivers go east to west. We'd spend most of our time portaging. Better to walk *without* carrying a canoe."

"What if we go by sea? Toel Ginu's on the coast."

I flicked water at her. "Rin canoes can't handle ocean swells. We'd drown."

"We could get on an itheran ship."

"How much money do you have?"

Nili looked in the leather purse on her belt. "Fourteen pann. My family mostly traded for preserves this summer. Yiro's growing so fast he eats like a wolf."

"So together you and I can afford passage on a toy boat." I sighed. "Look, you don't have to come—"

"I'm not backing out, Kako. 'Today we fly,' right? Or, well, hike."

"It probably won't work without Fendul. But I can't wait around for him to change his mind."

Nili stopped scrubbing. "Something's different. What happened at the lake yesterday?"

"I don't know. I keep . . . seeing things." I brushed my hair out of my face, leaving behind a wet streak. "I saw the scorched rioden alive again. I wasn't sure it even happened, but I had another vision at the shrine."

"Maybe you should tell Isu."

"She'll say the same thing as Fendul. That I'm lucky. I don't think seeing the land of the dead is ever a good sign. If the dead wanted to help, they'd make me immune to stab wounds. And bears."

Nili shrugged. "Well, I asked Orelein to travel somewhere other than the same boring itheran village, and he said no. So fuck him. I'm going with you."

Saying goodbye to Nili's family was the hardest part. I hadn't seen them all summer, and now we were leaving after only a few days together. I hugged Yironem and jabbed his ribs. "Listen to your mother. And stay away from floods."

"You don't," he muttered.

Hiyua gave me a long embrace, stroking my hair. "Be safe," she said before turning to hug Nili again.

No sound came from my plank house as we approached. I paused in the doorway to trace my fingers over the carved frame. The history of every family in the house was recorded there, stretching back generations upon generations. Only two hadn't ended, mine and Fendul's. I *knew* there was more to the world than this. I just had to get there.

Inside, thin bands of sunlight streamed through the shutters. Isu's bed was perfectly made. I stuffed a few things into my carryframe — a wool shirt and leggings, leftover trail food, a cottonspun blanket embroidered with the fir branches of my mother's crest. I kissed the hilt of my father's sword and placed it on the wall mount. I'd never learned to wield it, but I had both his knives on my belt. My flail had been a gift for my ninth birthday.

I hesitated over a bone needle. *Iren kohal*, I reminded myself. *Rivers keep flowing.* I couldn't stop, couldn't turn back. But even rivers took bits of the earth with them. I wrapped the needle in a square of sap-coloured silk and placed it in my purse.

"Is it too much to hope everyone went hunting?" I asked Nili as I did up the bindings on my carryframe. The words had just left my mouth when the door swung open.

Isu froze on the doorstep. "Where are you going?"

"South." I dropped the straps and straightened up.

She crossed the room with long strides. "Not after last night."

"What are you going to do, tie me to the shrine gate?"

"I'll keep you here until you demonstrate self-restraint. I can't allow you to represent the Rin to another jouyen when you insist on endangering and disgracing your own."

Nili put her hands on her hips. "Technically I'll represent the Rin since I'm older."

Isu cast her a cold look. "That's hardly an improvement."

"I *asked* you to come, Isu," I said. "You haven't seen your younger son since before the war."

"Things change." Her mouth made that thin line I knew too well.

"Maybe it's a good thing Dunehein left." I gave a hollow laugh and gestured at the plank house. "He seems to have fared better than his brother. What should I tell him? That even after we buried Emehein, *twice*, you still thought fighting the Dona was the right decision?"

Isu reeled as if I'd slapped her. "How can I make you understand the sacrifice we—"

"You can't. Ever. So stop trying."

"Kateiko—" She seized my wrist.

"Let *go!*" I tried to twist away. Nili wedged herself between us and forced Isu back.

Isu staggered away, hands dangling at her sides as if she wanted to forget they existed. I picked up my carryframe and gestured for Nili to follow.

"When will you be back?" Isu asked.

I paused with my hand on the door. "I don't know." And with that, I stepped into the glare of sunlight.

*

Nili and I left the plateau and made our way back down the mountain steps to the wide creek that curved around Aeti Ginu. A decaying hemlock log dyed the water red like tea. I dragged my feet over the shifting stones, mostly to fill the silence. Nili held back her usual chatter and hummed instead, twirling an arrow. The creek led to a dirt path that was slippery with moss. It wound past familiar landmarks — a waterfall pouring out cool spray, a hollow rioden tall enough to stand inside, the lake where Fendul fell through the ice when we were kids.

"I wish I could push him back in," I muttered.

The day was already warm. Our clothing was designed for humidity, spun from the fluff of cottonwood catkins. Nili had dyed hers reddish-pink and mine charcoal grey. We both wore open-backed shirts that knotted around our necks and waists, our leggings cut as far up the thigh as we could get away with. The one thing we didn't change was our leather boots, waterproofed with resin and tall enough to protect from itchbine.

We hiked more or less southeast, winding through steep valleys. Mounds of fluffy white clouds clung to the eastern peaks, but the sky was vivid blue, as if summer had never left. By late afternoon, the path faded to a rut, and we moved into single file. Stringy curtains of grey-green witch's hair brushed against our shoulders. Ferns snagged on our carryframes.

No one else had been here recently. There were no footprints or ashes to be seen. After a few more hours of unchanging forest, the path began to slope down. Bitaiya Iren, a wide, listless river, glittered through the trees ahead.

"We have a small problem," Nili called.

I'd lagged behind, trying to scrape a clod of mud off my boot. "What?"

She pointed at the river. "The bridge is gone."

I groaned. The fishing weir was still there, a lattice fence staked into the riverbed from bank to bank, used to trap salmon swimming upriver. But the bridge that once crossed the water alongside the weir was now just two sections of sagging wood, one on each bank, with a long gap in between.

Nili treaded cautiously onto the near end of the bridge. She examined its edge. "Looks like axe marks. The splinters have worn smooth. It's been gone awhile."

"Kaid." I put my hands behind my head. "Rin warriors must've destroyed it to slow down the Dona-jouyen."

The Dona war had been in spring six years ago, a month before lightning burned our sacred rioden and storms damaged the route south. Bitaiya Iren would've been bursting with snowmelt. Even a river flood hadn't stopped the Dona. I'd seen the body of a scout who made it to the top of Aeti Ginu.

A crumbling smokehouse nestled among a stand of cottonwood. I set down my carryframe and wandered over. The roof had caved in on one side. Lichen covered stone firepits among the rubble. As a child I spent weeks here at a time, smoking salmon in autumn and rendering smelt oil in winter. The smell of smoke and oil was long gone, replaced by rot and animal droppings.

I peered at the symbols on the doorframe. The Rin kinaru, three fish to indicate a smokehouse, and crests of families who fished this spot. One stood out. Tall, proud fireweed — the flower of warriors. My father and I both had it around our kinaru tattoo. He'd helped build the smokehouse. I hadn't been allowed to return here after that disastrous year. The Storm Year, we called it. Very inventive.

Nili pulled off her boots and sat on the bridge remains, dangling her feet in the water. It looked tempting. My hair stuck to the small of my back, and my feet already felt damp. I was halfway to the river-bank when the ground gave out.

"Ow! Aeldu curse it!" A splintered trapdoor held my thigh fast in the earth. I pushed against the ground. Rotten wood crumbled under my hands.

"Kako!" Nili dashed up the bank. She flung her body down by the hole and seized me under the arms. I scrambled out, clods of dirt falling away behind me.

"Who leaves a cache unmarked?" I grumbled. I rinsed blood off long gashes on my leg and picked out the largest splinters.

I gave the trapdoor two solid blows with my flail. It crumbled into fragments. I flopped onto my stomach and rummaged around until my fingertips grazed coarse fabric. I pulled up a heavy sack and dumped it out, expecting fishing gear.

I found weapons. Rusted daggers, decayed arrows, a machete with rotten leather wrapped around the blade. "Weird," I muttered, pulling off the leather to examine the iron.

Nili poked through them. "You're lucky you didn't get a blade in the foot."

"These must be from the Dona war. No one ever came back to claim them."

"Which side left them here?"

The fine hairs on my neck rose. "I don't know." I stuffed the weapons back in the sack and dropped it into the cache. It fell with several metallic clanks.

Nili sat back on her heels and looked at me. "You okay?"

I rubbed my foot through my boot. "Nei. I twisted my ankle."

She wrinkled her nose, but didn't say anything.

I lay back on the ground and covered my eyes to block out the sun. "We may as well stay here for the night."

"Then I'm gonna hunt some dinner." Nili stood and wiped dirt off her hands. "If you fall into anything else, make it the river. You could use a bath."

∗

I woke at sunrise and stared at the tent walls glowing with light. Shifting patterns played over the canvas. Nili sprawled next to me, one leg uncovered by the blankets. Her slow breathing filled the tent. I ran my fingers over the embroidered threads on my blanket, knowing the fir branches of my mother's crest better than I remembered the touch of her hand.

As I got used to our utter solitude, I began to register other sounds. The bridge remains creaked. Dew dripped onto the tent. Anwen Bel insulated itself in a sleepy cocoon. Plants and animals grew, died, turned back into earth. At times like this I heard voices on the wind, in the rustle of evergreen needles or the chatter of running water. Today, I heard murmurs like people talking through solid wood, but no matter how hard I listened, I couldn't make out the words.

Our ancestors were buried all throughout these woods. The Rin were the oldest jouyen in the Aikoto Confederacy. All Aikoto had been Rin once, thousands of years ago, until people left to settle other stretches of coastal rainforest. New jouyen rose and fell. Borders and allegiances shifted. We lost and regained parts of Anwen Bel, but always the Rin held the central region around Aeti Ginu.

A few itheran races tried to settle in Anwen Bel's edges. Only one kind lasted. They sunburned easily, so they liked the rainy climate. They lived and died by mountain goats — milked and ate them, spun and dyed their wool, carved their horns into tools and jewellery. The herders I traded with wintered on the plains beyond the eastern mountains. In summer, we met at Vunfjel, a seasonal village where their goats grazed the cooler alpine pastures.

Ninety years ago, all seven jouyen in the Aikoto Confederacy allied with the goatherds to fight a newly-arrived race of itherans. People called it the First Elken War. Two great forces locking antlers. The war was about trade routes — nothing that even mattered. In the north, the Rin fought alongside the Tamu-jouyen, who lived on two peninsulas of Anwen Bel. In the south, we fought alongside the Iyo-jouyen, our historic allies.

Not everyone agreed with the war. Some Rin and Iyo wanted to make treaties instead of fighting. They split off and formed an eighth jouyen, the Dona. They left their families, homes, sacred dead, and wandered the rainforest. No other jouyen would give them land. The Second Elken War passed, then the Third, and still the Dona-jouyen wandered.

Six years ago, the Dona tried to settle near Aeti Ginu. Behadul declared war on them instead. They'd abandoned our confederacy, he said, and their return offended the spirits of Rin who died in the Elken Wars. So we killed the Dona. Our own blood relatives. No prisoners. They put even more of our blood in the ground. Then, like we hadn't suffered enough, the storms hit.

"Can you stop making it so wet?" Nili mumbled.

"Huh?" I looked around the tent. Fog hung in the air. Nili's hair stuck to her forehead in dark brown clumps. "Oh. Sorry."

Nili stretched. Her knuckles grazed the tent, disturbing the dew. She rolled over and snuggled into the blankets. "Kako . . . why did you light the lantern during the star rain?"

"Ai. It's stupid." I sat up and put my arms around my knees. "Fendul said something about proving if Aeldu-yan was real."

"So you wanted to call the aeldu to the shrine."

I nodded, looking at the dancing shadows. "But if they're trying to communicate, why not show themselves? And why now, after so many years?"

"Maybe it's all they can do. Maybe you weren't ready before."

"I didn't think you believed in them."

She shrugged. "Just because they haven't spoken to me doesn't mean they won't to you."

"Nei. It's just a myth. I gave them a chance and they didn't come." I pulled aside a tent panel and looked out at the forest. "Spirits don't need to haunt us. Memories are enough."

I stepped outside, wincing at my ankle. The crisp air bit my skin, and I was about to reach back into the tent for my cloak when movement caught my eye. I snapped my head around and saw a figure disappear into the cottonwood thicket behind the smokehouse.

"Nili," I whispered. "There's someone else out here."

Nili seized her bow and shoved past me. I grabbed my throwing dagger and limped to the smokehouse, but nothing moved in the trees. I stood still, listening. When that failed, I called out. No response.

Nili returned, shaking her head. "The only tracks are ours from yesterday. You sure you saw someone?"

I stared into the forest. Branches stirred in a cool breeze, giving nothing away. "I'm not sure of anything these days."

❋

We gave in and swam across Bitaiya Iren, balancing our carry-frames on our heads and using the fishing weir to keep from getting swept downriver. We might've walked the riverbank all the way to its headwaters or its mouth and not found a single intact bridge. I wasn't strong enough to hold back a whole river so that we could cross on foot.

On the far bank, the vegetation grew so thick that we couldn't find the path. We aimed southeast as best we could. Rain filled our footprints with muddy water. Pushing through the overgrowth, we made slow progress. I wished I'd brought the machete. Not long after crossing the river, I clambered over a fallen fir and my ankle gave out again.

"You can't go on like this," Nili said, clearing the tree with ease.

"I'm not going to sit around in the rain all day." I pushed myself out of the muck and sat on a boulder. Silvery-green fir needles stuck to the mud on my cloak.

Nili rolled her eyes. "Bludgehead. At least ice it."

I pulled off my boot, revealing a swollen and bruised ankle. I froze raindrops into a chunk of ice, wrapped it up in my cloak and held it to the bruise.

"Maybe you could attune," Nili said. "You could walk on three legs and not use the injured one. I can strap your carryframe on your back."

"You know how I feel about attuning." I didn't look up, focusing my attention on the shock against my skin. Cold was real. This body was real. Not my other form.

"Kako, you can't avoid it forever."

"Watch me."

Isu said attuning was a gift from the aeldu. Every Rin connected with an animal and from then on we could take its shape at will. Some gift. I liked having hands.

"There's no reason you—" Nili sighed and paced in a circle. "Would you prefer I make you a walking stick?"

"Nei."

Nili groaned. She tipped her head back and stared skyward, ignoring the rain that fell on her face. "Are you being intentionally difficult?"

"Nei." I glanced up from under the damp hair that fell into my eyes. "Maybe."

Nili strode off into the trees, disappearing behind a cluster of bushes.

A hot wave of guilt rolled over me. "I'm sorry, Nili," I called.

"Glad to hear that."

I heard sawing and then a snap. Nili emerged from the bushes, carrying a cottonwood branch almost as long as she was tall, covered with shivering leaves just starting to yellow. She began stripping away twigs with smooth strokes of her knife.

"You're seriously making me a walking stick."

"I seriously am." Leaves accumulated around Nili's feet, followed by curling tendrils of bark. The smell of cut wood filled the air. Finally, she sheathed her knife and held out the staff. "There. If you're gonna act like a stubborn old woman, I'm gonna treat you like one."

✳

Dunehein and Emehein were the closest I had to siblings. We lived in the same plank house, shared fishing grounds and traplines, traded in Vunfjel together. Emehein was fourteen years older than me, already an initiated antayul by the time I was born. He taught my water-calling lessons whenever I got too impatient to listen to my mother. We'd sit in the snow and he'd talk me through seeing the flakes with my eyes closed. I remembered his deep, steady voice better than his face.

Dunehein, eleven years older than me, took me wandering deep into the rainforest. He showed me wolves lounging outside their dens, ospreys soaring in the sky, bears fishing in river shallows. With him around, I was never afraid. Sometimes he even let me tag along when he spent time with an Iyo girl, a trader who came to our settlement every summer before we left for Vunfjel.

Isu didn't come to Dunehein's wedding. She considered marrying into another jouyen to be abandoning the Rin. She reminded him how loyal his brother Emehein was, training with their father's battle axe since he was strong enough to lift it. After the Dona war when we buried Emehein the first time, Isu stored the axe in a rioden chest instead of taking it south to Dunehein.

Sometimes, during those first years of Isu raising me, she slumped forward at the fire as if a spirit was pulling her into the earth. At second glance she stood straight as ever, her long braid snapping back and forth as she tossed kindling onto the flames. Once I asked if the aeldu were invisible. She spilled the broth pot and sent me out to spar with Fendul. That night I heard her insisting to her husband's spirit that if Dunehein wanted the axe, he would've come for it.

As Nili and I got further from home, I couldn't shake the sense we were being followed. I kept seeing motion in the corner of my eye or hearing stones rattle. Once we turned to see a massive grizzly bear watching us, but the rest of the time I wasn't so sure it was animals.

"No one's come this way in years," Nili reassured me.

"How can we know that when we haven't been here?" I pointed out.

The only thing definitely following us was a grey deluge. I held creeks back so we could cross, water swirling at the edge of a chasm around our legs. At night I dried scaly sprays of rioden needles to pile under our woven bark mat. We sealed the tent panels with sap, but water leaked through every corner we missed.

Southeast was simpler in theory. We'd go left around one mountain and right around the next, but valleys and creeks and cliffs kept sending us off-course. All we had to go by was the position of the sun. We climbed slopes to get a better view, but the snowy eastern range never seemed to get closer or further.

Late the fourth day, rainclouds broke to reveal a thin blue sky. Only then did we notice the change in the air. "Can you smell that?" Nili said, sniffing random trees.

I could. It was like nothing I'd ever smelled. The trees looked different too. As soon as I noticed the blue-green needles of salt spruce looming over twisted pines, I knew what was coming. I felt the weight.

We made our way through the thinning forest and stopped on a bluff. Beneath us was a strip of rocky beach. Beyond that lay more water than I ever imagined. It stretched out as far as I could see to either side, sparkling orange under the setting sun. Hazy mountains were just visible across the water.

Nili put her hands on her hips and looked up and down the shore. "You said we'd go *around* the inlet."

I navigated down the bluff, grabbing fistfuls of shrubbery and digging my staff into the ground. Rocks rattled under my feet as I crossed to the water. I dipped my hand in, took a sip, and spat it back out. I stuck my tongue out repeatedly, trying to get rid of the salt taste. "It's definitely ocean," I called.

She followed my route down. "How far west d'ya think we strayed?"

"No idea." I ran a hand through my hair. "If we follow the shore east, we'll find the end eventually. I think."

"May as well make the most of it, ai?" She dropped her carry-frame, peeled off her boots, and waded into the water. "Aeldu save me, that's cold!"

I sighed with half exasperation, half amusement and followed her in. The cold soothed my throbbing ankle. My hair floated around my hips, brushing against clumps of seaweed that drifted back and forth with the tide. "I just dried your clothes from all that rain."

"Better dry yours too." Nili stuck her hands in the water and flipped them up.

I gasped as freezing water hit me. "You did not!" I whipped my arm through the air. A wave erupted from the surface and collided with Nili. I ducked when I saw her about to splash me again, but the splash didn't come. She stared open-mouthed at something behind me.

An enormous creature surfaced out in the deep water. Its marbled grey body flowed into a split tail like a fish. Another leapt from the water, droplets streaming off its flippers, and crashed back down with a torrential spray. *Whales.*

Rin who traded on the coast told stories about all sorts of creatures — playful dolphins, turtles the size of humans, squid lurking in the deep. I'd never seen any. My fur-trapper family always traded in the inland mountains. Seventeen years in the coastal rainforest and I'd never touched the ocean until now.

3.

STORM YEAR

I lay awake long after Nili fell asleep. Wind gusted over the promontory where we'd tied our tent to a salt spruce. When I closed my eyes, whales drifted past, etched into my memory. The lap of waves on the beach faded into the splash of flippers. I clung to a whale's speckled skin, the ocean rolling below us . . .

A twig cracked.

I snapped out of my dream. Nili stirred but didn't wake. I drew my flail and crept out of the tent. Cold air cut into me, whipping my hair around my shoulders.

The tip of the promontory was bare. I peered into the tangle of spruce and pines around our tent. "Who's there?" I called, swinging my flail in warning.

A figure stepped into the moonlight. Short dark hair, perfect posture, sword on his belt.

I hurled a chunk of ice at Fendul. It thudded against his chest and bounced away. "What in Aeldu-yan are *you* doing here?"

Fendul rubbed the spot where I hit him. "Most people say hello."

"Don't sneak up at night!"

"I planned to approach you in the morning. I thought you were asleep."

"I was. Thanks for waking me, mudskull." I crossed my arms, the flail's spiked head swinging by my hip. "That was you at the smokehouse, wasn't it?"

"Yes. My father sent me to bring you home." Fendul gestured at the inlet. "I knew you wouldn't turn around until you got stuck."

"We're not stuck. I was aiming for the ocean. I just found it a few days early."

"Kako." He shifted his feet, opened his mouth, closed it. Wind rustled through the forest, swirling ferns against our legs. "Listen, it's not fair to drag Nili along."

"Nili wants to come."

"She doesn't have family in the Iyo. Why would she care—"

"Because we both want Dunehein's help." The words escaped before I could stop them.

"You—" He pressed his palms to his temples. "Kaid. So that's what this is about. Aeldu curse it, Kateiko."

I took a step backward, more stunned by his swearing than his anger.

"You want to marry into the Iyo-jouyen like Dunehein did." His words were almost lost in his frustration. "How long have you been planning this?"

"Since Nili and Orelein split up this spring."

He shook his head. "I should've figured it out sooner."

"We're not going to right away. I can't until I'm eighteen. We just wanted to make the arrangements—"

"But only okorebai or okoreni can approve marriages between jouyen. Is that why you asked me to come? You were using me?"

"Don't talk about *using* people. You ratted me out so you'd look like the perfect okoreni saving Nili—"

"It had *nothing* to do with that—"

"Then what?" I cried. "You knew I'd never be allowed to go after that!"

"The autumn equinox is in three days. You couldn't have waited to visit the shrine? And don't say you went for the star rain," he cut me off. "I know why you lit the lantern."

"It's my family's shrine as much as anyone's! I should be able to go when I want!"

"Kako, I'm trying to look out for you, but there's not much I can do if you're determined to run headfirst into the ground."

"Maybe I should ask for your help next time. Oh wait, I tried." I hugged my arms closer to my body. "I'm freezing. I'm going back to sleep."

"I'm not leaving," Fendul called after me.

"*Fine.* But I hope you brought your own tent."

✳

I stepped into dense fog the next morning and smelled cooking meat. Orange light flickered on the point, but the ocean and sky were lost from sight. I headed in the other direction. Mist choked the forest, drifting along in spectral tendrils. My snares were empty. I thought about the limited preserves in my carryframe and searched the undergrowth instead, finding dewy mushrooms and late-season huckleberries.

Nili and I always talked of travelling. Seeing islands, the dry south, the northern tundra where the sun never set in summer.

I'd daydreamed of going with Leifar, a nineteen-year-old itheran goatherd and my recurring romantic fling, from Vunfjel to his town on the wide eastern plains, but he said it wouldn't be appropriate unless we married. I didn't care that my elders wouldn't approve the marriage. I just didn't like Leifar nearly enough for a life of rye sourbread, prairie blizzards, and wet, smelly, bleating goats whose horns could take out my eye. At least when I trapped elk, they stayed in the same place.

Nili had been with Orelein two years when he asked her to marry him. She said no. A yes would've tied her to Aeti Ginu forever. After they broke up, I told her, *Let's leave*. We'd marry laughing young Iyo who'd teach us to sail the seas. Nili could get silks and a rainbow of thread only sold in coastal ports, the materials her embroidery skill deserved. We'd meet people and eat food from places we never imagined. This summer, I told Leifar I wasn't coming back.

I was stripping grey bark off a cottonwood to get at the soft, edible inner layer when I heard voices. I returned to the campsite with my scarce pickings. Fendul had built a sputtering fire at the tip of the promontory. A hare carcass lay at his feet. Nili sat bundled in her cloak, bleary-eyed and messy-haired, chewing and looking anywhere but at him.

"I made breakfast." Fendul offered me a strip of meat.

"Don't you ever sleep?" I brushed past him and sat next to Nili. "Traitor," I told her.

"M'ungry. Too foggy t' hunt," she said around her mouthful.

I peered at the meat that was still cooking. The fat had barely melted. "Fen, your fire sucks." I dried a handful of kindling and tossed it on the fire. Sparks leapt into the air, glowing in the fog.

"Why is he here?" Nili asked once she could speak again.

"Apparently he let us wander around the forest for four days so we'd decide the smart option is to go home."

"Your mistake was thinking Kako is smart," she told Fendul. I jabbed her with a stick and she yelped.

"Neither of you are, or you'd remember this is a dead end." He took the stick and drew in a patch of mud. The eastern mountain range was a vertical line, the inlet a horizontal line to its left. The two didn't quite touch. "See this gap between the inlet and the eastern range? That *was* the route to the border crossing. It's all wasteland now."

"So we'll go around east," I said. "We're already in mountains. They're just taller out there."

"Kako, listen." Fendul leaned forward. "This winter will be bad. I can't imagine why else a snowcat came so far west. We can't risk travelling through those mountains this late in the year."

"Then we'll carve a canoe and cross the inlet."

"You hadn't even seen the ocean until yesterday, let alone rowed on it. Please don't try."

I popped a couple of berries in my mouth. They tasted like salt. I spat them out. "Fine. I'll take my chances with the wasteland."

Fendul ran a hand down his face and muttered something. "Right. See for yourself. Then we're turning around and going home." He stood up and dusted ash off his breeches. "Eat and let's get moving."

I made a face at him, but when he left I plucked a strip of cooling meat off the rocks.

*

I wanted to hate that Fendul was with us. I tried to sulk, but it didn't have any impact. He kept a polite distance and gave us time alone at lunch. It felt strange, given that I shared a house with him, so Nili and I resorted to mocking him when he wasn't listening.

We had a full day of monotony, cutting back northeast along

the inlet. Fog turned to rain. Rain turned to dry air. I thought it was good news when the inlet narrowed, but just before sunset, we crested a steep hill and saw it.

Dead earth. Not just dead — mangled. Blasted apart, blackened and scored with rifts across a flat valley until the ground balked at its abuse and rose into abrupt mountains. Boulders had been wrested out of the earth and tossed aside like handfuls of pebbles. Skeletons of trees dotted the landscape. What had been the riverbed of Oberu Iren was a dried, cracked rut.

Everyone remembered the Storm Year. It was the first summer I was away from home without my parents. I remembered standing on a mountain peak, the wind whipping through my hair as lightning split the sky. The thunder sounded like a distant cry for help as the far reaches of our homeland burned. The earth shook until fire burst forth from the ground, colliding with snow in plumes of steam. The sun turned red and then rain poured down as the sky drowned in smoke. Trees were buried under avalanches of ash.

The worst didn't reach us in the north, but itherans muttered oaths and herded their goats down the slopes, retreating to their town on the plains. I remembered Isu's arm around my shoulders as we watched the earth turn inside out. Her body trembled. I thought the world was ending.

Anwen Bel healed. It always did. The scorched rioden on the shore of Kotula Huin was one of the few remnants of the Storm Year. But on the crest of this hill, we were faced with a part that couldn't heal. The forest's guts had been ripped out and laid bare.

"My father and I came to check on it last year," Fendul said. "The elders think it's cursed."

"I don't believe in curses."

He gave me his favourite exasperated look. "It doesn't matter what we believe. We could be out there for days without food or water. We don't even know what's on the other side."

I shrugged. "Isu and Hiyua would've told us if it's impassable."

"Hiyua doesn't know how bad it is. Isu . . ." Fendul glanced down. "She knew I wouldn't agree to take you."

"Wait. *Wait*. She never wanted me to get to Toel Ginu to see Dunehein at *all*?"

Nili waved her hands to get his attention. "So what are we supposed to do? Stay cut off from the entire southern half of the Aikoto Confederacy?"

"We'll probably have to marry into the Tamu-jouyen," I muttered. I kicked a rock and it bounced away down the hill.

Nili's mouth twisted into a knot. "You told him?"

"I figured it out," Fendul said. "Look, give me some time. I'll talk to Behadul, and maybe we can go after the snowmelt—"

"Nei," I said. "I'm not going home to spend all winter seeing the land of the dead. *Nobody* will marry me if I go insane."

Fendul gave a small shake of his head. "Don't be dramatic."

"Don't be an ass." I shrugged my carryframe off my shoulders. "I'm going to gather food."

✳

It was well after dark when I returned to our campsite with a satchel of mushrooms. Blue light glowed through Fendul's tent. Nili had set up our tent under a cottonwood stand. I looked forward to crawling under the blankets and falling asleep, but when I pulled back a panel I found Nili awake.

"It's strange," she said as I ducked inside. "Sitting on the edge of this. It feels like . . . nothing. Like the air is dead."

I knew what she meant. I could feel it in the water. I'd tried to call some in the woods, but it was sluggish, like calling sap.

"Nili? Is Kako back?" Fendul asked. "Can I talk to the two of you?"

"Nei," she said. "I'm busy talking to the trees."

I pulled back the panel again. "Hurry up. You're letting the cold in."

Fendul squeezed inside. I draped the blankets over our laps. He'd brought his irumoi, a wooden rod covered with glowing blue mushrooms. It felt like when the three of us shared a tent on hunting trips as children, except now our knees bumped every time we moved.

"There's something I should tell you." Fendul flipped the irumoi between his fingers. The light swung over the tent walls. "My father and I came south when the storms began to calm. He wanted to know what caused them."

"Earthquakes," I said. "We've been over this. Quakes triggered volcanoes and avalanches, ash in the sky messed with the weather, and it all combined in a giant fucking mess. Even itherans say it's happened in their mother country."

"This is different. When I saw this wound in our homeland, I knew we had to change something. Stop the spiral that got us to that point. Itherans don't . . . react quite the same way."

I leaned forward, my hair spilling into my lap. "Wait, was that . . ."

"That's when I first attuned. The day I saw the wasteland."

"You never told me that," I said softly. I knew it happened that summer, but almost every Rin adolescent attuned in the Storm Year. I was eleven, Nili thirteen, Fendul fourteen.

"I knew it was an animal following us," Nili said suddenly.

I gaped at Fendul. "Seriously? What about 'attuning only for war and spiritual purposes'?"

"Looking after the jouyen is a spiritual purpose." He drew himself up taller, but his cheeks looked dark in the faint light.

Nili rolled back laughing and jabbed her finger into his chest. "You're never — allowed to tell me off — for attuning again."

He waved her off. "Let's get back to the issue at hand. Please."

"Yeah, what do you mean we have to change?" I asked. "The storms were just a fluke."

"Maybe not. My father thinks it was . . . well . . . vengeance."

"Who'd want vengeance on us? All our enemies are dead."

Fendul rubbed his arm through his woolen shirt, at the exact spot of his okoreni tattoo. "Some people are bitter about the Dona war."

"*I'm* bitter. Rin only split off to form the Dona-jouyen because they didn't want to fight some stupid trade war. So what did we do when they wanted to come home ninety years later? We massacred them."

"It's not that simple, Kako."

"Hang on," Nili said. "Fendul, don't say you think the aeldu were punishing us. Only, like, four Rin believe that, and they haven't been right in the head since the Dona war. Even Behadul doesn't listen to them."

"It wasn't the aeldu punishing us." Fendul dropped the irumoi on the blankets and leaned back on his palms. "Half the people who formed the Dona-jouyen were Iyo, remember. That means we killed people with Iyo relatives. Relatives still alive today."

"You think *Iyo* caused the storms?" I scoffed. "How? They only have water-callers, just like us."

He shrugged. "That's just what my father said."

I threw my hands into the air, hitting Nili's arm. "Okay, suppose they did — now what? They'll attack Rin on sight? My cousin *lives* with them."

"Dunehein joined two years before the war. They accept him as Iyo. We don't have that protection."

Nili tossed her long tail of hair. "You're just trying to scare us into not going."

Fendul pressed his hands to his head. "I want what's best for both of you, but I don't know what that is." In that moment it seemed like the thread holding him together unravelled, letting all the pieces of him loose to float into the air.

My stomach twisted. "You could try trusting us."

"If that's what you want." Fendul looked like he was about to say more, but he picked up the irumoi and rose to leave. "Please think about what I said."

Nili and I sat in the dark until we heard him settle into his tent. Then we curled up under the blankets, leeching each other's body warmth. Dead air stirred the leaves outside. Dead water stagnated in the dirt below us.

"Isu wants me to marry Fendul," I said.

"Nei!" Nili burst into giggles. "You couldn't possibly!"

I stuffed a blanket into my mouth to muffle my laughter. "She told me this summer. Pretty sure she was afraid I'd run away with 'that skinny itheran goatherd.'"

"But Behadul can't stand you! Fendul would never marry without the okorebai's approval."

"Not to mention, *ew*."

"Well . . . he's kinda lush, if you're into uptight, hare-nerved—"

"Shut up shut up!" I kicked her leg. "If you tell Fen, I'll tell him you snuck off from the autumn equinox ceremony last year to tap Orelein in the woodcarving workshop."

"You *wouldn't*." Nili sounded horrified.

"I swear on the aeldu I would. Then neither of us could look Fendul in the eye."

"You'll have to tap him with your eyes closed." She erupted with laughter as I jammed my elbow into her ribs. "Just imagine it. Your husband would be Okorebai-Rin one day. What would you do?"

"I wouldn't be an aeldu-cursed coward like Fendul. I'd make sure the elders listened to me. Why, what would you do?"

"I'd let myself visit the Iyo so I could marry someone else."

I snorted. "Yeah, good luck with that."

❋

The year Dunehein married into the Iyo, he promised he'd come back to visit, but the next summer he fell ill and couldn't travel. The summer after that was the Storm Year. No Iyo came north and we didn't dare travel south. We couldn't even tell Dunehein his older brother had died in battle. I waited, year after year. The Iyo never came. An alliance that had lasted thousands of years fell silent.

Behadul forbid Rin from going to them. *We cannot afford to lose anyone else*, he said, like we'd keel over as soon as we neared the border. When traders came from the Tamu-jouyen, our neighbours to the west, I asked if they'd had contact with the Iyo. They cast wary looks at Behadul and said our politics weren't their business. It took three years of passing messages just to find out Dunehein had survived his illness.

Until now, it'd been unspoken knowledge the Iyo were angry at us. Fendul admitting it meant acknowledging we did something wrong. No one had any idea how long they planned to stay away. Isu sent me to Fendul whenever I asked, Fendul sent me to his father, and Behadul was always busy. The eldest elder pretended she couldn't hear me. Hiyua was the only adult who agreed with Nili and me that after six years, the Iyo must at least be willing to talk to us.

I didn't expect to fix anything. Whatever was going on between Behadul and the Okorebai-Iyo was far beyond me. I just wanted to live somewhere that didn't feel like slow isolated death. As I huddled in my tent next to Nili, I resolved I'd talk to Fendul. Explain it properly. Not yell.

I stepped out into a grey drizzle, facing a limp sunrise over the mountains. I pulled up my hood, wondering why our campsite looked so empty. Then it clicked. Fendul's tent was missing.

"Nili. Nili, wake up."

She stumbled outside, pulling her other boot on. "What—" a yawn split her question in half. "What's going on?"

"Fendul's gone."

Nili turned in a circle, squelching in the mud. "He's probably just hunting."

"With all his belongings?" But what I'd mistaken for a rock was actually a satchel sheltered by bushes. Nili crouched next to me as I pulled out spare waterskins and enough dried meat-and-berry slabs to last for days. "He knew we'd need food to cross the wasteland . . ."

She stopped bouncing on her heels. "Then why leave now? Do you think he heard us last night?"

"We insult him all the time." I rummaged around again and pulled out a curved ram's horn engraved with a kinaru. I sucked in a breath. "Shit."

I'd only ever seen the Rin horn in two places — mounted over the hearth in our plank house or at Behadul's side. I didn't know who made it, but I hoped the horn had done them more good than it did the ram.

"What in Aeldu-yan does that mean?" Nili said. "If Fendul's going home to Aeti, he'd never hear it."

I pressed my lips to the opening at the horn's tip. "It means we have to hope there's someone else out there."

4.

WASTELAND

I grew up in a rainforest. The Rin had a word for people who can call water but not one for "desert." Running out of water was not a problem I expected to have, yet we passed rock after rock scrubbed clean even of lichen. We climbed over lava flows solidified into black streams, scratching our hands on burst bubbles of rock. I stood in Oberu Iren's cracked riverbed and imagined fish swimming around my shoulders.

My first impression had been wrong. The region wasn't dead. Things grow from death. Scavengers feed on carrion, seeds take root on fallen logs. Here there was an absence of life. No birds circled overhead to thieve away our scraps. Nothing wriggled in the dirt.

With midday sun beating down it was hard to resist taking long swigs from my waterskin. My tongue felt stiff and I struggled to swallow our dried food. Sweat evaporated from my skin. The heat faded at night, but we gave up travelling in the dark after Nili stumbled over the edge of a rift. We tried lashing our tent to a tree. Its limbs crumbled into dust at the touch of a rope.

"Kako," Nili said on the second day as we rested in the shade of a boulder. She sat with her chin in one hand and just looked at me. Nili, who made it everyone else's business when she was hungry or tired or sore, hesitated to complain.

"There has to be something here." I laid our waterskins in front of me, crossed my legs, and closed my eyes. My mother taught me how to seek water. Eventually, calling it became as natural as picking up a stick. That's easy when the stick is visible.

I spread my mind out like flowing sap. I focused on pebbles pressing into my legs. Still air against my skin. Nili's shallow breathing. I slipped back to the inlet, searching for the break of waves and the tang of salt.

Colourful spots danced across my sight. My fingers cramped. I forced them to stay open. Pain throbbed from my head to my feet — then it was gone and I was floating. Green washed over the world. Lush woods shimmered around me, bending like weeds in a lake. Soft ferns kissed my skin.

Faces laughed as if in mid-joke. One turned to me and smiled.

I coughed. Thorns stabbed my lungs as I spat up water. Someone rolled me onto my side and pulled wet hair out of my face. I flinched — was one of those people touching my hair? When I opened my eyes, I saw Nili crouching over me.

"What happened?" I croaked.

"You passed out." She sat back and tapped her foot against a rock. "You okay?"

"Sure." I wiped my mouth and lay still until the pain subsided.

Nili nudged me back into the shade. "Here." She handed me a waterskin.

The unexpected weight nearly caused me to drop it. Even the outside was damp. Fat drops rolled down the smooth hide. "Where—" I shook my head and just drank. Cool, clean water slid down my throat. "I was afraid it'd be salty."

"It's not seawater. I dunno where you pulled it from."

"Forest, I think. It felt like the whole place was underwater." I tried to recall the faces, but they blurred like a dream in the moment after waking. "And I saw people."

"Who?" She paused halfway through retying the ribbon around her hair.

"Never seen them before. I think they were . . . itherans."

In all the summers I spent trading with the itherans in Vunfjel, I'd never asked where their aeldu lived. I knew they had a sacred stavehall in their town on the plains. Maybe spirits drifted over the mountains sometimes and got lost in the wasteland where even dead things didn't belong.

✳

I awoke the next morning to warm slobber on my hand.

"Euhhh." I wiped my hand on my cloak and opened my eyes to see a charcoal grey fox, its white-tipped tail twitching. "That's disgusting."

The fox shifted, limbs rearranging, fur melding into tanned skin and Nili's reddish clothes. A grin split her round face. After the first few times attuning, people learned how to shift with clothing and weapons intact. However, complex items like our carryframes, with all our supplies, took too much effort. Fendul must've shifted into a crow just long enough to track our route and then followed us on foot. I pushed aside the pang of thinking about him.

Nili jabbed me. "Wake up. I have something to show you."

I pulled the blankets over my head to block out the morning sun. "Tell me instead."

"*Nei.*" She pulled me up. Years of archery made her stronger than she looked. She prodded me up a slope of rubble and pointed south.

I squinted at a smudge of dark green on the horizon. We must've missed it in the twilight when we made camp. I rested my forehead on her hair. "Thank the aeldu."

We kept our course fixed on that smudge. I smiled at the first dusty sapling I saw, baked greyish-yellow but pushing up from the dirt with all the determination of youth. Before long, we stood on the border of two areas — blackened trunks where a forest fire swept through behind us and a line of healthy conifers in front.

I stepped into the green shelter and breathed in the scents of wood and sap. The familiar tingle of water thrummed against my skin. I raised my hand and let a narrow stream fall from my palm. Nili captured a mouthful, droplets splashing over her chin.

As we made our way through a pass between two hills, a low rumble began to build. We emerged on the edge of a steep canyon, the walls eroded into uneven rectangles as if carved by a jagged knife. The whole fleet of Rin canoes laid end to end would barely bridge the gorge. Far below, rapids pounded over boulders, sending up sheets of white spray.

"The bad news," Nili called, "is we'll die crossing. Good news is we won't die thirsty."

If the river had a name, no one ever used it. It was just the border between the rainforests Anwen Bel and Iyun Bel that also served as the border between Rin and Iyo territory. I only knew of one bridge over it, and I had no idea which direction it was in. Our view up and down the canyon was blocked by dense foliage. I hoped desperately the bridge had survived the storms.

"I'm never hoping for water again," I said. "What do you think? East or west?"

Nili pointed east. As we trekked, I wondered what would've happened if the wasteland spread as far as the canyon. Surely nothing could disrupt such a huge river. I could barely hear Nili over the roar echoing up the cliffs.

She stopped when we reached a hemlock hanging off the bank, its roots knotted into the dirt. "Maybe if I climb out there to get a better view—"

"I . . . don't think that's necessary." I grabbed her shoulders and turned her sideways.

A pair of immense rioden stood by the bank like gateposts. Even if we linked hands we couldn't reach halfway around one. Wooden steps spiralled up the nearest trunk. Our gazes moved up and up to the underside of a bridge high in the trees. My neck hurt from looking at it.

"*Yan taku*," Nili said.

"I'll try not to take you out if I fall." I took a deep breath and put my foot on the first step. A chain of carved symbols wrapped around the tree, parallel with the stairs. I tried to read as I climbed, but they were mostly archaic crests obscured by moss. Once my legs started burning, I gave up and focused on keeping my balance.

By the time I reached the top, I must've climbed fifty times my height. I stumbled onto a platform of thick timbers and out to the bridge. Nili kept up and was right behind me. Wind whipped past and cooled the sweat on my brow. The whole world was laid out around us. Rolling green forest and white-capped mountains with teal slopes before us, cracked brown earth behind us. The gorge was a seam carrying glacial water into a viridian mist. I felt like my spirit was free of the earth itself.

An osprey whistled and I finally stirred. "Is this how you feel when you dance?"

Nili nodded. "But this is better."

Among crests on the ornate railing was a symbol of a kinaru with outstretched wings, its head turned to the side. The symbol of tel-saidu, an old name for air spirits. The Rin believed in two types of spirits — our aeldu in the dead world, and saidu, which inhabited the living world but had little to do with humans. Saidu were the elemental beings that controlled the forces of nature. They made the weather and turned the seasons.

When I was nine, just after Dunehein's wedding, I plied his new wife with questions about the route to her home at Toel Ginu. She said the sky bridge over the border was once a shrine where we asked tel-saidu for mild winters or strong tailwinds while canoeing. That was all she knew about it. These days, it was just a bridge.

When I had asked Fendul about it later, he explained that the Rin had once revered air spirits. Our crest, a kinaru with its head and neck straight, was a modified tel-saidu symbol. That crest and the shawl dance were all that remained of the old ways. The saidu went dormant hundreds of years ago, around when we began building shrines for the aeldu instead. Fendul didn't know which happened first.

All I'd really wanted to know was how we built a bridge so high in the trees. He didn't know that either. After the Storm Year, I'd asked him how saidu could make such powerful storms if they were asleep. He didn't know *that* either, but suspected the saidu didn't mean to cause them. That the storms happened precisely because they'd been dormant so long.

Nili rapped the solid timber railing. "Why isn't this rotten? Or covered in lichen?"

"We just walked through volcanic ruins and you're worried about lichen?" I wandered along the bridge. Most symbols were older than memory. Past the midpoint they turned to Iyo crests. "Once we step off this bridge, we're in Iyo territory."

Iren kohal. Rivers keep flowing. I knew what a future in Anwen Bel looked like. It was as barren as the dry riverbed of Oberu Iren, cut off from life and death alike.

"Sure you want to do this?" I called back.

Nili spread her arms. For a second she glided on the wind with invisible wings. "Today we fly."

❋

Mountains faded into hills as we curved southwest through the Iyun Bel rainforest. A day in, the auburn rioden and brown-barked hemlock grew thicker. I saw fewer needled fir and more leafy alder. Fewer mammals, more slugs. Water dripped from puffy mushrooms. On the second day, the forest ended.

"What in Aeldu-yan . . ." I stepped into an open valley. Wind whistled past.

A swath of trees had been reduced to rotting stumps, scattered alder saplings, and a layer of vibrant purple fireweed. A lazy creek flowed at the bottom, almost wide enough to be a river. We made our way down the slope toward a cluster of buildings on the bank. Woodchips crunched in the dirt. I circled the buildings and checked each doorframe.

No engravings. It was like speaking to someone only to be stared at in silence. Itherans didn't label their homes, but the smooth boards were closer to plank houses than the log cabins of Vunfjel.

Nili kicked a hemlock cone. "This place is creepy."

We put as much distance behind us as possible, pulling up our hoods against the heavy rain when we set up camp. Nili returned with a plump grey-feathered grouse, muttering about hunting in the dark. I struck my flint against my dagger until the sparks ignited a handful of dry lichen. I'd just dropped it on a pile of kindling when I heard a *clop-clop-clop* from the west.

We looked up as three riders came down the path, faces hidden by black hoods. I didn't know of a single jouyen that kept horses. The rider on the left carried a longbow and the others wore swords. The archer called out, but I couldn't understand the words.

"*Hanekei*," I called and raised my hand.

"Who goes there?" he said, switching into Coast Trader.

We only used the trade language with itherans. Every jouyen in our confederacy spoke dialects of Aikoto. Trader had some Aikoto words, some from the goatherds' language, and some I didn't know the origin of. The archer's accent was unfamiliar, but I could make out two rearing elk emblazoned on his leather armour.

The swordsman on the right scoffed. "Just a couple'a wood witches," he said gruffly.

"A couple of what?" Nili said, bemused.

"Young women should not be out alone at night," the archer said.

"We're fine." A prickle of irritation rose along my neck. "What are *you* doing here?"

"Poachers," the swordsman said suddenly, turning his horse and trotting past me. He seized the limp bird from Nili's hands and held it up by the neck.

"Ai, that's our dinner!" Nili grabbed at it, but he lifted it out of reach.

"We received reports that viirelei were poaching near the abandoned logging camp," the archer said. "Hunting is restricted in these lands to those with a permit."

I raised a hand to shelter my eyes from the rain. "Our jouyen has a historic agreement with the Iyo. We're allowed to hunt on their lands."

"Permits must be granted by the province. It is within our rights to remove poachers from said land how we see fit—"

"Are you threatening us?" My other hand strayed toward my dagger.

The third rider, a gloved man, finally spoke. "Only if you force our hand."

"We'll leave in the morning," Nili said. "Just give us back our food."

"Can't do that, missy." The gruff man placed his sword in front of Nili's neck, pulling her against the horse's shoulder. "Shoulda thought of that before you killed something that don't belong to you."

I went still. Nili stared at me with wide eyes.

"Let her go."

"You are in violation of—" the archer began.

"Shut up!" I yelled.

The swordsman dropped the grouse into the mud. "Nobody will miss some law-breakin' wood witches. Let's just be done with 'em."

"I'm not fucking around! I said let her go!" I pulled my dagger from its sheath.

In an instant, the archer nocked an arrow and aimed it at my chest. "Sir, your command."

Rain beat down, running down my sleeve in cold rivulets. The fire hissed. Light flickered off our blades. The gloved man's horse tossed its head. My arm trembled as my pulse beat through it.

Nili shoved the swordsman's hand away and ducked. I threw my dagger. It whipped through the air and thudded into his heart. His body slid from the saddle.

Pain exploded through my throwing arm. I whirled toward the archer just as Nili's arrow pierced his chest. He toppled back and fell hard.

The gloved man drew his sword. "Ai!" I shouted. He turned.

My hunting knife struck him below the collarbone and ricocheted away.

I drew my flail as he bore down on me — but his horse pulled aside at the last second. The man slammed his hilt into my head. I crumpled. Something cracked against my leg as hooves thundered past.

"Leave." Nili's voice rang through the rain-soaked trees.

I struggled to see through blood sticking my eyelashes together. Nili had an arrow set on the gloved man. He cast a swift glance at his companions and spurred his horse into the woods.

Bloody bone shards jutted from my shin. My lower leg bent like I had a second knee. I lay back in the mud and let pain wash over me.

"Kako." Nili cradled my head in her lap. "Kako, are you okay?"

The world spun like I'd done a flip underwater. "I . . . think so . . ."

She fumbled with the stopper of a clay vial. "Drink this."

I caught a sharp scent like unripe berries. I only drank tulanta when I was desperate. The name meant 'gate water' for a reason. "I can't — Nili, if he comes back—"

"Kako, please. Just take it." She held the vial to my lips. I gave in and swallowed the sour liquid, trying not to throw it back up.

Nili brushed damp hair from my face. "You'll be fine. I'll take care of you."

The last thing I heard before succumbing was the loud, mournful cry of a horn echoing across drenched forest and into the night.

5.

ITHERANS

I curled up on the lake floor, clinging to the soothing dampness. Water caressed my skin. Slippery weeds entwined my limbs. The weight of the lake bore down on me, pressing me into the cool earth. Specks of algae shuddered in murky green light, rising toward the surface as if seeking out the sky.

"Kateiko."

I clamped my hands over my ears. Something pulled them away. I wanted to stay under, but my body drifted up in a cloud of algae, toward the flickering sun—

"Kateiko. Can you hear me?"

"Shut up," I tried to say. Water poured into my mouth. My spine arched as I gasped.

I broke the surface. A man filled my vision. The edges of his hair were aflame. Water fell hard and fast on my face, but he burned bright.

"It's you." I jerked up. "I saw you in the wasteland. You smiled at me in the forest."

"You do not know me," he said, but I saw fire in the corners of his mouth.

"Am I dead?"

"You tell me."

Suddenly there was pressure under my shoulders and knees. A jolt shot through my leg. I rose into the air and was set on something warm and smooth that snuffled under me. I scrabbled around, latching onto tangled hair — and then I let go, nearly falling off.

"Go south to the creek," the man said. "Follow it west until you find a house. Tell the woman there Tiernan sent you."

"I understand," Nili replied, sounding far away.

Then there was warmth at my back and an arm around my stomach. Smudged lines slid past. The creature moved rhythmically, each thud of its feet reverberating through my body.

I drifted out of awareness and woke on a hard surface. Everything was dark except for a glow next to me. The burning man. He backed away, but I reached out.

"Stay with me," I said, the words thick as if my mouth were full of cottonwood fluff.

He linked his fingers into mine, his warm skin an anchor as the world spun. I tried to fix my eyes on the wall, but it bowed in and out until it was swallowed by shadows. Seconds, minutes, maybe hours passed — until white light spilled into the room. I turned my head and saw a figure illuminated in a doorway. Silver hair cascaded over billows of pale glowing fabric.

The story of Orebo surfaced through the fog of my mind. Orebo adored the moon and longed to keep some of its beauty for himself, so he turned into a bird and flew into the sky. He broke off a moonbeam, but it shattered into a thousand shards, each one becoming a star. There, wrapped up in the blanket of night, stood a fragment of the moon.

✳

I was aware of movement, light that came and went, a throbbing in my head. Cool water was tipped into my mouth, followed by liquid that tasted like evergreen needles. Voices faded away and ruptured back in.

My eyes were glued shut when I woke again. I rubbed them until they opened. The world was sideways. A ceramic pitcher and mug were set atop a table at eye level. I was on my side in a soft bed, a scratchy blanket rubbing against my skin. Log walls, slat floor, empty shelves. Sunlight streamed through a glass window.

A woman sat in a chair under the window. She had pale skin and arched eyebrows. The lightest hair I'd ever seen fell in waves over her shoulders. I was no good at guessing the age of itherans, but I put her at maybe thirty. She was examining a pile of fabric in her lap.

"That's mine," I said, recognizing Nili's leaf embroidery. I sat up. As the room pitched, I realized my belt was gone. Panic gripped me until I saw it hanging from a nail in the wall, my weapons and purse still buckled on.

She handed my cloak over. It was stained with blood and mud. "I was going to wash and mend it, if you'd like."

"Where's Nili? Is she okay?" I demanded.

"She's in better shape than you." Her face crinkled with a smile. She rose, poured water from the pitcher, and pressed the mug into my hand. "I'll fetch Nisali. Stay put."

I set the mug down as soon as the door shut. I pulled off the blanket, went to stand — and stopped in shock. My left leg was held straight with a splint, bandaged from knee to toes and stiffened with what smelled like cottonwood resin. I was still staring when the door burst open.

"Kako!" Nili swept me into a hug. "You look like death. Not in the good aeldu way."

"Thanks." I held up a handful of my hair. The brown strands were matted with dried blood. "Ugh. What in Aeldu-yan happened?"

Nili shut the door, dragged the chair next to the bed, and sat down sideways. A long gash crossed her forearm near her feather tattoo. Her hair hung loose, not tied back with its usual ribbon. "What do you remember?"

"Drinking tulanta and seeing a lot of weird stuff."

"I blew the Rin horn. You were bleeding everywhere, and . . . I was scared, Kako. A man came on horseback and sent me to get a healer." She gestured at her arm. "That's how I got this. Running in the dark. Stupid way to get injured."

"Where are we now?"

"In the man's house." Nili made a face. "I can't pronounce itheran names."

"Was that his wife?"

"Nei. His neighbour. She's the healer."

I fiddled with the filthy hem of my cloak. "What happened to the riders?"

"Well, one fled." Nili seemed intent on examining her fingernails.

"And the others?"

She hesitated too long. "Kako, maybe you should go back to sleep."

"Nili—" I grabbed her wrist, but she pulled away. "Nili. I killed someone, didn't I."

Nili strode to the window. She rested her elbows on the sill and stared out, sunlight glowing on her dark hair. "So did I, if it makes you feel better."

"Aeldu save us." I pressed my hands against my face. "The itherans know?"

"Yeah. The man's burying the bodies."

"Yan kaid. Fuck." My voice was too loud in the cramped room. I needed to get outside. I prodded my bandages. Nothing. "Nili. Nili!"

"What."

"I can't feel my leg."

She finally looked back at me. "The healer gave you a strong dose of some herb. You probably can't feel much of anything."

"That's comforting." I poked my other leg. She was right. I grabbed my right knee and swung my leg off the bed, followed by the left. I tried to stand and promptly fell over.

"Bludgehead." Nili heaved me off the ground and back onto the bed. "I thought not walking was implied."

I groaned and flopped backward. "So I'm supposed to just stay here? For how long?"

"I don't know." She fiddled with a lock of hair. "A month. Maybe more."

"A *month*?" Out of nowhere, I felt exhausted. Colourful dots of light danced in front of my eyes. I took Nili's suggestion and went back to sleep.

*

It was dark when I woke again. I swung my legs off the bed and knocked over something soft. My boots. I pulled on the right one, pushed myself onto one foot — and toppled into the far wall, landing on my wounded arm. I cursed and fumbled open the door latch.

A man sat in the next room, legs stretched out, a book open on his lap. A tallow candle on the table dripped into a metal holder. It bathed the room in a warm glow that didn't pierce the shadows. The man didn't notice me, giving me a chance to study him. Unkempt, shoulder-length brown hair. Stubble on his jaw. Tanned, scarred skin. He wore muddy boots and a leather jerkin over a frayed tunic and trousers.

As ragged as he looked, I was far worse. My hair was tangled like a bird's nest. The grey cottonspun of my clothes looked brown. Dirt coated my arms, legs, stomach, every bit of exposed skin. I crunched when I moved. At least he couldn't smell me over the oily stench of tallow.

"Hello," I said.

He snapped the book shut. "Good evening."

I hopped forward, using the wall for balance, and collapsed into a chair. Every step sent fire through my shin — though not as much as I expected, given how it'd looked before bandaging. "Where's everyone else?"

"Nisali is sleeping in my yard. Marijka has gone home." His accent was thicker than the woman's. He dipped his head. "My name is Tiernan Heilind."

I nodded back, glad to have learned itheran customs from a young age. "Kateiko Rin. Um, I think I was in your bed. Sorry — if you wanted to sleep—"

"Do not apologize. I put you there. I mean—" He shook his head. "Never mind."

The corners of my mouth twitched. "Thank you."

"Thank Marijka. Without her you would not be walking." He gave me a grave look. I felt suddenly embarrassed for smiling. "Nisali told me what happened."

I looked down at my dirt-encrusted nails.

Tiernan rose and slid the book into a slot on a shelf. "Those are not the first bodies I have buried in these woods," he said with his back to me.

"We didn't do anything wrong." My words tumbled out in a rush. "I'd never seen those men before—"

"By law, soldiers have the right to kill poachers. It is not a right often exercised."

"Whose law? This is Iyo territory."

He turned and raised an eyebrow. "That is a matter of contention."

"So what are we supposed to do? Let the next itheran we meet slit our throats for some invented crime?" I stood up and immediately regretted it.

"I recommend not provoking any more soldiers. And not putting weight on that leg."

I glared at him, then limped toward another door and outside onto a porch. I stumbled through the gap in the railing — and fell down a set of steps. Pain stabbed through my shin. I crawled with my two good limbs until I collapsed in the grass.

Charcoal black blanketed the sky, speckled with white needle-points. I traced constellations with my fingertip. Orebo, curled around the one star he managed to keep. A kinaru in the northern sky. The sword of the tel-saidu, which was silly, because why would air spirits need weapons?

If only no one invented weapons.

Every time I irritated Isu, she sent me to practise combat with Fendul. We spent countless hours throwing knives until we could sink them into the fissures of cottonwood bark. After I took out a duck in flight, Fendul said he'd better not piss me off anymore.

My first throw had been perfect. I could blame my second throw on the balance of my hunting knife, the arrow that sliced my arm, the moving target — but maybe I was afraid to strike true again. I'd taken a man's life. One moment he could feel the breeze on his skin and taste rain in the air. The next moment it was gone.

Fendul had told me to practise with my flail more. *You won't always have distance on your side*, he said. But I was afraid of what it'd be like. The sound of an iron ball shattering bone. The tug of spikes tearing through flesh. I'd hesitated, and it nearly cost me my life.

✳

"Did you sleep out here?"

I looked up at Nili's face against the grey sky. "I didn't sleep."

"Me neither." She lay down next to me. Rain formed puddles in the grass.

We couldn't be more than a few days' hike from Toel Ginu. Dunehein and the Iyo would be arriving there soon from their autumn fishing trips and settling in for winter. We were so close to the place we might someday call home and to people we might one day marry — but we couldn't get there.

"What are we going to do?" I said, and felt Nili shrug.

When the puddles submerged my arms, I finally sat up. We were in a wide clearing. The tiny log cabin and a stable nestled against the trees. A silver horse with a black mane and tail grazed in a paddock. A rough plank building rose almost twice the height of the cabin, its windows set high in the walls.

Tiernan emerged from the cabin and disappeared into the plank building. I'd forgotten about him by the time he came over and laid a pair of crutches in the grass.

"Marijka suggested them." He walked off before I could thank him.

I inhaled the smell of alder, recognizable by its bright red wood. "He's better at carving than you," I said, expecting Nili to protest, but she said nothing.

We moved our tent further into the woods that night. Tiernan lent us goat-wool blankets and a glass lantern. I practised with my crutches until I could hobble over tree roots. Evergreen needles and yellow leaves stuck to the resin on my bandages. Marijka laughed at the sight when she came to check on me.

Tiernan said that we could hunt on his property, but Nili seemed reluctant to touch her bow, and most days my snares came up empty. Instead, we foraged mushrooms, crabapples, and milk-white ghost-blossom. Nili waded in the creek, using her toes to dig up duck potatoes that floated to the surface. I unwrapped the bloody rawhide from my dagger grip and burned it in the forest. Rin custom dictated a dead person's blood had to return to the earth so their spirit could pass into Aeldu-yan.

More than once Nili woke screaming, her face damp with sweat and tears. I kissed her hair and wrapped my arms around her shaking body until she drifted off. I couldn't sleep. Wind and rain whispered to me in the shelter of the trees. During the day, Nili disappeared for hours, most of which I spent at the creek spinning shapes out of water and disturbing the fish.

"Where do you keep going?" I asked finally.

"Away." She didn't say another word. Sometimes I thought the silence was worse than her screams.

One afternoon, Nili turned up at the creek. "Marijka invited us to have dinner with them," she said, tying sinew cord to her bow and the other end to an arrow. "She asked us to bring fish."

"I can ask Tiernan if he has a net."

Nili shook her head. She stood knee-deep in the creek and loosed an arrow into a squirming salmon. The cord kept it from escaping. The set of her mouth betrayed how hard she had to concentrate.

Rin and Iyo had such close ties that travellers were granted automatic permission to hunt or fish on each other's land. I wasn't sure how sharing game with itherans who lived here fit into the agreement. Few of the old laws seemed to work anymore.

Marijka was on Tiernan's porch peeling apples when we arrived with the gutted fish. Her hair was pinned up in a bun and she wore a pale blue bodice and apron over a simple white dress. She smiled and waved us over.

"Hello, Marij— Mar—" I couldn't get the syllables right.

"Ma-*rye*-kah," she said with a laugh. "Like the grain. Call me Maika if it's easier."

"What should I call Tiernan?" I asked, settling on the porch steps.

She crinkled her nose and smiled. "Ah . . . I'd stick with his full name."

When the apples were done, we went inside, carrying the porch bench in with us for extra seating. Marijka seemed to know her way around, taking pots from hooks on the wall and tins of foreign herbs from the cupboards. Tiernan put the salmon on a grate over the fire, and the cabin filled with the familiar smell of roasting fish.

I hadn't paid much attention to the room before. The rough table and stone fireplace took up most of it. A few nails were hammered into the wall for cloak hooks, but there were no ornaments on the mantel. A ladder near the bedroom door led to a loft I couldn't see into. I paused by the bookshelf, wondering what Tiernan had been reading. The Rin didn't have books. I only knew of them because a goatherd's daughter used to read me folk tales while our parents bartered.

"Interested in theology?" Tiernan asked.

I wondered if he was making fun of me. "I don't know what that is."

"The study of religion. Or religions, as it may be."

"Like spirits and the dead and stuff?" I fiddled with a piece of hair behind my back. "You could say I'm interested."

"Nei, let me get it," Nili's voice interrupted our conversation. She reached for a tin on the top shelf. "I'm taller. I have to be. I'm tired of being the shortest in our jouyen."

"You're most certainly not taller." Marijka wiped floury hands on her apron. "Come here and we'll see."

They stood back-to-back, Nili stretching up on her toes. Tiernan set a wooden spoon on their heads and pushed Nili back down. It was ever so slightly higher on Marijka's side.

"Sorry, Maika. Nisali's got this one." Tiernan winked at me as Nili puffed out her chest.

I watched Nili chatter with Marijka as we prepared dinner. It was the first time she'd smiled since we got here. It reminded me of how she acted with Hiyua back home. Maybe Fendul was right — maybe I had dragged Nili along with me.

By the time we sat down, my stomach was eating itself. After days of muddy roots, dinner looked incredible and smelled better. Flaky salmon, rye flatbread with fruit preserves, steamed vegetables and herbs, spiced apple cake, even creamy goat cheese. Nili and I were hard pressed to stop thanking them.

"Tiernan, would you get some water from the rain barrel?" Marijka said as we cleaned away the dishes.

"I can do that." I put out my hand and filled the bucket she held.

She tilted it so water splashed against the sides. "Thank you," she stuttered.

I shrugged, but caught Tiernan looking at me before he turned away.

Marijka gave us herbal tea in chipped mugs. She'd brought seeds from Nyhemur, the plains beyond the eastern mountains, and grown them here in her garden. I drank slowly, taking what comfort I could from the heat. Getting stuck in the wilderness with two itherans wasn't the life we left home for.

Nili and I weren't abandoning our families. If Behadul and the Okorebai-Iyo sorted their problems out, we'd go home to visit. Otherwise, in a few years Yironem would be old enough to follow us to the Iyo. Maybe even Hiyua and Isu would remarry if it meant being with us again. But that day, if it ever came, wouldn't be soon enough.

"Can I ask you something?" I said. "How would you get into the north from here?"

Nili set her mug down too fast, knocking it against the table, and looked at me strangely.

Tiernan pulled a square of paper from between two books and unfolded it on the table. It was covered with strange ink markings, but as he ran his finger over the creased paper, the lines began to form recognizable shapes in my mind. It was an old map. Oberu Iren was still marked.

"We are here, near Tømmbrind Creek." He pointed. "This river up here is the Holmgar canyon. How far north do you want to go?"

I pointed at a river near Aeti Ginu, since the mountain itself wasn't marked. "There. We crossed the wasteland beyond the sky bridge. I wouldn't go back that way, but I don't know a way through the eastern range."

"The nearest pass through the Turquoise Mountains had some trouble two years ago. No one uses it now." Tiernan scratched his jaw. "The easiest way is to buy passage on a ferry—"

"We've been over that," I said quickly. I didn't want to admit we didn't have the money. "Itheran ships don't make port anywhere near there."

Tiernan exchanged a glance with Marijka. "Or you could take the tunnels."

"There's a network through the mountains," she explained. "People use them to cross to the province of Nyhemur."

I'd never heard of any tunnels. "Where do they come out?"

"Here, here . . ." Tiernan pointed at several places. One was north of the wasteland. From there it'd only be a few days back through the forest to Aeti Ginu.

"Is it safe?" I asked. "No floods or avalanches?"

Marijka studied me over her mug. "It should be safe now. But you'd have to hurry before the snow hits."

✳

"What was that about?" Nili said in our tent. "Are we going home?"

"I'm not." I rolled onto my side to look at her. "Nili . . . I know something's wrong."

She stared back, the lantern casting odd shadows on her face. "I'm fine."

"Nei. You're not. Neither am I." My dam crumbled. Tears streamed down my cheeks. "I don't think we can take care of each other anymore. You should be with your family."

"I'm not going without you."

"I can barely walk to the creek. My leg won't heal before winter." I brushed my fingers over her hair. "Maybe I'll come get you next year, or if you decide to stay with the Rin . . ."

Nili gave a choking laugh. "That'd be a fun conversation with Ore. 'Sorry about bleeding your heart. I changed my mind. Wanna get back together?'"

"Orelein still loves you. He should just be happy to have you home."

"He loves who I was before." She fingered the tangle of woolen blankets. "I don't . . . feel like me anymore."

"Well, you don't need him. Hiyua and Yironem love you no matter what."

"What are you gonna do?"

Briefly, I thought of Tiernan's books. "I don't know. If I'm stuck in the south all winter anyway, I can wait for the right time to approach Dunehein. Like when I'm sure the Iyo won't shoot me full of arrows."

"I'm afraid to go alone," she said quietly.

"Maika will take you to the end of the tunnel. I asked while you were busy. That's where you've been going, isn't it? To see her."

"Sometimes." There was a long pause, then Nili pulled a bundle out of her carryframe. "I started this over summer and just finished. It's a bit late for the autumn equinox, sorry."

I'd completely forgotten about the festival. I unfolded the bundle and gasped. A cottonspun shawl, black outside and white inside, embroidered around the hem. "Nili, I can't wear this — I'm not a dancer—"

"No one's around to stop you. You deserve to fly, too."

"Wait. Hold out your hand." I took something from my purse and dropped it on her palm.

Nili held up a chain with a silver pendant. I'd twisted snare wire into the shape of a leaf, framing three water droplets that shimmered in the firelight. She spun it, mouth half-open with wonder. "I didn't know you could do this."

"I had a lot of spare time this summer in Vunfjel. I traded my furs faster than Isu, and I could only spend so long chasing goats with Leifar." I draped it around her neck, did up the clasp, and gently pulled her hair out from under.

Nili brushed away tears of her own. "We were supposed to fly together, Kako."

"We'll see each other again. I promise."

That night, a charcoal grey fox and a silver-blue wolf slept curled around each other in a tent as the forest slept outside.

6.

FIRE & WATER

Nili and Marijka left with Tiernan's horse, our tent, and the Rin horn. I lay in the clearing that night searching for stars, but clouds blocked them from view. Tiernan stopped next to me on his way into the cabin.

"Come inside," he said. "It is too cold to sleep in the open."

I limped in after him and eased onto a chair, leaning my crutches in the corner. I didn't know what to do without Nili to fill the silence.

"Would you like to take a bath?" Tiernan asked, avoiding my eyes. "I can set up the wash basin and go to the workshop."

Heat flooded into my face. I'd been bathing in the creek, but I wound up covered in mud within hours anyway. "Nei. Thank you, but — I'm tired now."

"Ah." He scratched his jaw. "Well. You are welcome to take the bedroom."

"I'll be more comfortable out here. Please. I'm used to sleeping on the ground."

"If you prefer." He gave me a stilted nod. "Goodnight."

I waited until the bedroom door closed, then curled up by the hot coals and pulled the blankets over my head, wondering if a person could die of embarrassment.

When I looked outside the next morning, frost coated the grass with glittering crystal. *Rivers keep flowing, even under ice.* My first task was making a net before the autumn salmon run ended. I peeled fibres off brittle, frozen ropeweed stems and knotted them into cord. After Tiernan offered to come fishing with me, I decided my next task should be getting to know him.

"How old are you?" I asked on the way to the creek, stumping along on my crutches.

"Thirty-two. And yourself?"

"Eighteen after the winter solstice. How long have you lived here?"

"A year. The cabin used to be a fur trapper's lodge."

"Where did you live before?" When he didn't answer, I said, "I've never met itherans from this region. Only in Vunfjel, far north in the mountains."

"'Itheran' is not an accurate term," he corrected. "You would have met Sverbians. Nowadays most people in this province are Ferish."

"What's the difference?"

"Some came from Sverba and some from Ferland." He looked like he was trying not to laugh. "Our mother countries are not so far apart, but we have very different cultures. For example, the Ferish believe a single god reigns over everything."

"Oh, *those* itherans. They don't come to Anwen Bel anymore. We drove them off in the First Elken War." Distracted, I stumbled over a rock. Pain shot through my leg. "Are you Sverbian?"

"Yes. But it is impolite to ask."

"How else am I supposed to know? People say Ferish are darker, but you have dark hair."

"Most Sverbians look like Maika. Not all." Tiernan stepped aside to let me pass through a gap between trees. "You can also tell us apart by our accents."

"But you sound different from Maika."

"She was born near here, in Nyhemur. I immigrated from Sverba just twelve years ago."

My jaw fell. "You crossed the ocean? I've never met someone actually born in Sverba."

"I have never lived with a viirelei, so we are on equal ground."

"'Viirelei' isn't accurate either," I countered. "It literally means 'they of the west.' The Rin-jouyen is part of the Aikoto Confederacy. The Nuthalha Confederacy to the north and the Kowichelk to the south don't even speak the same language as us."

Tiernan inclined his head to me. "Fair point."

After that we only spoke out of necessity. I spent most days at the creek, determined to intrude on his privacy as little as possible. I built a fish smoker out of stones and whittled a long-handled rake to dig duck potatoes from the creek bed. We shared a few meals, but usually Tiernan was in his workshop from morning to night.

Thoughts lingered at the back of my mind. When I swept the cabin, I pretended to push them out the door. I finally pulled a book from the shelf, a wood-covered tome carved with a leafless tree with nine branches and nine roots, only to see lines of meaningless symbols inside. I wanted to ask Tiernan about them, but my tongue remained stuck in place.

Most nights, I lay awake listening to water drip into buckets under leaky spots in the roof. Voices murmured quiet as a heartbeat. I felt rain freeze into gentle sleet, a slow change like watching clouds cross the sky. I wondered if it was snowing in Anwen Bel.

Tiernan showed up one day leading a horse by the reins. Its saddle was askew, mud up to its knees, leaves tangled in its black tail.

"I found her wandering the woods with a limp," he said. "The other must have fled."

I recognized the nut-brown coat and white patch between its eyes. The archer's horse. I leaned against the paddock fence and watched Tiernan clean its hoof with a metal pick. "What are you going to do with it?"

"Take care of her until someone comes back to claim her."

"Do you think someone will come back?"

"No. If the survivor told the truth, he would be punished for abandoning his comrades. And shamed for fleeing from two young girls." Tiernan glanced up at me. "He likely claimed the others deserted."

I ignored the comment about my age. "You seem to know a lot about those soldiers."

"I know where they came from," was all he said.

Half a month after Nili and Marijka left, I heard a woman's voice outside. Marijka was grooming Tiernan's silver horse. She said they made good time and parted at the bank of Bitaiya Iren. That night, I dreamt Nili and I sailed across the sky as great birds.

※

Alder and cottonwood shed their autumn foliage, showering the field with yellow leaves that drowned in the damp. Marijka stopped by with apples and squash from her garden. Flocks of geese passed overhead in v-formations like honking arrows shot across the sky. The first snow fell, only to be washed away by rain.

I stopped one afternoon by the paddock, leaning on the fence to rest my leg. Tiernan was chopping a hemlock and stacking it by the cabin. The thud of his axe echoed across the clearing. I spun water in lazy spirals, then formed it into a bird and let it flutter through the fence posts.

"You should be careful," Tiernan said.

I hadn't noticed him watching. "What about?"

He came closer, resting the axe on his shoulder. He'd taken off his jerkin. His tunic, damp with sweat, clung to his chest. "Magic is not looked on kindly in this province."

My bird dissipated. "It's not magic."

"It is to those who do not understand it."

"What's not to understand? It's a tool." I pointed at the axe. "It's no different from that."

Tiernan spun the axe forward and stopped the blade a finger-width from my neck. "Do you not fear a tool in the wrong hands?"

I stayed still, barely breathing, until he pulled the blade away. "I'm not going to stop just because other people don't like it."

"That is the attitude which cost the lives of two men."

"They were going to kill us first!" I snapped. "You keep saying I shouldn't do this or that. What would you know about it?"

Tiernan's grey eyes searched mine. Then abruptly, he walked off. "Come."

"What—" I grabbed my crutches and hurried after him.

He stopped at his workshop, leaned the axe against the wall, and unlocked the door. I shuffled inside. Sunlight filtered through high, soot-stained glass panes. Cluttered tables ringed the room. Carpentry tools hung on the walls. There was a hole in the roof above an iron brazier. It seemed perfectly normal—

—until flames erupted from the brazier.

Blazing heat washed over me. I squinted in the light. And as suddenly as it appeared, the fire vanished, leaving the scent of smoke.

I whirled on Tiernan. "How did you do that?"

"Magic."

I resisted the urge to whack him with a crutch. "So you're a . . . jinrayul? A fire-caller?"

"Among less interesting things."

The burning man. I recalled how Tiernan looked the first night I met him. In hindsight, I knew I'd only seen the campfire behind him, perhaps a candle on the table as I lay on his kitchen floor, but a fitting delusion it had been.

I wandered around the workshop. Books and papers were strewn everywhere. A map as wide as my arm span was nailed to the wall. Symbols on the dirt floor flared with light as I stepped on them. "What are people so worried about? Getting blinded?"

"I am what is considered to be the wrong hands."

As I turned, something caught my eye. A sheathed sword tossed on a table. My stomach felt like it dropped out from under me. "You're a soldier."

He hung the scabbard on the wall. "I was a mercenary. There is a difference."

"Yeah, soldiers kill because they're told to. You kill because you're paid to."

"Do not condemn me so easily. A soldier would have turned you in for murder."

I tried to back away and stumbled on my crutches. "Why show me all this?"

"One day you will have to choose between who you are and who you want to be known as. Both options have consequences." Tiernan gestured around. "These are mine. Isolation, distrust, and fear."

"Maybe people are afraid because you threaten them with axes."

That prompted a smile from him. "Are you afraid of me, Kateiko?"

"Nei," I lied.

"Good. There are too many other things to fear in the world."

※

Tiernan's words echoed in my head as I washed duck potatoes on the porch. I was scared of a lot of things. That the living — or the dead — would come for me. That Nili was broken beyond repair. That my leg wouldn't heal. Maybe I wasn't afraid of Tiernan, just confused.

"Perhaps you can help me," Tiernan interrupted my thoughts.

I fumbled my grip on a potato. "With?"

He shifted his weight from foot to foot. "I want to dig a well before winter, but I do not know where."

"Why do you want a well? You have a rain barrel."

"Wells freeze less."

"You can just melt—" I rolled my eyes. "Whatever."

I brushed my hair from my eyes and glanced around. The clearing was full of water, in every blade of grass, in the horse trough, in the air. I pointed at a spot. "There's your water."

He turned. A torrent exploded higher than the workshop roof and crashed back to the ground. The brown horse whinnied and reared. Water flooded across the grass and pooled by our feet.

"That's for singeing my eyebrows off," I said.

Tiernan laughed. It was the first time I heard him laugh outright — a rich, deep sound that shook his shoulders. "You are a goose among the pigeons, Kateiko."

"Is that an insult?"

"Only if you dislike geese." He leaned against the porch railing. "Scholars with years of practice do not have that kind of strength."

"I have years of practice. I'm trying to get better than my aunt. She can hold up a river just by glaring at it."

"Can all your people control water?"

"Nei. Maybe a quarter. I mean, the rest could learn, but it's too much work for everyone to bother." I flipped the duck potato between my fingers, then pointed it at the workshop. "What do you do in there all day?"

"Research."

"Can I see?"

Tiernan raised an eyebrow. "It is dangerous. You might be bored to death."

I threw the potato at his chest.

Once the well was dug, we settled into a rhythm. Chores in the morning. Afternoons in the workshop. The books in there were full of illustrations — cities surrounded by stone walls, hills terraced like steps, plains covered with sand. In one tome, I found a sea creature that looked like one from Rin legend, but Tiernan said the book was of Sverbian myths.

He began to ask for my help. Draw this rune in the dirt. Judge whether that line was straight. He preferred to burn wood rather than call fire, so I dried logs whenever rain gusted into the woodpile. He measured everything from the height of flames to the composition of ash. When I asked why he just said, "To make it burn better."

I watched his scarred hands glide across sheets of paper, sketching diagrams in black ink. Sometimes crumpled diagrams went into the brazier. Sometimes they became patterns on the floor that flickered into life. He smiled more those days.

Tiernan cleared a table for me. I sat on a stool with my broken leg stretched out, tinkering with scraps of wood and wire while he asked me things I'd never given much thought. If I could extract pure water from tea or broth, if steam and ice were harder to control than liquid, if I could control salt water. The answers turned out to be *yes*. After I forgot about an orb of water and left it hovering in midair, he told me off for being irresponsible — then had me demonstrate how I did it.

*

"I can't believe you light fires by hand," I said, huddled up with my cottonspun blanket. The embroidered fir branches curved around me like an embrace.

"Call me old-fashioned," Tiernan said as he turned the logs. "Will that be too warm?"

I shook my head. Cold wind pierced the cracks in the cabin, driving rain and snow into the kitchen. At night it sounded like spirits trying to break in. My dreams were haunted by spectres that whispered in unknown languages. I hadn't slept through the night once in this room.

He set down the poker. "Goodnight, then."

"Tiernan." I wasn't sure what prompted me to speak. Maybe that the wind was louder than normal. Maybe that we wouldn't have many nights left together. "How long were you a mercenary?"

"Ten years."

My voice was nearly drowned out by the crackling fire. "Did you ever kill anyone?"

Tiernan sighed. He pulled up a chair, rubbing the dark stubble along his jaw. "More than you would like to know."

"Who were they?"

"Soldiers. Criminals. I would not trouble you with the stories of an old swordsman."

I studied him as he stared into the fire. There were lines at the corners of his mouth and a scar across his fine, straight nose. He wasn't old, but he looked worn, like a rag wrung out too many times. "How do you deal with it?"

"I distance myself from their memory."

I rubbed the scar on my arm. "I keep thinking about that soldier. Wondering if he had a family. But why should I care? He didn't care about us. We were just some wood witches no one would miss."

Tiernan stopped midway through stoking the fire again. "Did he call you that?"

"Yeah. What does it mean? Is that why you told me not to call water in front of people?"

"No." His knuckles were white around the poker. "It refers to your ability to shift forms. Some people think that means viirelei are . . . less than human. It is a disgusting term."

I was too confused to be offended. "Then they know nothing about us."

"Clearly not." He spoke in a low voice. "I am sorry, Kateiko. I should not have blamed you for provoking them."

"So it's okay they tried to kill us, but not that they insulted us?"

"That is not what I meant." Tiernan pinched the bridge of his nose. "I do my best to go unnoticed. I forget that for some people there is no escaping it."

I tugged at a stray thread on my blanket. "I can't forget about him. I left home because everything there reminded me of the dead. Yet here I am."

"You will not forget. You must accept what has come to pass." Tiernan rose to his feet. "Where is the blade?"

I pointed to where my belt hung by the door. "It's the double-edged one."

Tiernan unsheathed my dagger, a simple steel blade. He flipped it into the air and caught it. "This is Sverbian work."

"It was my father's. He traded for it in Vunfjel."

"In my culture, we name a weapon after it takes a life." Tiernan held the hilt out to me.

I took it reluctantly. "Is that supposed to help?"

"Weapons are tools. They have power, but you must not let them have power over you. To name it is to be in control."

"Did you name your sword?"

He nodded. "Hafelús. From an old Sverbian myth. It is the torch on the boat that ferries spirits to the land of the dead."

The light from the fire reflected off the blade, just like that night in the rain. I closed my eyes and imagined the shimmer of sunset on a lake. "Nurivel."

❋

Marijka bunched my bandages into a ball. "All right. Try walking."

Slowly, I paced up and down the kitchen, uneasy without the crutches. I'd grown used to them in the month and a half since breaking my leg. The skin on my calf was tender and the muscles had shrunk to nothing. "I think it's healed."

"Good." She began cleaning up her supplies. "I'd tell you not to rush it, but from what Tiernan tells me, that'll make you start racing deer."

I ducked my head and smiled. "Thank you. Not just for helping me, but Nili . . ."

"You girls have been through so much." Marijka kissed my cheek. "Come visit me when you feel up to the trip. I'm just down the creek."

I waved from the doorway as she crossed the field, a brimless white bonnet over her hair and a white shawl on her shoulders, like a ghostblossom among the yellow leaves. Then it was just Tiernan and me. My legs felt too bare in my cropped leggings. I'd been stuck huddling in my cloak, unable to wear my full-length woolen leggings over the bandages.

"What are you going to do now?" Tiernan asked, filling the kettle from the well bucket.

I'd played this conversation over in my head too many times to count. I just shrugged.

He set the kettle over the fire. "You planned to visit your cousin, correct?"

"Something like that."

"You should, if that is what you want." He stood with his hand on the kettle, ignoring the heat that must be seeping into his skin.

What I wanted didn't seem possible anymore. I ached knowing Toel Ginu was so close, but Fendul's warning about the Iyo had worked its way into my mind. Maybe Dunehein didn't want to see me. He never came looking for me. Without him, I wouldn't be allowed into the settlement long enough to meet someone to marry. Then I'd be stuck in the south alone until spring, at the mercy of any itheran soldier who found me.

Abruptly, I opened my purse and pulled out the silk packet I'd brought from my plank house in Aeti Ginu. I unfolded it on the table to reveal the bone needle. "That belonged to my parents. It was the ceremonial needle for their wedding marks."

Tiernan's eyes flickered to my tattoos. Aside from the kinaru and fireweed on my arm, a fan-shaped pattern below my collarbones marked me as an antayul. A Rin tattooist gave them to me at my initiation the autumn after I first attuned.

"Nili and I hoped to marry into the Iyo-jouyen. We don't have the approval of our okorebai or okoreni though. It was only a faint hope."

"You are quite young for marriage." He folded the silk back over the needle.

I rested my elbows on the windowsill and gazed outside. "It's the only way to get out."

Tiernan was silent. The kettle whistled. Finally, he said, "You are welcome to stay here."

"What?" I turned, knocking a tin off the sill. It clattered to the floor and rolled away.

"You will need to build up strength before travelling." He seemed focused on pouring water into the teapot. "I cleaned the loft out for you. Now that you can climb the ladder."

"I thought you expected me to leave."

Tiernan set two mugs on the table. "It gets lonely in these woods."

And so autumn passed, and winter began.

7.

WINTER

The loft was cozy with a peaked roof and a glass window. It wasn't high enough to stand in, but it was deep enough that I wasn't afraid of rolling over the edge in my sleep. Heat rose from the kitchen to warm it. I hung my kinaru shawl from the rafters so I saw it every morning.

I relished being able to move again. I carried a ladder around and stuffed moss between the logs to insulate the cabin. Marijka showed me the glass building where she grew herbs. The cloudy panes set in a wood grid warped the view of the trees. I ran around the clearing to see my footprints in the snow, but even that exhausted me.

Fendul was right about one thing. Winters were getting worse. I spent days tanning furs — scraping the flesh clean, rubbing in a slurry of animal brain, then stretching, drying, and smoking the hides — so they were supple but wouldn't rot. The smell made me want to vomit. I sewed rabbit-skin gloves and a mantle from the black fur of chubby marsh rats, set aside the best pelts for trading, and stitched the rest into blankets. Technically, I was only allowed to trap on Iyo land for food, but I figured if I ate whatever wound up in my snares, it wasn't breaking any laws.

"What did you eat last winter?" I asked Tiernan one day. Salmon and duck potato were Rin staples, but I hadn't gathered enough to last until spring, and the vegetable bins in his cellar were down to rutabaga and wild onion.

"Not much, to be honest." Tiernan scratched his jaw. He did that a lot, whenever his face grew dark with stubble. "Maika gave me preserves, but mainly I bought supplies in Crieknaast. I planned to go soon."

"Can I come? I've never been to a town that big."

"It is several hours on horseback. Can you ride?"

"On a horse? Nei. I don't have one anyway."

He raised an eyebrow. "There is a mare in the stable."

I stared at him. "You can't expect me to ride that dead archer's horse."

"You can never overcome your fears if you avoid them, Kateiko."

That's how I wound up in the paddock staring at a horse whose head was as big as my torso. I jumped back as the giant creature snuffled at me. "I don't trust intelligent things."

"You have to trust her before she will trust you," Tiernan said. "Do not think about her previous rider. Horses have histories of their own."

"What've you been calling it?"

"Cefal. It is just Sverbian for 'horse.'" He had a slight smile. "She is yours to name."

"What did you name yours?"

"Gwmniwyr."

"Goomni—" I shook my head. "Do Sverbians spit and decide it's a name?"

I looked into the mare's huge brown eyes and remembered what Tiernan had said about the power of names. I wondered how many battles the horse had survived. She deserved a name to carry her away from that.

"How do you feel about Anwea?" I asked. Anwen Bel was the calmest place I knew.

The horse nuzzled my face. Her whiskers tickled.

Tiernan led us around the paddock while I got used to the reins and saddle. After the first day, I was sore. After the third, I could barely walk. Just when I got Anwea to follow Gwmniwyr through the woods, fat snowflakes began to fall.

✳

I stared at the roof late into the night listening to windowpanes rattle and branches creak. The wind whistled a single word. *Look.* My cousin Emehein always said that in antayul lessons, when he was helping me find water with my mind. He'd make me close my eyes. *Look, Kako.*

A gust slammed into the cabin. Icy air burst in. I scrambled up and felt my way to the loft edge—

Warm light flooded the kitchen. The outer door swung on its hinges. Tiernan dashed out from the bedroom below me and shouldered it shut. An orb of fire followed. Eddies of snow settled around him.

"I knew it," I said.

Tiernan jerked. The orb flickered. "Gods' sakes, Kateiko." He shook snow out of his dark hair. He was in trousers and a thin shirt, still half-asleep. "Knew what?"

"You don't always use old-fashioned fire." I lay on my stomach with my arms over the edge and grinned at him.

"Have you ever tried to light a candle in a hurry?" he grumbled.

I waved my hand back and forth, evaporating the snow. "Come up here. Bring your fire."

At first I thought he'd refuse, but then he set his foot on the ladder. The orb bobbed up after him. He sat with his back to the wall, elbows resting on his knees.

I rolled onto my side. "I can never sleep through snowstorms. It feels like the world is awake and wants me to be awake too."

Tiernan glanced at the window webbed with frost. "Is it warm enough up here?"

"It's fine. I just . . . can't stop thinking."

He was silent for a moment. Then he said, "Do you want to tell me about it?"

I fiddled with a lock of my hair draped across the floor. "What do you think . . . happens to people after they die?"

"Most of my people believe spirits sail across the ocean to a land of abundance."

"Wait. You came here over the ocean."

"I assure you I am not dead." Tiernan reached toward me. I stilled as his hand went near my hair, but he just touched his fingers to my wrist. He was surprisingly warm. I felt a twinge of disappointment when he pulled away.

"What do *you* believe?" I pressed.

"Honestly, I am not sure. I would like to believe Thaerijmur exists. But then so might Bøkkhem."

"Isn't *bøkkhem* a curse word in Sverbian?"

"It is a barren flatland inhabited by spirits the god Bøkkai has stolen. It is also a curse word, yes."

I crinkled my nose. "Getting stuck there forever does sound like a curse."

Tiernan shrugged. "Ferish priests say some spirits live in the sky and some underground. I have heard many beliefs. None seem more or less plausible."

"Rin elders say the land of the dead is right here. Everyone whose blood flows into the ground winds up in Aeldu-yan. We can't see it, but the barrier is weaker in winter." I waved my hand through the air. "There. I just hit someone's great-great-grandparent."

"Parallel worlds do not work that way."

"You just said you don't believe in that stuff."

"There is . . . a theory." He laid my embroidered blanket on his arm and pinched it against his sleeve. "Imagine worlds are fabric. Two pieces next to each other, made from different cloth. They fold around each other, but never join."

"What if you unravelled them and wove them together?"

Tiernan gave me an amused look. "I do not recommend that."

I gazed at the crackling fire orb. "So there could be another world we can't get to."

"Maybe several. Theological scholars call them *shoirdrygen*, or splintered worlds. I doubt any are filled with the spirits of the dead. They are probably more like our own."

"I think . . . I might've . . . seen one."

He leaned forward. "Where?"

I recounted the incidents at Kotula Huin's shore, the shrine, and the wasteland. "I saw you the third time. Before I knew who you were."

Tiernan gave me a long look, like the first time he saw me call water. He seemed about to ask something, then shook his head. "Perhaps your ancestors were warning you."

"It's not funny."

"You passed out, Kateiko. You probably hallucinated and your mind forged a connection to the memory when you met me."

"That's what I figured." I sighed. The wind howled, scraping branches against the cabin. "But I don't know what to believe."

❋

Just before sunrise, I carefully opened the door. Snow formed a wall as high as my knees, packed into the porch. I stepped onto the drift, walked across the stiff crust, and stuck a tallow-soaked torch into the snow. Silence weighed down. Even the horses were quiet in the stable.

When I left home, there were only two explanations for what I had seen. One, I was losing my mind. Two, I really had seen Aeldu-yan. The second scared me more. Years after my parents' blood flowed into the ground, I'd accepted that all I could do was focus on living. *Rivers keep flowing.* I couldn't get lost among the spectres and shadows again.

I hadn't considered a third possibility. A world the Rin had no stories about.

Sunlight burst over the hills. The torch ignited at a spark from my flint, blazing like a tiger lily among the whiteness. I undid my cloak and let it fall. Underneath, I wore my kinaru shawl with the laces knotted around my wrists.

I repeated the chant from the Kotula Huin ceremony, my voice building as I tried to recall the pounding of drums in a distant valley. I spread my arms and called on the snow, lifting waves that swirled around me in wide circles. Light reflected off the white inner layer of my shawl and refracted through thousands of snowflakes.

Icy wind gusted across the clearing, tearing at my shawl. Tongues of flame licked up snowflakes and spat them out as steam. The wind stung my eyes, burned my lungs, clawed at my skin, but I clung to the driving snow. Then I looked to the hills and the pink sky.

Nothing. No visions. No rifts. If there was another world, I was cut off from it.

I slumped to my knees. The torch hissed out. The wind stilled. Arcs of snow settled around me and melted on my skin.

❋

Tiernan entered the kitchen not long after sunrise. I was curled by the fireplace with my embroidered fir blanket, fingertips pressed to my mouth, skin flushed with cold. "You must be freezing," he said.

"Mmm." I stared at ashes banked over the coals. I heard him pull on his boots, go outside, and come back in.

He tossed a split log in the fireplace and raked back the ashes. "That was quite the storm. We will have to hold off going to Criek-naast for a few days."

"Mmm."

Tiernan crouched by the fireplace, blocking my view. Flames began to crackle. He turned to face me. "Kateiko."

I rubbed my eyes. "Sorry. I didn't sleep."

"Did the wind keep you awake?"

"You could say that." I held out my hands to soak up the warmth. "I kept thinking about what we talked about last night."

"It confounds dedicated scholars. My explanation was not nearly sufficient." He pulled a book from the shelf and flipped through it. "There may be something of interest to you in these."

"I already looked through them. There weren't any pictures."

"Reading the words helps."

My cheeks felt as hot as the crackling log. "I don't know how to read."

He raised his eyebrows. "Why not say so before?"

I bunched my sleeve in front of my face to muffle my voice. "I didn't want you to think I was stupid."

Tiernan closed the book. "There is a difference between stupidity and lack of education. One can be remedied."

From then on, he spent the evenings teaching me. We started with Coast Trader letters since it was the only language we shared. It took some time to wrap my mind around the idea that each letter corresponded to a sound, not a meaning like Aikoto symbols. I spent my spare time tracing letters in the snow until I saw them when I shut my eyes.

One evening, I asked how to write my name. Tiernan tapped the quill against his hand as he thought, then dipped it in the inkwell and wrote several strokes on a scrap of paper. "That is an approximation of the sounds."

"Huh." I studied his precise strokes, the ink shining in the candlelight.

He added another set of letters under the first row. "Sverbian is harder to spell. That says 'Marijka Riekkanehl.'"

I matched the letters to their sounds, making silent motions with my mouth. "But I thought that was a 'j' sound." I pointed at the first word. "Like 'jouyen.'"

"It is always pronounced as 'y' in Sverbian. Coast Trader writing was adapted from Ferish. It does not work well with other languages."

"That doesn't make sense." I pushed the paper back at him. "Do your name."

Tiernan patiently added a third line. I thought the strokes of his name had a sort of quiet dignity. Mine seemed haphazard and aimless in comparison.

"Sverbian second names come from your parents, right? The goatherds in Vunfjel didn't use them much."

He nodded. "Riekkanehl means 'daughter of Riekkan.' Heilind means 'son of Heile.'"

"That's more exciting than Rin." I rested my chin in my hands. "My mother was Sohiko and my father Mikiod. What would that make my name?"

"Sohikoehl. I think you will find Rin easier to write."

"It'd be easier to teach Anwea to write." I let my forehead fall onto the paper. Sleeping poorly had caught up to me. "I'm never going to understand this."

He gathered up the spare paper. "It has been a week. Most people take years to learn."

"I don't want to wait years."

"Theological treatises are not a good starting point. You need to practise the basics first. A carpenter must know his tools before he can build a house."

Most of Tiernan's books were in Sverbian. The Trader ones were full of words I didn't understand even when he read them aloud. Staring at the pages felt like glimpsing another world, both seeming to hold something important just out of reach.

I sat up. "Where would I find something easier to read?"

"Crieknaast. Maybe. Even the newspaper there is in Sverbian."

I realized he was smiling. "What?"

Tiernan tapped his forehead. "You have ink there."

I rubbed my forehead and saw a black smear on my palm. "Please, let's go. The paths are clearing up."

"Honestly, I am not sure I can eat fish all winter anyway." He put the stopper on the inkwell and began packing things into a writing case. "To bed with you then. We have a long trip ahead."

8.

CRIEKNAAST

I woke to water dripping on my face. No matter how hard I tried to seal the cabin, I always missed some spot. Clumps of melting snow slid off evergreens around the clearing, so I left my fur mantle and just wore my cloak. Tiernan carried his sword, Hafelús, for the first time I'd ever seen, which made me uneasier than I cared to admit.

He'd pointed out Tømmbrind Creek's headwaters on a map. It flowed southwest from the mountains to the ocean, parallel to the Holmgar canyon. Crieknaast was on its banks, but instead of following the water, we took a narrow road through the woods. I was glad to avoid the valley of stumps Nili and I had encountered.

It was a painfully slow journey. Anwea was just as likely to nibble the underbrush as she was to follow Gwmniwyr. I wasn't used to giving instructions to another living thing. My limbs ached when we stopped for lunch, but I held back my complaints. Eventually the slush gave way to mud. After being so isolated, it was a shock to see other riders.

"How often do you make this trip?" I asked Tiernan.

"Every few months, whenever Maika comes to sell her herbal tinctures. The inn has the closest you will find to a real Sverbian pub in this province."

"You always say 'this province.' Like that should mean something to me."

"My cabin and Maika's house are in the north of Eremur. Crieknaast is in the northeast. Eremur has its own government, but is officially a territory of Sverba."

"Says who?"

"Sverba." He smiled wryly. "No viirelei nation living within Eremur recognizes it as a province."

"How far does it cover?"

"Everything west of the Turquoise Mountains, from the Holmgar south to the Hårengar."

"The . . . heron river?" I chewed my lip. "That's all the way into Kae and Yula territory. Most of the southern half of the Aikoto Confederacy."

The sun was setting by the time we drew near. One minute we were surrounded by forest, the next we rode through fields of winter rye, the steep hills scattered with log cabins and herds of shaggy white goats. Mountains loomed on the eastern horizon, their jagged peaks lit by orange sunlight. Our shadows stretched out in front of us.

Crieknaast's main street ran alongside the water. Dirt roads split into a web of houses, frost-blackened gardens, and muddy lots stacked with logs. The town smelled like wood and horses and fresh bread — but it was quiet. There were no playing children or scrounging dogs like in Vunfjel. I thought maybe it was just the season until I saw Tiernan's expression.

A boy helped us stable the horses at the inn. Tiernan had explained how the place worked, including that it had communal rooms separated by sex. As we left the stable, he told me the inn was called the Tømmbrind Arms.

"As in . . ." I held up my arms.

"As in a coat of arms." He nodded at the design etched on the pub's glass windows.

A rush of noise poured out as he opened the door. Loud voices, clattering dishes, scraping chairs. The pub was a low room with a stone fireplace, long tables, and smoky air glowing with candlelight. Tiernan spoke to a man behind a counter. Sverbian reminded me of rattling stones, harsh and musical at once.

I pulled a handful of coins from my purse and paid two iron five-pann. I didn't need to save them for betting with Nili anymore. The innkeeper brought steaming bowls of stew and mugs of tea. As we took our seats, two men hastily looked away. I thought they were staring at me until I heard a mutter of "Heilind."

"Do people know you here?" I whispered.

"A few." Tiernan leaned over to a stocky blonde woman. "What happened?"

She started to reply, then looked at me and switched into thickly accented Coast Trader. "The lumber camp up in the mountains. Massacred a few nights ago."

Tiernan closed his eyes, jaw clenched tight. "Who was behind it?"

"That be the mystery, innit? Came like bats in the night. No one left alive to talk. One of 'em councillors from the capital is in the town hall now, sorting it with Mayor Vorhagind."

"The Council is here?" Tiernan put his mug down so hard tea sloshed over the edge.

"What's the Council?" I asked.

"They run the provincial government from the capital city, Caladheå," he said. "The mayor knows better than to call on them."

"What else can he do?" said one of the men watching us earlier.

"Fifty of our men are in the military. The least Caladheå can do is send them back when we need them."

"Not much good our boys can do," the woman said. "People say it's Suriel come back. You know, that angry ghost up in 'em mountains."

I drew a sharp breath. "There's a spirit up there?"

"Ask him." The other man pointed at Tiernan. "That be your specialty, right, mage?"

"I have no dealings with spirits." Tiernan made a point of turning his back on the men. "We will leave straight after going to the market tomorrow, Kateiko. We should be safe in town, but it is best not to linger."

I barely slept that night amid the murmurs and shuffling of itheran women. The thought of a furious spirit lurking outside town swirled around my head until I felt dizzy. Maybe the aeldu had been trying to communicate for months and couldn't until the barrier thinned in winter.

※

We were leaving the Tømmbrind Arms after breakfast when the innkeeper waved us over. I couldn't understand the conversation, but Tiernan's face went from wary to annoyed to resigned before he strode outside.

"What's going on?" I asked, hurrying after him.

"The mayor asked me to come to the town hall."

I stopped in the middle of the street, leaning to balance out the heavy pelts in my shoulder bag. "How does the mayor know who you are?"

"I worked for him as a mercenary." He turned and walked backward. "Are you coming?"

The town hall was wedged between the main street and the

creek, surrounded by dead flowers and slushy puddles. I followed Tiernan up creaking timber steps and under a huge set of elk antlers mounted above the doors. A woman ushered us into a sparse room where three men hunched over a table strewn with papers.

Their low, harsh discussion cut off. The man in the centre straightened, showing a burly chest and a bristly yellow beard. "Thank you for coming, Heilind. I trust you heard the news. We are short on time. Councillor Montès is here from the capital and is now consulting with his aides."

"Should she be here?" one of the other men said with a nod at me.

The bearded man waved a hand. "'Tis fine. Here be how things stand. Took us three days to reach the lumber camp after that blizzard. Found twenty men, throats slit as they slept. The ones who woke were cut down by swords. All tracks lost to the melting snow. Montès thinks a lumberman went mad, but one man cannot do all that."

I shuddered. I wouldn't sleep well tonight.

"I know what you are thinking, Vorhagind," Tiernan said. "But Suriel has lain low for more than two years."

"This be not the first time since the Dúnravn massacre." Mayor Vorhagind pulled a map from the papers and drew two marks. "A mine collapsed this summer. Thirty men crushed to death. Bad accident, we thought. But slit throats be no accident."

Tiernan leaned over the map. "*Någvakt bøkkhem,*" he swore.

I peered over his shoulder. A red cross glistened on either side of the creek at the foot of the mountains. I didn't know how aeldu could kill anyone, let alone in summer when the barrier was thickest.

Tiernan tapped the crosses on the map. "You have men stationed here, yes? Pull them out, now. Your best hope is to abandon Dúnravn Pass."

Vorhagind shook his head. "There lies our issue. Councillor Montès is pressuring us not to close the tannery that lies up that way.

'Tis good for trade in Caladheå. And truth, my townsfolk need the money. By the time we rebuild somewhere else, the fur trapping season will be over."

Tiernan sighed and rubbed the back of his neck. "What do you want from the Caladheå Council?"

"Military support. Our militia here has too few men." Vorhagind spread his hands. "Traders from the Iyo nation told us Suriel was active again. They were right two years ago."

"Spirits don't carry swords," said the other aide.

"An army helmed by a spirit does," Tiernan said.

"Mayor Vorhagind, what did the Iyo call Suriel?" I shrank back when everyone looked at me. "Did they say it was an aeldu?"

"Something like that, missy. Saidu, I think it were."

A chill went up my neck. Saidu weren't limited by season like aeldu were — they *made* the seasons. They'd been dormant for centuries, but maybe the Storm Year caused one to finally wake.

Vorhagind put his hands on the table and leaned forward. "We need evidence Suriel is behind this. Caladheå will not send help otherwise."

Tiernan stepped back. "No evidence will convince the Council this was done by a magical being."

"We are not mages, Heilind. Montès may believe it from you."

"I have nothing to offer you," Tiernan said. "I am sorry, Vorhagind. You knew how the Council would react."

Vorhagind gave a heavy sigh. "I knew. But I had to try. Right, then—"

He was interrupted by a knock. An aide opened the door. Three men pushed past, all with black hair, all shorter than everyone else in the room. A faint spicy scent followed them in. They fit everything I'd heard about Ferish.

The one in front held his loose black robe away from the muddy floor. He had a receding hairline and a pinched face as if he'd been drinking cranberry wine. When he said something to Vorhagind, it took me a moment to realize he was speaking Trader.

"Let us move to the main hall, Councillor Montès," Vorhagind said, but the robed man's attention had strayed to Tiernan.

"Ah, you found a mage," Montès said. "What a relief it must be for the cumulative years of education in Crieknaast to double overnight."

Tiernan put a hand on my shoulder. "Time to go," he said in a low voice.

Montès's gaze slid to me. "Keeping company with the natives, Heilind? How nice to see you enjoying the countryside, dirt and all."

Everyone flinched. I was a moment behind, held up by his accent, but a hot flush of anger swept over me when it clicked.

Tiernan's hand tightened. "*Don't*," he said into my ear.

I glared at Montès and shoved past the men. I didn't stop until I reached the dead flower beds outside the hall. Cold wind gusted down the street, whistling through the drainpipes.

"I am sorry you had to hear that," Tiernan said behind me.

"It's not him I care about." I took a deep breath. "First the mayor asks for your help, then a councillor calls you by name. Is there something you need to tell me?"

He gazed at the towering white mountains. "I have dealt with the Council before. I will not again. That is all that matters."

✳

The market was almost enough to distract me. I felt like I was in a huge twisting rabbit burrow, weaving down narrow aisles and popping outside through gaps in the wall. Warm light streamed over high wooden barriers between clusters of tables. Chickens squawked, goats knocked their horns against shuddering pens, crested blue jays scavenged crumbs from the dirt. I kept stopping to look at glassy-eyed fish or metal buckles or cloudy jars of preserves.

It wasn't until I was surrounded by so many people that it hit me how out of place I was. The women all wore their hair pinned up under knit bonnets. Under their cloaks, I glimpsed white dresses and coloured bodices. In Vunfjel, it was common for girls to wear leggings and braids while herding goats. I kept my hood up over my unbound hair and tugged my cloak low around my ankles.

I kept losing track of Tiernan. His cloak and boots looked just like anyone else's, if more worn. As I watched him buy saddle and bridle oil, I was struck by the beauty of the scene — Tiernan talking with a merchant, sunlight spilling through wide doors, water blowing off the roof outside. Then he glanced up and met my gaze. I whirled away and knocked over a girl carrying a basket of lye soap.

In one stall, I found a few crates of books, spines creased and pages rumpled. Every one I flipped open had the angular symbols I'd come to recognize as Sverbian writing. "Do you have any books in Coast Trader?" I asked an elderly woman sorting pots of ink.

"Sorry, dear," she said with a smile. "Not much call for that 'round these parts."

My disappointment faded when I came across a clutch of wire racks hung with sheets of pale leather. A boy about my age perched on a stool, stitching a goat-skin glove.

"That's good," I said. "Better than I could do."

"Yeah?" He grinned. "Just killing time. Need any leather?"

"Actually, I'm selling pelts. Do you deal in fur?"

"Depends. Where do you trap?"

"Down the creek. I have permission to hunt on an itheran's land." I pointed at Tiernan a few shops down. "Ask him if you want."

"Nah, that be good enough for me." He swept his tools aside and patted the table.

I pulled a bundle of marsh rat pelts from my shoulder bag and spread them out. "They're already tanned. I just don't have time to track down a furrier."

The boy examined the fur and flipped them over to check the underside. "Not bad, but furriers are wary of pelts we don't tan ourselves. I can offer forty pann apiece."

"They're worth a half-sovereign each. You won't find any nicks or damage."

The boy's lips quirked up. "Forty-five pann and you tell me the name of the person who tanned these."

"Good enough for me." I grinned. "I'm Kateiko. You?"

"Ingard. Nice to meet you." He counted coins from a canvas purse. "Bit of advice, the new tannery by the mountains pays better. They ship straight to Caladheå and the old countries. Fur be worth a lordling's ransom there."

"Isn't it bad business to tell me that?"

"Doesn't matter to me." Ingard rested his elbows on the table. "My little brother works at that tannery. I don't care who sells where as long our wages get paid."

I wrinkled my nose. "I couldn't work in a tannery all the time. Smells awful."

"That's why they built it so far away. I throw my brother straight in the bath when he gets home." He turned as a little girl dashed up, yellow braid flying. "*Vanek*, Thyja?"

"Ingard, Ingard, *cijmmag*!" She seized his hand and dragged him into the aisle.

Everyone was heading outside, even the merchants. Tiernan appeared as we stepped into howling wind. The streams of people merged, flowing down the street to the town hall where Montès and Vorhagind stood on the steps. One of Montès's aides seemed to be translating his speech into Trader.

"After much deliberation, the mayor and I concluded there is no need to dispatch the military to Crieknaast," the aide said, pausing to hear the next line. "We believe the attack on the lumber camp was an isolated incident. We will be investigat—"

"What about the mine?" someone yelled.

The aide kept speaking as though nothing had happened, but a gust drowned out some of his words. "The new tannery near Dúnravn Pass will remain active until further notice—"

The crowd erupted into shouts. I stood on my toes and peered over everyone. Mayor Vorhagind shook his head and sliced his arm through the air. I realized with a shock he was telling them he disagreed, even though it meant publicly opposing the Council.

Councillor Montès rounded on him. The aide stepped aside as the two men began to argue, Vorhagind punctuating his words with sharp, sweeping gestures.

A clamour broke out near the steps. Voices mixed with the wind until my ears were filled with a dull roar. Montès backed away and stumbled on his robe. Vorhagind spread his arms to hold back the crush of people, just as my hood blew off and hair swirled in front of my eyes.

I clamped a hand over my hair in time to see Montès retreat inside. Vorhagind held up a hand to the crowd, ushered the aides in and disappeared after them. The doors slammed shut. A man leapt onto the steps and began addressing the townspeople.

"Kateiko, we need to leave," Tiernan called.

Before I could reach him, Ingard scooped up the little girl. He patted her braid and spoke into her ear. I could only make out one word. *Kinaru.*

"What did you say to her?" I asked.

"The story about Suriel's birds that eat kids. Only thing that makes her behave."

"Kinaru don't — oh. Fuck." My body went cold as if I'd jumped into a glacial lake. I whirled to Tiernan. "I know what Suriel is."

Tiernan's dark brows knit together. He hadn't heard me.

I had a moment of agony. I'd need to get closer, but his hair gusted around his face. If he were Rin he'd hold his hair aside — but of course itherans had no idea about our taboos. I seized his elbow and dragged him across the street into an alley.

"The Iyo called Suriel a saidu," I said once we were sheltered by timber walls. "We call them spirits, but it's not the right word. Saidu aren't dead like aeldu. They're not really *alive* either."

I broke off. How could I explain something all Rin understood from childhood, growing up with stories about saidu? I could barely explain in my own language, let alone a muddled trade language.

I started over. "Saidu are elemental spirits that control the forces of nature. Weather, seasons, all that. There'd be dozens in Iyun Bel, living in the forest and rivers and mountains. My elders say we don't see them because they're sleeping, but the Iyo must think a tel-saidu has woken. An air spirit. Maybe the blizzard was a warning."

The same look crossed Tiernan's face as when we were in the town hall. "This wind—"

I grabbed his hand. "The tannery. We have to get them out—"

"We cannot risk getting involved, Kateiko."

"They'll die if we don't! You're a soldier. Aren't you supposed to protect people?"

He pulled out of my grip, anger flashing across his face. "They will not listen to us."

I spun away and scanned the street. "Ingard!" I shouted, spotting him with the girl on his shoulder. I pushed through the throng of people and shook his arm. He gave me a confused look before following me.

"Someone has to go to the tannery and make them leave," I told him back in the alley. "I think Suriel is real, and here now, planning another attack. Is there anyone who can—"

"How do you know?" Ingard interrupted.

"The wind. It's a sign. Suriel—" I faltered when I saw his expression.

"They can't just up and leave. They'll lose their jobs."

"Better than their lives."

"Our jobs be our lives." Ingard glanced at the little girl. "Our father was in the mine that collapsed. That's why our brother works at the tannery. We can't afford for it to close."

I felt a sudden ache in my chest. I knew the bitterness in his voice too well.

"Did the mine collapse right after that windstorm this summer?" Tiernan asked.

"Yeah, but it were just an accident. A rockslide came down the mountain."

Tiernan gave him a hard look. "Would you stake lives on that?"

The girl wriggled in Ingard's arms. "Ingard, you hafta get Dåmar. The tall lady said so."

Ingard bit his lip. "It's not that easy. Only people who don't believe in Suriel took that job. I could get all the way there and half of 'em would refuse to leave."

I turned to Tiernan desperately. "Vorhagind can make them leave, can't he?"

"Yes. But he cannot speak to them while he is busy with Montès." Tiernan paused. "The workers might accept an official writ, but you will have trouble getting one right now."

"Can't you write one and say it's from Vorhagind?"

"Getting arrested for forgery is not high on my list of priorities, Kateiko."

"If you can get a writ, I'll take it," Ingard said. "I know the way. I just need to find someone to look after Thylanniga and the shop."

Under his skepticism I saw fierce determination. He could leave now and rescue his brother, but he was willing to risk the wait so we could save everyone.

"Meet me here when you're ready," I said.

The wind almost knocked me over when I stepped into the street. The shouts had become a chant that crept along my bones. I weaved through the crowd only to find barrel-chested men blocking the steps to the town hall. I tried to squeeze past, but it was like pushing aside ancient rioden. They barely glanced at me. I ducked under the railing instead.

My hopes fell immediately. A man stood under the elk antlers, arms crossed, a wooden truncheon in one hand.

"I need to speak to the mayor," I called.

"No one goes in or out," he said. "Not until the councillor changes his mind and calls the military."

"You can't keep everyone locked up in there!"

He glanced at the door. "Looks like I can."

"Aeldu save us. I don't have time for this." I vaulted over the railing and landed in a puddle, splashing everyone nearby. I shoved past them and strode to the back of the hall. The gardens there were empty. Everyone had converged at the front like scavengers on carrion.

A thin strip of dirt separated the wall from the creek, not enough to stand on comfortably. I tossed my cloak on the ground and stepped into icy water to my thighs. Choppy waves splashed against me as I waded toward the nearest window.

"This is not what people mean by backdoor diplomacy," Tiernan called from the bank.

"Just make sure no one comes." I stepped onto the dirt ledge, gripping the windowsill for balance, and dug my fingernails under the frame. It stuck fast.

"Kateiko, you have no idea what you are getting into."

"I'm not — letting them — die." I winced as my nail tore. I jumped back into the creek and tried the next window, and the next.

Finally, one slid up with a groan and shower of paint chips. I swung a dripping leg over the sill and tumbled through the narrow opening. My knee knocked into something. The room was full of dusty stacked crates. I pressed my ear to the door but couldn't hear anything over banging shutters and the churning creek. I crept down a dim corridor and cracked open the far door.

The woman from that morning stood behind a desk, clutching a stack of papers, staring out the window. She tossed the papers onto the desk when I entered. "You can't be in here," she hissed. "How did you even—"

"I need to speak to the mayor. It's urgent."

"You can't. He's with the councillor." She glanced back at the window, looking out at the crowded street and unnatural wind. "I could take him a message," she said finally.

I gritted my teeth. "Tell him — tell him the viirelei girl with Tiernan Heilind says Suriel is an air spirit. The wind means he's going to attack again. Vorhagind has to sign a writ to close the tannery. We'll take it there. He just has to write it."

The woman gave me a piercing look. "Wait in there. Keep quiet."

I retreated into the corridor and slumped against the wall to wait. Exhaustion dragged my body down. I hadn't slept properly since leaving Aeti Ginu more than two months ago, kept awake by whispers on the wind. This explained why.

The chanting faded, replaced by a single male voice. I wondered what was happening out there. If I was doing the right thing.

Ingard's brother and all the others would be out of work. I'd never depended on a wage, but things worked differently in Crieknaast.

I heard faint yelling. The chanting from the townspeople grew louder. I was sitting on the floor with my feet against the wall when the door opened.

"Here." The woman held out a folded paper sealed with red wax. "Vorhagind says to tell the workers he'll find 'em new jobs."

I scrambled up. "Thank you so much."

"I can't help you get out. That be the militia captain guarding the door."

"It's okay." I remembered to bow my head before hurrying down the corridor. I slid out the window into the creek and wrenched the frame shut, clutching the paper to my chest.

My cloak was still on the bank. Tiernan wasn't. As I wondered if he would've left town without me, a drop struck my face. And another. The sky had clouded over while I was inside. I glanced down and saw wet dots speckling the paper.

"Nei. Shit. *Taku taku taku*!" I pulled the water out before the ink ran, but I couldn't keep that up forever — not once I handed it off to Ingard. "Kaid! What do I do?"

A memory flashed into my head. Tiernan's workshop, after he told me off for forgetting a water orb. I explained how a fragment of thought kept it in place even when my conscious mind forgot. He asked if I could keep water *out* as well as *in*, but I never gave it much thought after proving I could. It was simpler to waterproof things with resin or fish oil rather than splinter my mind all over the rainforest.

That wasn't an option now. I wove a barrier around the paper, making sure every bit was sealed. Raindrops slid off like it was made of glass. I grabbed my cloak and ran.

Ingard was in the alley, holding the reins of a scruffy horse. "Did you get it?"

I held the writ out with both hands so the wind didn't snatch it. "It's waterproof. Don't ask how."

He tucked it into his breast pocket. "Where's your friend?"

"I don't know. It doesn't matter."

Ingard was mounting his horse when a rider appeared at the end of the alley. Panic flared through me, wrapped up in a memory of glinting swords, charging horses, mud and water. I squinted into the grey sheets of rain.

Tiernan and Gwmniwyr.

"I thought you gave up on us," I called.

"I cannot let a young boy ride into danger alone," he said.

I broke into a smile, a broad, genuine one untainted by sarcasm or bitterness. Riding with them was out of the question. I'd only slow them down. It was in their hands now.

※

I couldn't stay in town. I felt too anxious, too out of place. I couldn't understand anything the militia captain said, but it didn't seem like the crowd was leaving any time soon. I asked a woman how far it was to the tannery and she said two hours' ride in good weather. So I went into the woods. I tried not to think about how it'd be snowing near the mountains. I tried not to worry as even in the foothills, rain-drops turned to stinging snow and still the wind didn't let up.

I went back to town when I guessed four hours had passed. The crowd around the town hall had thinned, but most people were still there, sitting in the mud with hoods and shawls over their heads. Even if Tiernan hadn't warned me about calling water in front of people, there was no way I could protect them all.

Five hours passed. I followed the main street to the east edge of town and climbed a log pile to get a better view. Six hours. Night fell. Finally, firelight came down the hill.

I ran to meet them, maybe twenty people loaded onto horse-drawn sleighs. Tiernan rode at the front with a torch, wet hair plastered to his face, blood on his knuckles. He steered Gwmniwyr off to the side and dismounted. The silver gelding was as calm as always.

"Everyone is here," he reassured me. "A tree fell on the road. Startled a horse into breaking a sleigh. We had to redistribute everyone, travel slower."

Ingard rode up with a boy of about fifteen seated behind him. They slid off and waved the sleighs on as the four of us walked together, shielding our eyes from the snow.

"Ingard told us what you did," Dåmar said to me. "Is Suriel a real spirit?"

"Yes," Tiernan said when I hesitated.

"Kinaru don't exist though, no matter what your sister thinks," I said.

I fell back with Ingard as Dåmar and Tiernan went ahead with the horses. "I brought you something." I handed him a heavy burlap sack.

He gave me a confused look. "What is it?"

"Two rabbits and a cloud weasel. You can sell the furs even if you don't need food. Just be careful if anyone asks where they came from. I'm not . . . sure I'm allowed to hunt here."

Ingard looked at me, his mouth half-open. I had a sudden wrenching fear he'd turn me in. He probably had to report poachers all the time. I was such an idiot—

He leaned over and kissed my cheek. "Thank you, Kateiko."

A warm blush spread over my face. I hoped neither Tiernan nor Dåmar had glanced back.

9.

MOTHS OF ALL KINDS

Tiernan refused to stay in Crieknaast. Not even to spend the night before travelling.

"I thought you were only worried about Suriel attacking the pass," I said.

"Crieknaast is on the verge of a political catastrophe," he said. "We have done all we can. You have to trust me now, Kateiko."

If I had trouble riding in daylight, it was twice as hard in the dark, thrice in a snowstorm — at least until I let Anwea navigate. We stopped at a gristmill outside town to load the saddlebags with flour and rye groats before moving on. Once we were in the woods, Tiernan summoned a fire orb to light the way.

The weather eased about halfway back. My ears rang after so many hours of wind. I was sliding off the saddle with weariness when a flock of squalling birds hurtled past, skimming the ball of fire and vanishing into darkness. Anwea snorted and skittered back, jerking at the reins.

"*Wala, wala,*" I soothed. "*Dayomi.*"

Tiernan reined in Gwmniwyr. "Are you all right?"

"Yeah, she just . . ." I strained my ears over the fading shrieks. "What's that sound?" A faint rumbling came from the southwest.

The fire winked out. "Get off the road."

I dug my heels into Anwea's side. She shied into the underbrush, branches snagging my cloak.

A company of riders approached, two abreast between tangled walls of trees and bushes. As my eyes adjusted, I saw rearing elk sigils emblazoned on their breastplates. My breath caught in my throat.

The man in front raised a hand. They slowed to a halt. "Where are you headed?"

"Due west, near Tømmbrind Creek," Tiernan said. "Are you riding to Crieknaast?"

"Yes." He looked at Anwea. "Have you met trouble on the road?"

"She was just spooked by birds. Hush, Anwea." I hoped to the aeldu none of the soldiers recognized her or me, but as I turned her away to hide the white patch on her forehead, my eyes strayed toward the captain's.

He held my gaze for a moment, then nodded and raised his hand again. I counted twenty horses as they passed, churning up mud and snow.

"A messenger must have left hours before us to reach the capital to ask for troops so quickly," Tiernan said after the storm of hooves faded.

"I only saw one of Montès's aides outside the town hall. Maybe the other turned on Montès and called the military himself?"

"Maybe. But that is not nearly enough men to challenge Suriel."
He sounded uncertain. I was surprised how much that unsettled me.

✳

I woke to see Tiernan moving about the kitchen. I lay still and watched him through half-closed eyes. I'd trudged into the cabin well into the night and gone to sleep on the floor. It wasn't until he went outside that I realized he'd draped my fir branch blanket over me.

Tiernan didn't return. I lit the fire and stared at the spines of his books over a breakfast of hot tea and cold fish. Eventually I went to the workshop and found him shuffling through papers.

He glanced up. "I should go see Maika. Would you like to come?"

My legs screamed for me to refuse. "Sure."

Twigs and needles littered Marijka's yard. A hemlock near the greenhouse leaned at an angle, trunk splintered, whole branches torn off. The trees along the creek were a jagged wall of icicles. Fog clung to the valley like a nesting bird.

Marijka answered the door with rolled-up sleeves and stained hands. She led us into the kitchen and went back to dicing herbs. The windowsill and mantelpiece were lined with plants. Delicate leaves trailed over the sides of clay pots, the wood underneath stained red and yellow with pollen. Her house smelled different every time we visited. This time, it was deep and earthy, like soil after a rainfall.

I half-listened, adding comments to Tiernan's retelling of events as Marijka pulled glass jars from neatly organized shelves or twisted bundles of roots from the ceiling. She worked with a calmness that seemed to come from more than just practice. Watching her was like gazing into the depths of a still lake.

"We had stories about all kinds of spirits back east in Nyhemur," Marijka said. "None about elemental beings though."

"They're old, old beliefs," I said. "Tel-saidu cause wind, anta-saidu bring rain and snow, edim-saidu grow forests, and jinra-saidu cause fire. The world swung out of balance when they went dormant. Weird things started happening. Like all those storms we had six years ago."

Marijka looked thoughtful. "I suppose it'd be easy for an air spirit to create a blizzard if snow was already falling, but causing a rockslide seems much harder."

"Honestly, I hope the Iyo got it wrong." I fiddled with a set of metal scales. "Suriel's the only saidu who's woken so far. In the stories he was always odd, but not violent. If the first saidu to wake went crazy . . . that's bad. Really bad."

"You already knew of Suriel? The Iyo nation only mentioned him two years ago."

"He's been around longer than anyone knows. Thousands of years at least, probably forever, always living in the Turquoise Mountains. I didn't make the connection at first because we don't call him Suriel. He's not a 'he,' either. I don't know where that idea came from. Saidu aren't male or female."

Marijka smiled slightly. "That's our doing, most likely. There's no good term in Sverbian."

"Well, most saidu never interacted with people. Sometimes they listened to our rituals asking for good weather or foraging, but that's all. Suriel was one of the few who learned human language, and one of the last to go dormant, something like six hundred years ago. That's when the stories end. Or so I thought. After those storms, the Okoreni-Rin told me another story. I'd completely forgotten about it until Ingard mentioned kinaru.

"Ninety years ago, a Rin boy named Imarein came south to fight the Ferish in the First Elken War. He was the only one of his family who survived. I know that's true since it's recorded on his plank house. Afterward, Imarein went . . . wrong in the head. The Iyo told him about windstorms deep in the mountains and he became convinced Suriel had woken. So when he was — I forget, sixteen, seventeen — he left to find Suriel. He didn't come back. Everyone thought he'd died.

"Imarein turned up ten years later, missing half his fingers and toes. He'd shaved his head and inked over his family crest, leaving just his kinaru tattoo. According to him, he found Suriel's mountain and tried to climb it. A blizzard struck, but he kept climbing, black with frostbite, half-starved, swept off cliffs by wind and snow. When he finally reached the top, Suriel praised his devotion. Imarein said he'd been living there ever since.

"The Iyo believed him. The Rin didn't. I mean, he spoke in bird calls half the time. *Something* was wrong. Imarein got angry and left. That's the last time anyone saw him. People stopped talking about it because they didn't want anyone to copy him. No Rin has seen Suriel since."

I stopped tilting the scales and looked up. Tiernan sat rigid, hands clenched, staring out the window at the snowy yard. The kitchen felt too warm. Marijka and I had sweat on our foreheads.

"Your people mentioned none of this," Tiernan said.

"What difference would it make? No one in Crieknaast would've believed it. Storms don't usually wind up with people's throats slit."

Tiernan rose from his stool. "Maika, I need to go cut down that hemlock. Don't want it coming down on the roof." He strode out the door.

I stared after him. "What was that all about?"

"Don't worry about him." Marijka tipped a bowl of crushed red-brown roots into a pot over the fire. "What did you think of Crieknaast, all that trouble aside?"

I turned back to her reluctantly. "It might be nice if I spoke

---

112

Sverbian. I didn't expect all the women to be in dresses though. It wasn't like that in the north."

"Ah, rural folk are more lax. Some call us backward," she said with a smile. "No one will mind as long as you're covered. When I first came through Crieknaast on the trip from Nyhemur, I made the mistake of rolling up my sleeves to treat a woman with itchbine rash."

"What happened?"

"She recovered, but insisted her children were traumatized and her husband scandalized." Marijka held up her bare arms. "I had no idea these could drive a man to attend stavehall rites. The clerics should thank me."

I clamped a hand to my mouth to stifle a giggle. "I can't imagine you offending anyone."

She laughed. "I'm not infallible, I guarantee that."

"Why'd you leave Nyhemur?" I rested my chin in my hands as I watched her work.

"After I finished my medical training, I got a herbalism apprenticeship in Caladheå." She sniffed a spoonful of dark paste before adding it to the pot. "Tiernan and I made the trip together. He originally immigrated to Nyhemur, but there were better prospects for both of us here in Eremur."

"I didn't realize you'd known him that long."

"Well, I barely saw him for years. Mercenaries are like migrating geese. Every time they pass through town, you wonder if it'll be the last." Marijka rapped the spoon on the pot, maybe harder than necessary. "I never expected him to settle down."

"I'm not sure he has. He owns more carpentry tools than furniture."

"You're welcome to stay here if you need somewhere else to go."

"I don't mind living with Tiernan." I frowned, remembering Leifar's parents didn't like him being in my tent when I traded in Vunfjel. "Do itherans consider it . . . inappropriate?"

"No — well, yes, but it's not anyone else's business, and that's not what I meant." Marijka sighed and wiped her hands on a rag. "Maybe it's not my place to say this, but be wary of getting involved with Tiernan. You saw in Crieknaast how his work follows him."

"Everyone at the tannery might be dead if I hadn't gone with him."

"I'm not lecturing, Kateiko. I just want you to have options."

It was odd for people to be concerned about me when my future had no impact on theirs. No jouyen reputation to uphold, no aeldu to appease. Tiernan cared in his own way, but that way usually involved a lot more opinion.

"Thanks. I'll remember that." I smiled and gestured at the pot. "Do you need help?"

✳

The temperature plummeted. Lethargic snowflakes piled up in the clearing. I went to the creek with my net and found solid ice from bank to bank. Tiernan showed me how to make rye into sourbread or thick dark porridge, but eating grain all winter didn't appeal to me, so he carved two rods and agreed to come ice fishing.

When a day dawned with cloudless sky, I gathered our gear and waited outside while he fed the horses. Sunshine dazzled my eyes. The air was clear enough to see frost on evergreen needles a stone's throw away. A deer stared at me before bounding off, flinging up clouds of white powder.

I twirled Nurivel with my gloved hand. Once, using my throwing dagger had been as natural as walking, but my arm felt tight where the soldier's arrow had sliced through. I aimed at a cottonwood with grey bark like cracked mud. Nurivel sank into the tree, missing my target by a finger-width.

Then I saw the itheran.

He stood in the forest watching me. Tanned skin, black hair pulled back from his face and draped over his shoulders, longbow on his back. No elk sigil. Possibly Ferish. He didn't look very old, maybe early twenties.

The man pulled my dagger from the cottonwood. "Your form is poor."

Cold air caught in my lungs. "It's good enough." I stayed still, trying to decide whether to yell for Tiernan or just run.

He came forward and held out Nurivel. "Does Heilind no longer live here?"

"He does. Who are you?" I took my blade back but didn't sheath it.

Just then Tiernan emerged from the stable. He stopped short. "Rhonos!"

Tiernan's face split into a grin. The men strode toward each other and embraced, clapping their hands on each other's backs. All I could do was stare.

"This is Kateiko," Tiernan said. "She is staying here awhile."

"Rhonos Arquiere. Pleasure." He bowed stiffly and turned back to Tiernan. "I have news from Caladheå."

"We were just heading to the creek. Tell us on the way." Tiernan slung his axe over one shoulder and the rods over the other.

I was struck by the contrast between the men. Rhonos was light on his feet while Tiernan trudged through the snow. Rhonos's green cloak was bright as moss next to Tiernan's faded one. Yet they fell into conversation as if picking up from yesterday.

"There has been an incident in Crieknaast," Rhonos said, and I snapped back to listening.

"I know about Suriel," Tiernan said. "We left the day Montès tried to keep the tannery open. We passed soldiers heading there."

"Then you were lucky. The military received a report that Montès was being held hostage in the town hall. They broke him out and the townspeople rose up in protest. Now the soldiers have closed off the town."

Tiernan's hand tightened around the axe. "How many dead?"

"Forty-three Crieknaast residents and five soldiers."

Their words were like a flood of ice down my back. "Do you know who was killed?"

"No," Rhonos said without looking at me. "At least the Council is paying attention now. They are organizing an inquiry into Suriel. Montès will no longer be able to control the proceedings."

"The rest of the Council is no better," Tiernan said. "They would not believe Suriel exists if he knocked down Caladheå's Colonnium gates."

"They will not be able to deny it much longer. Rumours are circulating that Crieknaast is not the only target. Suriel's soldiers have been spotted as far away as Rutnaast."

"Where's that?" I asked, scurrying to keep up with their pace.

"It does not concern you," Rhonos said.

"How exactly does it not concern me? I have family in this region."

"Yet you clearly cannot read a map of it."

"Rhonos," Tiernan said. I felt a flash of spiteful pride it wasn't me getting told off for once.

"The Council is calling for people to testify," Rhonos said as if he hadn't heard anything. "Your name will come up sooner or later, Tiernan."

"Sooner, I expect. Montès knows we were in Crieknaast." Tiernan sidestepped a boulder. "I know how it will go. They will deliberate for weeks and do nothing."

"The Council will not ignore you. They will come knocking at your door."

"Let them. They cannot force me to testify."

"Do you not have a duty like the rest of us?" Rhonos put a hand on Tiernan's shoulder.

Tiernan shook him off. "What of you? Are you staying for the inquiry?"

"No. I am headed to southern Eremur for the winter." He glanced at the sky. "I hope the weather holds."

"Stay for a meal," Tiernan said. "With any luck, we'll have fresh fish."

I immediately wondered if I could get away with releasing all the fish back into the creek. Or burning lunch. Or serving it raw.

Rhonos shook his head and pulled up his hood. "My ship leaves this afternoon."

"At least stop in and see Maika."

"I will. Farewell." Rhonos turned to me. "May our next meeting be less . . . unexpected."

I waited until he disappeared among the trees before saying, "How did you become friends with him?"

Tiernan shrugged. "Moths of all kinds flock toward the same light."

"Moths are dumb." I slung the fish bucket over my elbow and stuffed my hands into my pockets. "What's so bad about an inquiry?"

"Politics is a game no one wins." He gazed into the snowy woods. "If the Council does send the military after Suriel's soldiers, I do not want to be near the blade when it falls."

"Do you make a habit of ignoring your friends' advice?"

"Rhonos is a ranger, a young one at that. He wanders remote lands, comes back after a year, and thinks he still understands the government. Caladheå will offer us no protection."

✳

Fishing distracted me for the rest of the day, but when the coals were dying after dinner, I finally had to face the thoughts I'd been avoiding. Forty-three townspeople had their blood in the ground. Some might be people I had told to come back to Crieknaast.

I knew the fear in Ingard's eyes when I said Dåmar was in danger. I helped raise Nili's brother after their father and sister were killed in the Dona war. Yironem was thirteen now, but Rin could be sent to war as soon as we attuned. The morning Nili and I left Aeti Ginu, I begged the aeldu to keep him from attuning as long as possible.

I sipped my tea. It was cold. I held a hand over the mug until steam rose from the surface, but there wasn't much point. The only tea Tiernan had was painfully weak.

The porch creaked. I heard Tiernan stamp snow off his boots before he came in carrying his axe. Melting snowflakes glittered in his hair. I could never tell if he was in the mood to talk, but when he took a whetstone out of his pocket, I realized he'd chosen not to stay in the workshop.

I dove in before he changed his mind. "I have to go back to Crieknaast."

"Why?" Tiernan braced the axe against the table and began sharpening it.

"To find out if Ingard and his siblings are alive. I know the town's closed, but—"

"Kateiko, the military will be all over Crieknaast," he said between the slides of his whetstone. "Do you want to risk sneaking into a town where you will be one of the only viirelei? You saw what soldiers did to you just for poaching."

I flinched. "How else am I supposed to find out?"

"Why does it matter so much? You only met that boy once."

"It's not about that." I set down my tea and went to the window, looking at moonlight on the snow. "I could never forgive myself if

I sent Ingard to rescue his brother, only for them to come back and . . . If we were wrong, Dåmar might've been safer at the tannery."

The grating stopped. "And if you do not get the answer you want?"

"I'll deal with that when it happens."

"You have your whole life ahead. Do not throw it away so easily."

"I won't pretend I'm not scared." I pressed my hand against the pane. Frost crackled out from my fingers. "But other things scare me more. I wake up most nights in a cold sweat because I hear voices in the wind and don't know what they're saying. You said I won't forget. That I have to accept it. I can't do that unless I know the truth."

Tiernan set down his axe and came toward me. The frost melted and ran down the glass in rivulets. "There is another way. I know people in Caladheå who may have heard something about the riot and who was killed."

"How far away is Caladheå?"

"Four hours by horseback."

"I won't ask you to come. Just tell me where to go." I ran my finger through water pooling along the sill. "Even if I never see Ingard or his family again, I need to know."

Tiernan slumped into a chair. "It is not that simple. You are likely not in Eremur's birth records. Unregistered viirelei cannot enter Caladheå alone."

"Who would I have to go with?"

"An itheran. The law is . . . well, it was written to accommodate settlers with viirelei wives."

"Then where do I register?"

"The Colonnium. In Caladheå."

"Aeldu curse it." I paced across the room, knotting my fingers into my hair. "That's the stupidest law I've ever heard."

He clasped his hands in front of his forehead. "If it matters so much, I will take you."

"I can't ask you to do that, Tiernan."

"Rhonos was right, in a way. The Council will not forget about me." He rose and took his cloak from its peg. "I need to talk to Maika."

"Now? Why?"

"She might want something from the market," he said without meeting my eyes. "Try to get some sleep."

10.

SLOW DESCENT

There was a knock at the door just as Tiernan and I finished breakfast. Marijka came in carrying several bundles of fabric. "Morning. Kateiko, I brought you something to wear."

I wiped my hands on a rag. "Maika — you didn't have to do that—"

"It's fine. I just lengthened an old dress." She unfolded some white fabric to show me a blue hem. "There are slits in the skirt so you can ride. Come, try it on."

In the bedroom, Marijka helped me put on all the different layers. An unbleached linen chemise, grey woolen skirts, the hemmed white dress with tight sleeves that hid my kinaru tattoo. A stiff dark blue bodice cinched the fabric, curving under my collarbones to cover my antayul mark.

"Itheran clothing is so complicated." I held my hair aside while she laced the bodice. "I think I'm wearing an entire goat."

"You can skip the underlayers in summer," she said. "As long as you wear a bodice and white dress, you're considered decent."

"Did Tiernan suggest this last night?"

"Yes. He wasn't sure you'd want to wear them, but I knew it bothered you in Crieknaast."

I stared at the log wall. "It hasn't sunk in yet I'm going to Caladheå."

"I'd go to Crieknaast for you if I could." Marijka pulled the lacing tight. "I should be there. I try to see sense in the Council's actions, but when they won't even let medics in to do our jobs—"

"Maika—" I pressed my hand to my chest. "I can't — breathe—"

The pressure eased. "I'm sorry, Kateiko. I don't mean to take it out on you."

"Nei, it's okay. Take out whatever you need."

She laughed and knotted the lacing. "There. Should I put up your hair?"

I went suddenly, completely still. Nili and Hiyua were the only ones outside my bloodline who'd touched my hair. No rule said itherans weren't allowed — it just didn't happen. Leifar tried once and quickly learned better.

I always felt like I saw Marijka from a great distance, like she was one of Orebo's stars giving its light to the world and none of its secrets — but for a moment, the light had cleared and I saw *her*. Beneath the endless patience, she was as frustrated as me. I wanted to give back something of myself, even if she'd never know what it meant.

So I nodded. She brushed my hair with a goat-horn comb, working through the tangles, and pinned the pale brown locks to my head. The slight tug on my scalp made my eyes prick with tears.

My parents always braided their hair. Sensible, modest, standard for daily wear. As an antayul, my only options were a braid or no hairstyle at all, so I left my hair loose even though I was forever fighting to keep it tidy. But the Rin were far away now. I had to learn a new set of customs. *Rivers keep flowing, far from their source.*

I wrapped my arms around Marijka's small frame. "Thank you so much."

"It's the least I can do," she said. "I hope you find good news."

✳

Gwmniwyr's black tail swished as he plowed a path through the snow. Anwea followed behind, breathing white puffs of air. She and I seemed to have met a compromise. Neither of us wanted to be in the cold longer than necessary. My hands felt thick and clumsy on the reins.

"Explain Caladheå," I said to distract myself. "Last I heard from the Iyo, it wasn't capital of anything."

Tiernan considered that. "What do you know about the settlement of this region?"

"By itherans?" I paused to think. "My friends in Vunfjel said Sverbians landed on the east coast, migrated across the continent, and settled in Nyhemur two hundred years ago. The Ferish landed on this coast much later. They built a trading post near Tamun Dael, the Tamu-jouyen's settlement up north, but it's gone now."

He nodded. "Most posts failed. Barros Sanguero, lord governor of the New Ferland Trading Company, tried to claim the land where Caladheå sits now. He built a stronghold near the Stengar river mouth to protect the company's port."

"Protect from what? Bears?"

"Other merchants," Tiernan said, but I saw the flicker of a smile. "The Ferish used brutal means to control trade routes. Sanguero was by far the worst. A Sverbian-viirelei alliance killed him ninety years ago during the First Elken War."

"I know about the war. There was a . . . schism? Is that the right word in Coast Trader? Some Rin and Iyo refused to fight, and split off to form the Dona-jouyen. But every other jouyen in the Aikoto Confederacy got involved."

He glanced up from adjusting the reins. "Right — you mentioned a Rin boy went to find Suriel after fighting in the war. I had forgotten your nation was involved."

"We mostly fought in the north. The Okorebai-Rin and a hundred others died near Tamun Dael." I ducked a hemlock branch drooping with snow. "My family helped build Caladheå after the war. They lived there awhile to protect the Iyo."

"Nyhemur sent settlers, too — Sverbians who hoped a strong port could fend off further Ferish invasion. Sverba declared Eremur a province so it could establish its own military. Caladheå has been the capital ever since."

I thrust out a hand. "See, that's what I don't get. The Iyo let others settle in Iyun Bel, but it's still *their* land. How do you declare a province on top of it?"

Tiernan shrugged. "With fundamental disregard for others' rights, I suppose. The political situation is . . . tense."

"I'd be tense if someone moved into my yard and expected me to obey their dumb laws."

"You can thank the Ferish for those. They control the Council these days."

I frowned. "How did *that* happen?"

"Sheer numbers. Famine hit Ferland and thousands of immigrants landed here in a matter of years. There were so many that a group calling themselves the Rúonbattai formed to try to drive them out."

"Thousands? Just how big is Caladheå?"

Tiernan gestured ahead. "See for yourself."

My words faded as we crested a hill. I reined in Anwea and just stared.

A flat plain sprawled out ahead, ribboned by a river feeding into a bay. Caladheå ringed the coast like creeping lichen. Timber structures hunkered among rust-red buildings, linked by twisting grids of roads. The white sails of ships in the bay were furled like flowers on the edge of bloom. Far to the east, hazy mountains nudged the sky, little more than bumps on the horizon.

I pointed at a massive stone building with a domed tower. It overlooked the city from a hill on the east edge, its snowy grounds surrounded by a stone wall. "Is that Sanguero's stronghold?"

"Yes. The Colonnium houses Council Hall and Eremur's military headquarters now." Tiernan pointed southeast. "Rutnaast, the town Rhonos mentioned, is in the far corner of the Roannveldt plain on the shore of Burren Inlet. If you were still wondering."

I grimaced. "Thank you."

We rode down a steep slope and across the tip of the plain. Ice floes drifted around thick pillars supporting a stone bridge over the Stengar. A crude guardhouse stood on the near riverbank. Soldiers with glinting spears waved us on, stamping their feet to keep warm. Two elk reared on their grey leather breastplates. Tiernan quietly explained grey uniforms distinguished city guards from the military proper, who wore black.

Riding into Caladheå felt like a slow descent into deep water. We were in the old Sverbian quarter, Tiernan said. Itherans swirled around us as we wound past timber buildings. Men drove horse-drawn sleighs, women carried packages tied with twine, children in wool hats and mittens squealed as they threw snowballs. A scrawny girl clutching a bundle of folded papers yelled, "Two pann! *Caladheå Herald*! Two pann a newspaper!"

The place *stank*. It was easy to see why by looking into the gutters. The reek of piss and goat dung melded with meaty tallow, sour vinegar, fermented cod, decaying offal, things I couldn't identify. I could only imagine how bad it must be in summer.

Tiernan stopped at a building that reminded me of Crieknaast's inn with a steep roof and white window frames. A creaking sign carved with a barren tree hung over the door. I slid down from Anwea, hoping no one saw me stumble when my skirt caught on the stirrup.

"The Blackened Oak," Tiernan said. "It was the Golden Oak until it burned down."

"Did you have anything to do with that?"

He gave me a disapproving look. "What do you take me for?"

The scent of rye bread and roasting goat in the pub was a blessing. The long tables were unmarred, but the stones around the fireplace were scorched black. The air seemed oddly clear. I realized there were glass lamps on the walls instead of candles.

A man with pale skin and a bushy yellow beard wound across the crowded room, wiping his hands on a stained apron. "*Hijke*, Tiernan! You're the last person I expected to show up with a young lady."

A rare smile crossed Tiernan's face. "Good to see you too, Nhys."

"It's been, what, six months? I thought you'd forgotten where the place was. What brings you back?"

Tiernan nodded at me. "Kateiko is trying to find out if a family from Crieknaast survived the uprising. Have you heard any news?"

"He's convinced I know everything," Nhys whispered to me. "Truth, I do, just not about this. Hang on." He went behind the bar and bent over to search under it.

I glanced around while we waited. Three hooded figures gambled with black shark teeth. A man in a patched cloak slumped across a table. He was so still I mistook him for a pile of rags. Two girls in white fur cloaks sat next to longbows taller than they were.

A boy with a striped hat and twitching hands moved his lips as if talking to a ghost. A woman with short brown hair fed scraps to a shaggy dog while a group of men argued in Sverbian, pounding the table so hard the plates rattled.

Nhys came back with a folded paper. He smoothed it out and gave it to Tiernan. "Check this. Probably won't help. Less than half the names be in there."

I peered over Tiernan's shoulder to see blocks of tiny meticulous symbols. "What is it?"

"Crieknaast obituaries," Nhys said. "Got it from a woman who slipped past the soldiers."

Tiernan was silent, then the paper crumpled in his grip. "Only the militia are listed. So the Council is censoring the newspaper now. Gods' sakes, there could've been children in that crowd."

"Please don't remind me," I muttered.

"No one else from Crieknaast has come by the inn," Nhys said. "You want news, there be only one place to go."

"I knew it might come to that." Tiernan ran a hand over his hair and sighed. "Is Rhedoch Quintere still the regional liaison?"

"Aye, far as I know." Nhys looked at him closely. "Did Rhonos tell you—"

"Yes." Tiernan's eyes flickered to me. "We will go to the Colonnium anyway."

I drew a sharp breath. "I thought you didn't want to go near there."

"There is no other option. If you want the truth, we will get it." He turned to Nhys. "Do you have space to keep our horses?"

Nhys nodded. "I'll send the stablehand to tend them."

I put my hand on Tiernan's elbow. "You don't have to do this."

"We will get it," he repeated.

✳

I buried my hands in my pockets against the cold. The eastern district of Caladheå felt subdued compared to the bustling Sverbian quarter. I jumped every time a sleigh swished past, leaving deep tracks between rows of brick buildings. Nearly everyone in this district had dark hair and was shorter than Tiernan or me — Ferish, I assumed. Some women were small enough I could've used them as armrests.

A long, straight avenue bordered by skeletal trees led up the hill toward the Colonnium. I paused halfway up to look back at the sprawling city and the ocean beyond. Seagulls floated on the icy breeze, their calls haunting the air.

Looming iron gates that looked too heavy to move stood open at the top. Rearing stone elk rose from pillars at each side, their hooves lashing out in eternal combat. Guards stood stiff and motionless. They all wore fawn-coloured breeches and deep blue coats with the elk sigil embroidered on their sleeves. Their spear tips formed a perfect row. I shuddered at their blank expressions as we passed.

"Why aren't they wearing armour?" I whispered.

"Colonnium guards are the highest-ranked soldiers in Eremur," Tiernan said. "They live and train within these walls. The lack of armour is meant to prove their bravery."

"That's stupid."

The Colonnium stretched across the grounds, its domed tower rising up against pale sky, arched windows glittering among cream-coloured stone. The entire Crieknaast market would fit in one of the wings flanking the tower. Colourful flags fluttered on iron poles. I felt like a speck of dust as we crossed a vast snowy lawn and passed by an erupting fountain. I sensed moving water underground, kept warm by machinery I couldn't fathom.

Tiernan stopped me on the wide stone steps. "You will have to uncover your head."

Arguing wouldn't get me out of it. Frosty air stung my neck as

I lowered my hood. I felt a rush of gratitude to Marijka for putting my hair up.

Tiernan pushed open the heavy doors. I stepped into a marble hall ringed with pillars that rose toward the soaring ceiling like ancient trees. Across the room, sweeping stairs led to a set of grand doors. The entire place felt cold. Cold white walls, cold light filtering through glass panes, a cold taste of steel. Even the candles in iron brackets looked like icicles. Guards stood at every entrance.

A man seated behind a desk beckoned us forward. "Please declare yourself and relinquish all weapons," he said in a flat voice with the trace of an accent.

Tiernan unsheathed Hafelús and placed it on the marble. "Tiernan Heilind. Mage."

The clerk's manner changed instantly. He rose and drummed his fingers on the desk. "I'll have to summon a guard to escort you—"

"I know. I have been registered as a mage for over a decade. Get on with it."

The clerk rang a tinkling silver bell. I set my flail and knives on the desk. He gave me a look and rang the bell again.

A voice called out. "What, Gélus, I'm coming—" A guard strode through a high archway, her spear tapping on the polished red-brown tile.

"You're needed for an escort." Gélus's hands shook as he shuffled papers.

The guard pointed her spear at him. "You realize this is an utter waste of time."

"Yes, madam."

"And this flimsy thing would do nothing if one of them," she swung her spear around to point at us, "decided to go on a magical rampage in Council Hall."

Gélus's papers scattered across the tile, soaking up slush tracked in from outdoors. "Yes, madam, but it's the law."

The guard sighed and kicked a paper toward Gélus as he crouched down. She turned to Tiernan and me. "I am Pelennus, and I'll be your escort. Where are you going?"

"The Northeast Liaison," Tiernan said.

"I'll show you to a waiting room. You might even get out in time for the spring fair."

"Quintere will see me."

She shrugged. "If you say so."

As we walked down a long gallery in the south wing, I couldn't take my eyes off Pelennus. She had a proud face with auburn hair pulled into a tight bun and wore the same uniform as the male guards. She was the first woman I'd seen in Eremur not wearing a skirt. Her steps were perfectly timed with the tap of her spear.

"Quintere's probably in the pavilion," she said over her shoulder. "He hasn't been back to his office all day."

The gallery opened into another wide hall, its floor inlaid with a pattern of white tiles. I glanced up and realized the entire ceiling was covered with a swirling mosaic. Pelennus strode to a set of glossy wooden doors and knocked.

A man with a pointed black beard answered. "What is it? The captains will be here any — oh. Heilind." His face paled. "Come in."

The glare of sunlight on a polished table stung my eyes as I stepped in. Flames crackled in a marble fireplace. I took off my gloves, grateful for the warmth.

Quintere walked past a row of padded chairs lining the table. He pushed aside a plate of half-eaten bread and cheese and began sorting through a pile of maps. "I have a meeting soon, so this will have to be quick. What do you need?"

"A list of the civilians killed in Crieknaast last week," Tiernan said.

Quintere stopped, holding a handful of papers in midair. "I'm not meant to give that out."

"The Council cannot suppress it forever. Not unless they plan on killing all the witnesses, in which case we will not need a list."

"It's just until this inquiry is over. People might get upset if they think—"

"Think what?" I said before I could stop myself. "That the military butchered almost as many people as Suriel? I think that justifies being upset."

Quintere looked stunned. "Those are my orders."

"I am not going to interfere with the inquiry," Tiernan said. "We are simply trying to find out if a family is alive. You owe me that much, Quintere."

"That may be, Heilind, but I can't give out classified information to civilians, especially not to viirelei."

"What does that have to do with anything?" My hands curled into fists. "All I want to know is if some people died so I can mourn them properly. Isn't that more important than hiding the truth?"

Quintere set down the maps, adjusted a paper on the polished table, and took a round metal device from his breast pocket. "The captains are late. I'm going to step outside and ask your escort if she knows where they are."

It felt like something had been ripped away from me. "You're just going to leave?"

He gave a slight bow. "I'm sorry I cannot be more help, miss."

"Fucking coward," I muttered as soon as the doors shut. "What's he afraid of?"

Tiernan gave me a hard look. "He just bought us a few minutes."

"What good does that do—" I fell silent as he seized the paper Quintere had singled out.

His eyes scanned back and forth. "No one by the name Dåmar or Thylanniga is listed."

I clamped a hand over my mouth. "What about Ingard?"

He paused a moment too long. "Did he tell you his second name? Or his father's name?"

A chill washed over my body that even the roaring fire couldn't stave off. "Nei, he never said — aeldu save me, if he—"

"Wait. His father died in the mine collapse. There may be—" He rifled through the pages, pulled out a tattered sheet and held them side by side. "Ingard Gjellind was killed in the uprising. That boy's father would be Gjelle, but there is no Gjelle listed as dying in the mine."

"He's still alive." Even as I said it, it didn't seem real. "His family is still alive. Thank the aeldu—" I crumpled against a chair.

It felt wrong to be relieved. Dozens of families grieved in Crieknaast. I could only hope none had lost their last source of strength and protection in the world — a parent or sibling struggling to keep a family together.

"Kateiko." Tiernan's voice sounded odd. "There is a note here. A troop of soldiers rode to the tannery the day after the uprising. They found the entire place destroyed."

My eyes widened. I stepped closer to peer at the scrap of paper. "We were right."

"Whatever happened in town, you helped save those people from certain death at Suriel's hands." He glanced up at me. "That is worth something."

I flung my arms around him, but quickly pulled back. "I'm just glad they had a chance." I lowered my eyes. "And that I didn't make Ingard lead his own brother to his death. I . . . honestly don't know if I could've dealt with that. Maybe that's selfish of me."

Tiernan laid a hand on my shoulder. "It is human."

11.

CALADHEÅ

"Anywhere else you need to go?" Pelennus asked in the mosaic hall.

"Well—" I glanced at Tiernan. "Maybe I should register in the birth records. So you won't have to come with me next time."

He inclined his head. "If you like."

"You want the Office of the Viirelei, then," Pelennus said. "Follow me."

On the way out of the pavilion, I saw Quintere talking to two men in plate armour. He met my eyes long enough to give a hint of a smile before gesturing the men toward the meeting room.

Pelennus led us back into the gallery, up a steep staircase to a balcony, and past identical doors with engraved metal panels. She rapped on one and stuck her head in. "Visitors for you, Falwen."

"Tell them to wait," a man's voice replied.

Pelennus closed the door and shrugged.

I leaned over the wrought-iron balustrade. The gallery was

filled with statues of soldiers on horseback, holding up swords or spears. Three elderly men were deep in conversation. From their loose, black robes I guessed they were councillors. Frost-coated windows looked out on the sprawling lawn.

Tiernan fiddled with his gloves and kept looking over his shoulder. I wanted to say something but didn't know what. I fidgeted with my bodice instead. After hours of riding, the boning felt out of place. I caught Pelennus watching, and she looked away as if in boredom. Two voices murmured in Falwen's office, then I heard the door open.

"Fuck," Tiernan said under his breath.

He never swore in Coast Trader. I spun to see who'd come out. An itheran in a long black coat and stiff-collared white shirt stared directly at us.

"Who's that?" I whispered.

"Ignore him." Tiernan put his head down so his dark hair covered his face.

"I don't think that's an option."

The man crossed the balcony with a warm smile. "Heilind! I barely recognized you."

Tiernan leaned against the balustrade. "Yet you never change, Councillor."

My jaw fell. The man was nothing like Montès or the doddering old councillors in the gallery. He was tall for an itheran, with a strong jaw and sharp gaze. Straight black hair fell past his broad shoulders.

"Who is this lovely lady?" the man addressed me.

"Kateiko," I stammered.

He lifted my hand and kissed the back of it, showing several ornate rings on his fingers. "It is a pleasure to meet an acquaintance of Heilind's. I am Councillor Antoch Parr."

Pelennus rolled her eyes.

"I heard you were in Crieknaast," Parr said to Tiernan. "Montès's handling of the situation was a disgrace to the Council."

"Gods forbid the Council go a month without disgracing itself. The entire political body would die of starvation."

"Rest assured I am personally looking into the military's actions." Parr twisted one of his rings. "Speaking of which, an inquiry into Suriel is set to begin in the new year. I hope you might be willing to speak on behalf—"

"Not a chance." Tiernan set a hand on his empty scabbard. "Do me a favour. Make sure the Council knows I have no interest."

"Of course. Please let me know if you change your mind." Parr gave me a deep bow. "Miss Kateiko, I apologize for the intrusion. Pelennus, good day." He strode down the balcony and entered a door near the staircase.

I smacked Tiernan. "What's your problem?"

Tiernan glared at me and rubbed his arm. "What?"

"He was perfectly polite."

"Politicians will say anything to persuade people to do what they want."

I glared back. We returned to waiting in silence.

The door finally opened again. A man beckoned. "Come. Hurry up. The mage stays outside."

He was unmistakably viirelei, tall and wiry like Fendul with cropped brown hair, but he wore a long-sleeved white shirt and a brocade waistcoat that hid his tattoos. It unnerved me to not know which jouyen he was from.

I stepped into a room that felt cramped despite its size. An entire wall was plastered with maps. Long ink lines stretched far overhead. Wooden cabinets were wedged into every available space. The only respite was a set of tall windows that looked onto a covered stone loggia, the mountains and thin blue sky visible in the distance.

The man sat behind a desk and pointed at a chair. "My name is Falwen. I represent every Aikoto jouyen from the Haka in the north to the Kae in the south. Whatever you need goes through me."

I perched on the hard chair. "That must be a lot of people."

"It is. I am very busy. So be quick." He spoke as fast as possible, and his Trader was flawless.

"I want to register in the birth records."

Falwen gave me a hard look. "Name and jouyen?"

"Kateiko Rin."

"A respectable jouyen. Once." He went to a cabinet and rifled through a folder. It looked nearly empty. "Are there others with you?"

"Nei. No Rin, I mean. That mage outside brought me into the city."

"Does the itheran government know you are Rin?"

"Nei."

He took out a larger folder and sat back down. "No Rin has lived in Eremur since the Second Elken War sixty-eight years ago. Few itherans remember the Rin-jouyen even exists. If you encounter trouble, at best the military will interrogate you. Do not ask the worst. From now on, to itherans, you are Iyo."

"Wait — just like that? What about my Rin tattoo?"

"Keep it covered. If you are forced to show it, lie. Make up a meaning."

I shrugged. I'd planned to become Iyo anyway, and if it made getting past the city guard easier, I wouldn't argue.

Falwen laid a blank paper on the desk, dipped a quill into an inkpot, and asked a rapid string of questions. My birthdate, marital status, the description and location of my tattoos, my role in the jouyen.

"Antayul," I said to the last one. "Will I need an escort if I come back to the Colonnium?"

"No. Water-calling is considered a lower form of magic." His hand streaked across the page. "Attuned form?"

"I'm not telling you that."

Falwen stopped writing. "Something to hide?"

My fingers tightened on the folds of my skirt. "A wolf. Silver."

On another paper, he took notes about my family and everyone I knew in the Iyo, then handed me a creased list. "Choose a second name. If you cannot read, I will assign you one."

"Can't I use Iyo?"

"Not here."

I tried to make sense of the writing, but it disintegrated into a jumble. "Do I have to choose from this list?"

"Not if it makes you hurry up."

"Sohikoehl."

Falwen's harried expression slipped into surprise. "Sverbian. How provincial." He jotted it down and stamped a sigil in red ink. "Listen carefully. You were born within Iyo borders but raised in the far north. That will explain your utter lack of knowledge about the south. Your family died of illness. Not in war. Understood?"

"Yes."

He filled out a palm-sized card, stamped it, and placed it in front of me. "This is your identification. It allows you to enter Caladheå. Do not lose it. That is much more paperwork."

I picked up the stiff card. I recognized my name and a string of numbers. "Is that all?"

"Yes. Now get out. And close the door."

Tiernan was waiting on the balcony when I emerged. "That was fast."

"Tell me about it." I waited until Pelennus looked away before waterproofing the card.

I knocked clumps of snow off leafless branches as I walked down Colonnium Hill with Tiernan, feeling more at ease with my weapons back on my belt. "I'm sorry about before. It's none of my business why you don't like Councillor Parr."

"Perhaps meeting him was for the better. I will rest easier if it dissuades the Council from seeking me out."

"Does that mean we can stop at the market before going back?"

He shrugged. "I don't see why not."

I stuck close to Tiernan as we walked deeper into Caladheå. There were no timber buildings like in the old Sverbian quarter, just red-brick structures packed into tight rows. From a single street corner, I could see more people than in all Aeti Ginu — talking, laughing, yelling, buying food or newspapers or fabric flowers from children on the sidewalk.

I began to play a game with myself, guessing who was Sverbian or Ferish. Quickly, I figured it out by their clothing. Sverbian women wore simple brimless bonnets, either white or the same colour as their bodices, and the unchanging white dress. Ferish women wore brimmed bonnets decorated with lace and ribbons, and dark patterned dresses that rose high on their necks. Ferish men had stiff-collared shirts and coats like Parr instead of a jerkin and cloak like Tiernan.

The street suddenly opened into a vast courtyard framed by tall brick buildings. People flowed in and out of laneways between rows of wooden stalls. The lanes were the only part of this district that didn't feel vertical. A spired building loomed over the square, grey towers grasping at the sky like talons. I'd seen a drawing like that in one of Tiernan's theological books — a *sancte*, he called it, a Ferish holy building. The peal of a bell echoed slow and deep.

"Wait," Tiernan said. "I want to show you something."

He led me along the edge of the square to a narrow shop with grimy windows. I stepped into a forest of books — shelves of coloured leather packed to the ceiling, coated with dust, small enough to fit in my pocket or too large to fit in my arms. Flickering lamplight illuminated the deep corners of the room.

I turned in a circle. "Yan taku."

An elderly shopkeeper with a starched collar bowed stiffly. "Good day. Looking for anything in particular?"

"I want a book written in Coast Trader," I said.

He blinked as if he'd just noticed I was there. "What's the point?" he muttered.

"We will browse alone." Tiernan nudged my elbow.

I edged into a gap between shelves, looking at gilt lettering on the covers. "I didn't know there was this much to write about."

"If you have thought it, someone has written it." Tiernan ran his finger along the spines. "What do you want to read?"

"I don't know. My friend in Vunfjel used to read me folk tales. I liked one about a fox that played pranks on people."

"I do not know that story."

"You must've had a boring childhood. What did you read?"

"History books. And atlases." Tiernan glanced at the carved signs nailed over the shelves. He pulled down a thick book, balanced it on his forearm, and flipped it open to a map covered with curving lines. "I liked dreaming about all the other lands out there."

"I guess you were born to travel." I tilted my head to study the map. "Do you ever miss Sverba?"

"All the time." He shut the book. "Fiction is upstairs."

We climbed a creaking staircase to the second floor. Tiernan guided me to the mythology section where I pulled out book after book until I found one in Trader, the length of my hand with a worn green cover. It even had an illustration of the crafty fox stealing a fisherman's bait.

I hugged it to my chest and made my way back down the steep stairs. A woman in a fur coat and floral print dress was buying a book at the counter. She didn't haggle, just handed over a few coins.

As soon as she left, I held out the book. "How much is this?"

The shopkeeper glanced at Tiernan. "Sure you want to buy her that, sir?"

"How much?" I repeated.

He squinted at the book through his spectacles. "Quarter sov."

I took a copper coin from my purse and set it on the counter. The man picked it up with a rag and rubbed it clean. I clamped my tongue between my teeth and shouldered the door open.

"I apologize," Tiernan said out in the frosty square. "I would have taken you elsewhere if I knew he would act that way."

"It's not your fault." I focused on stowing my book in my shoulder bag so he couldn't see my face. "At the rate I read, his blood will be in the ground before I need to go back."

We wandered down a laneway where merchants crammed under low roofs, selling every item imaginable — painted ceramic dishes, wool stockings, liquor in green bottles, coloured lace, pots of ink, silk handkerchiefs, bins of dried fruit, brass buttons. I stood still as people flowed around me. Snatches of different languages and the scent of meat and spices wove together like the bolts of patterned cloth on display.

"Show me some of your Sverbian food," I said. "Something that reminds you of home. Just . . . nothing with animal heart."

Itherans in Vunfjel ate hearts from the mountain goats they slaughtered. Tiernan had been confused the first time he saw me gut a rabbit and bury the heart. The thought of eating a sacred organ made my stomach twist.

The hint of a smile crossed his face. "How much do you trust me?"

"I trust you not to kill me with food. I'm still not sure about the axe."

Tiernan led me to a stall radiating heat from a stone oven. He spoke in Sverbian to a woman rolling out sheets of dough. She stopped long enough to take our coins and hand us steaming dark brown pastries wrapped in paper.

"Careful. The inside will be—"

"Ah!" I spat out my mouthful.

Tiernan sighed. "Hot."

I flailed my hand in front of my mouth and sucked in cold air. "What did you call this? *Blødstavgren*?" I asked when I could speak again.

"Yes. *Blødstavohl* in rye pastry. It is a traditional midwinter dish."

"Goat blood stew, right?" I bit off a cooler chunk of meat and swallowed when I noticed Tiernan looking at me. "You didn't think I'd like it!"

He chuckled. "I did not expect you to know what it meant."

"There are plenty of things to learn just by listening, you know."

"Including how to not burn yourself."

I elbowed him and walked off with my pastry.

After passing stall after stall of itheran merchants, I saw something jarringly familiar — the Iyo dolphin crest embroidered on a square of leather nailed to a wall. I stepped into the shop, brushing past a rack of tawny elk-skin cloaks.

A woman with a dark brown braid and friendly wrinkles around her eyes raised a hand. "*Hanekei*."

I smiled and returned the greeting. She didn't comment on my accent. Maybe she thought I was from the Tamu-jouyen. They sounded like us, even though Iyo were closer in customs.

Her cloak was plain. It went against etiquette for embroiderers to adorn their own clothes. Nili always decorated mine when she got bored. Iyo embroidery wasn't as well-regarded as Rin, but the woman's stitching was sturdy. I picked out mittens edged with cloud weasel fur as a gift for Marijka. I wanted something for Tiernan, but nothing seemed right.

"Do you have any makiri?" I asked on sudden inspiration.

"Only a few. Itherans don't buy them." She opened a box and showed me an assortment of stone figurines the length of my thumb. "My daughter carves them."

"They're beautiful." I had to admit Iyo were better at stonecraft. Carvers from both jouyen worked small to show their skill, but Rin made makiri out of wood instead. I sifted through seals and water-fowl, common attuned forms among Iyo, and chose a grey wolf speckled with mica, ears alert and one paw raised.

"How far is Toel Ginu from here?" I asked after we settled on a price and I was counting out sovereigns and iron pann.

"Five, six hours on foot. You might be able to see the fires during the Yanben ritual."

I thanked her and kept wandering. With the last of my money from selling furs in Crieknaast, I bought paper packets of herbal tea from an Iyo man and opened them up to breathe the familiar smell. I was just walking off when I saw an itheran boy swipe a tin and sneak back to his laughing friends.

"Ai!" I grabbed his arm. "Put it back before I tell the shopkeeper."

He wrenched away. "What you gonna do, wood witch? Bite me?"

"Fuck you. Just put it back."

"Ooh, she's got a mouth on her!" The boy laughed. "I like a bit of mouth on a girl. Better dull those canines first though."

"*Kaid ne aeldu,*" I spat.

One of his friends lurched toward me. "What'd you say?"

"Doesn't matter." I stood my ground, even though his arms

looked twice as big around as mine. "Just tell him to give back what he stole."

"Go ahead. Call the Elkhounds. See who they believe." The big one grabbed a fistful of my cloak. I cringed, waiting for the blow——

——and a sword slid in front of his throat.

"See if they get here before you bleed out," Tiernan said.

The boy released me like he'd been burned. The first one spat on the cobblestone, dropped the tin, and pushed through the crowd, his friends close behind.

Tiernan sheathed Hafelús. "*Cijmmag. Taena.*" He seized my elbow and dragged me away.

I tried to pull out of his grip. "I didn't do anything wrong!"

"I know."

"Then why do we have to leave?"

"Gods' sakes. What is your plan if they return with the city guard? I thought this was one place you could not get in trouble——"

"Ow. Tiernan, you're hurting me."

He let go instantly, but he didn't slow his pace. The crowd thinned as we wound through the streets. I heard the faint toll of the sancte bell.

"I'm stopping here," I said when we came to a park. I tromped through the snow without waiting for an answer and climbed a slope to a stone gazebo.

The coast sprawled out to either side, rising to white hills in the distance. Docks jutted into the water like the teeth of a comb. Ships rocked in the bay, their masts tilting back and forth. I watched a galleon set sail and shrink to a speck on the horizon before I heard footsteps.

Tiernan drew forward and stood in the wide gap between pillars. "I am sorry, Kateiko."

I rubbed my elbow. "What would you've done if those boys fought back?"

"Knocked them down."

"Like that wouldn't draw the guards' attention."

Tiernan shifted his feet. "Even I lose my temper from time to time."

"On my behalf? That's sweet." I wrapped my hand around a pillar and swung back and forth. "What will I do when I don't have a big scary ex-mercenary to rescue me?"

"Develop a better sense of self-preservation, I hope."

"Ai, that reminds me." I pulled the wolf makiri from my pocket. "As thanks."

Tiernan held it up. The mica sparkled in the sun. "What is it?"

"A makiri. You put it on the mantelpiece, and it protects your home from cruel spirits. I don't believe in them, but . . . you have no ornaments."

"It will look nice above the fire. Thank you, Kateiko." He tucked it into an inner pocket of his cloak.

Orange light glittered on the waves. A chill breeze came off the ocean. I drew my mantle tight and pulled off my gloves to breathe on my fingers.

"Give me your hands." Tiernan removed his gloves and wrapped his hands around mine. Warmth spread up my arms and through my body like running sap.

"How did you do that?"

"Magic."

I laughed and looked into his grey eyes. "You're not the wrong hands for magic. Not at all."

12.

YANBEN

Tiernan placed the makiri on the mantel when we returned to his cabin. It watched over us in the evenings as we sat side by side with my book. I followed along the page and listened to Tiernan's voice fill the kitchen, the words laced with his accent. My mind drifted away to worlds where animals talked and warriors beheaded giant serpents.

Three days after we returned from Caladheå, a soldier rode into the clearing.

He carried a spear and wore the blue Colonnium guard uniform. His horse stopped in front of the cabin, white clouds emerging from its nostrils. Clumps of snow stuck to the feathery hair around its feet.

"Tiernan Heilind," the soldier called.

I ducked behind the stable and peered around the corner. There was no answer. I didn't know if Tiernan was even home. Maybe he'd gone to the creek—

—then he strode outside and yanked the cabin door shut. "What is it?"

"The Caladheå Council summons you to testify regarding Suriel."

"I made it clear I will not go."

The soldier dismounted and took an envelope from his breast pocket. "Here is the writ."

Tiernan unfolded the contents. "Signed by all twenty councillors except Parr. So they do not even listen to him." He held up the paper. "Is there any legal ground for this?"

"The Council holds the right to summon witnesses. Refusals to testify must be made in person in the Colonnium."

"I have done exactly that." Tiernan tore the paper into quarters and dropped it onto the snow. "What more do they need, a signature in blood?"

The soldier stepped toward the porch. "My instructions are to bring you back."

"I will not be intimidated by the Council. I am no longer theirs to command."

"Don't make me do this, Heilind." The soldier pointed his spear at Tiernan's chest.

An orange glow radiated from Tiernan until he blazed like the sun. The spear erupted into flames. A wave of heat rolled across the clearing, melting the snow down to the dead grass.

"The next person may find my aim less accurate," Tiernan said. "Now get off my land."

The soldier flung the spear away and swung onto his horse. I flattened myself against the stable wall until the hoofbeats faded, and then I bolted.

❋

I banged on Marijka's door. I heard faint footsteps, then it swung open. "Can I stay here awhile?"

Her smile turned to confusion. "Of course. Come in."

The kitchen smelled like evergreen needles, cool and sharp. "What are you making?"

"Anaesthetic. Painkiller," she added, seeing my blank look. "A man came from Crieknaast after the uprising and bought my entire supply. I hope he was able to get back into town."

I shuddered. "Can I help?"

"Here." Marijka slid a stone mortar of dried leaves across the table. "You can grind more needlemint."

The scent burst out even stronger as I pulverized them with a pestle, giving me the urge to sneeze. "Is this what made my legs numb?"

"Yes. It's native to Sverba, so naturally it grows best in the snow." She took a glass bottle from a shelf and measured clear liquid into a jar. "Not that I don't appreciate the company, but did something happen?"

"A soldier came looking for Tiernan. The Council is summoning him."

Marijka set the bottle down and looked at the ceiling. "Gods help us. That must've been a conversation."

I rubbed my boot against my other heel. "Was . . . Tiernan in the military?"

"Not as an enlisted soldier. But yes, most of his contracts came from Cáladheå."

A cold weight settled in my stomach. "How could he fight on their side?"

"He asks himself that every day." She tapped the mortar. "'Grind' is a few steps down from 'obliterate.'"

"Sorry." I eased off the pressure. "But doesn't it bother you?"

"It's not as simple as taking sides. Life brings us together with people we never expected to stand beside. Sometimes we have to distance ourselves from those who once stood by us." Marijka stopped rummaging through a drawer. "I think you know that, or you wouldn't be here."

"Here in your house, or in Iyun Bel?"

She shrugged.

We spent the rest of the afternoon grinding leaves and mixing them into jars of vodka. Marijka explained that the alcohol preserved the herbs. The brännvin Rin bartered from Sverbians was vodka flavoured with fennel, but she said with a smile that probably shouldn't be used as medicine.

Marijka settled by the fire with some sewing after dinner. I wandered around the kitchen looking at her ornaments. A wooden rack on the wall held a row of ceramic plates painted with snowy landscapes. Marijka said they were pictures of Nyhemur where she grew up.

I bent over to look at a figurine of a horse with its mane streaming in the wind. Firelight glinted on the polished wood. "What do these symbols carved in the base say?"

Marijka glanced up. "Tiernan's name in Sverbian writing. He made it several years ago."

"Huh. I thought he only carved practical things."

"Practical." She clamped the needle between her lips while untangling the thread. "That's a good word for him these days."

My eyes traced over the horse's powerful legs, flared nostrils, alert ears. I could almost hear the thud of hooves on frozen soil, smell sweat on its hide, feel the strain of muscles under its skin. I never would've guessed Tiernan could make something so beautiful.

✳

The cabin was dark when I returned. Light filtered through the sooty workshop windows. I crept across the clearing, squishing through the muck, and nudged open the door. I collided with a wall of heat.

Tiernan sat on the workshop's dirt floor, elbows on his knees, head in his hands. The brazier burned with a dull glow. Amber-coloured tallow candles dripped onto the tables. His jerkin was tossed over a stool, and his damp tunic clung to his skin.

I unclasped my fur mantle and edged forward. "Tiernan?"

He looked up at me as if I were oceans away. "Kateiko. You left."

"I was by the stable earlier. When that soldier came. Why didn't you tell me you fought for Caladheå?"

Tiernan rubbed the bridge of his nose. "I did not want you to be afraid of me."

"I'm not. Too many other things to fear in the world, remember?" I took off my gloves, knelt, and wiped a streak of ash from his face. He stiffened.

"You have to understand," he began. "No. You do not have to, but I hope you will. I came to this land with no connections, no money, nothing but my sword and magic. I could barely speak the trade language. The military was reliable work."

"Why did you leave it?"

The brazier flickered. "It is not a story I would trouble you with."

"Please. I want to know." I shifted into a cross-legged position, ignoring the mud on my boots, and took his hands. His skin burned against mine.

Tiernan looked down at the dirt. "I met a man when I arrived in Eremur. Jorumgard Tømasind. We took several contracts together. He was . . . the kind of swordsman you wanted at your back in a fight. The kind of friend you wanted by your side at your wedding.

"Jorum and I took a contract from the Council two years ago. A company of soldiers was investigating anomalies in the Turquoise

Mountains. Dead cragsmen, odd weather. Iyo traders in Crieknaast warned us not to enter Dúnravn Pass. We went anyway.

"The wind picked up as we rode into the mountains. It raged through the peaks until an avalanche blocked the pass — in mid-summer. The captain refused to turn back. We were stuck for days while scouts searched for another route. Jorum was ready to give up, but I insisted we see it through.

"Riders came out of nowhere and attacked in the night. They slaughtered half our men before we realized what was happening." Tiernan's voice slipped. "Jorum was with me, but I lost him in the fray. I escaped to Crieknaast with two men. A few more showed up days later, starving and frostbitten. Jorum never came."

"Did you go back to look for him?"

"More than once. I finally found his body preserved by the snow. He had been cut down by a blade. I carried him back to Crieknaast for a proper funeral."

I felt a pang deep in my chest. No wonder he'd been bothered by the story of Imarein Rin climbing a mountain in a blizzard. I held his hands tight, not caring about the scorching heat. "I'm sorry for snapping at you in Crieknaast. About protecting people."

He shook his head. "You could not have known."

"What did the Council do?"

"Refused to acknowledge the truth. They blamed the attack on rogue cragsmen, but those were trained soldiers. I saw the sigil on their shields. A black bird with spread wings, its head turned aside. Falwen confirmed it was linked to the spirit the Iyo traders warned of. A few politicians believed it was a planned attack, Vorhagind and Quintere among them, but it was not enough. That is when I left the military."

I tried to piece everything together. It felt like holding a handful of iron links with no way to forge them into a chain. Saidu were territorial, I knew that much. They claimed a home and scuffled over borders. Legend says that back when they were awake, the worst weather — earthquakes, volcanic eruptions, coastal floods — was the result of those scuffles.

But saidu never cared about humans in their territories. Suriel had allowed Imarein to live on his mountain, the heart of his land. Either he was less tolerant of itherans or something had changed since Imarein's time. Now Suriel was willing to kill people to keep them out of Dúnravn Pass. Storms didn't work, so he sent human soldiers. Speaking our language without speaking.

That part made sense. In theory, he could've filled the pass with a permanent storm, but even the strongest saidu had limits, especially when affecting elements other than their own — in this case, a tel-saidu using wind to move snow. Suriel would've needed time to recover before making another storm. It was more efficient to send soldiers. Unusual, but then, he'd always been unusually involved with humans.

"Why would anyone fight for Suriel?" I wondered aloud. "Mounted soldiers must be itherans. Your people never revered tel-saidu like mine did."

"Money, ambition, bloodlust. The same reasons anyone becomes a mercenary. Suriel must have a human captain who commands in his name and manages the practical aspects of war."

"Who, though? Imarein would be over a hundred now. And in the stories, Suriel only spoke to people he deemed worthy. I have no idea how an itheran would earn his trust, unless — ai, never mind. If I don't know something about saidu, you definitely won't."

Colour rose in Tiernan's cheeks.

Realization hit me like floodwater. "You knew. In Crieknaast. You knew what Suriel was before I told you."

"I knew. Just not about Imarein."

"Why didn't you tell Mayor Vorhagind?"

"I did. Two years ago, as soon as I made it back from Dúnravn. He accepted a spirit might be responsible for the massacre but was skeptical about the avalanche. Crieknaast has always suffered severe windstorms."

"He believed me."

"Vorhagind trusts viirelei. More than he trusts mages, apparently."

My eyes narrowed. "So you knew he might listen to me, but you still didn't want me to go back into the town hall?"

Heat pulsed off Tiernan. "Montès would have dragged you to Bøkkhem and back if he found out you interfered. You have no idea what he has done to viirelei. I hope to the gods you never find out."

I opened my mouth, then stopped. I could hardly lecture Tiernan for protecting me after he lost Jorumgard. And he'd helped rescue the tannery workers after a little nudging. "Maybe it's good the Council summoned you. It's another chance to convince them."

"To do what? Suriel went quiet until Crieknaast expanded into the mountains. Sending a military detachment will just provoke him further."

"But no one out there is safe. Vorhagind's the only one who knows what the wind means, and Rhonos said Suriel's soldiers aren't just near Crieknaast."

"I will not suffer another inquiry. I had to publicly relive every violent moment of a massacre only to be told that my closest friend, a renowned swordsman, was killed by a hermit with a hatchet. Once was enough."

The workshop felt like the inside of a steam vent. My shirt stuck to my skin. The brazier had grown brighter and brighter until it blazed like a bonfire, illuminating the wood grain of the walls and the high soot-stained ceiling.

"I'm sorry," I said. "It's your decision."

For the first time that night Tiernan's eyes focused on me. "I told you I do not know what to believe about the dead." He took a shuddering breath. "People believe what gives them comfort. Nothing gives me comfort, so I believe nothing."

Tears pricked my eyes. I wanted nothing more than to stroke his tangled hair, to touch his spirit and say I understood — but I couldn't bring myself to move. So we stayed there with our hands together until the candles sputtered out and the brazier dimmed. When we finally rose, I hid the blisters on my palms.

※

The next day, Marijka spent over an hour in the workshop with Tiernan. I heard voices but couldn't make out the words. When she came outside looking frustrated, I asked what was wrong, but she just shook her head and said, "I fix bodies, not minds."

Sometimes Tiernan was in the workshop when I woke and was still there when I went to bed. I struggled to read in there, distracted by his questions — about Aeldu-yan, my visions of that parallel world, the voices I heard in the wind, and other things that didn't seem related. How I learned water-calling, if any Sverbians I met up north used magic, if we farmed or dug wells on Aeti Ginu.

"Tiernan," I said gently when he asked about attuning. "Remember saying it's rude to ask what kind of itheran someone is?"

He apologized and returned to burning perfectly-measured pine rods. His silence unnerved me. He went to the door every time a noise came from the woods, then seemed to forget what he'd been doing. That night, I found him standing in the clearing as if listening to the wind.

His questions turned to experiments. I'd fill an engraved basin with water while he timed me or measured its temperature. Sometimes I did it while standing on a rune. The glowing symbol sent tingles over my skin, like the crackle in the air during a lightning storm, and water leapt to my call as if it were anxious to please me. I liked the feeling, but was always exhausted after, and had to stop so I had energy left to check my trapline.

"Don't go," Tiernan said one day. For a moment I was the water wanting to please *him* — but an ache had settled deep in my muscles, and it was cruel to leave wildlife trapped in my snares. He was staring at the floor runes when I left.

✳

Snow drifted down, covering the circle he'd melted when the soldier came. Rain washed away the top layer. After the cabin flooded, I tried to form a barrier around it but couldn't sustain it for more than a few hours. I got used to drying the floorboards while I read folk tales. I took down Tiernan's book with the nine-branched tree on the cover, trudged through two pages, and gave up.

On the evening of the winter solstice, I went into the workshop. "Will you go for a ride with me tonight?"

Tiernan set down his quill. "Where?"

"It's a secret."

He gave me a look, but agreed. We bundled up in our warmest clothes. Snow had built up in the woods, so we rode along the creek until I smelled the ocean. We tethered the horses just before the inland forest gave way to a dense tangle of salt spruce. The branches of the tallest trees didn't start until several times my height, but I'd rigged a cottonwood by slingshotting rope over a branch. I grabbed the rope, braced my boots against the fissured bark, and started climbing.

"Kateiko—" Tiernan said.

"Come on. Once you reach the branches, it's easy."

He said something in Sverbian I didn't want to know the meaning of, but followed me up. We sought footholds on leafless limbs until they were barely strong enough to hold us. My clothes were covered in sweet-smelling resin by the time I turned around.

We stood above the canopy of North Iyun Bel, the ocean and forest like an endless dark blanket around us. Treetops swayed under the moonlight. I could see the lights of Caladheå and silhouettes of ships in the bay. It was silent except for rustling evergreen needles and the slow beat of waves.

Kujinna kobairen. Today we fly. The solstice was one of the few times I truly felt Rin.

"Tonight is Yanben," I said. "On the longest night of the year, Aeldu-yan and Eredu-yan overlap. The worlds of the dead and living unite, and we commemorate those we've lost." I fished a torch from my flail sheath and held the tallow-soaked end out to Tiernan.

"Is that a good idea?"

"You're a jinrayul. I'm an antayul. We'll be fine."

The torch burst into flames. I murmured in Aikoto and tossed it into the canopy. A treetop ignited, flames slowly catching on wet wood.

I pointed across the bay to South Iyun Bel. Far on the horizon, orange pinpricks of light burst into existence, glittering in the clear winter air. I wondered if Dunehein was out there with the Iyo. If he knew his brother Emehein's blood was in the ground.

I offered a torch to Tiernan. "Each person makes their own beacon."

He stretched his arm out to take it. Branches creaked under us. "What do I say?"

"Whatever you want the dead to hear."

Tiernan spoke into the darkness. The only word I understood was *Jorum*. He lit his torch and flung it into the forest. A second treetop caught fire next to mine.

We stood in silence, balancing under twinkling stars. Moonlight reflected on the rippling ocean. We floated in a crystal sphere that was the same upside down, east to west, north to south, dead to alive.

At the edge of my hearing, gentle words drifted back to me on the wind.

13.

SKAARNAHT

My fishing line drifted back and forth with the current, nudging against a circle in the ice. Snow crunched. I turned to see Marijka.

"Had any luck?" She brushed off a boulder and sat down.

I tipped the fish bucket forward to show her two creek trout. "It's something."

"Say, Kateiko . . ." Marijka tapped her mittens on her knees. "Would you like to come to Caladheå for the new-year festival?"

"What do you do for it?"

"Well, I always attend rites at the stavehall in afternoon, but at night people celebrate. Music, fireworks, that sort of thing. I thought you might be going a bit crazy out here."

I tugged at my hair and tried to laugh. "More than a bit."

Winter was a social time for Rin. During those long nights, I heard stories about aeldu and saidu, learned the history of the jouyen, watched embroiderers and woodcarvers make goods to trade for wool and steel. Tiernan was in better spirits after Yanben but couldn't hold a conversation about anything other than his research. Maybe in Caladheå I'd run into more Iyo, get a feel for what they thought of Rin without intruding on their homes at Toel Ginu.

A few days later, I put my dress on over the woolen underlayers and fumbled through lacing the bodice. I braided my hair after giving up on the pins. On the way down the loft ladder, my feet tangled in the skirt and I tumbled to the floor in a heap.

Tiernan raised an eyebrow. He was seated at the kitchen table with a book. "Perhaps you should stick with your normal clothes."

"You're always telling me not to attract attention."

"Yes, no one will notice you gangling about like a newborn fawn."

I ignored him as I made tea.

Everyone from the outlying lands must've been in the city. A rumble of voices carried down the street as Marijka and I rode toward the Blackened Oak. We squeezed into the pub and sat on a bench made of split logs with bark on the edges. Nhys greeted us with a warm smile and hurried off to mop up a spill, pausing to glare at a patron lighting a pipe from the fireplace.

"The clientele is eclectic, but Nhyskander makes the best *blød-stavohl* in Caladheå," Marijka whispered with a smile.

I believed her. The stew was rich and thick, goat's blood bringing out the savoury taste of the meat. I was more fascinated by the patrons though. A group of itherans took up most of our table with a card game, their laughter echoing off the low ceiling. The man in the patched cloak was slumped over as if he hadn't moved since I was last there. Everyone had red cords around their wrists.

"You're welcome to come to the stavehall, but the rites are in Sverbian," Marijka said as we left, joining a stream of people that parted whenever a sleigh would whisk down the street.

"Ai . . ." I held up my bag, heavy with pelts. "Actually, I wanted to go to the market."

"Will you be able to find it?"

"Plenty of people to ask for directions." I swung my arm out and hit a passerby.

Marijka grabbed my hand as the woman glared at me. "The stavehall's on the way. I'll direct you from there."

The stavehall was a tiered timber building surrounded by snowy lawn. Everything about it was triangular, from its numerous gables to the shingles covering its walls and roofs. The handrails on the steps were draped with crimson cloth. With peeling white paint and a sagging porch, it looked as out of place among identical brick shops as grass trapped between flagstones. The Colonnium's domed tower rose behind it.

Eighty years ago, after the construction of Caladheå, Ferish immigrants flooded the coast. We had an uneasy truce for a decade until a Ferish naval captain tried to seize the city, declaring the Colonnium and its surrounding land had been stolen from Ferland in the First Elken War. The Sverbian-Aikoto alliance fought back. We almost won. Then in late summer, the driest time of year, fire ripped through Caladheå. People later realized it started in a dozen places at once.

I gazed at the highest gable, carved with the leafless nine-branched tree from one of Tiernan's theological books. "Is this one of Caladheå's original buildings?"

Marijka nodded. "We're on the border of Førstown and Bronnoi Ridge, the old Sverbian and viirelei districts."

"I've heard of this stavehall. Antayul in my family helped save it from burning in the Second Elken War, after they realized our district was lost."

"Then we owe your family." She gestured at the brick shops. "Ferish took over Bronnoi Ridge. They would've taken the stavehall grounds if they could."

I imagined flames tearing down the street where we stood. The Rin had buried their dead near Toel Ginu and returned north. They forced Fendul's great-great-grandmother, Okorebai-Rin at the time, to promise we'd never live in the south again.

"Was that the same fire that burned down the Blackened Oak?" I asked.

Marijka smiled. "No, that was recent. Better not ask Nhyskander about it."

She dropped two pann into a rattling metal basin on the sidewalk. An elderly man in a white cleric's robe handed her two red cords from a bundle and inclined his head to me. He must've heard me talk about the stavehall. I'd have to be careful if I was going to pass off as Iyo like Falwen advised.

"What's this for?" I asked as Marijka knotted a cord around my wrist.

"We call tonight Skaarnaht, which means 'Red Night,'" she said. "The knot represents the link between the old and new year. It's bad luck to remove it before midnight."

I waved my arm back and forth and watched the ends flutter. "So if you already have bad luck, you'll lose it and get more bad luck?"

"Don't lose it." She laughed and shook a finger at me. "I'll meet you at the steps of Nen Divinus, the sancte in the city square, at five o'clock. Once night falls, it'll be too hard to find each other."

Marijka headed into the stavehall, and I headed downtown. Caladheå was decorated for the holiday. Fir boughs and knots of blood-red berries hung over doorways. Garlands of scarlet ribbon wound through fences, stark against the snow. Most shop windows were dark, but dozens of white-garbed people sold cords. I flowed along with the crowd, watching the endless stream of faces. I felt too tall among delicate women who walked with ease in long skirts. A gangling fawn indeed.

The snow had been cleared in the square, revealing a circular pattern of white and grey cobblestones. Stocky men nailed boards into a platform near the sancte. I wandered laneways criss-crossed with ribbon until I found the Iyo embroiderer. As we haggled, I learned her name was Segowa. Ingard had told me the white winter pelt of a cloud weasel fetched the same price in Caladheå as a marsh rat twice the size, but I didn't believe him until I held the sovereigns.

A strange energy filled the market, as if the loud conversations and laughter were a sheet of ice holding in an undercurrent of whispers. Women held their purses close. Men spoke in rapid Coast Trader littered with foreign words. As I wandered down a narrow street, the sky blocked out by buildings, I caught a fragment of conversation.

"—Crieknaast all over again. Damned mess," a man said beside me.

I whirled in time to see the back of his head. I pushed through the throng, keeping my eyes fixed on his felt cap until a towering man with a furry hat blocked my view. I stood on my toes, thinking I'd lost him, until I saw him hold a door for his companion.

Voices spilled out of the red-brick building. It had boarded-up windows and a drainpipe covered in dripping icicles. The paint on the sign was flaking away, but I could make out an otter with a bottle in one paw. I pushed the door open and entered a room choked with pipe smoke, packed with people at round tables and a bar along the back wall. The only light came from sputtering candles that lit the place with an orange haze.

My hopes plummeted. The patrons were mostly men, and every single one had removed his hat. I lowered my hood and edged along the wall. A few people looked at me suspiciously. Everyone was in high-necked Ferish clothing. My boots stuck to the floor like it was coated in sap. By the time I reached the far end, finding the man with the felt cap seemed like a lost cause.

I glanced down the bar. A guard in a blue coat sat on a stool, spear leaning against the counter. I wondered why a Colonnium guard was downtown — then I recognized the auburn bun. Pelennus stared straight ahead, hands around a pewter mug. A man with stringy black hair and flushed cheeks leaned against the bar, talking so loudly I could hear him over the crowd.

"That uniform don' suit you. Shouldn' you have an apron or somethin'?" He pounded the counter. "Barkeep! Don' you have a nice apron for the woman?"

The barkeeper ignored him. Pelennus took a sip of her drink.

"The Antlers are no place for a lady. Lady elk don' even grow antlers! Iss not right, you know?" The man leaned closer. "How 'bout you show us a differen' rack instead?"

Her hands tightened around the mug.

"How about you shut your fucking mouth?" I said, and Pelennus finally looked around.

"Wha's it to you?" he slurred. "Wanna join the Antlers too? Maybe the Elkhounds will take you. Bitches and wood witches, what a match."

I crooked my right arm, thrust my fist upward, and slapped my other hand twice against my right shoulder.

The man's face twisted. He lurched away from the bar, grabbed my elbow, and pulled me close. He reeked of alcohol. "Lis'en here, I won' be insulted by some flea-bitten little—"

"Don't touch me!" I tried to shove him away. He twisted my arm and I cried out.

Pelennus was on her feet in an instant. She drew back her fist and slammed it into his skull. He dropped like a sack of rotten brassroot.

She shook out her arm. "Thanks. I've been wanting to do that for a while."

"Uh . . ." I looked down at the man.

"I'm not allowed to use force on civilians until they assault someone." She rolled the man onto his side and loosened his collar. Only when she stood up did she notice the faces staring at us. She slammed her spear into the floorboards. "What are you looking at?"

Everyone turned away. The clank of mugs resumed.

"Thanks." I rubbed my elbow.

She looked at me closer. "Weren't you at the Colonnium a few weeks ago?"

I nodded. "Pelennus, right?"

"That's my surname. Call me Iannah. I'm off duty." She gave me a clipped bow.

I returned the gesture. "Kateiko R— Sohikoehl."

"Now there's a mouthful. Koehl okay?"

"Um . . . sure?"

"Well, Koehl, let me buy you a drink." Iannah glanced at the man, who was drooling onto the floor. "Non-alcoholic. Some people start the festivities too early."

I hesitated, then slid onto a stool. She flagged down the bartender, who poured a mug of cloudy brown liquid from a kettle warming on an iron stove. Iannah clanked her mug against mine. I put my face into the steam, inhaled the scent of spices and took a sip.

"Ginger mull," she said, watching my expression. "You can get it watered down."

It took all my willpower to swallow without spluttering. "Nei. I like it. Thanks."

"We made it every winter back home. Too strong for most city folk."

"You're not from here?"

Iannah shook her head. "Born in Laca vi Miero on the other side of Burren Inlet. Been in Caladheå almost nine years." She tipped her mug toward me. "What brought you here?"

"Just . . . seeing the city." *Lie*, Falwen said. "I was born near here but grew up in the north. I'm going to the square in a few hours for Skaarnaht."

"Going to be a hell of a night," she muttered. "Maybe I'll see you there. I'll be on duty."

"I didn't think Colonnium guards served anywhere else."

"They're pulling us down the hill for the night. Council's making a speech." She nodded at the pub. "Only reason you'd find me in the Drunken Otter."

I shifted on the hard stool. "There must be nicer pubs nearby."

"Not really." Iannah nudged the unconscious man with her boot. He groaned. "You here with your mage friend?"

"Nei, I'm with someone else. We're only here for the night. I wish I could stay longer."

"Why don't you?"

I wrapped my hands around the steaming mug. Why, indeed? I had enough money to stay at the Blackened Oak a few nights. "I don't know what to do here."

Iannah gave me a long look. Her green eyes stood out against her light skin. "Tell you what. I have tomorrow off. If you're still in town at noon, meet me by the Colonnium gates."

"Really? You must have better things to do."

"I've never seen someone give such an impressive two-hand salute. And that," she held up her mug, "is worth celebrating."

*

Iannah walked me back to the square and left to find her captain. I waited on the steps of Nen Divinus, watching a teenage boy go around with a long pole lighting glass lanterns as the sun dipped toward the horizon. Marijka appeared just after the bell tolled five times. We went to the docklands to find somewhere quieter for dinner, over which I told her about meeting Iannah. She warned me not to mention it to Tiernan.

Night had fallen by the time we returned. The square was transformed, packed with people all the way from Nen Divinus down the laneways. I could barely hear Marijka over the noise. The sancte's portico was lined with torches to illuminate the newly-built platform where a couple in brocade robes performed a slow dance with complicated hand movements. On the corner of the stage, a man plucked a stringed wooden instrument with a bent neck.

"They get the boring Ferish culture out of the way early," Marijka said, and I grinned.

We saw one performance after another. Two soldiers in full armour gave a sword-fighting demonstration, the clash of blades echoing off the brick. A woman recited a poem I couldn't understand, but her voice carried me away like a raging storm. Actors in exaggerated costumes gave a silent performance that sent waves of laughter through the audience.

Then space was cleared by the platform, and two lines of people formed as a new group climbed onstage. Three men with drums strapped to their hips, a red-haired man with a flat handheld drum, two women with fiddles. They all looked Sverbian except for one, the tallest, and when he turned our way I saw the dark blue Iyo dolphin painted on his drum.

Exuberant music flowed over the square. A riotous dance began of people linking elbows and spinning in and out of the lines.

Marjika laughed and clapped along. For a moment, I saw part of her that was young and wild and glowed like the stars, and the world didn't seem quite so big.

Someone grabbed my hand. A boy with golden hair and a face full of laughter pulled me into the dance. I thought for a second it was Ingard — then our elbows linked and I was twirling, flung toward the line where someone else swung me around and back out. My hood slipped off and my brown braid whipped through the air as I spun like a leaf in a gale.

I collided with a wall of onlookers at the end. The golden-haired boy stumbled toward me and kissed my hand. I didn't know if I blushed or if I was just sweltering from exertion.

There was no way to get back to Marijka without getting crushed. I escaped to the edge of the square to catch my breath. Elkhounds marked by grey leather armour stood with shields and spears along the shop walls. I climbed on a windowsill and clung to a drainpipe while I looked over everyone's heads. A row of Colonnium guards in blue was spaced across the steps of Nen Divinus. Iannah's severe bun shone in the firelight.

I followed the scent of roasting meat into the packed laneways. I bought strips of venison and a glass bottle of amber liquid that the shopkeeper assured me didn't have alcohol. Then I took a deep breath and headed for the sancte. "Am I allowed to stand here?" I asked as I drew up alongside Iannah.

She shrugged. "Don't see why not."

I offered her a strip of meat. "Hungry?"

She arched an eyebrow and accepted it.

"So you just stand here all night?"

"Until something goes wrong."

I passed the bottle back and forth with Iannah. She said it was called cordial. It tasted like sour apples. Light poured out of coloured windows behind us, spilling rainbows on the stone. The faint drone of chanting inside mingled with the soaring music.

We had a good view of the platform. The women tapped their feet, fiddles cradled against their shoulders. The drummers' mallets bounded through the air. The Iyo man couldn't stay still, stamping his feet in a dance that carried him around the stage. His dark hair was spiked up like a shark fin that bobbed with the music. He laughed as the red-headed itheran swatted his hair with a mallet.

After I cooled off, I went into the crowd, dodging people swinging half-full bottles. By the time the dance ended there was still no sign of Marijka. The musicians left, and three figures in black robes climbed onstage, followed by Colonnium guards.

An old man with more wrinkles than face stood at the edge of the platform and raised his hands. His voice was surprisingly strong. "Good evening, blessed new year, *Ciårva Skaarnaht*. I am Councillor Brasius Obolèto. On behalf of the Caladheå Council, thank you for coming. . ."

I tuned out his speech and squinted at the men behind him. Montès and Parr. Good thing Tiernan didn't come. I stood on my toes, searching for Marijka, but snapped back to attention when a ripple went throughout the crowd.

"—with great distress I report Rutnaast has fallen to a grievous attack. Had the mayor called for aid sooner, the military may have been able to prevent—"

"Crieknaast called for help and got a massacre!" someone shouted.

"The events in Crieknaast were a terrible tragedy," Obolèto said. "Nobody regrets the losses more than us. The inquiry regarding Suriel will be expanded to include Rutnaast—"

"How many will die while we wait?" another person called.

"*Ikken naeja!*" a man shouted. Voices repeated the words until they echoed across the square. A boy next to me with the first scruff of facial hair raised his fist as he shouted along.

"We will do everything possible to protect the citizens of Eremur—" Obolèto struggled to speak over the chant, but the noise only grew. People pressed in around the stage. I could barely breathe, let alone move.

A woman got on someone's shoulders and addressed the crowd. "It's been a month since Crieknaast! Our brothers and sisters lay dead and still the Council demands evidence! We need action, not empty words!"

Obolèto stepped back a second before a bottle shattered at his feet. The guards moved in.

"*Ikken naeja! Ikken naeja!*" The woman pumped her fist into the air.

A man leapt onto the platform, raised an iron cudgel, and charged at Obolèto. Parr twisted the man's arm behind his back and brought him to the ground before the guards could react.

A trumpet shrilled. The doors of Nen Divinus swung open. Light spilled out, silhouetting figures in deep blue robes as they flooded into the portico. A man rushed up the steps wielding a knife. Iannah's spear cracked against his ribs.

I lost track of her after that. All I could see was swinging spears, red elk on silver shields, tangled arms and legs. Screams pierced the night, high and guttural like dying animals. Someone stumbled into me. I fell, soaking my skirt with slush, and put my hand into a pool of blood on the cobblestone. I scrambled up and tumbled down a laneway with the crush of bodies.

Sobbing met my ears. I spun and saw a child under a table. I crouched down. "Where's your family?"

"I don't know," she gasped.

I scooped her up, avoiding her dark curls. "*Wala, wala*. It's okay." I pressed her shaking body against mine and kept moving. The trumpet sounded again.

"*Akesida! Hud ulan!*" Someone grabbed my sleeve.

Segowa. The Iyo embroiderer. I stumbled into her stall. A young woman sat on a crate, holding a wailing baby wrapped in otter furs. A lamp flickered on a shelf, the air thick with the smell of fish oil.

I set the girl down. "You'll be safe here, okay?"

"Tema," the young woman addressed her mother. "You have to find Aire before he gets into trouble."

Segowa pointed at me. "*Akesida*. Are you looking for anyone?"

I nodded. She beckoned, climbed on a table in front of her shop, and swung up onto the roof. I scrambled up and followed the long row of stalls back toward the sancte. Parr stood alone on the platform, directing soldiers into a wall of shields.

The square was chaos. People bottlenecked in the streets leading out. A man wrested a spear from a Colonnium guard and swung it at his head. The guard ducked and took him out with a kick to the knees. Glass shattered somewhere. A lantern flickered out.

The bell tolled from the tower of Nen Divinus. Midnight. The new year.

Light exploded on the horizon. I ducked as a crash of sound rolled over the city. Brilliant red sparks filled the sky. Another burst followed, rumbling like thunder.

I spotted Marijka at the end of the laneway, her white bonnet glowing under the fireworks. "Maika!" I yelled. "Maika!" She turned and pushed toward me. I dropped to my stomach and pulled her up onto the roof.

Segowa scanned the crowd. During a flash of light, her mouth formed a silent curse. She leapt off the roof. Moments later, she returned with a man slumped over one shoulder. Marijka and I grabbed his cold, slippery hands. He groaned as we hauled him onto the roof and back down the laneway.

"Airedain—" The young woman rose as we staggered into the stall. The curly-haired girl was still there, wrapped in an embroidered cloak two times her size.

Segowa pulled shut the heavy folding door. Marijka and I laid the man down. Only in the light did I notice his dishevelled crest of hair. The Iyo drummer. He was younger than I'd thought, tall and skinny like a sapling.

"It ain't so bad," he said with a weak smile. His face was pale. A long rip marred his black leather jerkin, glistening red in the lamplight.

Segowa sliced open his jerkin and tunic with a bone knife. I turned the little girl aside so she didn't see the gash between his ribs or the blood that ran onto the cobblestone.

"Let me treat him. I'm a medic," Marijka said.

The Iyo women turned to me.

I nodded. "She's helped me."

Marijka knelt next to Airedain and examined the wound. "I could stitch it, but it might get infected. Do you trust me to try something else?"

His dry chuckle turned into a cough. He spat blood. "If you can fix me."

"Kateiko, I need water," Marijka said. "As hot as you can make it."

Segowa handed me a bowl that I filled with steaming water. Marijka cut the red cord off her wrist, scrubbed her hands, and rinsed the gash.

"Hold him down," she told Segowa and me. "This will hurt."

We gripped Airedain's arms. He sucked in a rattling breath as Marijka pressed her hands onto the wound. I leaned down with all my weight as he convulsed. A stream of cursing spilled from his mouth, a tangled mix of Aikoto and Sverbian.

"Keep as still as you can." Marijka's voice was flat.

Airedain clenched his teeth, the muscles in his neck taut. I twined my fingers into his. Segowa whispered into his ear. His pulse skittered like a sparrow.

I didn't realize it was over until Marijka leaned back. The bleeding had stopped. The torn flesh was fused together, leaving a jagged red line across his ribs.

"Yan taku," I muttered. "You never told me you could do that."

"It's better for the rest to heal naturally. Be careful not to reopen it." Marijka bandaged the wound with clean linen from Segowa.

Airedain pulled himself up and leaned against a crate. Damp hair stuck to his forehead. His breathing was ragged. "Never thought I'd be healed by itheran magic. Thanks."

"If you weren't such an idiot—" the young woman began.

"Enough, Lituwa," Segowa said.

Lituwa scowled and unlaced her shirt to feed her squalling baby.

"Aeldu bless your blood," Segowa said to Marijka. She put a hand on Airedain's shoulder and kissed his hair. "My son. Thank the aeldu."

I wasn't surprised the three were related. They all had high cheekbones, thin lips, and dark brown hair, though Airedain's clothes looked Sverbian and the women wore traditional shirts and leggings, their hair neatly braided. Lituwa must've been the one who carved the wolf makiri I gave to Tiernan.

Curious, I read Airedain's tattoos. The one in the centre of his chest was partially covered by bandages, but I recognized the drummer symbol, a circle with four points like sunbeams. He had a pattern of arrowhead leaves around the dolphin crest on his arm. No marks for marriage or children.

I glanced at his face and realized he'd caught me looking. He grinned.

We huddled in the stall as shouts and explosions ruptured the air. Light flickered through cracks in the walls. Segowa handed out fur-lined cloaks to use as blankets and took up a post by the door, clutching a glinting dagger.

I pulled the curly-haired girl into my lap, trying to get comfortable with the wall pressing into my spine. Her sobs had quietened, but she kept casting scared looks at Airedain. "What's your name?" I asked.

"Mida," she said in a tiny voice.

"Do you like snowflakes, Mida?" I held out her hand and traced a pattern on her mitten. A snowflake as big as her palm appeared, shimmering in the lamplight. Her mouth formed a circle. I looked up to see Lituwa's eyes fixed on me.

"Rin, right?" she said. "Falwen said one finally turned up."

No point lying. "Yeah. I came south to visit my cousin Dunehein. Just never made it to Toel Ginu."

"The shrine carver's husband?" Airedain said. "I always forget he used to be Rin."

"You know him?" I asked too quickly.

"Me? Nei, not really. We moved to Caladheå the summer he joined the Iyo. Liwa here moved back to Toel after a couple years though."

Lituwa nodded. "I saw Dunehein and his wife a few days ago. They're in good health."

My shoulders eased. "They're not here, are they?"

"Nei. Most Iyo don't care about Skaarnaht. I just came to see my little brother perform." Lituwa jerked her chin at Airedain.

He touched his ribs and winced. "Too bad I won't be playing again for a while."

"You were very good," Marijka said. "The Skaarnaht dance is one of my favourites."

"It's nothing compared to the spring equinox." Airedain winked at me. "Music, dancing, alcohol, and a thousand people packed into the Toel shrine. You should come, Rin-girl. I'll be healed by then."

"Maybe." I felt too warm all of a sudden.

The fireworks eventually stopped. The noise faded into a dull rumble. Lituwa's baby fell asleep in her lap and Mida nodded off in mine.

Not long after the bell tolled one, a woman's voice echoed down the lane. "Mida! Mida, where are you, darling?"

Segowa heaved open the door. She stepped outside, raised a hand, and called out. I stood up, balancing Mida's limp form on my shoulder.

A Ferish woman with wild eyes and a rumpled bonnet shoved past Segowa. She clapped a hand to her heart. "*You* — what are you doing with my little girl?" She pulled Mida out of my arms, throwing the embroidered cloak on the ground.

"The lady saved me, Mama," Mida said sleepily.

"Poor thing. You don't know what you're saying." She kissed Mida's dark curls. "Ugh, you even smell like them—"

The woman cut herself off. Her eyes travelled from me, past Lituwa and Airedain, to Segowa behind her. Her gaze settled on Marijka, who just raised her eyebrows.

"You should keep a better eye on your daughter," I said.

She glared at me and strode out of the stall.

14.

INQUIRY

When I woke up in the Blackened Oak, dawn was just breaking. I stumbled downstairs to the pub, groggier than aeldu rising. People nursed injuries and talked quietly. I looked at the ceiling, trying not to stare.

"What was everyone chanting last night?" I poked at my rye porridge. Even honey and huckleberry compote couldn't make it appealing.

"It's Sverbian for 'not enough.'" Marijka sighed. "I wouldn't have brought you if I knew things were so bad."

"Actually . . . I'm going to stay for a few days."

"Is that wise?"

"I want to know what's going on. The Iyo are caught up in all this, too."

Marijka tapped her clay mug. "What should I tell Tiernan?"

"Tell him I'm staying. It's not your responsibility to explain my decisions."

She smiled wryly. "If you're not back in a week, I'm sending him to search for you. Then he's your problem."

I waited until we were alone in the stable before asking the question nagging at my mind. "Maika . . . why didn't you heal me like you did Airedain?"

"I did. Your tibia was shattered."

As I stared at her, something clicked. "Tiernan said without you, I wouldn't be walking."

She nodded as she adjusted Gwmniwyr's bridle. "I'm no expert, but I do what I can."

I flung my arms around her. There weren't words enough to thank her.

After Marijka left, I wandered down empty streets toward the ocean. Fog coated the city. Every shop window was dark, shutters closed tight. I followed the peal of the sancte bell into the square. It was like a beach strewn with driftwood after a storm. Broken glass crunched under my boots. A few stalls had caved in, tattered garlands hanging from the wreckage. Red cords littered the ground like drops of blood in the slush. Grey-armoured Elkhounds stood guard at each laneway.

Several stalls were blocked by tables propped on end. A hunched man swept clay shards into a pile. The *skritch*, *skritch* of his straw broom filled the square. I peered into Segowa's shop through the half-open folding door and saw Airedain sitting on a crate, blanketed with an ash-grey caribou hide.

"Morning," I said in Aikoto. His Trader was better than mine, but I missed speaking in my own language.

His face cracked into a grin. "Am I glad to see you. Liwa took her kid back to Toel Ginu and I'm bored stiff." His Iyo accent was nice, a little softer than Rin.

I edged past a stack of crates in the entrance. A dark stain marred the cobblestone where he lay the night before. "How're you doing?"

He was pale except for the purple half-moons under his eyes. "Better now I got some tulanta in me. I'm grateful to your friend, but I sure wish she carried painkillers."

"You wouldn't be able to move if you took her painkillers." I perched on a crate. "Did you sleep here?"

"Sleep? Nei. Have I been pissing into a bucket? Yeah. At least if looters come, I got something to throw at 'em."

"Ew." I glanced at a ceramic pail under a table and shuffled my feet away. "Are you and Segowa staying in Caladheå?"

"My tema will. Liwa wants me to go back to Toel." He ran a hand over his hair. Pieces of the crest stuck out in every direction. "They carried eight bodies out of here. I got lucky."

"My aunt would say the aeldu were looking out for you."

"Or Aeldu-yan didn't want me." Airedain stretched. His grin turned into a grimace. "Maybe I'll go back for a while. Depends on this inquiry."

"What do you think they'll do?"

"I'll tell ya what they shouldn't do. Challenge Suriel again. Fucking pigeons ignored our warnings once already by going to Dúnravn. The bludgeheads' memories are shorter than burnt lamp wicks."

I drew back. "My friend was at Dúnravn. They thought they were doing the right thing."

"Then your friend's a bludgehead too, ain't he? You must know the saying about saidu. 'The wind dies a thousand deaths.' The Iyo have stayed out of that pass for centuries."

"Wait. The earliest I've heard of Suriel waking was ninety years ago, when he spoke to Imarein Rin."

Airedain shook his head. "Suriel didn't wake — Iyo elders say he never went dormant. We call him Ainu-seru. The mountain owl. Stayed awake while other saidu slept, just turned cranky and hid on his mountain peak. When itherans showed up he got *really* pissed off. S'why Crieknaast has always been so fucking windy."

I had so many questions, but his eyes looked unfocused and he was shivering. I picked up a clay mug from the ground, filled it with hot water, and pressed it into his hands.

He held it up in thanks. "I tell ya, one thing I miss about Toel is having antayul around."

I stayed with Airedain until it was time to meet Iannah. He assured me Segowa would be back soon, but the image of him huddled in the shadows followed me through the streets. *Lucky*. Was that the best we could hope for?

Iannah was leaning against the stone wall around the Colonnium grounds when I arrived. She wore her blue elk-sigil coat, but carried a sword instead of her spear. Long pieces of hair hung loose from her bun.

"When did you get off duty?" I asked.

"Eight." She yawned. "I think."

"We don't have to go anywhere today—"

"No. I need to get out of here." She pushed off the wall. "I forgot everything's closed today though," she said as we walked down the hill.

"I don't want to be in a crowd anyway." My eyes flicked to her sword. "I have to ask you something. Did you — stab anyone last night?"

"No. Why?"

"I was with someone that got hurt. Badly. I know it's your job, but . . ."

Iannah stopped walking. "I have to do lots of things civilians don't like. If it bothers you, leave. But my job is to keep the peace. Best way is to stab as few people as possible."

I gave her a half-smile. "Where do you like to go that's quiet?"

She looked at me closely. "There's one place, but it's not somewhere most visitors go."

"As long as I won't get stabbed."

So we headed outside the city and south along the bay where the ground rose into craggy hills. My back was slick with sweat when we reached a bluff overlooking the ocean. Boulders were strewn about like grains of sand scattered across the earth. Behind us, the Roannveldt plain faded into mist.

Iannah went straight to a hunk of red stone and climbed up like it was a ladder. I followed more slowly, seeking footholds on the salt-stained rock, cursing my skirt. The dull roar of waves rose toward us. A warship drifted in the bay, white sails spread to catch the wind.

"It sounds like the earth's pulse." I loosed the ribbon from my braid and ran my fingers through my hair until it billowed around me.

"I grew up inland," Iannah said. "Never saw the ocean until I left home. Sometimes I come here to remember there's a world outside the Colonnium."

She had a way of speaking that made the words flow together, something I'd noticed among all Ferish. I studied her face. She had a sharp jaw and a long nose that ran perfectly straight from her brows. If itherans could attune, she'd turn into a rust hawk.

I winced as soon as I thought it. Attuning was intensely personal. I didn't even know the second form of every Rin.

Turning away, I saw an open structure further along the bluff.

It was little more than a flat roof supported by stone pillars. A grey slab occupied the centre. "What's that?"

"The Hollow Sepulchre. A war memorial."

We slid down from the boulder and weaved past the rubble, stopping several paces away. I recognized a few words carved under the roof overhang. The slab was waist-high, unmarked, the rough width and length of a person.

Iannah unsheathed her sword and set it on the dirt before stepping onto the smooth stone floor. She turned and saw me standing motionless. "You can enter if you leave your weapons."

"In my culture, people aren't allowed to enter another nation's shrine."

"It's fine. Really." She held out her hand.

I set my flail and knives on the ground. Then I took Iannah's hand and crossed over the border into the memorial. She didn't let go as we walked to the tomb.

"Caladheå was built on a lot of spilled blood," she said. "My grandfathers are buried near the city. You'd think we'd learn to stop killing each other."

"Someone told me this morning people have short memories."

"They do." Iannah nodded at the tomb. "It's empty as a reminder that anyone could end up in there, but nobody comes here anymore."

I thought of the dead soldiers buried near Tiernan's cabin. *Dead.* The word scratched inside my skull like a thorn. I wondered if Iannah knew them. Suddenly I felt sick. I pulled my hand from her grasp and walked to the side of the memorial facing the foggy ocean.

It felt like the whole of Aeldu-yan had been stuffed into the hollow slab behind me. We were falling, all of us falling one by one. The further I ran, the deeper I spiralled into something I couldn't escape.

✳

That evening, Iannah took me to a shop crammed between buildings as if it was built in an alley. She simply called it Natzo's. The red-brick walls were decorated floor to ceiling with spoons. Long-handled wooden spoons, tiny silver spoons, ceramic spoons painted with delicate flowers. Iron vats lined a brick counter, puffing steam from under their lids. Iannah explained the contents and translated my request for Natzo, the short, balding Ferish shopkeeper. *Spianèʒi te choionne*, she called it, which I didn't try to pronounce.

Iannah took a notched steel spoon from the wall and found an empty table lit by a tallow candle. I chose a copper spoon with an etched handle. We both had flat wheat noodles, mine in clear broth, hers in opaque green. I'd never eaten wheat — it didn't grow here. I tried to mimic how she twisted noodles around her spoon.

"I didn't mean for today to be so depressing," she said.

"It's not your fault." I tried a mouthful and winced. The spicy broth stung my lips. "Did you always know you'd become a soldier?"

"Yeah. I could knock down most boys in Laca vi Miero. Came to Caladheâ to join the military academy when I was fourteen. Soonest they let people in. Knocked down most boys here and enlisted a year later."

"What's the academy like?"

"Brutal. Long days sparring in mud and rain until we were bruised like last year's crop. Still better than boarding school." She pointed at my flail with her spoon. "What about you? Not many civilians carry those."

I pulled my cloak over it. "We get our first weapons when we turn nine. Civilians don't exist among my people."

"If this inquiry goes wrong, they won't exist here either."

"Everything seems to rest on that. I hate not knowing what's going on." I rested my chin on my hand. "You must hear all sorts of things at the Colonnium."

Iannah rolled her eyes. "I swear people forget guards exist from the way they talk in front of us."

"So you know everyone's secrets?"

"Some." She paused with her spoon above her broth. "A Sverbian councillor used to fund a radical militant group called the Rúonbattai. During elections he pretends it never happened. And the Southeast Liaison got thrown out of a dinner last month for implying a Nyhemur diplomat's wife looks like a goat."

I clamped a hand to my mouth so I didn't spit noodles over the table. The corners of her eyes pulled back in amusement. I wondered if she ever smiled.

"What're you doing tomorrow?" Iannah asked later when we got up to leave. The street was black outside. Rain battered the windows.

"Nothing yet."

"I'm off duty in the afternoon. If you come by around one, I'll show you something." She covered a yawn. "Right now, I need to sleep."

❋

"Please declare yourself and relinquish all weapons," Gélus droned.

"Kateiko Sohikoehl. I'm here to see Pelennus." I placed my identification card on the desk along with my weapons.

Gélus looked down at them and back up. "Oh, you again." He consulted a paper covered with tiny writing. "Pelennus is off duty."

"I know." I stared at Gélus. He stared back. I sighed and retreated into a corner.

A low murmur seeped out from the doors across the hall, rising and falling like the tide. More guards stood in the lobby than last time. I edged behind a pillar, relieved when Iannah showed up. Her hair was tidy again, but she still looked tired.

She led me through winding corridors until we emerged outside. I stepped onto the lawn to look at the back of the Colonnium. A balcony spanned the second level, its roof supported by wide-spaced stone pillars. I realized it was the loggia I saw from Falwen's office.

Iannah stopped at a door in the central tower. She took out an iron ring loaded with keys, turned a rusted one in the lock, and yanked the handle. The door groaned open. I ducked under a spiderweb and followed her up a creaking spiral staircase. Freezing rain gusted in from narrow slits. She held a finger to her lips before unlocking the door at the top.

I stepped onto a ledge and gasped. We stood just below the domed ceiling of a massive hall sculpted from cream marble. Ice coated the windows. The black-robed figures below looked tiny, facing each other from behind two long polished tables. A man with a yellow beard stood in the centre like a leaf snagged on the antlers of clashing elk.

"Are we allowed to be here?" I whispered.

"I have the key, don't I?"

I peered over the iron railing. At one end of the hall was an elaborate chair carved from the same gleaming black wood as the panelling behind it. "Why is that seat empty?"

"It was the seat of the Ferish lord who built this place," Iannah whispered back. "He stationed archers on these ledges to protect him during the First Elken War. Didn't help much. The Sverbian-viirelei alliance killed him on the back lawn while he was executing prisoners. After the Second Elken War, Ferland and Sverba formed the Council so one person would never hold that much power again."

"Does it work?"

"Not really."

I squinted at the yellow-bearded man. "Ai, that's the Crieknaast mayor."

The discussion drifted up to us, distorted by echoes. Montès and a man with white-blond hair were asking questions. Vorhagind gave weary replies marked with half-hearted gestures. Parr sat straight-backed, hands folded in his lap. His black hair was pulled back, showing a scarlet hem around his neck. Most councillors had grey hair or none at all. Montès's balding head gleamed in the cold light. The elderly man who spoke at Skaarnaht dozed in his seat.

I frowned. "It's all old itheran men."

Iannah snorted. "Welcome to the Council."

"What's that red hem on Parr's robe mean?"

"Ex-military. Served for eighteen years, six as a captain. He fought in the Third Elken War and through the height of the Rúonbattai resistance. Retired when he got elected."

"Crieknaast and Rutnaast are both on routes through the Turquoise Mountains," the pale-haired man said. "You sent messengers to warn other border towns about Suriel, correct? What did these messages say?"

"That all our industry near Dúnravn Pass be destroyed," Vorhagind answered. "That every incident was preceded by terrible storms, the like of which we have not seen since the Dúnravn avalanche two years ago."

"Do you mean to imply those are related, or is your retirement plan to write the farmer's almanac?" Montès asked. I had to pay close attention to understand his accent.

"The viirelei believe Suriel is linked to the wind," Vorhagind said. "They warned us of him twice and were right both times. I trust them to read the signs."

"That would be the one thing viirelei can read," a dark-haired man said. A laugh rippled through the room.

"Ass," I muttered.

Montès tapped the table. "Why did Rutnaast's mayor ignore your warning? Did he distrust you, or simply distrust viirelei?"

"I can only speak to my decisions." Vorhagind's words carried an edge. "I would suggest you ask him yourself, but he is a touch too dead to respond."

"A terrible loss indeed. Do you fear for your safety, Mayor, over there by the mountains?"

"I would be fool not to in these times."

"And if someone told you to abandon your town's primary trade route and industries to appease a spirit, you would?"

"I have, and would again."

Montès rose to his feet. "My fellow councillors, a month ago I hesitated to doubt such a dedicated mayor, overlooking his order to barricade us in the town hall, but it is plain to see now. These storms have driven the poor man mad with fear. Even his staff seem addled, haunted by tales of ghosts. The people of Crieknaast worry about their mayor's soundness of mind."

"That's not true!" I hissed as a clamour erupted. Iannah raised an eyebrow. I bit hard on my tongue.

Parr's clear voice cut through the others. "Montès would have us believe citizens are dropping dead of their own accord — a witless, deluded, and dangerous view."

Montès raised his hands, wide sleeves draping like cocoons, until the room fell silent. "Mayor, you consulted the mage Tiernan Heilind after the lumber camp incident, did you not?"

"Aye, as due his involvement in the Dúnravn expedition." Vorhagind sounded like he was speaking through gritted teeth.

"Heilind vehemently proclaimed the existence of a spirit after that expedition." Montès's voice was smooth as silk. "He now refuses to testify. I assume he is no longer willing to corroborate a story borne of paranoia and children's bedside tales."

"Fucking *takuran*." I gripped the cold iron railing. Iannah raised her other eyebrow.

"Proof be in our funeral sites and the ruins of our towns." Anger filled Vorhagind's voice. "Go look, if you dare step out from behind your guards. But do not butcher my townspeople again, or we *will* stand against you."

Shouting erupted below. Words blurred like driving snow, too thickly accented for me to understand. Half the Council leapt to their feet, leaning over the tables and brandishing fists.

Parr stood up, raised a massive tome, and dropped it on the table. The *whump* resonated throughout the marble hall. A stack of papers spun away and fluttered to the ground. The oldest councillor jerked awake. Everyone snapped silent.

"Crieknaast called for aid and we gave them death," Parr said. "Rutnaast called for aid and we gave them nothing. Caladheåns have made it clear they will not accept inaction, and I do not intend to fail them too. We know these towns lie in a warpath. Have you forgotten how many soldiers died at Dúnravn?"

Parr placed his fist over his heart. "Eremur suffered three wars because we turned against each other. We may not survive a fourth. We must stand together on the front lines and face our common enemy. Councillors, we swore an oath to our citizens. Do not fault them for demanding we fulfill that oath."

A murmur rippled down the tables. One by one, the councillors took their seats. Montès was the last, adjusting his robe before lowering himself into his chair.

Iannah looked up at the domed ceiling. "People think history's forged on battlefields. Sometimes it's decided in this room."

The sleet had faded by the time the Council pushed back their chairs. Iannah and I slipped down the spiral stairs and through the Colonnium to the south gallery where Falwen's office was. We sat on a bench between the statues of soldiers on horseback, stretching our stiff legs. Orange light glowed through ice crystals on the windows.

"Montès only did that to get back at Vorhagind for humiliating him in Crieknaast," I said.

Iannah shrugged. "He's petty enough for that, but it's more complicated. Montès got elected twenty-three years ago, just before the Third Elken War. You must know what happened there."

"Um . . ." I would've if I was Iyo like she thought. The Rin didn't get involved, so neither did any other northern jouyen. "I know the Ferish started it."

"Not the ones in government. Ferish rebels held a coup because they were angry about treaties the Council signed with Sverba and your nation. The Sverbian Rúonbattai tore Caladheá apart in retaliation. Ever since then, Montès has done whatever it takes to keep soldiers in the capital."

"Even when they're needed elsewhere?"

"Crieknaast has eight thousand Sverbians. Caladheá has a hundred thousand residents, mostly Ferish. Guess which matter more to him."

I frowned. "Who else is testifying?"

"Rutnaast refugees. Dúnravn survivors. Nobody with political influence." Iannah glanced at me. "What'd you say before? 'Takuran'?"

I gave a harsh laugh. "It means someone so foul they have to be buried in shit because dirt rejects their blood. Don't repeat it."

Voices echoed through the gallery as a group of councillors entered from the lobby. They must've lingered in Council Hall and just left. Parr was among them. He put his hand on a councillor's shoulder, said something, and strode to the nearest staircase up to the balcony.

"I have an idea." I dashed across the room, boots slapping on the tile. A man jerked aside as my skirt swirled against his robe. Iannah ran after me, sword swinging at her hip.

"Councillor Parr," I called, catching up to him at the top of the stairs. "May I speak with you?"

"Miss Kateiko." He brightened. "What can I do for you?"

I twisted my hands behind my back as he pulled out a silver key. "I was just wondering . . . no one from the Iyo-jouyen is testifying at the inquiry, right?"

"No, not as far as I know." He unlocked a door and beckoned Iannah and me through.

Inside, dusk light filtered through tall windows overlooking the pillared loggia. A map with flowing gold script covered an entire wall. The other walls were lined with paintings in gilt frames — portraits of sombre itherans, vases spilling over with colourful flowers against dark backgrounds, ships in hazy ports at sunrise.

Parr gestured toward two padded benches around a low table. "Please, take a seat. Excuse my manners. I have a meeting soon, but I can spare a few minutes."

He strode past a heavy carved desk, undid a clasp at his neck, and hung his robe on a hook. Underneath he wore a black silk waistcoat, a white collared shirt, and black breeches. A triangle of deep green silk showed above his breast pocket. A slender knife sheath peeked from under his waistcoat hem. I wondered if he always carried it, or just since Skaarnaht.

Parr turned back, catching my glance. "Now, you were saying?"

I edged forward, sinking into a rug, and perched on a bench. "Sir, maybe it would be helpful to consult people who actually know what Suriel is."

He rested his hands on the back of the other bench. "We have a scholar of viirelei studies attending who is an expert on local mythology."

"With all respect, Councillor, anyone who says saidu are a myth isn't who you should ask. The Iyo have known about Suriel since long before itherans arrived."

Iannah, still standing, tilted her head. The permanent blank expression of Colonnium guards was aggravating.

If Parr was surprised, he didn't show it either. "Falwen and I discussed the idea briefly. We concluded it unlikely the Council would agree to invite a viirelei."

"Couldn't you persuade them? The Sverbians might agree."

"Perhaps, but they make up only a quarter of the Council, and the inquiry schedule has already been drawn up. I would have to request an extension, and find a viirelei both knowledgeable and willing—"

"Falwen could send a messenger to Toel Ginu." If I was pretending to be Iyo, may as well go all in. "He probably didn't press the issue because the Crieknaast events didn't affect us. But my friend, another Iyo, nearly died in the Skaarnaht riot. My people can't avoid this anymore."

Parr deliberated a moment, then crossed to his desk and scrawled on a slip of paper with a white quill. "I suppose it cannot hurt to try. Pelennus, would you do me the favour of delivering this to Falwen? My apologies — I know you are off duty."

Iannah took the folded paper and gave a clipped bow. I dipped into a curtsy like Marijka taught me, but Parr's voice stopped me at the door.

"Actually, Miss Kateiko, if you would stay a moment."

I looked at Iannah. She shrugged.

After she left, Parr said, "I learned something from Mayor Vorhagind yesterday."

"What, sir?"

The dim light cast him into silhouette against violet sky. "A young viirelei woman acquainted with Tiernan Heilind broke into Crieknaast's town hall. She advised the mayor to oppose the Council by abandoning Dúnravn Pass."

I froze. I couldn't think. My heart thudded against the stiff boning of my bodice.

"Do you know what happened in Rutnaast?"

"Nei, not — entirely."

"Half the ships on Burren Inlet sank in a storm. Vorhagind warned Rutnaast to abandon their port. They did not. A day later, soldiers bearing Suriel's sigil sailed down the inlet. Rutnaast no longer exists."

Parr slowly crossed the room. "The world owes a great deal to people who are not afraid to break the rules." He opened the door and bowed. "Have a pleasant evening, Miss Kateiko."

✳

I met Iannah again the next afternoon. We followed a cobblestone path that started in the docklands and wound down the coast. The next day she brought dull practice blades and taught me sword-fighting stances in the fields behind the Colonnium. I challenged her to spar hand-to-hand, no weapons allowed. She trounced me every time, pinning me in the snow even though I had a palm of height on her.

Iannah slept strange hours around her midnight-to-noon post, so I had a lot of time alone. My horse, Anwea, seemed to know the paths across the Roannveldt and trotted happily through slush and muck. I spent an evening in Segowa's stall helping Airedain cut hides. Segowa gave me amber-coloured sapsweet and showed me what they made with my furs.

I wondered aloud how two people managed the shop. A single blanket took weeks to embroider. Nili, Hiyua, and the other Rin embroiderers spent all winter sewing goods to trade with itherans. Segowa explained that she and Airedain only made the items that had to be tailored in the shop — cloaks, gloves, slippers. Things like blankets and purses were made by her daughter or nieces in Toel Ginu.

I didn't press them about Dunehein. Knowing he and his wife

were alive was enough for now. Making a good impression on the Iyo in Caladheä seemed like my best way of easing into diplomacy. *Self-restraint*, as Isu said.

One day I woke and realized my birthday had passed. I didn't know the exact date, just that it was half a month past Yanben. Any other year wouldn't have mattered, but I was eighteen. Old enough to marry outside my jouyen.

I mentioned it to Iannah later, trying to sound offhand. We sat on a brick wall bordering a park, watching people pass. Snowflakes swirled around as if afraid to meet the earth.

"Doesn't matter unless there's someone you want to marry, right?" she said.

I kicked my heels against the wall. I couldn't explain without admitting I wasn't Iyo. "I just feel like I should be looking."

"No rush." She picked a burnt corner off her bread. "My oldest sister got married at sixteen. She sounds miserable in her letters."

"You must want to get married eventually."

"Can't. Female soldiers aren't allowed to be courted by men."

I crinkled my brows. "That sounds . . . lonely."

"Not like I have time for romance. Easier to just not think about it."

"Oh, come on. Like you can shut your brain off. Or your eyes." I pointed at a young man with dark curly hair and broad shoulders. "You don't think he's lush?"

Iannah gave me an appalled look. I laughed.

I expected her to return to the Colonnium at sunset, but she insisted my birthday couldn't go ignored. She stopped at a grocer and made me wait outside, after which I made her come back to the Blackened Oak where it was warm. This inn didn't have communal rooms, so we weren't worried about disturbing anyone. We kicked off our boots and sat cross-legged on my bed. Iannah unbuttoned her coat and tossed it over a stool. Underneath she wore a sleeveless white shirt that showed her curving muscles.

"Hold out your hand." Iannah counted small green objects into my palm. "Salted beans. You have to eat one for each year you're turning. It's a Ferish tradition."

I rubbed a finger over them, feeling the grit of the salt. "Can I drink water in between?"

"Only after every tenth one."

"You're making that part up."

She grinned. I'd never seen even the trace of a smile on her lips before. "I did twenty-two without any water."

"Fine. Watch." I started eating the beans one at a time, crunching them between my teeth. I wanted water after six. At ten my mouth tasted like bean-flavoured salt. I glanced down at the last eight — and tipped them all into my mouth at once.

Iannah burst out laughing as I choked them down. She tossed me a waterskin. "Here you go, Koehl. Well done."

I drank until the sting of salt was rinsed away. "I don't want to get any older."

"Don't complain. You got to skip the first seventeen years." She held out the bag of beans. "Hungry?"

＊

The sky was clear and bright the next day, so I waited for Iannah outside the Colonnium. I stood by the courtyard fountain watching water bubble up and fall into a wide basin. On a platform in the centre was a bronze statue of a man, one foot resting on an anchor. He wore a triangular hat and held a scroll over his head. I crouched to read a plaque on the base.

"Sir Gustos Dévoye. Captain of the *Péloma*," said a voice next to me.

I jerked up, twisting my knee. "Oh — Councillor Parr. I didn't hear you coming."

He gazed at the statue, politely ignoring my pain. "Dévoye was one of our most famous naval captains. He founded Eremur's first trading port."

"Found it? Was he lost?"

Parr chuckled. "Some speculate he was."

I glanced around the empty courtyard. "Why are you out here, sir?"

"Fresh air eases my mind." He rubbed his thumb over a silver ring on his finger. "I have good news, although just as likely you have heard already. Your nation agreed to send your second-in-command as envoy."

"The proper title is Okoreni-Iyo." I twisted my braid behind my back. "Just . . . might be good to remember."

Parr bowed. "I hope that does not rattle free from my mind in the next three weeks."

"Three weeks? How long does an inquiry take?"

"Far too long." He sighed. "Let us hope nothing else goes wrong in the meantime."

As I walked through the city with Iannah later, I told her it was my last day in Caladheå, but I'd be back for the Iyo testimony. "You know where to find me," she said. I went to see Airedain, but Segowa said he had gone to Toel Ginu. I fell asleep that night dreaming of silent gusts swirling between mountain peaks.

15.

HOUSE OF THE DEAD

I heard the thud of the axe before I saw Tiernan. He was by the cabin splitting logs with rhythmic blows. His beard had grown out. I hadn't noticed before, but without a tan he was almost as pale as Marijka. He looked up at me and went back to work. I took my time brushing Anwea's sleek brown coat in the stable. Gwmniwyr whickered in the next stall.

Tiernan rested the axe on his shoulder as I approached. "You came back."

"Why wouldn't I?" I leaned against the cabin, inhaling the woody scent of hemlock.

"Maika said you were spending time with a viirelei family."

"And the guard who escorted us through the Colonnium." I wasn't going to lie, no matter what Marijka said.

"You have a knack for encountering dangerous people."

"Like you?"

"That is different." Tiernan swung the axe into a log, loosed the blade and swung again.

I folded my arms. "You're mad at me."

"It is none of my business who you spend time with."

"But you *care*." I stepped forward, crunching through the snow. "Aeldu curse it, Tiernan. Is that so hard to admit?"

He tossed the split wood aside and balanced another piece on the block. "She is a soldier, Kateiko. What do you think will happen if she learns you are lying about being Iyo? Or that you killed one of her comrades?"

"I'd tell her why. Maybe she'd understand."

"She has to follow Council orders."

"What would you have me do? Live in exile? Some people like having friends." I regretted it even before I saw his wounded expression. "I'm sorry. I didn't mean that."

He turned away. "You should go see Maika."

✳

The woodpile was overflowing when I returned. I crept across the clearing and hesitated on the porch before knocking. Tiernan opened the door and returned to his book. I climbed the loft ladder and lay awake late into the night, huddled under my fir branch blanket, listening to the fire fade into lifeless embers.

A cold snap had North Iyun Bel in a chokehold. As the weather squeezed the breath from the forest, Tiernan and I circled each other in uneasy dissonance. He brought firewood in every morning and then went to his workshop. I spent hours curled up with my book, speaking the sounds aloud. My voice felt thin inside the empty cabin. I started a story about a wise woman who healed the sick, but the words were too complicated, and I gave up halfway.

My breath froze into icy filaments on my mantle when I ventured out to check my snares. More often than not, they were empty. Everything hid in warm burrows. When I tried to tug an unlucky squirrel free, the brittle wire snapped and sliced my wrist. As I sucked away the blood, something occurred to me. I dashed back to the clearing, almost forgetting to grab the squirrel, and burst into the workshop.

Tiernan looked up. "Your game is bleeding on my floor."

"Nei, that's me." I dug my heel into the frozen dirt to bury the red drops. "Tiernan, where did Suriel's army come from? I mean, who are they?"

"No one knows. I would guess mercenaries from Nyhemur or the south."

"So they could be anyone, right? They could wear a different sigil and no one would recognize them."

Tiernan set down a paper. "What are you getting at?"

"Maybe those soldiers in the woods weren't from Caladheå. That's why they didn't care about killing Nili and me. That's why no one ever came looking for them."

"Why would Suriel's men be here?"

"No idea, but they mentioned poachers near that valley of stumps up the creek, and the only traps in this area besides mine are years old. So why ride to an abandoned logging camp at night? Why kill us except to keep us quiet?"

Tiernan ran his finger over the wall map. Then he lifted his sword down and buckled the scabbard around his waist as he strode toward the door. The fire in the brazier sputtered out. "Get your cloak."

"I'm already wearing it," I muttered. I tossed the squirrel into the snow and hurried after him to the stable.

After hours of riding with only creaking saddles, snuffling horses, and crunching snow to break the awkward silence, I was almost relieved to reach the camp. Almost. Skeletal alder grasped at the sky like effigies. Ice suffocated the creek.

"This place has been abandoned for years," Tiernan said as we approached the buildings on the bank. "Log drivers used the creek to transport lumber. They passed Maika's house every day. When the Storm Year began, they fled."

I shivered. "Can't say I blame them."

He reined in Gwmniwyr among saplings poking through white drifts. "Do you feel anything?"

"Other than creeped out?"

"Auras. Lingering magic. There might be some trace of Suriel."

"Nei. I haven't seen anything this side of the sky bridge." The cold leeched moisture from the air, but I felt the familiar tingle of water in the blanket of snow.

Tiernan rode up to a building and pressed his hand to the wall. The air shimmered like a scorching summer day, warping the planks. He flinched as light erupted through cracks in the wall. I shielded my eyes, but the negative image was seared inside my eyelids. A long-necked bird with spread wings, its head turned to the side.

"Oh, fuck," I said.

Snowflakes skittered over the frozen creek. Wind flooded down the valley and slammed into us, almost knocking me from the saddle. I grabbed the reins as my hair whipped around my face. Icy needles stung my eyes until I could barely see through the blinding whiteness.

"Hold on!" Tiernan shouted.

A ring of fire erupted around us. I flung my arms around Anwea's neck as she reared. Waves of snow drove into the flaming wall, sizzling into steam that poured into the sky. The valley splintered into shards of orange and scarlet and gold light.

I huddled low over Anwea until the wind stilled and the flames faded. I looked up to see a circle of scorched stumps surrounded by puddles. Woodchips and twigs floated in the water. Ash drifted through the air.

"Runic magic." Tiernan flexed his fingers. "More like a signature than a threat. Suriel has not been here in a long time."

"That's good, isn't it?"

"Maybe. We still do not know why his men were here." He turned Gwmniwyr around. The reins trembled in his hands. "We should go."

✳

I should've been relieved. I could return to Caladheå without fear. Without hiding from every soldier I saw or dreading the day Iannah learned I killed one of her comrades. Yet *someone* was buried in these woods because of me, and Suriel's reach seemed further all the time.

"Stay close to home tonight," Tiernan said. Then he returned to his workshop and left me wondering where home was.

I dug a chunk of alder out of the kindling box and sat by the fire while my squirrel stew simmered. The last time I whittled was on the shore of Kotula Huin when it was too humid to hold my hunting knife. In winter my hands never warmed. My fingers were clumsy around the rawhide grip.

Tiernan came in with an armful of wood and tossed a log under the stew pot. He paused to watch curls of wood fall at my feet.

"I'll sweep it up," I said.

"I did not know you whittled," he said, stacking firewood in the corner.

I grimaced as the bone blade slipped. "Apparently I don't."

He pulled up the other chair and sat down, leaning his elbows on his knees. "You need a proper whittling knife. That blade is too large."

I brandished it at him. "This is all I have."

Tiernan pushed my blade down and took his folding knife from his breast pocket. "Here."

I accepted it cautiously. The grip was pale polished wood, fire-branded with a curling design like filigree, still warm from his body heat. I swung the steel blade out from the notch in the handle. "You trust me with this?"

"I have seen you skin a rabbit." He adjusted my fingers around the handle. "Try to relax. When your mind is at ease, your hands will follow."

"Is that why you stopped carving?"

He pulled away. He was silent a long time, staring into the fire. Finally, he said, "I used to whittle when I travelled. Now it . . . is better if I do not."

I bit my lip as I looked at him. Soot had settled in the lines of his skin like a tattoo. "Tiernan . . . you don't have to go through this alone."

He gave a faint smile. "What prompted this sojourn into carving?"

"I don't know. It was stupid to try." I brushed woodchips off my legs. "I can't trap furs in summer. If I want to go back to Caladheå, I need something to sell."

"I see." Tiernan was halfway to the door by the time I realized he'd gotten up.

I twisted around. "Wait, aren't you hungry—" The latch clicked shut. I sighed. At least the stew would keep in the snow.

*

I woke to see the loft glowing green.

I grabbed my cloak and stumbled outside with one boot on. A shock of cold froze my nostrils. Tiernan stood in the clearing, a silhouette in the dancing light. I followed his footprints in the snow, hopping from one to another until I drew level with him.

The night sky shimmered as if the turquoise water of Kotula Huin was tacked to the stars. Curtains of light vibrated on the horizon, smudged upward like strokes from a paintbrush. White bursts winked in and out of sight.

"Can you hear it?" Tiernan asked.

I held my breath. The sky snapped like blazing fire. "The aeldu are loud tonight."

He turned, questions written on his face.

"Rin legend says on nights like this, we're in the house of the dead." I pointed at green and teal beams arcing across the sky like ceiling rafters. "They welcome us under their roof to shelter us from the cold."

"Do you believe the dead are out there?"

"I don't know." I hugged my chest. "I'm afraid if I start to believe, I'll get lost in that world and won't know how to come back."

"Kateiko . . ." Tiernan's voice was stilted. Heat radiated off his body. He smelled of woodsmoke. "Why did you bring me to Yanben?"

"Because you were already lost. And I wanted you to come back."

He took a step away. "Kateiko—"

"What changed while I was in Caladheå?"

The sky crackled. Tiernan's breath was shallow. "I missed you."

My brows crinkled. "I don't understand."

"I grew used to your presence." He rubbed the bridge of his scarred nose. He wasn't wearing gloves. "You said you hear voices in the wind. So do I, but your voice drowns them out."

"I didn't think you wanted me here." I shuffled my feet in the snow. "You were avoiding me. I was trying to give you space."

"So was I." He looked into my eyes. "I cannot keep you here. When Maika told me you met a viirelei family, I was relieved. You deserve the life you left home for."

"But you don't want me to be friends with a soldier?"

Tiernan gave another faint smile. "This old, scary ex-mercenary cannot protect you from everything."

"I'll come back. Yes, I want to spend time in Caladheå. It's the closest I can get to Toel Ginu for now, to seeing my family. But I'll always come back. I promise."

"You are too young to make such promises."

"Not anymore. I'm eighteen now." I pressed my cold fingers to my mouth. My eyes felt frozen open, but I didn't want this to end.

He turned toward the cabin. "We should go—"

"Tiernan." I caught his arm.

He stilled. The silver flecks in his dark beard shimmered in the turquoise light. Hesitantly, I rested my hands on his chest, feeling his heartbeat through his worn leather jerkin. Warmth flowed into my body as smoothly as poured water.

Tiernan folded his rough hands over mine. He let me linger a moment before gently pulling my hands away. "Come inside," he said, and his voice was the only one I heard.

✳

The cold snap broke the next day. I basked in warm sunshine that flooded the porch. The log cabin didn't have a proper doorframe, so I carved symbols in the railing with Tiernan's folding knife. A sun for the burning man, a wolf for the Rin girl, and a roof for a night spent in the house of the dead.

16.

ASHTOWN

Three weeks passed faster than I could've imagined.

Caladheå was in shambles when I arrived. Shop windows were boarded up, broken glass lay on the cobblestones, Elkhounds patrolled the streets. I kept seeing the same Sverbian letters painted on brick walls. I could guess the meaning. *Not enough.*

I went to the square with my newest batch of pelts and found Airedain minding Segowa's stall. "You must've come back for the inquiry," I said.

"Nei, just got bored at Toel." He flashed a grin that lit up the dusk. "Wotelem's testimony got delayed anyway. Inquiry turned into a bloody fucking mess."

I talked to Parr by the fountain the next day. He looked ragged, his Council robe wrinkled and his black hair escaping its ribbon. When I tracked Iannah down, she said people had shown up demanding to attend the inquiry and had been thrown out — but we could watch if I kept quiet under pain of a spear-shaped hole in my gut.

I arrived at noon and waited in the south gallery. Every time a guard looked my way I reminded myself there was nothing to fear. Iannah came straight after her shift, carrying her spear as threatened. My stomach was knotted like a fishing net as we climbed the stairs to the ledges in Council Hall.

Wotelem was the younger brother of the Okorebai-Iyo. He stood where Mayor Vorhagind had, fielding the Council's questions like a tree weathering a storm. His dark braided hair was coming in grey. He wore an unfastened vest to show the black tattoos on his arms and chest.

"Not one person has offered proof of these spirits' existence," Montès was saying. "You have no written records documenting them, nor have you seen Suriel with your own eyes, correct?"

"I have not," Wotelem said. "Nor have I seen the wind, yet I know to fear a storm."

"Caladheå is not a city of cowards who tremble at shadows in the night."

"Would you curse your god's name simply because you had not seen his face?"

Montès's face twisted. "How dare you. I will not be spoken to like that by a—"

"What are these spirits said to look like?" a pale-haired man interrupted loudly.

"Saidu cannot be seen unless they wish it," Wotelem said. "In ancient times, some took fixed shapes when dealing with humans. Nowadays, they could pass by as a breeze or a grass fire, noticed only by those who know how to look."

"Such as who?"

"My people's spiritual guides. The only living Iyo with the gift is too frail to leave Toel Ginu."

"Are there any active spirits besides Suriel?" The pale-haired councillor seemed intent on not letting Montès speak again.

"Suriel is the only saidu who did not go dormant. We believe it is because he had a close history with humans, while other saidu grew distant. He is no longer alone though. The others woke not seven years ago."

A murmur rippled down the tables. I leaned over the railing, not sure if I'd heard right. Iannah pulled me back.

Parr raised his hands for silence. "Why have no others made themselves known?"

"Most were killed within months of awakening, Councillor. You might call it civil war. We call it the Storm Year."

My stomach felt like it dropped to the floor of Council Hall. I rested my forehead on my hands. "Yan taku."

Iannah tilted her spear at my stomach.

The Rin said storms meant the saidu were at war, but it was a figure of speech. Saidu didn't kill each other. Whenever they scuffled over borders, one eventually surrendered. Behadul had declared the Storm Year a long, catastrophic fluke. It was more believable than the alternative.

My first thought was Behadul lied — but maybe he didn't know. Maybe the Iyo kept it secret and the only Rin who could sense saidu had died. Or something I hadn't thought of, like I didn't know about parallel worlds until Tiernan told me. I knew so much more than when I left home and yet I still understood nothing. I had more and more iron links that didn't fit together.

"Seven years," said a man with silver hair. "Is that not around the same time we stopped hearing of the Sverbian Rúonbattai?"

The pale-haired councillor waved a hand. "The Rúonbattai vanished eight years ago. I hardly think those are related."

"Okoreni-Iyo, what would compel the saidu to fight one another?" Parr asked. I smiled to hear he'd remembered Wotelem's title.

Wotelem spread his hands. "Look to the last one standing. Suriel has proven himself rogue. We suspect he turned them on each other."

"Yet their core purpose is managing the weather. Does killing each other not seem . . . contrary to their existence?"

"You are familiar with locusts? They begin as grasshoppers, then something we cannot explain triggers a change. They cluster together, destroying each other and everything in their path. The saidu were likely disoriented from waking. Suriel may have used that."

Parr looked disturbed. "And you believe he now has a human army fighting in his name? How does he manage that?"

"Through a human captain, I assume," Wotelem said. "Suriel has been known to trust a select few people before. I would sooner go to war with a thousand soldiers than fight Suriel though. People are breakable. The wind dies a thousand deaths and still returns."

✳

"Yeah, we got hit during the Storm Year," Airedain said that evening. "Lots of land torn up by the mountains. Nothing so bad as your side of the border river though."

We sat on the floor of Segowa's stall wrapped in furs. Airedain was sewing a shirt for her to embroider. Cold wind blew in from the ocean, bringing damp air that heat from the food stalls couldn't stave off.

"Why didn't you tell me the saidu had woken?" I asked.

Airedain looked baffled. "I thought you knew. What'd they teach you up north?"

"Enough for me to explain to the Crieknaast mayor what a telsaidu is. Your jouyen left that part out."

"Itherans get squirrelly when you talk about spirits other than theirs. The ones who believed it was a ghost stayed away."

"What about telling them kinaru eat children?"

Airedain threw back his head and laughed. "Aeldu save me, they're still telling that story? My friend Nokohin made that up 'cause itheran kids kept wandering off into the forest."

I couldn't help laughing. "Can I . . . ask something else? Why didn't any Iyo come north after the Storm Year?"

"We intended to," Segowa said. "The Tamu advised waiting. They said the Okorebai-Rin was . . . unsettled from your war with the Dona-jouyen. That he blamed Iyo-born Dona for convincing Rin-born Dona to fight you."

She paused to unstick her bone needle from a pelt. "Our okorebai instructed us to let your jouyen make the first move. Year after year, the Rin made no effort to approach us. I didn't expect to see one of you again in my life."

"I'm not supposed to be here," I admitted. "The Okoreni-Rin said you hate us."

"Ehhh." Airedain tipped his hand back and forth. "Nei, we just think you're kinda weird."

I flicked water at him. He laughed again.

"What's done is done," Segowa said. "We can't afford to dwell on the past."

"Right. No hard feelings." Airedain thumped the cobblestone. "I'll prove it. Wanna see my other job, Rin-girl? It's my first time drumming since I got on the wrong end of a spear."

"Ehhh." I imitated his gesture. "Sure, if you can handle being with someone so weird."

*

Airedain took me to a district called Ashtown near the southern docklands, explaining the name came from the constant layer of coal ash produced by huge brick-making kilns. I suddenly understood why he always wore black breeches and tunics. The hem of my skirt was stained dark by the time we arrived.

His workplace was a packed, smoky pub called the Knox Arms. A balcony on the second level looked down on a stage in the centre of the pub, a design I instantly knew to be influenced by Aikoto shrines. The furniture was like a mixed bag of old buttons. Crude pine stools, tables with finely carved legs, and soft padded chairs stood next to crates nailed together. The flickering oil lamps were made of glass or ceramic or brass.

I found a spot on the balcony and clapped along as drumbeats and soaring strings filled the room. Sverbians and Iyo jostled past. When a woman put down her fiddle and sang a lively piece, a few patrons climbed on a table and did some kind of dance involving a lot of high kicks and spilled drinks. Airedain bent over and held his ribs between songs, but when he was drumming it felt like the music coalesced into an aura around him, and he radiated pure joy. For a few hours, I shared his world and almost forgot about the one beyond those four walls.

I lost track of him while they packed up their instruments. When I saw him again, he was curving around an itheran girl's neck to whisper in her ear, fingers knotted in her golden hair. I pushed through the crowd to an outdoor terrace, rinsed ashy slush from the steps, and sat down. I breathed cool night air, a relief after inhaling pipe smoke for so long. Blue-white stars glittered overhead. I wondered if I could get used to living in Caladheå, then wondered what Tiernan was doing back in North Iyun Bel.

"Ai, Rin-girl." Airedain flopped down and leaned against the stone wall. He held a ramhorn mug of amber liquid.

I glanced around, but the steps were empty. "You shouldn't call me that in public. I'm Iyo, remember?"

"You Rin have been gone longer than anyone in this pub's been alive. No itheran's gonna know what it means." He elbowed me. "So, what'd ya think?"

"I'm impressed. Almost as good as our drummers back at Aeti."

"Not as glamorous as Skaarnaht, but it pays." He took a swig and held the mug out.

I sipped it and almost coughed it back up. "That's disgusting. It tastes like swamp water and misery."

"Sverbian ale. It gets better by the third or fourth mug."

I handed it back. "I was surprised you played something as major as Skaarnaht. You can't be more than, what, twenty-two?"

"Twenty." He looked pleased with himself. "But I've been drumming for fifteen years. Learned from my uncle back when I lived at Toel."

"Looked like you were learning a lot about that itheran, too. Am I keeping you?"

"Britte? Nei, she brought her friends tonight. Flock of fucking pigeons. I've been seeing her for two months and can barely get a moment alone with her."

"Why bother then?"

He grinned. "The moments are worth it."

We were interrupted by yelling in Coast Trader. "Hey! Fleabait!" We looked up to see a group of Sverbians on the terrace, leaning over the wall along the steps.

Airedain set the ale down. "The fuck do you want?"

"We want y'outta our city!" the man said. "You an' your filthy wood witch there! Your people brought this on us!"

"I got no idea what you're talking about, mate."

"*Någvakt rettai*! You planned this all along!" a woman shouted.

"*Aeldu dan någva*," Airedain replied lazily.

They understood well enough. A burly man vaulted down from the terrace and smashed a bottle on the wall. The jagged edge glinted as he staggered toward Airedain.

Without thinking, I leapt up and swung my flail into the man's arm. Blood spattered the steps. He lurched and swung a fist into my stomach. His next blow sliced across my forehead.

I stumbled, warm blood streaming into my eye. Airedain caught me and struck the man's nose with a *crack*. A second, third, fourth punch, and the man went sprawling.

Another itheran edged down the steps, knife in hand. I seized a bottle from the ground and whipped it at him. It shattered on the stone behind him.

Something flashed in Airedain's hand. With a few flicks of his wrist a steel blade snapped out. "Don't come any closer."

"Scared?" the burly man jeered, arm limp, blood pouring from his nose.

I heard footsteps, spun, swung my flail. A figure went down like a felled tree. Airedain's blade sank into someone's gut and came out dripping.

"We can't—" I gasped. The others were coming like a cloud of bats.

Airedain yanked me toward the street. "Run."

We ran. Through dark lanes and empty lots, scrambling over snowbanks, leaping an iron fence, and sliding on ice under a timber bridge. Cold air burned my throat. All I heard was our feet hitting the cobblestone, the shallow rasp of my breath, the rattle of my flail chain.

Airedain stopped in an alley filled with piles of frosty vegetable peels. I slumped against a wall and slid to the ground, cloak snagging on the brick. The lashes of my left eye were stuck together. Pain lanced along my hairline.

"You okay?" he panted, clutching his chest.

"Oh, yeah. I just wanted a closer look at the cobblestone I'm bleeding on."

"Lemme see." He peered at me in the dim moonlight. He unbuckled his jerkin, pulled off his tunic, and pressed it to my forehead.

"You'll freeze." I looked away from his tattooed chest. The spear wound had healed into an ugly scar across his ribs.

"It ain't far. Come on." Airedain helped me up. He wiped his blade on a vegetable pile before shoving it into his breeches pocket.

We hurried through a maze of alleys to a street lined with ash-stained brick buildings, all sharp corners and steep roofs and small windows. He unlocked a door and we climbed a cramped staircase into a shadowy room. Airedain took a tinderbox from a shelf and lit a lamp. The rank smell of fish oil jolted my memory back to Aeti Ginu.

Two unmade beds were crammed into the room, a washstand in the corner, floorboards covered with woven bark mats. A row of stone makiri lined a shelf above an iron stove, with a hole cut in the shelf for the stovepipe. Fur pelts hung on the walls.

Airedain pointed me to a chair and handed me a bucket. "Sorry to make you call your own water, but the well's freezing cold."

I set his bloody tunic on the table. "You live here?"

"Yeah. Every flat on this street is Iyo."

"Why not in a plank house?"

"'Cause the plank houses burned down. We got a chunk of Ashtown in a treaty after the Second Elken War, when the brown pigeons started moving into Bronnoi Ridge. The Council promised to build us something that wouldn't burn."

I held my hair aside as he washed my face with a rag. He worked gently, careful not to graze the strands with his fingers. After spending so much time around itherans, it was a relief to be with someone who understood the taboo.

"Thanks, by the way," he said. "You didn't have to take a bottle to the head for me."

"Seeing you almost bleed to death once was enough." I flinched as he dabbed at the cut. "Will Britte come looking for you?"

"Probably not." He wrung red water from the rag. "She ran off during Skaarnaht. Doesn't look good to be with a viirelei in a riot."

"She *left* you there?"

"I was still in one piece then. She'd have stayed if she knew I was gonna bleed out in my tema's shop. I think."

Airedain washed his hands, dug a wool tunic from a rioden chest, and pulled it on with a wince. I watched him move around the room, closing the shutters, lighting a fire in the stove. His crest of hair brushed the ceiling. He was even taller than Fendul, with wiry strength from drumming, but neither of us would've survived a longer fight.

"What was that blade you had?" I asked.

"A fan knife." Airedain pulled it from his pocket. Closed, it looked harmless, two auburn wood rods clasped together, but he showed me how they folded back into a handle for the blade hidden between them. "Gambled it off a sailor a few years back."

"Does this kind of thing happen often?"

"Nei. I've been in bar fights, but I always knew why." The blade and rods blurred as he flipped them around his fingers. "I've seen a couple of those pigeons at the Knox before. The owner Emílie will ban them, but the Elkhounds won't arrest 'em. They never do. Useless fucking mudskulls."

I unsheathed my flail to wash off the blood. "I wonder what they think we did."

"Dunno." He snapped the knife shut. "But you should stay here tonight. My cousin's in Toel. You can borrow his bed."

*

"Rin-girl. Let's go get breakfast. I'm starving."

I opened my eyes to see Airedain poking me with a drum mallet. I touched my forehead and made a face. "All right, I'm getting up." I sorted through my ashy clothing, grateful I'd worn leggings under my dress so I had something to sleep in.

I'd finally started sleeping through the night at Tiernan's, but the previous night brought the dreams flooding back. Rain, firelight, a sword at Nili's throat, and a rider bearing down on me. It'd been comforting to wake and hear Airedain's slow breathing in the next bed.

"Jonalin and I don't have much food here," he said. "My friend's sister has a flatbread stand in the docklands, if that's okay. She makes it with brassroot flour."

"Fine by me. I've eaten enough rye this winter."

I paused halfway through lacing my bodice. Airedain used his palms to shape his dark brown hair into its usual shark-fin shape, stiffening it with clear amber paste from a clay pot. The smell reminded me of the forest. "What is that stuff?"

"Pine resin and linseed oil."

I half-smiled. "You won't be able to do that after you get married."

"So I won't get married." He flicked his oily fingertips at me. "I don't think it's fair men have to grow their hair out after they marry."

"The Haka don't. You could marry into their jouyen."

"Not a bloody chance. They're weirder than you Rin."

Outside, the streets were grey with ashy slush churned by passing feet. Rotten leaves clogged the gutters, forming puddles covered with thin ice. Itherans either ignored us or cast us dirty looks. I put up my hood and stayed close to Airedain.

"Hang on," he said as we crossed a park full of gnarled trees and limp bushes. He picked up a soggy bundle of papers from a bench with broken slats. Black ink ran onto his fingers.

I peered over his shoulder. "You can read?"

"Little bit. Went to itheran school for a few years." He thumbed through the pages and then stopped. "Aw, fuck."

"What is it—" I fell silent as I saw the illustration. A white bird with spread wings, its long neck out straight — and next to it, a black bird with spread wings and its head turned. The Rin crest and the tel-saidu symbol Suriel had taken for his own.

Airedain's eyes moved slowly over the page. "Some itheran found the Rin crest on an old plank house in Bronnoi Ridge. Ruins from the fire seventy years ago. It doesn't mention the Rin by name, just says the symbol must be related to Suriel. Now itherans are claiming viirelei were behind those attacks — Crieknaast, Rutnaast, everything."

I reeled back. "There's not enough Rin to even *do* that—"

"I know. Guess the pigeons don't." He flipped to the front page. "It's today's newspaper. Those people last night must've heard about it early."

"Do you think someone wrote that because the Okoreni-Iyo testified yesterday?"

"Probably. Now they won't trust anything he said." Airedain crumpled up the newspaper and tossed it in the snow. "Itherans can't accept this is their fault. Fucking takuran."

"There's no way the Council can believe viirelei did it. The Iyo *warned* Crieknaast about Suriel. The mayor said so in his testimony—"

"How do you know what he said? It's a closed inquiry."

I bit my lip. "I have a friend in the Colonnium guard."

Airedain looked at me like I was covered head to boot with itch-bine rash. "You're friends with an Antler? What in Aeldu-yan is wrong with you?"

"I'm friends with Marijka, and she saved your life."

"Yeah, 'cause I got stabbed by a fucking Antler." He spat on the frozen ground. "Face it, Rin-girl. Someone hates us and wants the other pigeons to hate us, too."

❋

Iannah was by the fountain when I arrived at the Colonnium at noon. "What happened to you?" she asked.

"Drunken bar fight. I was neither drunk nor inside a bar."

She tugged my hood over the gash on my forehead. "Don't let anyone see that."

I flinched, more from shock at her hand going near my hair than from pain. "Why?"

"A viirelei was hauled up overnight for killing a Ferish man. Self-defence, he says."

I felt dizzy all of a sudden. "Who? What's going to happen?"

"Don't know. But they're keeping him here instead of the prison." Iannah turned as someone emerged from the Colonnium. Faint shouting drifted out.

We hurried up the steps and inside. Parr and Montès faced each other in the lobby, ringed by onlookers. Their voices echoed off the marble. The bald spot on Montès's head looked as smooth and glossy as a chestnut in the cold light. I positioned myself behind a pillar, hoping no one would notice me wearing a hood indoors.

"—needless distraction," Parr was saying. "You know Suriel is behind these attacks!"

"Viirelei have been trying to drive us from Eremur for a century," Montès said. "You fought their Rúonbattai allies for years. You know they always intended to stage a coup. This is it. They terrify our citizens with ghost stories to lure our army from the capital—"

"The Rúonbattai are gone. Be as paranoid as you like, but murder is a matter for the city guard—"

"We must make an example. We must prove we will not tolerate—"

"We risk civil war with every passing day! We *must* focus on Suriel!"

"So desperate to return to the battlefield, Antoch?" Montès's lips curved like a poisonous flower in bloom. "One might suspect you of warmongering, though I could not blame you. What do you have left but faded glory?"

Parr's voice went suddenly quiet. "You know nothing of war, Siego." He stepped close, bearing down on Montès with his full height. "Divided we are weak. How can we stop a spirit if we cannot even come together to fight his human army?"

"*Human*," Montès said. "A generous term. How many humans scratch their own fleas?"

Iannah grabbed my cloak the moment I stepped forward. "Not this time, Koehl."

Parr took a deep breath. "We will resume this discussion in the Hall, Councillor Montès." But as he turned away, I glimpsed raw anger in his eyes.

17.

SKAARMEHT

Segowa's stall was empty in the morning. I peered through a gap in the locked folding door. The shelves of embroidery tools were still there, but the valuable furs were gone. I leaned over to the next stall. "Do you know where Segowa is?"

"At the Colonnium with the rest of them, probably," said a man sorting cartons of wax candles.

I didn't understand until I arrived. The avenue up the hill was packed with people. Not chanting, not fighting, just sitting on the cobblestone. Colourful flags fluttered in the damp wind. Dark blue dolphin for Iyo, pale orange shark for Tamu on the coast of Anwen Bel, grey whale and roaring brown grizzly for Beru and Haka in the north, green heron and copper fox for Kae and Yula in the south. I'd never heard so many Aikoto dialects at once. The occasional Coast Trader word was as jarring as a stone in a bed of moss.

Colonnium guards lined the avenue between leafless trees, their bronze buttons winking in the sunlight. Three captains with red silk bands on their sleeves talked quietly. Clustered together, their spearheads really did look like antler tips.

A short distance off the road, Segowa and several others huddled around a bonfire. I crunched through deep snow over to her. "What's going on?"

"A protest," she said, ladling out broth from clay pots nestled in the coals. "The Council refuses to release the Iyo man who killed an itheran."

"Who are they? No one I asked yesterday knew."

"Baliad Iyo is a fisherman. I sold him mittens for his son last month. The dead man was a dockhand named Palut Cimarus."

I hugged my chest. "Isn't there anything we can do?"

"Yes." Segowa pointed her ladle at a crate of clay mugs. "We can take care of these cold and hungry people."

It was better than nothing. I helped a man with a whale tattoo on his neck carry the crate up the hill, and we joined other antayul distributing hot water. In the crowd, I saw the Iyo tea seller, a Tamu woman who visited Aeti Ginu sometimes, a few people from the Knox Arms. I crouched to hand a mug to a young boy, and as I straightened up I saw a guard shiver.

The guard wasn't much older than me, with short black hair and a thin beard, his ears and nose red from cold. The leather glove on his spear hand had a hole in the fingertip. Snowflakes gusted into the high collar of his blue coat.

Tiernan's words came back to me. *One day you will have to choose between who you are and who you want to be known as.* I suddenly understood it was more than a warning. It was a challenge. I didn't care if itherans feared magic or if other Aikoto thought I was betraying them. None of them were my people, yet we were all on that frozen slope together.

I stepped toward the guard and held out a steaming mug. I waited, my arm outstretched. "It's just water." I took a sip and held it out again.

He didn't move. Didn't speak. Wind swept across the hill, creaking in the gaunt branches, driving snow into his skin. Finally, he wrapped a gloved hand around the mug and drank. "Thank you," he whispered in stilted Trader.

I smiled. I noticed another antayul watching, a girl bundled in a deerskin cloak, barely old enough to have attuned. She looked at me with eyes wide as an owl, then held out a mug to a scarred guard missing an ear.

From then on I offered water to everyone. The guards who accepted nodded their thanks. Not one smiled, but I was used to that. When I found Iannah, she accepted a mug without hesitation.

"Keep your weapons under your cloak," she said quietly. "We have permission to use lethal force on armed viirelei."

I spilled hot water down my cloak. "Kaid," I swore and dried the fabric. "How can the Council condone that?"

"Their heads are stuck where it's too dark to see." Iannah spat on the cobblestone. "I'm expected to fight my own city while a war has started out there."

"So what are we supposed to do? *Not* fight back?"

"Pray to whatever god you believe in."

I snorted. "The only spirit I'm sure about is the reason we're here. I'd have better luck asking a mountain goat not to gore me."

Near the top of hill I recognized Airedain by his spiked hair. He was passing out dried lingcod from a hide bag. He gave me a long look over the crowd before turning away, as distant as the pale sky scarred by grey clouds.

"Sohikoehl," a voice called, then louder, "Sohikoehl!"

I whirled to see Falwen, Officer of the Viirelei. He stood in a cluster of people, standing out among all the fur and leather in a grey wool coat with brass fastenings. His hands darted like birds as he spoke rapidly in the Haka dialect. He ushered the others off and beckoned to me.

"Take this to Councillor Parr." Falwen clamped a quill between his teeth, rifled through a stack of papers, and pressed an envelope into my hands. The red wax seal showed a rearing elk under a spray of rioden needles. "If he is not in his office, find him."

"Why me?"

"You are here all the time. You are less likely to be questioned."

I glanced at the closed gates in the looming stone walls. "Am I allowed in there?"

"Yes. Show the guards that seal. And if you open that envelope, I will open you." He pointed his quill tip at my heart.

I backed away, all too aware he knew everything about me. The guards scrutinized my identification before opening the iron gates with a wrench that made my teeth hurt.

The Colonnium was silent. Gélus wasn't at the front desk, but I left my weapons, sensing the guards' eyes on me. I hurried to Parr's office and rapped on the heavy door.

"Come in," came the faint reply.

I edged inside. Parr was at his desk, sleeves rolled past his elbows, black hair loose over his shoulders. Morning light flooded the room, glinting on the gold script on the wall map.

"Councillor, Falwen asked me to bring you this."

He didn't look up from his writing. "Bring it here, please."

I padded across the rug. Parr slit open the envelope and pulled out the contents. I waited, not sure if I was dismissed. His desk was covered in the most beautiful craftsmanship I'd ever seen. A glass inkpot with swirled sides like a seashell, brass candlesticks, a three-masted ship made of black marble with white linen sails.

"A plea from the Okoreni-Iyo." Parr finally looked at me. His eyes went to my forehead. "Goodness, Miss Kateiko. What happened?"

I reached toward the gash. I'd parted my hair off to the side before braiding it, but it had shifted. My lie faded before it left my lips. "Baliad Iyo is going to be executed, isn't he?"

He set down the paper. "I will do everything I can to prevent that, but criminal matters are the jurisdiction of the city guard. The law is against us."

"The law is wrong. Blood in the ground doesn't put blood back in someone's veins."

"It may not come to that," he said gently. "Baliad has a clean record, and witnesses saw Cimarus attack him first."

"I heard Councillor Montès in the lobby yesterday." My chest felt tight. "We can't go on like this, sir. If viirelei are blamed for everything Suriel does, soon there won't be any of us left to blame."

Parr folded his hands in front of his face. "I know. We are at an impasse. Death lurks at our border and self-destruction lurks within." He shook his head. "What would you do in my position?"

I opened my mouth and shut it. No one had ever asked me that.

"I'd find out what Suriel wants," I said finally. "This isn't just about defending his territory. He tolerated itherans until the summer of the Dúnravn expedition. Something changed then. But killing us isn't the goal, or he wouldn't drive people away with storms first. We're collateral damage."

He fixed me with an intense look. "Do you think we would be safe if we avoided him?"

"Nei." I wondered if I was being tested. "He didn't care about Rutnaast until this winter. He keeps pushing further, and he has nothing to lose except human soldiers. I don't think he'll stop until he gets what he's looking for."

"Smart girl." Parr chuckled wearily. "Let us hope we survive long enough to figure out what that is." He rose and drifted across the room, stopping at a portrait of a young woman.

I followed and gazed up at her. She wore a high-necked black dress, hands folded in her lap, dark hair pinned up in soft curls. There was a trace of sadness in her brows. "Who is she?"

"My wife. She fell ill during the influenza epidemic, a year after our son was born. I was in southern Eremur fighting the Sverbian Rúonbattai when she passed away. She had already been buried by the time I returned."

"You must've loved her a lot, to keep her picture here." I knotted my fingers into my skirt, regretting my intrusiveness as soon as I said it.

"I was very fond of her." He rubbed a hand over his eyes. "My son left after I joined the Council. I have not seen him in half a decade. At times like this, I wonder if it was worth it."

"I'm sorry, sir." My voice sounded too quiet.

Parr gave me a tired smile. "Forgive me, Miss Kateiko. The Colonnium is a lonely place. I do not receive much company that is not demanding one thing or another of me."

I looked up at Parr, though I was nearly as tall as him. "Councillor, all I ask is you don't give up. We need you on our side."

He bowed. "I will be dead before I give up."

✳

The guard changed at noon. Iannah waved before heading through the gates. Segowa disappeared and returned with furs and blankets for the children. I sat on the edge of the avenue with a bowl of broth, the slush seeping through my clothes. I got up to pass out more hot water and restore feeling to my legs.

I was surprised how many other antayul offered water to the guards. My simple gesture had spread. The captains walked among the crowd, watching but not interfering. One shared a mug with another guard. The hill was bitterly cold even in the afternoon sun. Wind and damp took no sides.

Itherans joined the protest. Men and women smelling of fish, Sverbian clerics wearing white robes and iron pendants of the nine-branched tree, grizzled men with elk pins by their collars and missing limbs, Ferish youth that huddled together and offered uncertain smiles as I passed. A few carried sheets of wood or cloth painted with familiar letters. *Ikken naeja. Not enough.*

We gave food and water to anyone who sat on the stone avenue. Some came to the bottom of the hill and watched until the cold drove them off. The sun dipped through the sky like a sinking ship, casting shards of red and gold light into the ocean. Shadows stretched up the hill. Still we waited. Just after the sun vanished below the horizon, the gates creaked open.

Parr and Montès stood under the rearing elk statues. I glimpsed Iannah among the guards behind them. Parr was motionless, his head held high. A scabbard hung at his side. I'd never seen him with a sword, just the knife he wore under his coat.

They didn't say much. Only one sentence mattered. Baliad Iyo was to be hanged.

Silence hung over the hill like the moment between breaths.

A bow cracked. An arrow pierced Montès's chest through his Council robe. He toppled back, thudding to the ground.

Half the guards on the avenue thrust their spears forward in unison. The other half swept across the hill. A guard's spear hurtled through the air and sank into the snow just behind a fleeing figure.

I expected chaos like at Skaarnaht. Panic. Noise. Trapped bodies.

But no one else moved. The rows of spearheads were the jaws of a beast around us. My hand shook as I willed myself not to draw a weapon.

"What are you waiting for?" someone shouted behind the stone walls.

I looked into the eyes of the guard nearest me. A dark-haired man, square-jawed, maybe Tiernan's age. I'd given him water not an hour before. "Please," I mouthed. "Please don't."

The spear trembled in his gloved hands. He stared into my eyes, unblinking — then raised the steel tip. He returned his spear to his side, pointing at the sky.

I heard rustling. Other guards raised their spears. Across the avenue, all the way down the hill, steel lifted away from the crowd. I turned back to the gates. Iannah tapped two fingers to her forehead in salute.

Parr lifted Montès's body and carried him into the courtyard. The gates wrenched shut.

❋

Flame wove through the darkness. Wotelem carried a burning torch up the hill. Cracking sounds filled the night as people snapped off branches and lit them from the torch, passing fire from person to person until the entire avenue blazed. From the city it must've looked like a column of flame rising into the sky.

"Ai, Iyo-girl." Airedain held a burning branch in one hand. He pushed a bundle at me with the other.

I shook out the white linen square. In the flickering light I saw a dolphin outlined in soot. Instead of being curled like the Iyo crest, it was straight, flippers extended, forming a cross like the Rin kinaru. "Did you make this?"

He lifted one shoulder in a shrug. "Special flag for a special Iyo."

I smiled. I draped it over my mantle and stuck my cloak pin through the corners. Then I snapped off a branch and lit it from Airedain's.

We sat on frosty cobblestones under drifting snowflakes. Someone began to sing, joined by hundreds of voices until the night was thick with grief. Darkness curled through the crowd as the torches went out. When the cold sank into my bones, Airedain wrapped his arm around my shaking shoulders, his sleeve pressing against my braid.

I didn't notice the guards were gone until the sky turned red in the east and Iannah came back alone. I disentangled myself from Airedain, my legs stiff as planks. He glanced at her, but didn't say anything.

"Caladheå is going to war," Iannah said. "Parr had half the Council convinced. Montès's death tipped the vote. We're sending soldiers to Dúnravn and ships to Rutnaast."

My breath caught. It was a bitter triumph, but at least the military knew what they were facing this time. A seed of hope burst open in my chest, unfurling to meet the dawn.

"Did you catch the person who shot Montès?" I asked.

"No. They had a horse waiting in the streets. We have no idea who it was."

"What'll happen to you?"

"Guarding the councillors." Iannah leaned on her spear. "Longer hours, better pay, same damned Colonnium."

"I promised Tiernan I'd leave Caladheå when the inquiry was over." I wrapped numb hands around my elbows. "I don't know when I'll be back."

She shrugged. "Come by when you do. I'll be here until the end of time."

"I will. Promise."

"I have to get back. See you, Koehl." She saluted and walked off.

Airedain rose and stretched, his long arms dark against the brightening sky. "You don't have to go."

"There's nothing more I can do here. It's not our fight anymore."

"It never was."

As I gazed at him in the faint light, I was reminded of the autumn sunrise at Kotula Huin. *Today we fly.* I never would've guessed one vision would lead me to a foreign city at the dawn of a changing world. "Are you going back to Toel Ginu?"

"Nei." Airedain kicked at the dusting of fresh snow. "This was our land long before the pigeons arrived. I have work, a home, friends here. I ain't gonna let them drive me out."

"That could've been us instead of Baliad."

"I know."

"You're an idiot."

"I know." He grinned, but the light no longer reached his eyes.

Later that day as I rode into North Iyun Bel, I heard a horn in the distance, low and rumbling like an earthquake. I looked back and saw a column of soldiers riding onto the Roannveldt plain, the red elk banner snapping in the wind.

Eventually, I'd learn the Sverbians called that day Skaarmeht. *Red Morning*, the start of the War of the Wind. The Rin would never name it.

18.

SHOIRDRYGE

I pushed open the workshop door. "Tiernan?"

He looked past the brazier. Flames crackled higher than his head. No wonder he hadn't heard me in the stable. "Kateiko." The fire dimmed, licking at the brazier lip.

I leaned against the doorframe. "The Council declared war on Suriel."

"Gods willing, they will have more luck than before." Tiernan rubbed his temples. "Come inside. You are letting the cold air in."

I drew forward, holding my hands to the flames. "I thought the cold didn't bother you."

"Not in the way you think." His pale skin was streaked with soot and sweat, blurring into his beard. There were holes burned in his tunic and his hair fell tangled to his shoulders. His eyes traced over my forehead. "Do you want to tell me what happened?"

I almost said no. Everything I'd done might invite a lecture, and after leaving behind the bloodstains of one war only to find myself at the start of another, I was tired. But as I looked into Tiernan's eyes, I knew he'd understand. The gash on my face would fade into a scar and it'd be one more thing we'd have in common.

So we sat on the dirt, watching flames tremble like leaves, and I told him everything. He didn't question my friendship with Iannah, fighting itherans with Airedain, or my conversations with Parr. When I told him about calling water in front of Colonnium guards, he smiled and said, "I wondered which you would choose."

That night I unbraided my hair and put on my old winter clothes. I scrubbed ash from my dress and stored it in the rioden chest Tiernan had built me. As I hung my dolphin flag next to my kinaru shawl, a flash of white light caught my eye. I peered out the frost-etched window and saw Tiernan walking around the clearing, writing symbols in the air that glowed before fading away.

"What were those?" I asked when he came back inside.

"A warning," was all he said.

*

Two days later, a blizzard struck overnight. Amid the howls of a war horn, voices called the Rin battle cry. *Kujinna kobairen. Today we fly.* I pulled my embroidered fir blanket over my head and told myself it was my imagination.

A crash snapped me awake. I jerked up and slammed my head into a rafter. "Kaid!"

"Kateiko?" Tiernan called. "Are you all right?"

"More or less." I put my fingers to my forehead. They came away wet. "Fuck. Ow."

"Go back to sleep. I will check on the horses."

In the morning I had to climb a snowdrift to get out the door, nearly hitting my head on the porch roof. Grey clouds smothered the sky. Light came from everywhere and nowhere at once. A hemlock had blown over, caving in the workshop roof, its trunk splintered like a bone. Shards of wood littered the snow.

"A tel-saidu must've been angry," I said as we wiped wet, heavy snow off the ladder mounted on the workshop wall.

Tiernan gave me a reproachful look. "You should not joke about such things."

"I'm not joking. The Okoreni-Iyo said the Storm Year happened because Suriel started a war among the saidu."

"No one knows if Suriel caused it." He stood the ladder next to the hemlock and picked up a saw. "All that's certain is he did not take a side."

I craned my neck as he climbed into a cluster of green needles. "How do you know?"

"I have met viirelei scholars who study the saidu. They say Suriel went far north during the war, all the way to the tundra. He was not here for any of it."

"What scholars? Where?"

"Ingdanrad. A mage settlement on Burren Inlet, in the mountains near Nyhemur." He looked down. "You should not stand there."

I stepped back. "Maika's mentioned it. That's where she studied healing, right?"

"Yes. And where we met." The saw scraped. A branch fell with a *whump*, scattering needles everywhere. "People from any culture can study magic there. They live freely, unlike in Eremur where every mage is bound by law to register with the government."

"Why didn't anyone from Ingdanrad testify at the inquiry?"

Another branch hit the snow. "Several Sverbian mages were accused of helping the Rúonbattai massacre Ferish immigrants during the Third Elken War. The mages were murdered while in Council custody. Ingdanrad refuses to get involved in Eremur's politics anymore."

"You could've told someone else about the saidu war. Parr, Mayor Vorhagind — someone who'd tell the Council for you."

"My ties to Parr and Vorhagind are well-known. The info would have been traced back to me." A third branch fell. Tiernan clambered down and rubbed his beard. "I have no lumber set aside, but it will take too long to season any."

"Tiernan." I waited until he looked at me. "Why didn't you tell *me* you knew all this?"

He sighed. "Can this wait until my research will not get snowed on?"

I narrowed my eyes, but relented. "If you cut boards for a frame, I'll dry them, and we can patch it with bark. It won't be great, but it might last the winter."

❋

"*Bøkkai*," Tiernan swore from the roof. "Kateiko, could you bring me a *cwngeht*?"

"A what?"

He paused. "A chisel. There should be one on the table nearest the map."

I set down the hemlock bark I was cutting. As I rummaged through Tiernan's tools, an ink sketch caught my eye among pages of his fine handwriting. I dropped it like it scalded me. "Why is there a drawing of Suriel's crest in your notes?"

"For reference. Did you find the chisel?"

I moved under the yawning hole in the roof. "Tiernan, people tried to kill Airedain and me because of this symbol. If someone found this here, I swear to the aeldu—"

"I am not going to discuss this while I am on a roof."

"Then come down here."

"Gods' sake, Kateiko—"

"I'm serious," I said, raising my voice. "I've been patient, but it ends now. There's a war going on. If you're looking into Suriel, at least tell me."

I heard thumping, followed by the creak of the ladder. The door swung open.

Tiernan stood with a hammer in hand. "I am not looking into Suriel. My research takes me to the same places as him. That is all."

"What are you trying to *do*? You're not just burning stuff for no reason."

"Most people are happier not knowing."

I folded my arms. "Do I look happy?"

He glanced upward as if asking the sky for strength. "You are too stubborn for your own good. Come. Sit." He settled on the floor and rolled up his sleeves. I sat cross-legged across from him, ignoring how cold the dirt was.

"I told you about shoirdrygen, parallel worlds, but not how they are formed." He scraped up a handful of soil and shaped it into a mound. "Make a stream there, on top."

I put my fingertip on the peak. Water flowed down the slope and pooled at the base.

"Imagine that stream is the flow of history. Then a catastrophe alters it forever." Tiernan placed a pebble in the stream, diverting it into two paths. "Time itself is ripped apart. The world splits and two distinct timelines emerge. Hence the term 'splintered worlds.'"

I pulled my hand back. The stream stopped. "What kind of catastrophe?"

He brushed dirt from his palms. "An extremely limited number of mages can tap into the flow of time and see into the past or future.

Maika and I cannot. The process is unimaginably difficult and requires linking oneself so closely to time that it becomes as fragile as human life. Theological scholars' theory is that when a temporal mage is on the brink of death, two timelines form — one where the mage lives and one where they die."

"What happens to those timelines?"

"They form parallel versions of the original world. As they flow apart, history develops differently. Temporal mages tend to be extremely influential in war, politics, and religion, given their knowledge of the past and future, so their lives or deaths have monumental impact. If the inhabitants of one shoirdryge saw another, it would not look familiar."

Cold air blew through the hole in the roof, stirring my hair. I drew my knees to my chest. "That's what I saw in my visions."

Tiernan nodded. "The storms the saidu caused seven years ago did not happen there. You saw your sacred rioden tree alive because it was never struck by lightning. You saw the wasteland as forest because the saidu never destroyed it."

"That's what you're researching? Other worlds?"

"Specifically, how to reach them. I began looking for rifts into shoirdrygen when I was younger than you. I had no luck in Sverba, so I came here. A couple years after the storms, I began finding runes of a kinaru sigil at potential rift sites. It meant nothing to me until I saw Suriel's soldiers bearing it at Dúnravn. I stopped searching after that."

"Then what's all this for?" I waved at the brazier.

"I resolved to make a rift instead. Look." He held out his singed tunic sleeve. "You need water, soil, air, heat to grow flax before you can spin the fibres into linen. Too little will starve the flax. Too much will destroy it. The fabric of worlds is the same."

"Wait. All your experiments with my water-calling — I thought you were just curious. You were . . . using my people's skill for this? Using me?"

He was silent. At least he had the decency to look ashamed.

I flicked the pebble from the dirt mound. "Why not tell me sooner?"

Tiernan rubbed a hand down his face. "The shoirdryge is not a world like ours with different people. It *was* our world. As far as I can tell, it split off around ten years ago, when violence between the Rúonbattai and the Ferish was at its worst. My guess is one side had a temporal mage who died in battle."

"Wait — ten years ago means—"

"The worlds split after you were born. You exist there, but everything you know from the last decade may be different."

My heart fluttered like a frightened bird. "I . . . I need to think. Alone."

✳

I lay in the snow, staring at the darkening sky framed with barren branches. I ignored slush seeping into my cloak, my knives pressing into my back, rain sliding down my face. For all I knew, I was ignoring it in another world.

Ten years. Before the Dona war, before the Storm Year. So many people might still be alive. We wouldn't be cut off from the Iyo. I allowed myself to daydream, imagining all the ways my life might've gone.

Some things were set out from birth. I was an antayul because I was the eldest child of one, and I'd marry a non-antayul to keep our family's skill set diverse. But maybe in that world I had siblings. Maybe I learned woodcarving or embroidery, or went west for summer trading and sailed the ocean. Maybe I got Behadul's approval to marry Fendul and our eldest child would be Okorebai-Rin one day.

But all that meant missing good things in my life. I wouldn't have bonded with Nili and her brother, Yironem, while Hiyua and Isu hunted. I wouldn't even like Fendul if we hadn't spent hours upon hours sparring. Isu had given me unyielding instruction in calling water, setting snares, tanning furs — all the skills I needed to survive. The only reason I spoke Coast Trader so well was from spending so much time with Vunfjel kids. Even though I left Leifar the goatherd, I had enjoyed summers with him.

And the last half year wouldn't have occurred. I might've met Airedain, but not Tiernan or Marijka or Iannah. Never learned to read or ride. Never become the person I was now.

The summer of the Storm Year, when the sky and earth ruptured and fell into each other, I saw a silver-blue wolf nuzzling its dead pack member. For a moment we simply watched each other. Then lightning struck and it bolted. The next morning, I awoke with the body of the wolf. I yowled and thrashed until the tent ropes snapped. Isu coaxed me through returning to my own body, then held me tight and kissed my hair until I calmed down.

Every Rin had different ideas about attuning. Isu said our second form reflected who we were inside. Some people thought the form was a fluke. Fendul told me once he thought it happened when we related to another being. I never admitted it, but his version made the most sense.

Nili, Fendul, and I showed each other our attuned forms when we reunited that autumn. After that I refused to do it again. Leifar and the Rin canoe carver's apprentice I'd briefly been with had both asked what my form was. I hadn't told either of them. For years, attuning was nothing more than a painful memory. I didn't figure out what it meant until I started to think about leaving Aeti Ginu.

As I lay in the snow under creaking branches, I knew it was time to stop resisting. A wolf was the second body I'd been given. Maybe in another world the aeldu gave me something else, but I had to accept the one I had. *Iren kohal. Rivers keep flowing.*

✳

Light spilled out around the bedroom door. I raised and lowered my hand twice before knocking. The sound was so loud in the tiny cabin I almost bolted back outside.

Tiernan opened the door wearing the thin shirt and trousers he slept in. His hair was more rumpled than usual. "Kateiko. Is everything okay?"

"Can I come in?"

He stepped aside. It felt strange. I'd dressed in here with Marijka, slept in Tiernan's bed when I first arrived, been in the loft with him, but we'd never been in this room together. A tallow candle flickered on the bedside table like a dying beacon.

I perched on the bed, covered by the smooth otter fur I sewed into a blanket for him. "I'm sorry for running off. It's just . . . I realized my family might be alive."

"As might Jorumgard and a good many more of my friends." His grey eyes were heavy with grief.

I shivered. Even after drying my wool shirt and leggings, they were still cold. "There's . . . another you out there. That's who I saw in the wasteland." I tilted my head. "You were smiling."

"At least I am happy somewhere." Tiernan sat next to me and looked at his scarred, trembling hands. "I apologize for keeping so much secret. I find it . . . difficult to talk about."

I wrapped my hand around his. "I can't help with your work anymore. I'm sorry, I just . . . can't be part of that. But I want to help you through this, Tiernan."

"You help by being here." His voice was choked. "I close my eyes and see blood, hail, spears. My comrades dead in the snow. I hear their screams in the wind. Every winter puts me back in those mountains, fighting to keep two other men from freezing to death while we fled."

No wonder he always wrapped himself in heat like a cloak. My burning man. His hair fell over his eyes, shining in the candlelight. I dug my nails into the fur to keep myself from brushing it aside.

"What would you do if you got through to the shoirdryge? Would you stay there?"

He was silent a long moment. "I do not know."

"You don't think *I* should go."

"This is your homeland. You have family here. If you crossed to another world, you would never truly belong. I . . . had nothing left in Sverba. But Eremur will never be my home."

"I don't want you to leave," I said in a small voice.

Tiernan smiled faintly. "You are a braver person than I to face this world."

Brave. Not a word often used to describe me. Reckless or bludge-headed, usually. It felt strange to be called that by someone who'd travelled so far and fought so many battles, but suddenly I wanted to be brave. For both of us.

"I want to show you something." I let go of his hand and stood as far away as possible in the small room. He rose as well, but I shook my head. "Wait there."

My body shifted. My legs shortened, my face lengthened. Silver fur rippled over my skin. I fell forward and landed on paws. In the time it took to blink, I went from human to wolf.

I wasn't sure what I expected him to do. Back away, yell, look at me in disgust. Maybe hold out his hand like itherans did with their dogs.

He just looked at me the same way he did every day.

I shuddered, rising up on two legs, and whirled to face the wall. I buried my face in my arm as tears stung my eyes.

"Kateiko." Tiernan touched my shoulder.

I lowered my arm and turned back to him. "Thank you," I whispered.

"What for?"

"For not caring. For never calling me a wood witch, or . . ." I wiped my eyes with my sleeve. "I've only shown a few people that. Never an itheran."

"Kateiko." The way he said my name was the most beautiful thing I'd ever heard. "As if I did not know when you gave me the makiri. Or when I saw your carving on the porch."

"It's different though. Seeing it in person."

"I know." Tiernan's arms wavered by my sides before embracing me. A shock went up my spine as his fingers wove into my hair, pulling ever so gently on my scalp.

I slid my arms around him and inhaled the smell of woodsmoke. We were the same height. I was smaller than most Rin men and freakishly tall next to itheran women, but alone with Tiernan, I only had him for comparison.

Warmth soaked into my body. I closed my eyes, hardly breathing, hardly daring — but I nestled my face into his long unkempt hair, feeling the strands against my lips. For a while, I allowed myself to forget about this world or any other.

And so winter passed, and we awaited the dawn of spring.

19.

SPRING EQUINOX

Deep snow kept us at the cabin for a month. The frozen fog felt like a bubble that would burst if I moved too quickly. In the evenings, Tiernan and I took turns reading folk tales aloud. Sometimes I caught glimpses of strength and grace in his voice, only for it to disappear like a star that vanished the second I looked at it. He asked once, quietly, if there was any way I'd help with his research. He dropped the subject when I said no. Giving him a way to leave this world, to leave me, would be like putting my hand on a chopping block and letting someone else decide whether to swing the axe.

Marijka brought news from Crieknaast after the paths cleared. The military was taking hard losses, driven back by storms every time they tried to breach Dúnravn Pass. Suriel's men struck fast and retreated fast. People had started calling them Corvittai, a mix of the Ferish word for blackbirds and the Sverbian word for ghosts. I'd asked Marijka to search for Ingard, and she found him still at the tannery shop. His brother, Dåmar, had found work tending horses for the military. I thought about visiting, but after itherans attacked Airedain and me in Caladheå, I was afraid what they might do in a town hit so hard by Suriel.

The days grew longer. The first patch of yellow grass was covered by sleet within a day, but the melt had begun. Cold, clear water spilled over the creek bank. Blue and purple buds pushed through the snow like delicate spearheads. An idea blossomed with them.

I brought it up one evening while I swept woodchips around the fireplace. A crisp breeze made the flames sputter. "So . . . I was thinking about going to Toel Ginu."

Tiernan looked up from the bridle he was oiling. The smell filled the kitchen, savoury like broth. "To see your cousin?"

"Yeah. Airedain suggested I come for the spring equinox festival. It's the one night people from outside the jouyen are allowed in the shrine."

"Then you should go."

I twisted my hair behind my back. "I was hoping you'd come."

"Would I be welcome?"

"There were itherans at the vigil for Baliad Iyo. I'm sure no one will mind." I leaned on the broom, the straw crunching on the slat floor. "Please. It'd mean a lot to me."

Tiernan rubbed the bridge of his nose. "Very well. For your sake."

My lips twitched. "Don't look so grim. It'll be fun."

"Should we bring anything?"

I shook my head. "It's rude. A jouyen is proud to offer food and shelter to anyone who visits, even after a long winter."

"I should do something about this." Tiernan scratched his beard. "Make myself somewhat presentable."

"Nei, leave it. I like it."

"Maika says it makes me look like a lumberman."

"You're an educated lumberman." I giggled as he threw a handful of woodchips at me.

❋

The Roannveldt plain was silent except for the squelch of hooves. Shaggy white goats watched us pass from boggy pastures. A massive horse pulled a plow through a muddy field. My attention kept straying east, but fog held the mountains' secrets close.

Beyond Caladheå, the plain rose into steep hills capped with snow. In the depths of South Iyun Bel, we rode past alder and cottonwood bursting with new leaves. A thousand shades of moss grew on salt spruce that were as thick as cabins. Anwea and Gwmniwyr flicked chittering insects away with their tails. Catching up to a boisterous group of Iyo, we slowed the horses to a walk. A cheerful girl perched on a log directed us to a stable near the visitors' plank houses. In a pocket among bristling spruce, we found Sverbians rubbing down sweaty horses by a cluster of timber buildings.

"I knew you wouldn't be the only one," I whispered to Tiernan.

Seagulls squawked as we approached Toel Ginu. A rocky peninsula jutted into the ocean, steep cliffs dropping away to the water below. Dozens of plank houses stood in neat rows on the bluff. People were everywhere, talking in groups, carrying wooden casks and baskets of food, pounding torches into the dirt to mark paths. Children flew kites down the coast, colourful shapes skittering through the sky.

Tiernan gave me an encouraging smile. I led the way, searching for familiar faces. I had poor odds, knowing as few Iyo as I did—

"Kako!"

I whirled. A huge figure lifted me into the air and spun me around. I squealed until my feet hit solid ground.

Dunehein's chest shook with laughter. "Look at you! My little cousin, all grown up!"

I held up a lock of his wavy brown hair that tumbled past his elbows. "Aeldu save me, your hair! I barely recognized you!"

"Good, ain't it?" He beamed down at me.

Dunehein was a bear of a man with arms like tree trunks, towering a head taller than me. Last time I'd seen him his hair was cropped. His clothes were simple — knee-length breeches and a sleeveless shirt showing his tattoos. Kinaru on his left arm, wreathed by tiger lilies, the same as Isu. Dolphin on his right, just above the band of serrated salal leaves from his wife Rikuja's crest.

"Airedain said he met you in Caladheå. I wondered when you'd show up." Dunehein fixed me with a hard look. "Did you leave Aeti alone?"

"Nei. Sort of." I ducked my head. "Isu wouldn't come. I'm sorry."

"We'll talk about it later." He slung an arm over my shoulder. "Who's your friend?"

"Um — this is Tiernan. I'll tell you about that later, too. Tiernan, this is my cousin Dunehein."

Tiernan nodded, embarrassed. "Kateiko insisted I come."

"Sounds like the Kako I remember." Dunehein rumpled my hair. "Let's go to the shrine. Rija's hard at work, but she'll wanna see you."

The three of us made our way to the tip of the peninsula where a stone archway led to a small island. Rock pillars rose from the ocean, the cream and white and grey layers worn smooth by the waves. I peered over the cliff's edge. On a narrow strip of beach, a group of boys were throwing rocks into the water, almost invisible in the mist.

I cupped my hands around my mouth. "Ai, Iyo-boy!"

Everyone looked up, but only the one with spiked hair waved. "Rin-girl! You came!" Airedain yelled.

"Be careful," Dunehein teased as we crossed the bridge, waves churning underneath us. "That boy's trouble."

I rolled my eyes. "You have no idea."

We passed under the shrine gate, the rioden logs carved with leaping dolphins, and up a flagstone path into a salt spruce grove. The sweet scent of lilac filled the air as we followed Dunehein up timber steps and into the tiered shrine. It took my eyes a moment to adjust to the dim light. Sunbeams full of dust motes filtered down from high windows. The upper floors wrapped around each wall, leaving a hollow square in the centre so I could look straight at the roof from the ground. Normally the silence in a shrine weighed on my ears like deep water, but it was filled with the clatter of preparations.

Dunehein sent me upstairs to get Rikuja. I climbed a narrow creaking staircase, passing row upon row of carved symbols on the walls. Unlike Aeti Ginu, where family history was recorded on plank house doorframes and jouyen history was recorded in the shrine, all history for the Iyo was in the shrine. Every birth, death, marriage, battle, and okorebai for hundreds of years was written there. I wondered what they'd do when the walls filled up.

I found Rikuja on the third floor, sitting cross-legged on a high platform of interlocking beams. Her pale brown braid was woven with bark cord. She worked with deft movements, the *tap tap* of her chisel echoing off the ceiling.

"Rija?" I said.

She dropped the chisel. "Kako!" She leapt off the platform and swept me into an embrace, throwing aside the hair taboo in a single motion. "We heard you were in Iyun Bel! Dune was about ready to go searching for you."

I scrunched up my face. "Sorry. It's been a long process getting here."

Rikuja stepped back. "Oh, love, look at you. Tall and beautiful. You must have all the boys at Aeti Ginu tripping over each other."

"Nei, Nili's got that position. But I don't mind. Boys scare away all the hunting."

Rikuja laughed. "My work can wait. I have something to show you." She dragged me to a row of carvings that ended halfway up the wall. "Here."

I looked where she was pointing. Between a tiger lily and a salal leaf was a blank circle. Only then did I notice she wore a loose shirt to fit over her stomach. I clapped a hand to my mouth. "Rija — are you—"

"Yes." Her smile lit up the whole shrine.

I flung my arms around her and pulled back immediately. "Sorry, sorry, I should be more careful! How far along? This is the first one, right? Aeldu save me, what else did I miss?"

She laughed again. "Five months. First one. Don't worry."

I leaned over the railing. "Dunehein!" I yelled down. "What took you so long?"

He gave me the two-hand salute, slapping his shoulder twice in a perfect *fuck you*. I doubled over, the railing pressing into my stomach as my laughter echoed throughout the shrine.

✳

We had dinner with Dunehein and Rikuja in their plank house, clustered around the hearth with ten or so other families. It was chaotic and informal, passing everything around on platters to share with messy fingers. Salted lingcod drizzled with smelt oil, rye flatbread with huckleberry jam, fermented seaweed, pickled mushrooms and brassroot, deer sausage, cranberry wine. Tiernan, laughing, said some of it wasn't far off from what they made in Sverba.

He and Rikuja fell into conversation about woodcarving, so after dinner she offered to show him monuments around Toel Ginu. Dunehein and I slipped away to sit on his bed at the far end of the plank house. With woven bark mats, vellum lanterns, and the dirt platforms covered with fur blankets, it felt like being back in our plank house at Aeti Ginu.

The Tamu had promised to tell Dunehein that his older brother died in the Dona war, but I'd never been sure if my message got through. I braced myself for the worst. "Did you hear about Emehein?"

"Yeah. From the Tamu. Took a year though." Dunehein rubbed the back of his neck. "I wish my tema told me herself."

"I asked Isu to come. I'm sorry, she just . . . she didn't want me to come either."

"It ain't your fault." He wrapped massive hands around mine. "I should've come back for you. The Okorebai-Iyo told us to wait, and I didn't wanna push too much when I'd only been Iyo for a couple years. Then, well, the Rin never reached out. I kept thinking, next year it'd happen."

He was the same as I remembered, even his Rin accent intact. He'd always been like a brother to me. Emehein had been distant. Serious. Loyal enough to die for our people. Dunehein left when he was twenty, as soon as Rikuja was old enough to marry. We gave each other condensed versions of everything since then. I went over the last six months in more detail, leaving out the shoirdryge. Dunehein was the only person besides Nili I'd ever been completely honest with, but I wouldn't put that weight on him.

"I'll do whatever it takes so you can stay in Toel," he said. "Tokoda, the Okorebai-Iyo, knows what Behadul's like. Maybe she'll make an exception. Let you become Iyo without marrying in."

"I don't know." I covered my face with my hands. "I don't know what I want."

"The Iyo ain't perfect, but it gets harder the longer you're gone from your own kind. I see it when people come back from Caladheå. Like they can't call Toel home anymore." Dunehein frowned. "This Tiernan fellow. I'm not sure how to feel, Kako. Everything going on lately — it's not good, you know?"

"I trust him, Dune. More than I trust most people."

"I've got nothing against the man. I just want you to have somewhere stable when things get worse out there. You're strong, little cousin, but even the strongest bird has to land eventually."

I bit my lip. "What's happening here? Will the Iyo join the war?"

"Nei. Not this time. We used to have our own military regiment in Caladheå, but Tokoda disbanded them. No more fighting itheran wars, she said."

"It could spread. Crieknaast isn't doing well."

He shrugged. "Maybe. But I don't blame her. Both her kids died in the Third Elken War, the eldest only nineteen. That's why her brother Wotelem is Okoreni-Iyo."

I glanced at the families by the hearth and pictured Toel Ginu empty, the peninsula quiet except for wind and waves. I shuddered. It felt too much like Aeti Ginu.

Dunehein lay back on the bed, his light hair sprawling across the black fur. "Aeldu save us. I'm scared, Kako. What am I doing, bringing a child into this world?"

"You're doing a good thing. If we die, let it be to protect the people we love." I lay next to him and gazed at the vaulted ceiling. "If you have a girl, she'll get your tiger lily crest. Your bloodline shouldn't end with you."

He sighed. "None of this shit was happening when Rija and I decided to have a kid."

"Yeah, but that kid will have the toughest parent ever to protect it." I grinned. "Plus you, I guess."

Even his laughter sounded like a roaring bear. He shoved me off the low platform with a sweep of one arm. "Who knew you'd grow up to be such a brat?"

*

Night had fallen by the time we tracked down Tiernan and Rikuja. The stone bridge to the shrine glowed with torchlight, a fiery path through the fog. The gate fluttered with blue and white flags. Muffled music blended with the crash of waves.

A woman stood in the centre of the shrine steps as people flowed around her. Her silver braid draped over one shoulder. She wore a sleeveless shirt to show her numerous tattoos. If the interlocking lines on her arm didn't give her identity away, the respectful way everyone greeted her did. Her gaze glided over us, but she made no move to speak with us.

Airedain was right. Skaarnaht paled in comparison to the spring equinox. The shrine was packed with people dancing, drinking, hanging over balcony railings to watch the drummers in the centre of the room. Drumbeats pounded the walls and spilled into the night. Airedain wasn't onstage, so I squeezed along the edge of the ground floor until I found people serving drinks out of casks.

"What is this?" Tiernan asked as I handed him a frothing mug.

"No idea, but I'm positive it has alcohol."

He gave me an amused look. "You are a bad influence."

I clinked our mugs. The sap-coloured liquid tasted like spiced ale, a half-successful attempt to mask the swamp aroma. "To a night of bad influences and worse decisions."

I danced up a staircase and into the surging crowd. People pressed in from all sides, skin and cloth rubbing together. The spring equinox was the one night when no one cared about touching anyone's hair. I held my mug in the air and took Tiernan's hand as I moved my hips to the music. "Come on. Stop being uptight for once in your life."

"I don't dance."

"You do now." I spun, tossing my hair and kicking up my feet. He laughed and relented, moving with me until we were swept up in the current.

I closed my eyes and soaked in the noise, heat, smell of bodies in motion. For the first time in months, it was warm enough to wear my cropped shirt and leggings, my bare stomach and thighs kissed by the muggy air. The music was as familiar as my name, but the Rin shrine had never felt so alive. Neither had I. When I opened my eyes Tiernan was watching me. I grinned and turned sideways, one hand folded into my hair as I swayed back and forth.

Dunehein and Rikuja passed by and raised their mugs in silent greeting. I saw Rikuja's three brothers with their wives and children. Airedain pressed against an Iyo girl with his hands on her waist. Segowa pretended not to notice. Airedain's sister, Lituwa, danced with a man I guessed was her husband. Falwen stood stiffly by a pillar. There were people from every Aikoto jouyen, and a couple I thought might be from the Nuthalha and Kowichelk confederacies.

When Tiernan and I retreated to catch our breath, Airedain waved from behind a clump of people. "Back soon," I said into Tiernan's ear.

Airedain met me halfway. He had black cloth around his wrists and swirling blue lines painted on his skin, the Iyo drummer regalia, but wore his standard black tunic and breeches. He wrapped an arm around me, holding a mug in the air to avoid spilling it. "Rin-girl! Having fun?"

I scrunched up my nose and pushed him away. He smelled like alcohol and his skin was slick. "Gross. You're all sweaty."

He grinned. "Now you are, too."

"Ai, weren't you seeing that Sverbian girl, Britte? Do you have a lover in every town?"

"I've only been to three towns." He took a swig of ale. "So yes."

"Sleaze. I'm sure Segowa raised you better than that."

Airedain looked unfazed. "Britte doesn't care what I do outside Caladheå. Honesty's good for you. You should try it."

I crossed my arms. "What's that supposed to mean?"

He used his mug to point at Tiernan, who was watching us. "Why bring an itheran unless you're tapping him?"

My jaw dropped. Airedain threw his head back and laughed. I smacked his arm. "It's not like that. It's complicated."

"So uncomplicate it." He poked my ribs. "Does he even know?"

"M . . . aybe? Yes? I think so?"

"Aeldu save you. No wonder it's so fucking complicated, ai?"

I shoved him lightly. "Don't you have somewhere to be? Aren't you playing tonight?"

"Soon. When those old folks get tired. Wait — shit." Airedain stood on his toes to peer at the lower floor. The drums had stopped, replaced by a loud hum of voices. He downed his ale, pulled off his tunic, and thumped a hand on my shoulder. "Make that now. Get down there, this is gonna be good."

Tiernan gave me an odd look when I returned, but I ignored it and pulled him downstairs. The next drummers were onstage by the time we got there. Airedain winked as he strapped his drum around his waist. They raised their mallets—

Music pulsed through the shrine, a fast and heavy beat that rattled the window shutters. The floorboards vibrated until the building moved with the crowd. Arms and legs and heads churned around us. I pressed my back against Tiernan's chest, feeling his sweat on my skin.

"Kateiko—" His hands went to my arms as if to push me away,

but there was no room to move. So I stayed, tipping my head back onto his shoulder to gaze up through hazy torchlight as drumbeats resonated through our bodies.

A drummer shouted something. As people began to push backward, I realized what was happening. Space was cleared near the stage. Dancers spun into the empty circle, showing off to the cheers of onlookers before diving back into the fray.

"Rin-girl!" Airedain called, twirling a mallet and pointing it at me. "Show us what you can do!"

I froze for a second before someone pushed me forward, and then it was too late. I spun on my heel. As my arms sailed out, ribbons of water flowed from my hands and snapped through the air. I lifted my arms, twisted the whips together, and let them rise toward the high ceiling. The crowd blurred. I heard cheering, but I only saw Tiernan, his eyes fixed on me—

—before the shrine splintered and he was gone.

The faces behind him smudged. I fell and fell and fell. Everything slid out of view. The roof vaulted overhead. My body collided with the ground and the air burst from my lungs.

*

I awoke on something soft and smooth. Everything was dark except for warm light off to my side. I turned my head and saw Tiernan sitting on a stool, enveloped in firelight from a vellum lantern. Faint drumbeats and the smell of seawater drifted in on the breeze. "Where are we?"

"Dunehein's home. His bed, to be precise. He carried you here." Tiernan gave a faint smile. "Airedain came, too, with Rikuja and others I do not know. Many people care for you here."

"Where are they?"

"They just left. I asked to speak to you privately."

I sat up and groaned. My hands trembled. The entire world felt shaky and my insides felt tangled as a bird nest. "Why does this keep happening? I thought—" I knotted my fingers into my hair. "*Kaid*! I thought I left this all behind in Anwen Bel."

Tiernan looked at his folded hands, his hair falling into his eyes. "I assume you saw into the shoirdryge again."

"Yeah. You were there, then you weren't anymore. Because in that world, I didn't bring you here tonight."

"I . . . have a theory. But this time, it really is just a theory." He rose and paced away. "The most likely sites for a rift into the shoirdryge are those that seem . . . damaged. The death of so many saidu means the sites are not being repaired from our side, and the barriers grow thinner."

"But most of my visions didn't happen anywhere damaged."

"Not all are as obvious as the wasteland. Everything we do marks the earth. Plowing fields, lighting fires, digging wells. There is a common thread with your visions. Every one occurred while you used magic. Perhaps you pulled water from the shoirdryge without even realizing."

"That . . . would explain how I found water in the wasteland." I swung my legs over the side of the bed. "Are you saying I've been springing tiny leaks in our world for years?"

"Not exactly." Tiernan turned back to face me. "It requires an enormous amount of power to create a rift. Think of your magic as absorbing water into a sponge. It weakens the barrier enough for you to see through, but does no real damage."

"So why don't I get visions every time I call water?"

He rubbed his forehead. "That is where my theory comes in. I believe you are simply in the right mindset sometimes. Our minds focus just like our eyes. You expected to see another world and you found one."

"But I didn't expect to see Aeldu-yan tonight! I haven't in months!"

"Maybe not consciously. But your mind already learned how to see shoirdrygen. You were on sacred ground during a gathering of your people, just like your first vision."

"So this might happen every time I visit a shrine?" I tried to stand. My knees gave out.

Tiernan caught my arms. "Honestly? I do not know."

I leaned against him, burying my face into his shoulder. He was so warm I felt dizzy. "I don't want anything to do with other worlds. I want to live in this world with you."

"Kako," he whispered. Not once had he ever called me that. "I cannot ask you to stay with me—"

"I'm asking you, Tiernan. Stay with me in this world." I searched his grey eyes. "Please. I'm not asking for anything else."

Tiernan put rough fingers under my chin. He brushed his lips against my hair, sending lightning through my body. When he spoke, his voice was heavy. "I am sorry, Kako. I cannot give you that promise."

20.

SACRED GROUND

Tiernan, Dunehein, and I walked along the cliffs the next morning while Rikuja finished her carving. Wind battered the trees on the island until they bowed under the strain. I latched onto Dunehein's arm, partly so I had an excuse not to walk near Tiernan.

"My little barnacle," Dunehein chuckled. He must've noticed Tiernan and I had barely spoken all day. "You used to follow me and Emehein all over. Your tema sure showed us the back of her tongue after we swam in a river during the snowmelt."

"And then I wasn't allowed to swim with you anymore, so I went with Nili."

"Aeldu save us, I don't know how our parents coped. I could use you around when my little one comes."

I held my hair out of my face as gusts tossed it in every direction, the brown strands blending with Dunehein's. My cloak battered my legs. "I doubt Tokoda will let me stay."

"I spoke to her last night. She's willing to meet you." Dunehein glanced at the sky. "Stay another day, at least. Storm's blowing in."

The ocean had turned steely grey, its steep waves crested with white foam. The sky was scrubbed of colour like a worn rag stretched over the earth. I searched for dark clouds, but there were none. The wind seemed to come from everywhere at once.

"Something is wrong." Tiernan stopped, his face blank. He pointed down the peninsula. "There."

I squinted at the island. At first I couldn't see anything — then I noticed the curl of black smoke rising from the grove.

"Rija," was all Dunehein said.

Then we were running. Dodging boulders, tearing through scrubby grass, leaning into the wind. Onto the stone archway as smoke swelled into the sky. Under the log gateway with its leaping dolphins.

The thought flickered through my mind that the equinox was over. Not my shrine, not my jouyen. I threw that thought into the ocean and kept going.

Dunehein took the steps two at a time and wrenched open the doors. Searing heat and acrid smoke poured out. Flames consumed the far wall. I could just make out Rikuja on the second level, trapped between a burning staircase and a gap in the floor. She yelled to us over the crackle of burning wood.

I raised my hands — and remembered last night. My water fizzled into steam. I swore, choked on ash, and clamped my sleeve to my mouth. The charred stairs began to crumble. Boards crashed to the floor, spraying out embers.

Suddenly the heat faded. Tiernan stood next to me, glowing like the sun. Tendrils of flame pulled back to the corners of the shrine.

Dunehein pressed into the opening. Rikuja swung her legs over the railing, hung from the ledge, and fell into Dunehein's arms. He staggered and set her on the ground. I waved through the orange haze. Rikuja dashed toward me—

—and the balcony gave out with a groan of cracking wood. A pillar toppled and slammed into Dunehein, knocking him flat. A chunk of glowing timber landed on his arm.

"Dunehein!" Rikuja shrieked.

We sprinted forward. Rikuja pulled burning debris off his body while I grabbed the massive pillar, straining to lift it. Dunehein twisted around, but couldn't get a good hold on it. My eyes watered so much I could barely see.

"Watch out!" I spun my flail and smashed it into the smouldering beam over and over until it fractured. Sparks spat out in every direction.

We heaved the splintered fragments aside. Dunehein tried to stand, but one leg gave out. Rikuja and I swung his arms over our shoulders. The smell of scorched flesh made my stomach twist. Something crashed to the floor, showering us in embers.

I chanced a look back as we neared the open doors. Tiernan was silhouetted by blazing red and gold, hands up as if straining against an invisible wall. Flames closed in, swallowing the gap where Rikuja had been. I tried to shout, but there was no air in my lungs.

We stumbled outside. People flowed into the grove, Wotelem and Tokoda at the front. Someone helped us ease Dunehein onto the ground. Rikuja collapsed, gasping for breath.

"Rija." Dunehein kissed her forehead and placed a hand on her stomach. "Rija, are you both—"

"I think so." Her smile trembled. Tears streamed down her cheeks.

I spat ash and rubbed my sleeve across my eyes. "Tiernan!" I yelled. Figures passed by in the swirling black haze, fanning out around the shrine. Wind shrieked through the trees. I turned back and forth, ignoring the embers landing on my skin.

I didn't see Tiernan striding across the rocky ground until he was right in front of me. His skin was raw, hair damp with sweat, clothes streaked with soot. He caught me and pressed his hands to my head. I smelled my hair scorch at his touch.

"Kako. Are you all right?"

"Ow — yeah—" I said between coughs.

He turned to Rikuja. "Do you know what caused the fire?"

"Nei. I didn't notice until it was too late. A candle must've blown over—"

"*Bøkkai*," Tiernan swore. "Call off your mages!" he yelled as waves rose from the ground and crashed against the blazing building.

"Have you lost your mind?" Tokoda called.

"This fire is Suriel's doing! Fighting it is a death wish!"

Everyone stared at him. "Why should I believe you, itheran?" Tokoda asked.

"It's burning too fast to be an accident!" Tiernan knelt and pressed his hand to the dirt. A pulse of light shot across the ground. The shrine flashed blinding white. Plumes of smoke shifted in the sky, coalescing into the outline of a kinaru.

Cold fear washed over me. "Tiernan's right! They have to stop!"

"Let it burn, Tokoda," Dunehein said, grimacing in pain. "It ain't worth the fight."

Tokoda didn't respond. The top level of the shrine caved in with a terrible grating sound, launching sparks into the air. Flames rose from the yawning gap and collided with the onslaught of water. Steam drowned out clouds on the horizon.

"Suriel!" I shouted. "If we let the shrine go, will you let us live?"

Ash streaked past like scorched leaves. The air shimmered as heat rolled over us. My hair twisted like seaweed caught in the tide. I waited, barely daring to hope—

The hollow reply came from the air itself, sweeping over the island.

Yes.

Tokoda gave me a piercing look. "From the blood of the aeldu, I swear as Okorebai-Iyo." She raised a hand and strode into the black smoke. "Antayul! Fall back!"

The waves dissipated in midair. Searing wind rattled the island, bending trees until they cracked. I shielded my eyes as the blaze spiralled into a column. A salt spruce toppled onto the building. The second level collapsed with a groan.

Wotelem began directing everyone out of the grove. Two men helped Dunehein up and someone slung an arm around Rikuja. Tiernan and I stumbled after them.

We clustered on the stone archway. Tokoda and the antayul came soon after, thirty or so streaming through the haze, covered with soot and burns. Smoke billowed into the sky, casting a shadow over the island.

The air finally stilled. Flames stopped leaping toward the trees and settled into a steady blaze. The blackened husk crackled. Glowing embers drifted to the rocky ground.

"Everything was in there," Rikuja said in a strangled voice. "The Iyo's entire history — everything we've known for hundreds of years, gone—"

"Everything except us," Dunehein said.

※

We gathered at a flagstone firepit on the mainland. Rikuja kept coughing, but the healers said it should pass within a few days.

Dunehein's knee was dislocated. His skin was brilliant red on his left arm, the kinaru and tiger lily tattoos almost unrecognizable under blisters.

"It ain't nothing. Ladies like scars, don't they?" He winked at Rikuja.

"I like you alive." She leaned her head on his shoulder and stroked his long hair.

I ran my tongue across my teeth. I couldn't get the taste of soot out of my mouth. It didn't seem worth the effort to wash it off my skin. Whatever retribution the Iyo would inflict for entering their sacred ground, I doubted being clean would help. I mentally went through common punishments. Public shaming. Hard labour. Exile. Cutting off a finger — or worse, a person's hair.

"Kateiko Rin. Tiernan Heilind," a female voice said. Tokoda and Wotelem stood in front of us, a matched set of silvery hair and inked skin and serious faces. Neither carried weapons, but that wasn't much comfort.

I struggled to my feet and raised a hand. "Okorebai-Iyo. Okoreni-Iyo. *Hanekei.*" Next to me, Tiernan repeated my gesture.

"How do a Rin and an itheran know so much about Suriel?" Tokoda asked.

"We've dealt with him before," I said. "In Crieknaast."

"I know what you are," Wotelem said to Tiernan. "Only an Ingdanrad mage would know to look for one of Suriel's runes."

Tokoda folded her arms. "Suriel rarely leaves the mountains. The same can be said for itherans from Ingdanrad."

"I have not lived there for nearly twelve years," Tiernan said. "Caladheå lures Suriel west by provoking his anger. You are in the storm path."

"The Iyo leave Suriel alone and he leaves us alone. That is our way."

"Strange things are happening all over Eremur." Tiernan's voice was level. "Half a dozen of Suriel's runes exist in the western Roannveldt alone. Perhaps you know what I mean."

Tokoda's grip tightened on her arms. "The walls of the world may be crumbling, but Toel Ginu stands strong as ever."

"Not anymore," I said, wondering if the pounding of my heart was visible. "I saw through the barrier last night in the shrine. It's weakening."

Her gaze flicked to me, the wrinkles on her face like lines etched in stone. "If there was ever a jouyen who would see the world fall to ruin, it would be the Rin."

I bristled. "I left the Rin because I don't agree with them. I would've sooner abandoned Aeti Ginu than gone to war with the Dona."

"Yet you carry weapons onto another jouyen's sacred land. What else has Behadul taught Rin children? Do saidu follow you everywhere?"

The protest died on my lips. Maybe Tiernan was wrong. If my water-calling damaged the barrier, and Suriel was searching for weak spots — I felt sick.

"It's not Kateiko's fault." Airedain stepped forward and leaned against a stack of split logs. "I saw it, too. Yesterday morning, before they got here. A rock pillar collapsed into the ocean, but I swear for a second it was standing again."

My eyes widened. So I wasn't the only one.

Tokoda rounded on him. "You did not think to inform me?"

"Maybe if you mentioned it'd bring Suriel down on our heads, it'd have seemed more important," Airedain said, hanging his thumbs off his belt.

Dunehein rose to his feet, leaning on Rikuja. "Kateiko and

Tiernan saved our lives, Tokoda. You might as well blame me for the Storm Year because I was Rin once."

Tokoda eyed him. Finally, she gave an almost imperceptible shake of her head. "Never let it be said the Iyo do not appreciate those who aid us."

She turned to me. "Kateiko Rin. You may stay in Toel Ginu. Dunehein is responsible for you until arrangements are made with the Rin-jouyen. If I see Behadul again, I will mention he could do with listening to the youth of his jouyen on occasion."

"Itheran." She pointed at Tiernan. "In light of your actions, I will overlook your trespass onto sacred ground. You are welcome here as long as I am okorebai. The Iyo-jouyen values its alliance with our Sverbian neighbours. I daresay we will need each other soon."

Tokoda turned to leave, grey braid swishing, but paused and glanced at Airedain. "And you. Aeldu help me, boy. Just stay out of trouble."

✳

Tiernan pulled me aside that afternoon. We went to the cliffs where we couldn't be overheard. Scraps of ash drifted past like seagulls in the black smoke. "I have to say goodbye, Kateiko."

"What do you mean? I'm going back with you."

"Not this time. You need to stay with your family." He gazed at the horizon. The sky was still grey and flat. "You will be safer here."

I narrowed my eyes. "You don't get to decide where I go."

"This is not a point to be argued. I have entangled you too much already."

"What are you going to do? Lock me out? I'll sit on your porch until you let me in."

Tiernan turned away and slammed his fist into his palm. "*Någvakt bøkkhem.* Why must you always—"

He closed his eyes and took a deep breath. "I suspected Suriel was also looking for a rift into the shoirdryge all these years. Marking off sites as he found nothing. We must have come to the same conclusion — make a rift instead of finding one. That fire was nowhere near strong enough to tear through the barrier, but I cannot imagine why else he did it."

I stared at him. "Suriel burned down the shrine just to . . ."

"*That* is what he has been doing near Dúnravn Pass. Experimenting with rift magic. He killed cragsmen investigating the strange weather, massacred the military expedition investigating their deaths, and drove off anyone from Crieknaast who got too close. All so we would not find out."

"Then why come here?"

"Desperation. Clearly he had no luck in the mountains. The coast has been hit by severe storms these last few years. I did not realize how bad it was until Airedain mentioned the stone pillar collapsing. Suriel must have thought fire would do the rest."

"But he had to know antayul would try to stop it—"

"He probably hoped they would not get there in time. I doubt he expected a fire mage to interfere." Tiernan rubbed his temples, leaving streaks in the soot. "The question is how he found out so quickly the barrier is crumbling. Perhaps someone tipped him off."

A cold feeling grew inside me. "It could've been anyone. There were over a thousand people here yesterday — itherans, Kowichelk and Nuthalha—"

"However Suriel found out, my work will draw his attention eventually. I defied him by holding back that fire. A second time will not go over well."

"Who else knows about your research?" I grabbed his arms. "Tiernan, who else knows?"

"At least one person too many."

I shoved him. "Will you just fucking tell me? I'm sick of you only telling me things when you think I need to know!"

"Kateiko. Stop." Tiernan seized my wrists. His chest rose and fell unevenly. "It does not matter who. I will not take you into that storm with me."

"I won't let you face Suriel alone!"

"Listen. Yesterday was the first time I have seen you happy and at ease. You deserve a better life."

I stared at him, my pulse beating against his skin. "You heard Tokoda. If I mess up, it'll fall on Dunehein. I can't do that to him when he has a child coming. It'd be different if I married into the Iyo, but I can't stay here like this."

Tiernan released my wrists. "You have that option."

It took a moment to realize what he meant. "Tiernan—" I choked on his name. "I don't want to marry anyone here. Please let me come back with you."

Waves crashed against the rocks below. Smoke swirled past in the lingering breeze. Finally, finally, his shoulders slumped. "Then you should say farewell to your family."

21.

IREN KOHAL

Tiernan didn't go into the workshop the day after we returned. He finished the chores and lingered in the clearing until I hesitantly asked him to come hunting. He agreed just as hesitantly. He still read with me, but he was always distracted, like his mind was travelling the world without his body. Dunehein's words echoed in my head. *You've got a good man there, Kako*, he'd whispered as he hugged me goodbye. Yet I wasn't sure what I had at all.

A week after we returned, light flashed around the clearing and burned white against the trees. I dashed out of the stable. Tiernan burst from the cabin with his sword drawn. It was bright as day even though the sun had set.

"It is only me, Tiernan," a voice called.

I squinted across the clearing. A man walked toward us, hands up to show they were empty. Long black hair, green cloak, bow on his back. Rhonos, Tiernan's young ranger friend. He'd made it back from wintering in southern Eremur.

Tiernan lowered Hafelús. The warning runes faded. Darkness settled over us. "Gods' sakes, I was starting to worry."

The men fell into deep discussion in the kitchen. I set out mugs of tea and leaned against the wall to listen. Rhonos's hair was matted, his jaw covered by a long beard, and his skin lined with dirt. His accent was definitely Ferish, so when he unfastened his cloak, I was surprised to see a Sverbian-style leather jerkin over a tunic and muddy trousers.

"The navy has given up Rutnaast," Rhonos said. "None of the refugees want to return. The mines lie empty. Eremur will have metal shortages soon."

"Ingdanrad will suffer too," Tiernan said. "Do they plan to get involved?"

"No. They struck trade deals with mines in Nyhemur, but waiting out the war is a dangerous gamble. Suriel must know their mages could be his strongest threat."

"They must feel safe while his Corvittai soldiers are occupied in the west."

"It will not last." Rhonos laced his fingers together and stretched out his arms. "We could use their aid. If anyone knows how to destroy an elemental, it would be them."

"It's impossible," I said. "The wind dies a thousand deaths. The only thing that's ever killed a saidu is another saidu."

"Perhaps nobody else has tried."

"Yeah, because we're not fucking idiots—"

"Have you heard any news from nearby?" Tiernan interrupted.

"Plenty, but none good," Rhonos said. "A company of soldiers was ambushed returning to Caladheå. People say it was viirelei retribution for some fire down the coast."

The back of my neck prickled. "That can't be true."

"After viirelei assassinated a councillor, it would not surprise me."

"The Colonnium guard has no idea who killed Montès! Besides, that happened because your people sentenced an innocent man to death!"

Rhonos fixed his gaze on me for the first time that evening. "My people suffer alongside yours. I have no love for anyone in the Council, but the only group more fond of violence than the Sverbian Rúonbattai is the viirelei."

"*You're* the one talking about murdering the wind."

"The Iyo nation is not out for vengeance," Tiernan said. "Suriel caused that fire. We witnessed it ourselves."

Rhonos raised an eyebrow. "Why were you in a viirelei settlement?"

"He was with me," I snapped.

"Why was *Suriel* in a viirelei settlement?"

"I have no bloody idea." Tiernan swirled tea around his mug. "He was trying to burn a rift into the shoirdryge, but I cannot fathom why. The more I think about it, the less sense it makes."

Rhonos and I exchanged a glance, realizing Tiernan had confided in both of us about his research. I caught a trace of surprise in his expression.

"Regardless, Suriel's arm travels far and his eye reaches further," Rhonos said. "You will cross paths with him again and again, Tiernan."

"I am well aware. I just—" said Tiernan as he paced the room. "What am I meant to do, Rhonos?"

"You know the answer." Rhonos watched him levelly. "Every day you search for this rift is a risk. You are locked between forces who will throw you and everyone around you under the cart to lighten their load."

Tiernan ran a hand through his hair. "It is a lot to give up."

Rhonos stood and placed a hand on Tiernan's shoulder. "I trust you to make the right decision."

❋

I woke to grey light and the patter of rain. I climbed down from the loft and was about to light a fire when I realized Tiernan's boots were missing. The clearing looked empty, but the workshop door was ajar. I crossed the field barefoot, the mud and grass squishing between my toes. The rain was cool on my skin. I crept into the workshop. "Tiernan?"

He stood in the centre of the room, staring at a soot-streaked window. Water dripped through the bark patch on the roof. I touched his shoulder.

"Kako." It took a long time for him to focus on me.

"Have you slept?"

"No. I was . . . I had a lot of thinking to do." He reached for my hand and then pulled back. "I made my decision. I will cease trying to open a rift into the shoirdryge."

I looked into his eyes, hardly daring to breathe. "Tiernan . . . if you're doing this because you're afraid of Suriel, you'll always regret it."

"Fear was never enough to make me give up."

"What changed your mind?"

"Hope. Joy. Love." He ran his fingers along the iron brazier. "The Iyo lost their strongest link to the dead, yet life moves on. I must move on with it. You already knew what it took me half a lifetime to realize."

I longed to reach out and stroke his hair, but I couldn't bring myself to move. "Are you sure you want to do this?"

"I . . . Yes. Yes. I am sure." Tiernan began collecting papers off the tables. He handed me a stack and gave a faint smile. "Together."

Fire blazed up in the brazier. We held the papers over the flames and dropped them at the same time. They ignited and curled in on themselves, disintegrating into grey ash.

We gathered up years of work. Pages and pages of research and diagrams went into the fire. Tiernan set aside a few books and burned the rest. He erased the glowing symbols on the floor. Eventually all that was left was carpentry tools and the map on the wall. I didn't know how to feel when it was all over. I'd dreamt of this day since Tiernan told me shoirdrygen existed, but his expression spoke more of endings than beginnings.

The flames went out. I took Tiernan by the elbow and led him to the cabin. He slumped by the cold hearth, stretching out his legs like the first night I'd ever really looked at him. I lit a fire and put the kettle on. Rain drummed on the roof and slid down the window.

"There is something else you should know," Tiernan said.

"What's that?" I pulled out clay mugs, then turned to him when he didn't answer.

"I am sorry, Kako. I don't know how else to tell you." His head was bowed, hands pressed to his forehead. "I am going to ask Maika to marry me."

A mug slipped from my hand and shattered. Tiernan flinched.

"It will not be the first time." He gave a weak laugh, but his shoulders shook with what might've been tears. He pulled something from his breast pocket and placed it on the table. A golden ring, etched like knotwork.

"When did you—"

"Ten years ago. After she completed her apprenticeship. She said no." Tiernan rubbed the bridge of his nose. "I would not abandon my research. Maika was afraid I would leave and never return. She has no doubt given up on me, but I must try."

"She's been just down the creek the whole time and you—" I stuttered to a stop. "Tiernan, you're a fucking idiot."

"I know."

I backed away, clay shards cutting my bare feet. My ribs felt too small for my thudding heart. "I'm sorry, I — need to go."

❄

I took Anwea and fled north. Away from Tiernan, Marijka, the creek, and Caladheå — everything that had been part of my life since I crossed the sky bridge. We made it to the Holmgar just before sundown. I slid off Anwea and collapsed at the edge of the canyon. The river ran high from melting snow. I listened to water churn far below and wished I could flow away with it.

Where did it all go wrong? Even as I asked myself that I knew the answer. I tried to pinch the setting sun between my finger and thumb. Tiernan had always been just out of reach. Nothing had gone wrong because I never had him, from the moment I glimpsed a shadow of him in another world to the moment he cut out of existence in the shrine. The burning man who glowed too hot for me to touch.

In all the time we spent together, Tiernan's heart and mind had been with someone else. The day he showed me how to write her name before his own. The moment in the shimmering turquoise light of Aeldu-yan he confessed to missing me, just because I was the only one around to drown out his ghosts. And the spring equinox, after Airedain convinced me to be more forward — only for Tiernan to refuse me the same promise Marijka asked for a decade earlier.

Only one thing might've made a difference. If I never asked

Tiernan to come to the equinox festival, if he never saw the burning shrine, things might've stayed the same. But still I would not have Tiernan. He changed his mind for Marijka, not me.

Anwea snuffled my shoulder. I crinkled my nose. "I don't have any food for you. I didn't even bring any for me." I'd left my weapons at the cabin. Not one of my smarter decisions.

She nuzzled me again. I wrapped my arms around her neck. "So do horses feel heartbreak, or are humans the only ones stupid enough to — to fall in love with someone who doesn't—" Tears welled in my eyes. I pressed my face against Anwea's smooth hair and sobbed as the sun sank out of view beyond the ocean.

✳

I awoke to rain running off trees and dripping onto my face. The ground was wet around me and dry beyond that. I stared up into rustling leaves. "Seriously?" There were some things no one ever told me about being an antayul.

We slowly made our way back south. I foraged dandelions and peppery watercress while Anwea grazed. My hair still smelled like woodsmoke. I scrubbed it in an icy brook, brushing my fingers over the scar I'd gotten on my forehead from the drunken Sverbian in Caladheå. I slept against Anwea's warm flank, but by morning of the third day, I knew it was time.

Tiernan was on the porch steps, whittling a block of pale wood with his folding knife. He rose to greet me. A smile cracked across his face. "She said yes."

"Oh, Tiernan." I'd never seen him smile like that, like sunlight radiating from his body. I hugged him, careful to avoid his hair. "I'm happy for you." Some part of me truly was.

"It will be a small ceremony in two weeks," he said. "I understand if you do not want to stay—"

"I'll stay." I tried to return his smile. "When else will I see a Sverbian wedding?"

The days flew by. I tended Marijka's garden while she made arrangements in Caladheå. It gave me a chance to break down in solitude behind her greenhouse. When Marijka returned, she took me into her kitchen and showed me two rolls of patterned cloth.

"They represent the regions of Sverba our families came from," she explained. Hers was white criss-crossed with silver lines. Tiernan's was blood red with black lines. She fingered the soft woolen cloth. "I never thought I'd wear this."

"I can't believe Tiernan made you wait ten years."

"Truth be told, I had given up on him. But I believe in second chances." Her smile faded. "If we had wed back then, Jorumgard would've been Tiernan's *stjolvind*."

"His what?"

"A friend or relative who protects the groom from evil spirits." She refolded the cloth and slipped it back into the paper wrapping. "Rhonos agreed to be Tiernan's. In Nyhemur, a Ferish *stjolvind* is unheard of."

"That's the way of things around here." I handed her the packing twine. "Do you have someone like that?"

"The bride has a *stjolvehl*, but I have no relatives in Eremur." Marijka gave me a hesitant smile. "I hoped you might be mine, Kateiko. The evil spirits are just a myth, I promise."

My mouth fell open. I almost said no, until I thought about what it'd be like to get married without Nili at my side. I knew how it felt to be alone and far from home. Marijka had done so much I'd never been able to repay. "Of course. I'd be honoured."

Their wedding day dawned bright and warm. I helped Marijka lace her silver bodice over a white gown. I pinned a piece of jewellery I'd made — wire twisted into a crescent moon with shimmering water droplets — into her white-blonde hair. Her laughter filled the room when I explained how she looked like a shard of moonlight the first time I saw her.

Tiernan was more handsome than ever. For once he'd combed his hair and scrubbed the mud from his boots. Marijka had sewn the red and black cloth into a sash that he wore draped across one shoulder with a white tunic and black trousers. A nervous smile tugged at his lips. He looked younger without his beard, softer.

We gathered in the clearing among green grass and blooming purple and blue flowers. It was a small ceremony indeed. There were only a dozen of us. Tiernan and Marijka stood on either side of a cleric in a white robe. Rhonos and I stood next to them, avoiding each other's eyes. A handful of their friends, including Nhys from the Blackened Oak and a woman who played the fiddle, gathered round.

When I looked back on that day, I remembered it like pictures etched into my memory. Tiernan moving the ring from Marijka's right hand to her left. Sweeping her into a kiss that stung to watch. Rhonos and I knotting cloth around their wrists, white for Tiernan and red for Marijka. The new couple lifting joined hands with radiant smiles as everyone cheered.

We pulled out tables from the workshop and had dinner in the field. People stood up one at a time to tell stories about the couple. Marijka was a student at Ingdanrad when a young mage from Sverba showed up to do theological research. She taught him Coast Trader and he helped her practise Middle Sverbian. He was twenty-one and she was eighteen when they left. Nhys told a story that ended with, "Here's to a lovely woman and her husband, who I've never forgiven for burning down my inn," which left Tiernan burying his face in his hands and everyone else roaring with laughter.

Tiernan pulled me aside that evening. "I meant to talk to you about this sooner, Kako. The cabin is yours if you want it." He was moving to Marijka's so they didn't have to rebuild her greenhouse and replant her garden. I wondered how much it had to do with leaving his workshop behind for good.

"I can't stay here," I said. "Thank you, but . . . this was never a home to me."

Tiernan nodded. "Come visit sometime. I — we both care about you." He fiddled with the white cloth around his wrist.

"I'll always come back. I promised." I kissed his cheek. "Goodbye, Tiernan."

It was well past dark, candles sputtering on the tables, when Tiernan lifted Marijka onto Gwmniwyr and swung up behind her. Nhys said something in Sverbian. From the way everyone laughed, I was pretty sure I didn't want to understand. Their inebriated friends waved and called loud farewells as the couple rode off to their new home.

I stayed more from a sense of protection over the clearing than any interest in socializing. People eventually trickled into the workshop and fell asleep on the dirt floor. I lingered outside the cabin. I'd already packed my kinaru shawl, dolphin flag, and fir blanket into my carryframe.

"It gets cold overnight," Rhonos said behind me. "Come join us."

Rhonos had been civil all day, not mentioning our spat from his earlier visit. For what it was worth, he had a part in making Tiernan happier than I'd ever seen. I felt the edge of my dislike blunt as I followed him into the warm workshop.

Iren kohal. Rivers keep flowing. Life moved on. I had to move with it.

22.

IF IT DOESN'T HURT

I stood on the edge of North Iyun Bel the day after the wedding, gazing at Caladheå. The city of white sails. Two months after Eremur declared war on Suriel, I didn't know what to expect. I hadn't stayed in the capital long after Montès's assassination. All Rhonos knew was that the city guards were cracking down on viirelei.

"You don't have to stay," I told Anwea. I hadn't tethered her, but she seemed content to graze near the hollow log where I stowed my carryframe. "If you're gone when I get back, then . . . thanks for everything." I stroked her mane and tugged my bodice into place. It felt odd wearing my dress without all the warm underlayers.

Elkhounds stopped me at the bridge over the Stengar into Førstown, the old Sverbian quarter. They demanded to see my identification and asked where I was going, what I was doing, how long I was staying. I made up answers and showed them a stone dolphin token Airedain's sister Lituwa had carved as proof I was

Iyo. It didn't actually mean anything, but the guards lowered their spears. They hadn't given me nearly as much trouble when I arrived alone during the inquiry.

Caladheå was quiet. Sverbian protest words flaked off the brick walls. It felt like the city was holding its breath. People hurried through the streets without stopping. They'd gotten what they wanted, but I wondered how long the military could hold back the tide.

The Colonnium gates were shut. "No viirelei permitted until further notice," a guard said.

"What if I need to go to the Office of the Viirelei?"

He pulled a paper from an iron box mounted on the wall. "Fill this out to apply for an appointment."

My eyes traced over the flowing ink script. I could read maybe a quarter of the words.

Iannah always left the Colonnium on her days off, but since her post change I had no idea when they were. I spent two hours wandering the red-brick shops, terraced houses, and green parks of Bronnoi Ridge until I found Natzo's noodle shop, recognizing it by the smell of broth.

"Do you know Pelennus?" I asked the balding shopkeeper, speaking as clearly as possible. "Colonnium guard? About this tall, female, red hair?"

"Ah! Antler!" Natzo finally exclaimed. "She come once a week. Midday. You come back two days, yes?"

Two days. Iannah had always been one person in Caladheå I counted on to be in the same place, but the same war that kept her inside kept me locked out. So I went looking for the next closest person I had to a friend in the city.

✳

It was near dark by the time I found the Knox Arms, a single spot of liveliness in the dead streets. Airedain was onstage drumming with as much spirit as ever, like the music shielded him from all the turmoil of the world. I found a spot along the balcony to watch, but couldn't get into it like last time.

"Can I buy you a drink?" said a voice next to me.

I turned to see a brown-haired Sverbian boy leaning against the railing. "Why?"

His eyes flickered to my forehead. I couldn't tell if his recoil was from my scar or my question. "I dunno, it's polite?"

"Don't bother."

"Gods' sakes, are all viirelei so uptight?" He pushed off from the railing and left.

No one else talked to me all night. When the music stopped, I went downstairs, weaving past loud stumbling people and sticky tables littered with empty mugs. Airedain was packing his drum away in the back of the pub. I tapped him on the shoulder. "Ai, Iyo-boy."

He jerked upright, dropping a mallet. "Rin-girl!"

"What'd I say about calling me that in public?"

"Shit. Forgot, sorry." He scooped up the mallet and spun it. "Whatcha doing back in Caladheå? Thought you were done with this place."

I scrunched up my face. "Tiernan got married yesterday."

Airedain closed his eyes and exhaled. "Oh, fuck." He pulled me into a hug, careful not to touch my braid. His tunic was soaked, but I didn't push him away this time. "You wanna get out of here?"

I tilted my head up to look at him. The top of my head barely met his nose. "Sure."

The night had cooled off. Rain washed ash into the gutters, rinsing the city of its usual stench. I stuffed my hands into my pockets as we walked to Airedain's. Inside, he tossed his keys on the table and lit the oil lamp. The row of stone makiri gazed down at us.

Airedain uncorked a clouded glass bottle. "You're gonna need this."

I put my nose to the opening. It didn't smell like the brånnvin I was used to. "What is it?"

"Straight vodka. Alcohol is like love. If it doesn't hurt, it ain't strong enough."

I drank. My shoulders twisted and my throat burned like I'd swallowed embers. I handed it back. "Yan taku. That's worse than your swamp water."

"Effective though." Airedain held it up in mock salute and flopped onto his narrow bed. "So what in Aeldu-yan happened? I thought that man was pretty sweet on you."

I sat next to him, scuffling my feet. "Remember Marijka? The Sverbian who healed you at Skaarnaht? Turns out they have a history."

Airedain winced. "Guess people always go for their own kind in the end."

Something cold gnawed at my stomach despite the warmth of the alcohol. Tiernan never seemed to care I was a different race, but he never told me a lot of things. "What about you? I thought you'd be with Britte tonight. Did she change her mind about your other lovers?"

"Nei. She left me after she found out I wasn't playing the spring fair."

"Kaid. I'm sorry—"

"Don't worry about it." He ran a hand over his spiked hair. "Guess I know why she was interested in me. Whatever."

I frowned. "Why didn't you play the fair? You were looking forward to that."

"Some new fucking law against viirelei performing in public. I'm lucky to keep my job at the Knox. Emílie knows I need the money, but she'll get in trouble if the Elkhounds find out."

"That's ridiculous. Does the Council think you'll start a riot with a drum?"

"Dunno." Airedain picked at his rumpled caribou fur blanket. "I think they just don't want us giving the pigeons any ideas."

I pulled the bottle from his hands, took a swig, and shuddered. "Why do you put up with living in Caladheå?"

"'Cause I don't know what else to do." He leaned against the wall. "Liwa wants me to move back to Toel. 'You dress like an itheran, you drink like one, you even swear like one,' she says. Easier to deal with strangers thinking you're a freak than your own family."

"I'd prefer no one think I'm a freak." As I recalled the boy in the Knox Arms, an idea struck me. I put down the vodka and peered at my reflection in the cracked, cloudy mirror above the washstand.

"You're prettier than Marijka, if that's what you're thinking."

I laughed. "What? Nei, I just . . ." I unbraided my hair, pulled a section forward, and sliced it with my hunting knife. Long brown strands fluttered into the washbasin. I adjusted the length until it fell just below my eyebrows, concealing the scar.

Airedain studied me for a moment, then thumped the bed. "I approve."

"Good. I got this stupid scar because of you." I looked into the mirror again, running my fingers through the short strands. I'd never cut my hair in my whole life. Isu would be furious.

"You gonna . . ." Airedain gestured at the basin.

"Ai, yeah. Sorry." I gathered up the strands and tossed them in the iron stove.

"Where are you staying tonight?" he asked as I flopped on the bed.

"No fucking idea."

"You can sleep here, but one of us has to take the floor. Jonalin's in town this time."

I glanced at the other still-unmade bed. "I'm not convinced your cousin exists."

"He works as a dockhand. Even weirder hours than my jobs."

"Mmm." The last night I spent there felt so long ago. So much had changed, yet I was still drifting with nowhere to land. I sat bolt upright. "Oh, shit."

"What?" Airedain paused with the vodka halfway to his mouth.

I squirmed. "I told Tiernan I slept here once, and he gave me such a weird look after I talked to you on the spring equinox. Dunehein had been teasing me about you. I think Tiernan thought we — you know." My cheeks felt hot. "Slept together."

He threw back his head and laughed, his spiked hair crumpling against the wall. "Of all the wrong ideas to get—"

I punched his arm. "The thought of tapping me is funny?"

"Ow. Nei, I just never — aw, fuck. It's gonna sound bad no matter what I say." He rubbed his neck and squinted one eye shut. "I'd never make a move on a girl who's hung up on someone else. I called you into the shrine circle so Tiernan would have to pay attention to you."

"That's sweet. Too bad I ruined the moment by passing out."

"Probably didn't help his confusion that I jumped offstage as soon as I saw you go down."

"Aeldu save me." I gave a shaky laugh to hide the tears that wanted to emerge. "Well, it doesn't matter what Tiernan thinks. I never had a chance with him."

Airedain stared into the vodka. "Maybe it's better this way. Getting involved with itherans just complicates shit. We got enough to worry about."

"Ai, thanks for sticking up for me, by the way. With Tokoda." I drew my knees to my chest. "You never mentioned you'd — you know, seen things that shouldn't exist."

"Only once. Heard it first, actually. The echo sounded wrong." He shook his head. "We gotta look out for each other, Rin-girl. No one else will."

We stayed awake until the bottle was nearly empty. I didn't trust myself to make it to the latrine behind the flats, so Airedain looked away while I peed into a ceramic pot. "You're a city girl now," he said with a laugh when I dumped it out the window into the rain.

I eventually gave up on staying upright and slid onto the floor. Airedain lay next to me and tapped out rhythms on the floorboards. I sang a Rin song about Imaidu, the first person to attune, messing up the words so badly I gave up and curled into a giggling ball.

Jonalin showed up when the oil lamp was sputtering out. He looked about the same age as Airedain. Same dark brown hair, cut shorter, arms and chest corded with muscle under his tunic. He took one look at us laughing on the floor and went to bed. We kept our voices down after that. Airedain pulled the heavy caribou fur from his bed and draped it over us. I drifted into sleep with his hand on my elbow and the sound of his slow breathing next to me.

✳

"Hey, Koehl." Iannah stood in front of me wearing her blue-and-fawn uniform and her sword. "Good to see you."

"You have no idea." I got up from the sidewalk and hugged her. She went rigid, then placed her arms around me. I didn't say anything when her hands grazed my braid.

We squeezed behind a table in Natzo's. Everyone spoke rapid Ferish, so I wasn't worried about being overheard. Iannah stuck with her steel spoon and green broth. I switched to a whalebone spoon and *spianèʒi te papriconne*, wheat noodles in rust-red broth. It was so spicy my eyes watered.

"I never knew you were so attached to him," Iannah said after I told her about Tiernan.

"Neither did I for a long time."

It was hard to pin down when I realized I was in love. Maybe when I learned there was another Tiernan. I'd come to accept the man I knew — all his faults, all the ways he prickled my nerves, all the flashes of kindness. I didn't want him any different.

Iannah listened until I talked myself out. When talking turned to crying, she handed me a frayed handkerchief, paid Natzo four pann, and held my hand as we wandered west from Bronnoi Ridge. People's mouths tightened, but they kept their eyes down and their words to themselves. It was a relief after spending yesterday in Segowa's stall. Iannah kept her head up, slowing her measured pace to match my steps. Soft rain drizzled down and cleared away again.

She filled the silence with news. The military had abandoned Dúnravn, but Mayor Vorhagind enlisted cragsmen to guide a detachment north of the pass where they caught a camp of Suriel's Corvittai off guard. The navy sailed up Burren Inlet deep into the mountains, razing every port they found. Hit on both sides, the Corvittai funnelled down the central plains. Riders with Suriel's sigil were slaughtering farmers and goatherds in the eastern Roannveldt.

"That doesn't sound like Suriel," I said. "He always warns people first."

Iannah shrugged. "His army needs food. That's probably why they destroyed Rutnaast — to clear out naval traffic on Burren Inlet so they could smuggle shipments past. Now their supply lines are cut. Starvation wins out over following Suriel's orders. Food shortages will hit us, too. Caladheå already went through its stores feeding three thousand Rutnaast refugees."

"Where did all these Corvittai even come from?"

"Our ranks, mainly. We checked the bodies. A few are known political dissidents. My guess is the Corvittai captain is Ferish and recruited mercenaries to match. Easier to manage on and off the battlefield."

"So why does everyone still blame viirelei?"

"The Council won't admit the war has left the mountains and come down here." Iannah's lips pressed together. "They're okay with letting viirelei take the fall for razed farms and dead herders. Damned cowards."

I wondered what Airedain would say if he knew how much an Antler sounded like him. "Will you get in trouble if you're seen with me?"

She shook her head. "Who's going to stop me?"

By late afternoon, we wound up on the cobblestone walkway in the docklands. The tide was out, revealing barnacles on the timber piers. Barrel-chested men unloaded crates from a creaking merchant galleon. I saw Jonalin among them and waved. Chattering seagulls hovered overhead. The noise was reassuring. Whatever happened on land, ships still came and went.

"Do you ever think about leaving?" I asked.

"No," Iannah said. "There was nothing for me in Laca vi Miero. Other guards talk about returning to Ferland, but my grandparents left for a reason."

I lifted my face to the grey sky and wondered if it was raining in Anwen Bel. "I . . . have something to admit. I didn't just grow up in the north. I was born there, in the Rin-jouyen. Falwen registered me as Iyo so I could get past the Elkhounds."

Iannah's brow creased. "You're the nation who left Caladheá after the Second Elken War."

"You know about that?"

"Only from serving at the Colonnium. Rin aren't mentioned in our history lessons. That'd mean admitting you left because we razed your district." She tilted her head. "Why are you here if you're not Iyo?"

"I hoped it'd be better here." I closed my eyes as the ocean wind curled around me. "I keep wondering if I should go home."

"Nobody can decide that but you."

I thought about her words after she headed back to the Colonnium. She was right. But it was easier not to decide anything at all.

✳

I found a new rhythm as spring passed. I built a campsite on the edge of North Iyun Bel and stitched a tent out of deerskin, like the ones Rin made long ago before we bartered canvas from itherans. Anwea grazed on the slopes leading to the tip of the Roannveldt plain. Rain and fog turned my campsite into an island among soaring spruce.

In Caladheå, I kept my head down like Rhonos warned me to. Still, more than once Airedain and I fled from itherans who shouted at us on dark streets, only to run into grey-armoured Elkhounds who shoved us against brick walls and demanded to know what we were doing. The guards on the Stengar bridge stopped me every time I entered and left Førstown. Airedain told me not to bother trying to enter through Shawnaast, the western district overrun by Ferish.

I saw Iannah once a week on her day off. We met Parr in the square one afternoon as we hid from sheets of rain gusting onto the stalls. He greeted us with a smile and stopped to talk. Iannah said he was the only councillor who went out in public without a bodyguard. She claimed it was a political tactic, but from what I'd seen he could defend himself. Now that I knew to look for it, I could see the faint outline of the knife under his coat.

Airedain introduced me to some Iyo in Ashtown and the Sverbian musicians he performed with. I got used to the burn of brännvin, preferring the fennel-flavoured kind to straight vodka, and slept on his floor whenever I didn't feel up to the hike north. Iannah gave me an unimpressed look the first time I showed up with a splitting headache. I swore she talked louder that day.

Segowa paid me to collect dyestuffs from the forest. Alder bark for red and yellow, lichen for orange and purple, stinging nettle for green, hemlock bark for brown and black. My hands were stained for days from stewing cottonspun and bleached linen in a field behind the Iyo flats. It was just enough money to get my boots patched by a cobbler, buy sugar for Anwea, and keep a flask of brännvin in my bag.

Food prices went up as Iannah predicted, starting with itheran goods like rye, eggs, and goat milk. Ashtown flooded with viirelei selling a rainbow of forage. Orange salmonberries, leafy greens, red seaweed, golden brassroot for grinding into flour. After I saw Elkhounds arrest a Kae woman for selling tealhead ducks, I decided trapping wasn't worth the money. Instead, I quietly traded creek trout for crab and fish oil from Jonalin.

I hitched a canoe ride to Toel Ginu for the wedding of another of Airedain's cousins. I met Lituwa's husband long enough to learn his name and Airedain's friend Nokohin long enough to remember he made up the story about kinaru eating children. A few Rin who married into the Iyo-jouyen long ago welcomed me, but the gazes of other Iyo followed me. Dunehein, Rikuja, and I spent the rest of the night stargazing on the cliffs.

I visited Tiernan as promised. The first time, a fresh garden plot had been planted. The second time, he had Gwmniwyr harnessed to pull up stumps to clear land for a paddock. The yard burst with life. Neat rows of vegetables reached for the sky, vines climbed trellises, flowers spilled from the windowsills. It smelled crisp and sweet and tart in the clean air following heavy rain. Marijka invited me inside, but I politely refused.

It wasn't a life I'd call happy or healthy. I spent five days at my campsite shaking and coughing, too exhausted to maintain the waterproof barrier around my tent but too dizzy to climb onto Anwea. I went through my entire food store and couldn't see well enough to set a snare. Just when I questioned my sanity in not staying at Toel Ginu, Airedain showed up.

He built a fire, peeled off my wet clothes, and lent me a waterproof bark cape. Nothing ever tasted better than the roots he boiled into broth. When the rain eased, he hung my clothes by the fire and resealed my tent with resin. I asked between coughs if he had to return to Caladheå for work, but he said they could manage without him for a night.

And he did stay the night. He slept next to me in my cramped tent, his warm back against me, but all I could think was that he wasn't as warm as the burning man who was never mine.

It was a functional life at best. I watched ships come and go in the harbour while the days and grass grew longer. Storm clouds churned over the eastern mountains and tore themselves apart. Pinpricks of fire glowed on the Roannveldt, creeping west as summer approached.

23.

DESPERATION

When I went to meet Iannah one morning, the streets were flooded with soldiers. She pulled me into the trees along Colonnium Hill and told me some Ferish and viirelei had gotten in a fight near Toel Ginu. I asked her to walk me to Ashtown where I could hide out for a day or two. Instead, we found Airedain on the street outside his flat, shouting and throwing punches at two Elkhounds. One pinned Airedain's arms down, but he twisted free and smashed his fist into the other guard's face with a *crack*. His fan knife flashed.

Cold fear shot through me. "Airedain!" I shouted.

He whirled. A spear sliced through his arm. Blood sprayed over the cobblestones.

The guards seized him. They blurred into a tangle of glinting weapons, leather armour, grey and black cloth. Airedain spat out curses, twisting, kicking, knife ringing off steel.

Iannah wrenched them apart. She shouldered Airedain out of the way. "Go," she told the guards with a glare that could melt iron. They backed away and ran. To me she said, "Get him out of here. Hurry."

I wrangled Airedain's keys from his pocket. His sleeve was torn, the black dolphin tattoo underneath stained red. I dragged him to the door in the brick wall, fumbled the lock with shaking hands, and pushed him upstairs into his flat. "What in Aeldu-yan is going on?"

Airedain slammed a fist against the door. It rattled in the frame. "Fucking pigeons killed Nokohin!"

"Wait — your friend from Toel?" I tried to seize his wrist.

"He wasn't even a warrior!" He snapped his fan knife around, the blade spinning through the air. "If I find the fucking takuran who did it—"

"Listen, you bludgehead!" I grabbed his shoulders. "Don't go picking fights. You hear me? It won't bring Nokohin back—"

"How can you not be mad?" he shouted, wrenching away. "The bloody pigeons get away with it every time!"

"So you got in a brawl with the first soldiers you found? That's not helping!"

"What, you on their side now, Rin-girl? That Antler friend of yours get in your head?"

"Iannah's on *our* side. She just risked her post because you're too proud to run from a fight—"

He laughed. "Right, you don't have to care because it ain't your jouyen. Your bloody crest made itherans think this is our fault, but Iyo are the ones dying."

"Don't you do that to me!" I shoved him into the wall. "You think I'm not mad? Itherans tried to kill Nili and me. They didn't care which jouyen we're from. So yeah, I'm fucking mad!"

He glared back, clutching his chest. "At least you survived. Noko didn't! We're getting hit from both sides and this ain't even our war!"

"They made it ours." I curled my hands until my nails dug into them. "I know it hurts, Airedain. I *know*. But getting thrown in prison won't fix anything. Aeldu save me, the last time an Iyo killed an itheran—"

He slid down the wall into a heap, his tunic catching on the brick. His knife clattered to the floor. "I'm sorry, Kateiko. I just—" He put his head down and folded his hands over his neck. "I'm sick of worrying. Of being scared every time I go outside."

I slumped next to him. "I know. Me, too." I heard voices in the street and wondered if anyone had heard us. "I'm sorry about Noko-hin. I wish I could've gotten to know him."

"You woulda liked him. He was a better person than me."

"That's not hard," I said, evoking a strained laugh from Airedain.

"Fuck. Noko's parents will have to bury their last kid." He rubbed a hand over his eyes. He was crying. "It ain't supposed to be this way."

I leaned my head on his shoulder. "None of this is."

"They were heading to Crieknaast, the people leaving Toel. Noko's family goes trading every summer."

"Even now? It's a mess out there."

He nodded. "I saw him last week. He came by the Knox to see me play. You know what he said? 'I'm not afraid of spirits out there. I'm afraid of people right here.'"

We fell into silence. Sunlight streamed through the shutters, casting bright lines on our legs. The beams of light felt like tiny beacons. A vigil for the dead.

"Tell me about Nokohin," I said.

"He was an ass." Airedain laughed. "We were always getting in trouble for shit. When we were ten, we had a competition to see who could hit the Yula with more snowballs. Noko hit the Okorebai-Yula in the face and blamed me. My temal was furious. He took my drum away."

He flipped his knife around, tossing it up in the air and catching it, rods snapping against the blade. "But I loved Noko. He always told you exactly what he was thinking. Told me when I was being an ass. And he was one of the few people who visited me in Caladheå."

Airedain paused. "He loved kids. Wanted a bunch of his own, just hadn't found the right girl. My sister Liwa let him hold her baby before she let me. I went with him to Crieknaast a few times. He'd make up stories for itheran kids, and I'd play music to go along."

I smiled. "I see why you were friends."

"Noko was the first person I attuned in front of. Can't believe he's gone. Forever is a fucking long time."

"His blood will flow into the ground." I caught one of his tears before it ran onto his thin lips. "I don't know what happens to the spirits of the dead, but . . . their bodies stay part of this world."

He turned to me, dark brown eyes sparkling with water. "Who did you lose?"

"My parents, my cousin Emehein, all my father's family. A lot of bloodlines were wiped out in the Dona war."

"Aeldu save us. Your jouyen has had it rough," he muttered.

"It was a long time ago." I twined my fingers into his. His skin was warm and calloused.

"You're wrong," he said after a long while. His voice shook. "It ain't pride. I always run from fights when I'm with you. Just . . . when I'm alone, I don't care what happens."

"I care. So does your family."

"Dunno what they'd do if I wound up in prison. Or worse." He ran a hand over his rumpled crest of hair. "It's my nephew's first birthday in a few weeks. My tema would kill me if I missed it. Liwa would hunt me down in Aeldu-yan and kill me again."

"See? You have to be careful." I nudged him. "We'll get through this war. Just don't get in any more brawls."

One side of Airedain's mouth twitched up. "Gonna work some magic, Rin-girl?"

I gave a hollow laugh. "Yeah. But first, let me clean that spear wound."

❋

Airedain and the rest of the Iyo in Ashtown went back to Toel Ginu for the burials. Some stayed. Alone in North Iyun, I recited a death rite for Nokohin and the others. Iannah told me none of the survivors were arrested because the Elkhounds didn't know who they were.

On a cold grey day when the sky drizzled with all the enthusiasm of a graveyard, Segowa asked Airedain and me to mind her shop. I stayed in the back sorting lichen while he dealt with customers. Pale pigeons with iridescent heads waddled in the shelter of stalls, cooing softly, different than the dark grey pigeons I knew from the wild.

"The fuck do you want?" Airedain said around midday.

"I'm looking for Sohikoehl," came Iannah's voice.

"I dunno who—" Airedain turned. "That you, Kateiko?"

I brushed lichen from my skirt and ducked under colourful skeins hung from the roof. "Aren't you on duty today?"

"Councillor Parr pulled me off post to find you." Iannah leaned on her spear. "He wants to speak to you."

I leaned on a bolt of dandelion-yellow linen, feeling light-headed. "Why?"

Iannah glanced at Airedain. "He didn't say."

At the Colonnium, Antlers opened the gates without a word. Iannah's spear tapped on wet stone as we crossed the courtyard. She stayed by my side, through the cold marble lobby where the clerk Gélus took my weapons, all the way to Parr's office. I took a deep breath and knocked.

Parr answered right away, smiling down at us. His black coat and breeches were crisp as new leaves, a silver elk pin by his collar, but his eyes were bloodshot and his dark hair was wavy from the damp. "Miss Kateiko, how nice to see you. Thank you, Pelennus. That will be all."

I gave Iannah an apprehensive look as I stepped into the office. She shrugged.

Parr shut the door. "Come outside with me. I have just been enjoying the rain."

What I'd mistaken for windows were actually glass doors, propped open to let in the cool air. I followed Parr out to the loggia. Sculpted cream pillars rose into arches overhead. Water dripped off a high overhang. Guards stood some distance down the balcony, spears as rigid as the pillars.

Parr rested his arms on the solid stone railing. "My colleagues have offices in the pavilions. I prefer the view from here, particularly on the rare days that the mountains are visible."

Beyond the high wall around the grounds, the Roannveldt sprawled hazy green with crops. The Stengar meandered across the plain until it was swallowed by mist. I leaned against the railing. "I can't look east without thinking about what's happening there."

"A wise man keeps one eye on his enemies and one on his friends." Parr glanced at me. "Thank you for coming on such short notice, Miss Kateiko."

"Why did you want to see me, sir?" I was uncomfortably aware how much of a mess I was. My hands were stained orange from the lichen, skirt smudged grey with ash, boots covered in mud, hair escaping its braid, and my cloak needed patching. My head ached from drinking brännvin with Airedain the night before.

Parr deliberated over his words. "Are you still in contact with Tiernan Heilind?"

My hands tightened around the rough stone. "Sort of."

"I have urgent matters to discuss with him, but Heilind is, shall we say . . . unreceptive to Council emissaries. I hope you might be able to persuade him to meet me."

"I'm — not sure that's a good idea." I pressed my fingers to my lips. "He's intent on not returning to Caladheå. He just got married, you know."

Parr looked taken aback. "Did he? To whom?"

"Marijka Riekkanehl. Do you know her?"

"We have met. Well, best wishes to them. Nevertheless, that does not change the situation. I will visit Heilind if he does not wish to come here."

I gazed at the lawn below. "I'm sorry, Councillor, but Tiernan and I aren't on the best terms. I'm not sure he'd forgive me for bringing you to his home."

"Kateiko." His voice was heavy. "Do you remember saying you would find out what Suriel wants if you were in my position?"

"Yes. I remember."

Parr took my hand. His skin was warm in the damp air, the gems on his rings lifeless in the dull light. "I have been in contact with Suriel. I know what he wants."

My head jerked up. "You spoke with Suriel? How? When?"

"Within the last few days. A Corvittai approached me to nego- tiate. I requested to meet Suriel to hear his terms directly."

"A Corvittai? Who?"

"I promised to keep this person's identity secret. A condition of their trust." His hand tightened on mine. "The important part is Heilind is the only person who might be able to help."

The shoirdryge. It had to be that. I wasn't surprised Tiernan told Rhonos about his work, but Parr was the last person I expected to know. "Tiernan thinks Suriel's trying to get to another world," I said hesitantly. "Is that right?"

"Along those lines. His goal is slightly different than Heilind's, but he is willing to accept help. That is an opportunity we cannot let pass."

"Isn't there anyone else you can ask? Ingdanrad, or — or the Okorebai-Iyo—"

Parr laughed, but there was no humour in it. "Ingdanrad shut its gates long ago. As for the Iyo nation, that bridge has been burned until the river below flows thick with ash."

Every drop falling from the overhang prickled at my senses. I heard the patter on the stone loggia, tasted rain in the air, felt it nudge at my mind. "What would it mean for us, sir? If Suriel got what he was after?"

"It may mean the end of this war."

I'd asked Parr not to give up. And he hadn't, even as he faced down the entire Council, as the troops he'd once captained fell to the Corvittai, as everyone else turned on each other. I owed him the same.

"Then I'll take you to Tiernan."

*

The soonest Parr could get away from his Council duties was three days later. He said it'd look odd if we left the city together, so I agreed to meet him on the road into North Iyun. I worried that Parr might recognize Anwea as a military horse — for I was sure she'd belonged to a Caladheå soldier once, along with the elk-sigil armour taken by the Corvittai — but Iannah told me soldiers used all sorts of breeds. Eremur was too remote to be picky.

Parr arrived on a brawny soot-black stallion. As we rode, he kept up polite conversation, telling me the history of landmarks in Caladheå, asking if I'd had this or that type of Ferish food — yes to *papriconne* broth, no to a bread I didn't understand the name of. He steered us onto a new topic whenever I fell quiet. It was a nice distraction from what lay ahead.

I sensed the flow of the creek before I heard it. "Hold up a moment." I slowed Anwea to a halt, pretending to adjust the reins while I searched for a glimmer in the air. My palm tingled as I disabled the warning runes. "Sorry. It's just ahead."

Tiernan had explained how the runes worked after I set off the blinding light on my first visit. Apparently I'd been immune to the ones at his cabin because I was inside the circle when he set them. He'd tweaked the ones around Marijka's home so I could use water magic to temporarily disable them.

"Tiernan?" I called as our horses splashed through the creek.

He walked around the corner of the greenhouse, carrying a dirt-encrusted shovel over one shoulder. "Hello, Katei—" He bit down on my name. "What is he doing here?"

"Please don't be mad." I slid down from Anwea, pressing close to her warm body. "I brought Councillor Parr to speak with you."

Tiernan drove the shovel into the ground. "I have no interest in what he has to say. Nor should you."

"I would not do this if there was any other way, Heilind." Parr dismounted with practiced ease. "This regards Suriel. Let us put the past behind us. You dwell on the edge of a battlefield and I would not see you or your wife suffer."

Tiernan rounded on me. "You told him about Maika? What else does he know?"

"Nothing!" I said, my voice rising. "Tiernan, please hear him out. *Please.*"

He pressed his fingers to the bridge of his nose. "Come inside."

The kitchen looked almost the same as before. Among Marijka's flowers and herbs, I recognized clay dishes from Tiernan's cabin, his hunting knife by the fireplace, and the stone wolf makiri on the mantelpiece, sheltered by rubbery leaves. "Where's Maika?" I asked as we settled on rough wooden chairs.

"At Crieknaast's military hospital, cleaning up the most recent battle." Tiernan cast a pointed look at Parr. "Now, what do you want?"

"Your expertise." Parr laid his black riding gloves on the table. "Suriel has offered conditional peace. He wishes to access somewhere called the void. His air magic cannot break through all layers of the barrier around the world, so he requests the aid of a rift mage."

Tiernan was silent. Then he rested his elbows on the table and covered his face with his hands. "*Någvakt bøkkhem.* That means nothing good for any of us."

My brows drew together. "What's the void?"

"The space between worlds. Like the tiniest gap between adjacent walls. No scholar has found a scrap of evidence it exists."

"No scholar has studied rift magic as extensively as you," Parr said. "The Corvittai have known about your work for some time, Heilind. They came to me because they know we are acquainted."

Tiernan wasn't listening. He paced the kitchen, weaving around the roots hanging from the ceiling. His face took on that distant look I'd seen so often. "Of course. The shrine fire. Suriel knew exactly what he was doing."

I twisted in my chair. "What do you mean?"

"He only needed a force strong enough to tear open this side. The weak side. But why—" Tiernan snapped around to look at me. "When was the Toel Ginu shrine built?"

"Ai . . ." I chewed my lip. "Almost seven hundred years ago?"

He slammed a fist into his palm. "*Bøkkai*! I cannot believe I overlooked that."

"Overlooked *what?*"

"I thought Suriel was searching for the shoirdryge that split off a decade ago. I did not begin finding his runes until after that. But another shoirdryge split off more than six hundred years ago. It has drifted so far away that no one sees it anymore."

I stared at him. "Just how many of these do you know about?"

"Only those two." Tiernan ran a hand through his hair. "The new world is too close to get in between. Maybe Suriel was using the shrine as a sort of . . . focal point for the space between the older world and ours. It is one of the few structures in Eremur that precedes the split. Gods know what he will destroy next."

"That is a risk we will have to take." Parr leaned forward and placed his folded hands on the table. "Suriel did not divulge why he wants to access the void, but he does not plan to return. He says other air spirits from surrounding regions will divide up his territory and manage the wind. Our only hope of being free from his shadow is for him to depart this world."

Tiernan shook his head. "It cannot be done. You would have better luck throwing Suriel into the ocean and hoping the tides devour him."

"Caladheå cannot help. Ingdanrad will not. You may be able to."

"No," Tiernan said with sudden vehemence. "Were my previous refusals not sufficient? I will have nothing to do with a dangerous spirit the Council has angered time and time again."

"If that's what Suriel wants though. . ." I hesitated. "Maybe he'd stop attacking everyone."

"Until he becomes angered by my failure." Heat rippled out, shimmering around Tiernan. "I have turned away from that path. I will not go back to it."

Parr rose, his chair scraping. "Heilind. We could end this conflict once and for all."

Tiernan faced him down. The room felt too small. I stood, acutely aware I was between two men with years of military experience and a good deal more physical strength, and placed myself so they had to look past me to see each other.

"The Council did not allow us to leave Dúnravn Pass to call for reinforcements," Tiernan said. "They did not allow Crieknaast to abandon Dúnravn, or order Rutnaast to abandon the port. They did not make amends with Ingdanrad for letting mages be murdered in custody. All these chances, yet all I see is desperate men asking others to lay down their lives."

"Do not fault me for the cowardice of ignorant men," Parr said, his voice growing louder. "Montès is dead. He is no longer around to cloud their minds—"

"Montès was only the mouth of the political body. The inside had already gone to rot."

"Do not punish Eremur for a government that cannot govern. You are a better man than that, Heilind."

"My obligation is to my wife. You have no grounds on which to judge what kind of man I am." The plants around Tiernan began to wilt. The kitchen crackled as if embers had spilled on the floor.

Parr's hand slid under his coat hem toward his knife. After seeing him take down a rioter at Skaarnaht, I had no doubt he was still in practice from his combat days.

I stood still, faint from the heat, my skin damp with sweat. "Tiernan."

He looked at me in silence. Slowly, the crackling faded.

Tiernan turned his attention back to Parr. "If I ever want to be the kind of man who drives away his own family, I know who to ask for advice. Now get out of my home."

Parr's mouth formed a thin line. He picked up his gloves and strode outside.

I dashed after him, blinking in the harsh sunshine. "Councillor, wait!"

"I am sorry for wasting your time," he said as he crossed to the paddock. "I should have known better."

"Sir, let me talk to Tiernan." I reached out and caught his elbow.

Parr turned to me. "I can recognize a man who has made up his mind, Miss Kateiko. That said . . ." He reached into his breast pocket and handed me a small card. "This will grant you entry into the Colonnium. Please come see me if you ever need help."

It was stiff white paper with the rearing elk sigil stamped in red ink. Parr's name was written in bold strokes. I held it to my chest. "Thank you, sir."

"I would be glad to see a kind face again." Parr gave me a sad smile. His black hair shone in the midday light. "Farewell."

I waited until he'd ridden across the creek and out of sight. A breeze stirred around me, carrying the sweet scent of flowers and sun-warmed grass. The leaves whispered an invitation. I pressed my fingers to my lips and went back inside.

24.

SAIL

"I don't understand." I leaned against the kitchen doorframe. A breeze floated through the window, cooling the room. "Suriel never stopped you before. Why now?"

Tiernan took down one of Marijka's ceramic plates, painted with a chestnut horse pulling a sledge over snow. "I made a promise to Maika."

"That you wouldn't leave. Not that you wouldn't help anyone else leave."

"I also promised to take care of her. Nothing good can come from working with Suriel."

"You'd condemn everyone else to death instead?"

Tiernan replaced the plate in the rack. "I gave those people ten years of my life, Kateiko. Ten years of war and loss and futility. Maika is all I have left."

"What about me?" My voice cracked. "Suriel almost killed what's left of my family. Doesn't that mean anything to you?"

"Of course it does." He touched my chin. "But he is seeking the impossible. There is nothing I can do."

I slapped his hand away. "How do you know? You won't even talk to Suriel!"

He took a step backward. "Kako—"

"Don't call me that!" Hot tears stung my eyes. "Rhonos asked for your help, Parr asked — I thought if I asked maybe you'd agree, but you don't care what happens to anyone else! Maika would care!"

Tiernan stilled. I saw his heart pounding through his tunic. "Do not bring Maika into this. If she learns what Suriel wants of me—"

"What are you afraid of?" I pushed him back, forcing him into the centre of the room. "She's your wife! You're supposed to trust each other!"

He placed strong hands on my shoulders. "I will not risk my marriage over this—"

"Does she know who she married? A man who'd let the rest of the world burn?" I struck my fists against his chest. He grabbed my arms, but I twisted free. "You'd let — all of us — die!"

Tiernan dodged. A flowerpot shattered on the floor. "Kateiko, stop!" He pinned my arms down and wrapped his arm around me.

I struggled in his grip. I couldn't even move my head with my braid clamped to my back. All I could see was him, the scar across his nose, his tanned skin, the dark stubble along his jaw. I felt his warm breath on my cheek.

I slammed my knee into him. "I should tell Maika! I should tell her you don't care if Suriel kills us all! Are you afraid she'd leave you?"

Tiernan's grip tightened. "You will not speak to her about this. If you tell her anything, do not consider yourself welcome here again."

I stared into his grey eyes, the heat making me dizzy. He released me and stepped back. His hair was damp, my hair was damp, and I didn't know if it was sweat or humidity or just water rolling off me and colliding with the burning man I both loved and hated at once.

I strode outside, slamming the door, and spat on the grass until the taste of woodsmoke was gone.

✳

Our words played in my head as I crouched in the forest, eyeing ridge ducks on a pond choked with green algae. Maybe I never knew Tiernan as well as I thought, but Marijka knew him better than anyone and still she married him. So why was he afraid of her finding out?

I knelt, searching for a good angle through the trees. Soft lichen squished under my hands. I slid into a cottonwood stand, the catkins bursting with white seed puffs. Ducks charged at each other, splashing up water. Feathered ridges on their heads flared.

Then it hit me. Maybe Tiernan wasn't keeping Suriel from Marijka, but Marijka from Suriel.

Marijka studied at Ingdanrad. She was a mage. She knew Tiernan had been searching for a rift. More importantly, she was worried enough to refuse his marriage proposal. That meant she thought there was a chance he might succeed.

I readied my throwing dagger, Nurivel, its blade dappled with leaf shadows. It was muggy under the canopy, even so late in the evening. The solstice was only a few days away.

Every season had a day for uniting with others. The autumn equinox with other Rin after our summer travels, Yanben with aeldu, the spring equinox with other jouyen. For two hundred years, Jinben had been about uniting with itherans on the summer solstice.

A duck launched from the water. I threw my dagger. The duck

tumbled from the air and splashed into the shallows, wings twitching. The others skittered away squawking.

I was sure about one thing. Marijka would care.

✳

I went back the next day, slinking along the creek under cover of the overhanging trees. Tiernan was on a ladder cleaning leaves out of the gutter. The day after that a white dress hung from the laundry rope behind the house. Marijka's broad-brimmed straw hat poked over the top of tomato plants.

"Hello, Maika," I called.

She stood up and smiled, brushing dirt off her apron. Her hands were pink with sunburn. "Good morning, Kateiko. I'm afraid Tiernan's out hunting."

I stopped between the waist-high rows. Cottonwood fluff covered the soil like snow. "Actually, I wanted to talk to you alone."

Marijka tucked her trowel under her arm. "What about?"

"Did you ever help Tiernan with his work? All that stuff about shoirdrygen?"

"A little. I helped him translate Coast Trader texts in the Ingdanrad library. That was before I knew what he was trying to do."

"What about since then?"

Her eyebrows crinkled. "Has he been talking about this?"

"Not willingly." I shuffled my feet. Once I told her, there was no going back.

She trailed her fingers over narrow leaves and unripe orange tomatoes as I recounted the meeting with Parr and my fight with Tiernan. "This was all supposed to be over," she said when I was done.

"It could be. Once Suriel's gone, we'd never have to think about other worlds again."

"How can I—" She tilted her face toward the vibrant blue sky. "I left Tiernan alone for ten years because he wouldn't give up his research. How can I ask him to go back to it?"

"Offer to help. Then he'd know you trust him to stay once the rift is open. If he still refuses . . . maybe you can open a rift yourself."

Marijka set down the trowel and untangled the stems of two drooping plants. "I need to tie these up. I think I have twine in the greenhouse."

I followed her into the glass building. Water rolled down the warped panes into pollen-choked puddles. Marijka hung her hat on a nail and rummaged through a bin of tools. She took out a ball of twine, then put it down and sighed.

"Tiernan rarely talked about his research. He knew I didn't want to hear it. But . . ."

"What?" I came closer, ducking vines spilling from a hanging basket.

Marijka gazed out at the forest. Her pale hair was escaping its pins. "I went through Tiernan's notes while you were both in Toel Ginu. I think he figured out how to open a rift. He just . . . didn't."

My skin suddenly felt cold even in the sweltering greenhouse.

She stretched out her hand to look at her etched wedding ring. "I don't know if it was because of me, Suriel, or something else. Experimenting with magic is dangerous. Especially this kind."

"Could you do it though?"

"Alone? No. Even Tiernan would've needed help, and my healing magic isn't suited to this at all. If I went back to Ingdanrad and convinced other mages . . . *maybe* we could. It's a very small maybe."

I heard a nicker and turned to see Tiernan leading Gwmniwyr into the yard, their outlines distorted by moisture. I lowered my voice. "The war's coming, Maika. I've seen fires in the east. Everyone's in danger. Soldiers, civilians, people who've never seen magic or held a sword. This isn't just about us anymore."

Once she had reminded me of a still lake, but now something stirred deep in the water. "I swore as a medic to help people, but Tiernan's my husband. I have to talk to him before agreeing to anything."

I took a deep breath, imagining my life if I never saw Tiernan again. "He's going to exile me for telling you."

"He can't. This is my house, and you're my *stjolvehl*. Just let me talk to him first." She paused. "Although you probably shouldn't camp in the area tonight. Good chance of forest fires."

I wasn't going to argue. I headed for the creek while she went to the paddock where Tiernan was wiping sweat off Gwmniwyr's silver coat. By the time Marijka's yard was out of sight, the whisper of creek water blended with faint shouting.

❄

I retrieved Anwea and rode west along the bay, as far as possible until the coast veered north. Iannah wouldn't expect me for three days, and I'd told Airedain not to come looking for me. I stopped on a hill sloping toward the shore and fell asleep under my fir branch blanket and a roof of stars.

The tide was out when I woke, leaving shimmering pools on the sand. Anwea grazed behind me. I chewed a tough piece of dried marsh rat and watched waves come in. The hazy green smudge of an island rose on the horizon out west.

A cutter drifted past, faded red sails billowing in the wind. I wondered how far I could travel on a ship. If I could leave everything behind forever and find a new world across the ocean. If I could forgive myself for doing that.

Everything was so simple in my book of folk tales. The heroes slayed the monsters, saved the land, and fell in love. They always knew what they were supposed to do. There weren't any stories where every option was terrible.

"All right there, young missy?" a scratchy voice interrupted. An old itheran limped down the hill, leading a massive horse.

"I'm fine." My hand went toward my knives.

"No need for that." He stopped several paces away. "You're on my farmland, is all."

"Oh!" I scrambled to my feet. "Sorry, I'll leave right away—"

The man waved me back down. "Nonsense. Who am I to drive a soul from a good thinking place, eh? Just mind your horse doesn't trample the crops back that way."

Something genuine about him made me pause halfway through untangling Anwea's bridle. He was unarmed. His clothes were worn and faded. His horse looked placid, almost sleepy, the thick tufts of white hair over its hooves spattered with mud.

"I come out here sometimes meself to watch the ships pass," the old man said. "Makes all the other troubles in the world seem small."

I set the bridle down and brushed grass off my legs. "They're so beautiful. Drifting along like it's effortless."

"Ah, sailing only looks that way, missy." He squinted at the ocean. "When you've got torn sails, snapped rigging, and a flooded deck, keeping a ship aright is the hardest thing you'll ever do. If something ever seems easy, you're too far away to see how complex it is."

"Like flying." When I was young, Dunehein spread out a waxwing carcass to show me how the feathers worked together to keep the bird aloft.

"Sailors and seagulls, we're all just fighting the wind. Ah, well." He patted his horse. "Ain't nothing good in life that's not worth fighting for."

The old man bid me goodbye and headed back inland. The horse's brown head bobbed as it plodded after him. I thought about his words as the ship faded into blue haze where sky and ocean met, and I knew what I had to do.

Kujinna kobairen. Today we fly.

✳

I expected to have to sneak back into Marijka's yard, but she was alone on her garden bench, a bowl of greens in her lap and a paring knife next to her. She was gazing at the trees. By the amount of cottonwood fluff the wind had blown around her feet, she'd been there awhile.

"Don't worry," Marijka called when she saw me. "Tiernan's not home."

I drew close, afraid to step wrong in case he left a rune to set me on fire. "Where is he?"

"Good question." She gave me a weary smile. "He'll be back. He left Gwmniwyr, and he's loved that gelding longer than he's loved me."

My insides bunched together. "I'm so sorry, Maika—"

"Don't blame yourself for my husband's temper." She stretched, seeming to remember she had arms. "I'm sure he's fine. He's lived through far worse than a night outdoors."

I eased onto the bench, sore from riding. "I worked out a plan. You're not going to like it, but . . . at least you can stay here and wait for him."

Marijka listened carefully. "You're right," she said afterward. "I don't like it. Especially without running it by Tiernan."

"I'm not sure how long this peace offer will last, especially if Suriel knows Tiernan refused. The least I can do is try to learn something useful. Maybe it'll make Tiernan change his mind."

A small sigh escaped her. "Do what you need to. But please be careful."

✳

The Antler at the Colonnium gates held Parr's card up. He passed it to his partner. "That look authentic?"

"More likely than her being able to forge it," the other guard said.

"Doesn't mean she didn't steal it."

"Councillor Parr gave it to me." I failed to keep the edge from my voice.

The second guard looked me up and down, then pulled open the gate and pointed inside with his spear. "Keep your hands where I can see them."

I walked side by side with him across the lawn, holding my hands to my chest. A few people stared when we entered the lobby, but my attention was drawn to the marble staircase where three black-robed figures stood talking. Somehow the place felt cold even in summer.

"Where is Councillor Parr?" the guard called, and then everyone was staring.

One of the councillors opened the doors at the top of the stairs and spoke into the Hall. A moment later, Parr strode down the stairs, his robe sweeping behind him, its scarlet collar bright in the pale room. "What is it?"

The guard held out the card. "Did you issue an entry card to this viirelei?"

"Yes, as our esteemed Officer of the Viirelei does not have authority to grant entry to his own kind," Parr said as if commenting on the weather. "Was there a problem at the gates?"

"Not at all, sir." The guard bowed his head.

"Then I will gladly escort this young lady to Falwen's office.

Your diligence is noted." Parr plucked the card from the guard's grip and handed it to me. "Shall we, miss?"

In the south gallery with the statues, Parr glanced around before ushering me into his office. He closed the door behind us. "I apologize, Miss Kateiko. I did not expect them to give you so much trouble."

"It doesn't matter." I stared at the richly woven rug, trying not to let my anger or humiliation show.

He kissed my hand. "What brings you here? Is something wrong?"

"Nei, sir — well, sort of." I touched my skin where his lips had brushed. "I'm sorry. I didn't mean to interrupt your work."

"The Council is on a recess. I do not have to return quite yet. Please, sit." He settled on a padded bench and folded his hands.

I perched on the bench opposite him. "Councillor, I tried persuading Tiernan. He still refuses. But I know someone else who might be able to help."

Parr leaned forward, eyes fixed on me. "Who?"

I gripped my hands together to hide their shaking. "Name your source — the Corvittai who approached you — and I'll name mine."

"I cannot. The deal would be off."

"Then I want to talk to Suriel."

Parr twisted one of his rings back and forth, silent.

"Nothing against you, sir. But he's more likely to trust my people than yours. I need a guarantee this will end the war before I give him any names."

"Suriel is dangerous to face in person."

"I've met him before. I was in the Toel Ginu shrine when he burned it down. My family and I barely escaped." I held Parr's gaze. I could say that honestly without pretending to be Iyo. "I'll face Suriel again if it means getting rid of him forever."

"Then we share the same determination." He drifted to the glass doors. I trailed after him, and we gazed at distant mountains rising against grey clouds. "It is strange, the things that bring us together."

"Moths of all kinds flock toward the same light," I murmured.

Parr touched my elbow. In the still air of his office, his cologne smelled warm and layered like spiced wine. "Are you sure you want to do this, Kateiko?"

"I'm sure."

"Council will not be in session tomorrow. Meet me at dawn past the guardhouse on the southeast road out of Caladheå. We have a long journey ahead."

25.

SE JI AINU

Airedain would've let me stay with him, but I couldn't face his questions. I bought a wedge of flatbread in the docklands and watched the moon move through the sky. It was freeing to be in the dark with the city asleep behind me. I unbraided my hair and let the wind flow through it. Sailors and dockhands didn't seem the type to care. They worked bare-chested, laughing and swearing, paying no attention to the viirelei girl on the shore.

I headed southeast when the sky turned orange. It was Jinben, I realized. The longest day of the year. I waited in an alder copse, hands under my arms, wishing I'd brought my cloak. It was too muggy to wear it during the day, but my thin dress offered little protection from the breeze.

Parr arrived as the sun rose over the mountains. He was smart enough to wear a coat, his hair tied with a black ribbon. Too late I realized I'd forgotten to rebraid my hair.

"Where are we going, sir?" I asked as we set off toward the plain. He'd said I wouldn't need a horse, but I wondered how far we could get on foot.

"To my home first. I need to collect something."

"You live out here?" I glanced back. "But you came from the city."

"I did not go home last night," he said. Only then did I notice how tired he looked.

We turned off the main road onto a winding, dusty lane framed by draping willows. It felt secluded after the open plain scattered with hillocks and copses. I stopped short when the lane widened into a half-moon courtyard. "That's your home?"

A brick manor covered in trailing vines rose above the courtyard. I'd never seen anything like it. A square central tower, small rounded towers flanking the covered entrance, peaked green roofs across the wings. The brick might've been cream-coloured once, but time had weathered it grey. The garden beds held only damp soil and shrubs clinging to life.

"Parr Manor has been in my family for a century, even before Caladheå was built." He plucked a wilted petal from the flagstone and brushed off the dew. "It has seen better days."

"It's still incredible."

He gave a slight smile. "You are kind to say so."

We looped along a weed-choked path into sprawling grounds bordered by a dense hedge. On a stone terrace, scaffolding suspended an iron brazier. The bright wood looked newly cut. Parr removed a tinderbox from his pocket, ignited damp kindling in the brazier, then took hold of a rope and pulled hand over hand. A creaking pulley lifted the brazier high overhead. It swung back and forth into stillness, dark smoke curling into the sky.

"What's that for?"

"You will see soon enough." Parr stepped back and gazed south.

I stood on my toes but couldn't see over the hedge. Then he pointed up. A pinprick floated above the horizon. As it drew nearer, I realized it was massive. Impossibly so.

A colossal bird glided toward us. The pale underside of its wings camouflaged it against the sky. It swooped low, beat its wings with a rush of air, and landed with a *thump*. It shuffled across the terrace on webbed feet and peered down at me. Its eyes were bright red, chest cotton-white, everywhere else black as soot except for white mottling on its long neck.

I clamped a hand to my mouth. There was no mistaking it. I'd grown up hearing stories and seeing carvings all over Aeti Ginu. I'd worn a shawl of it while trying to see into the parallel world. I had it tattooed on my left arm, hidden under my sleeve.

"Nei. But — kinaru are a myth," I stuttered. Anyone who claimed to have seen one was assumed to have had too much alcohol or not enough sleep.

Parr stroked its feathers. The bird clacked its pointed bill. "Before seeing one, I would not have believed in them either."

"They're sacred to tel-saidu. Suriel trusts you with one?"

"My Corvittai source is too busy fighting this war to act as intermediary. This is the only way to reach Suriel at Se Ji Ainu."

"The Pillared Mountain," I translated, ignoring his stilted pronunciation. Se Ji Ainu was an Iyo name. I wondered who taught it to him. "That's where we're going?"

"Yes." Parr placed a hand on the kinaru's side. It hunkered down and he swung onto its sloping back, settling between its wings and neck. He extended a hand to me.

Today we fly. I climbed up behind him and wrapped my arms around his waist. The kinaru ruffled its wings.

Parr bent close to the bird's head. "Take us to Suriel."

The kinaru soared over the Roannveldt, riding columns of warm air. Everything was tiny below us. Fields of pale blue flax grew among a hundred shades of green, packed together like fish scales and laced with creeks that flowed into the Stengar. When I turned to look for Caladheå, it was already lost in the fog.

I squeezed my eyes shut, feeling the kinaru's muscles flex and its feathers stir. I felt my heartbeat against Parr's back. His hair gusted into me, but I soon gave up trying to avoid it. I relaxed into the sensation of my own hair streaming behind me, the graceful rise and fall of the bird, the beautiful abandon of being untethered to the earth.

The Corvittai had hit hard. Black fields speckled the plain where we landed to rest. I wandered through the ashes of a pasture, stretching my aching legs. Flies and the stench of death drew me to a muddy pit near a log farmhouse. Seven bodies had been dumped inside, five the size of children. When I stumbled back to Parr, he gripped my hand in sympathy.

"I still see the face of the first child I found dead in his mother's arms," he said. "That day, I resolved not to rest until the Sverbian Rúonbattai and their allies were gone for good."

I felt too sick to eat but didn't want to pass out while riding the kinaru. Parr shared a parcel of salt pork and dried fruit with me. In an unburnt strip along a creek, I found bushes laden with salmon-berries and sour chokecherries, which he accepted with a wry smile.

Flying again, the flatlands gave way to forest. We curved north-east, cresting the mountains. Cold air forced into my lungs until I could barely breathe. The sun was high overhead when I spotted a thick band of glittering blue. With a jolt, I realized where we were.

On Tiernan's maps, Burren Inlet formed a cross in the mountains with Rutnaast on the west and Ingdanrad on the east. We were above Dúnravn Pass by the north beam of the inlet. Somewhere down there were the bodies of Tiernan's comrades.

We rose up and up, passing the tree line, sailing over endless sheets of ice, craggy rock, pristine snow unblemished by humans. My arms were numb, but the thought of falling kept them locked. Then, beyond the tip of the inlet, I saw it.

A vast platform atop a precipice, marked at each corner by jagged pillars. The rock shelf sloped down to a basin of brilliant turquoise water that spilled over in misty waterfalls and plummeted into chasms. A dozen kinaru floated across the lake, wings folded close to their bodies. Fog swirled up and wreathed the precipice.

Our kinaru sailed forward and dropped. I had a sudden flash of fear we'd crash into the mountain — but the bird wheeled over the water and skimmed the surface back toward the pillared platform. It dipped its feet into the lake, sending up icy spray as it glided into shore.

I tumbled into the shallows and splashed up to dry ground. My legs were as stiff as wood. Parr inhaled as he stepped into the cold water. Sunlight barely penetrated the mist, and the wind bit my skin. I hugged my chest. Waterproof boots but no cloak. So I was only half an idiot.

Parr unbuttoned his coat and draped it over my shoulders, enveloping me in warmth. "I am sorry, Kateiko. I should have found you some warmer clothes."

"Thank you," I stammered through chattering teeth. I tried to dry his breeches and boots, but the water ignored my call. It clung to the fabric, blank and unyielding.

I turned in a circle. Nothing fed into the basin to replenish water flowing out at the falls. The lake should've been frozen. I sensed its weight on the stony lakebed, the stirring of fog, droplets rolling off the kinaru behind us, but none of it responded.

"Is something wrong?" Parr asked.

"Nei. It's nothing." I pulled his coat tight around my body.

He leaned close to speak into my ear. "Be brave."

I tried to remember everything Fendul had told me about Suriel, something that'd tell me how to approach him. None of the ancient stories probably mattered. Suriel didn't seem the same anymore. What was Imarein Rin like? Brave, yes, to climb this mountain in a blizzard. Reckless. And utterly devoted to tel-saidu, enough to leave home and our shrine to the aeldu, even after his whole family died in war. If Suriel wanted devotion, I could tell enough of the truth.

We climbed the slope, dripping onto the rock. The pillars seemed hewn straight from the mountain. I craned my neck to see their summits as I followed Parr onto the platform. He sank to one knee in the centre. I knelt next to him, not sure what I was looking for until the haze parted.

A translucent figure floated at the far end, twice the height of any human, surrounded by trails of mist. Its blurred silhouette shifted like smoke. The changing light made it look as if a hood covered where a face might be.

You have returned. The hollow voice flowed across the precipice, pressing in from every side, whispering along the fine hair on my skin.

"I have brought someone who may be able to help you, Suriel," Parr said. I clung to his clear voice, my only comfort under a blue dome that weighed down on icy peaks. We were two shivering moths caught in a glacial wind.

I swallowed several times before my throat worked. I spoke in Aikoto, partly to appease Suriel, partly so that Parr wouldn't understand. "Suriel. I'm honoured to enter your territory." In my peripheral vision I saw Parr glance at me, but I pressed on. "I was born to the Rin-jouyen, the children of kinaru. When my companion here told me you want to reach the void, I wanted to help. To serve tel-saidu as we once did."

Suriel replied in perfect Rin dialect. *What do you offer?*

"The rift mage you want, Tiernan Heilind, refuses to help. I know another mage who might — but before I bring this person to you, I have questions. If I may ask."

Prove your worth first.

My whole life since the Storm Year had led to this point. No Rin was better suited than me.

"For seven years, I've been listening to the wind. My jouyen says I hear voices of the dead, but I always thought it was something greater. I left home, crossed the wasteland, and stood on the sky bridge, my people's ancient shrine to tel-saidu. It moved me in a way nothing else has. I knew then why Imarein left the Rin. Last winter in Crieknaast, I witnessed your windstorms and realized the best way I could serve you was communicating your wishes to other humans.

"I convinced the townspeople of Crieknaast to leave Dúnravn Pass. I arranged for the Okoreni-Iyo to teach foreigners of your existence and your strength. In Toel Ginu, I told the Okorebai-Iyo to let you raze the shrine. You agreed to spare the Iyo's lives, and I knew then you're not just strong, but gracious, too. Today, I betrayed the man I love to come here to you."

Suriel drifted closer, pulling clouds of vapour with him. He bent low. His misty hand forced my chin up. I stared into the faceless void, intensely aware he could feel everything — my breath, pulse, body heat. I felt Parr's hand on my elbow, but couldn't tear my gaze from the spirit.

The icy hand withdrew. *Ask your questions.*

I swallowed again. "Why do you want to reach the void?"

All I heard was the wind and rippling calls of kinaru. Then Suriel said, *Swear not to repeat this.*

"I swear. On the blood of kinaru."

I am no longer welcome in this world.

"By humans?"

By saidu.

I inhaled sharply, choking on the cold air. Suriel had always been an outlier. Maybe he didn't fight in the Storm Year because it was about him. No one knew how many saidu survived or what else they might do to get rid of him. "So . . . if you reach the void, that's it. You won't come back."

Yes. My army will disband. Other tel-saidu will fight over my territory. Humans will survive the storms if they avoid these mountains.

It could fix everything — and I couldn't tell anyone. But if Iannah was right that the Corvittai captain was Ferish, then an itheran had earned Suriel's trust somehow. Maybe Marijka could, too. "Would you be willing to meet this other mage?"

Name a time and place.

Every day risked more deaths, but I didn't know if Tiernan was home yet. Marijka wouldn't go without telling him. "Noon, two days from now. At the valley of stumps along Tømmbrind Creek."

Suriel circled us slowly. *Bring the mage only. Not your companion here.*

"So he told the truth? He's not serving you?"

He is not.

Parr, kneeling next to me, watched Suriel in silence. He had no idea we were discussing him.

"I — have one request." My hands clenched. This was the one part I hadn't told Marijka. "Promise you won't harm this mage. Or Tiernan Heilind. I'll take any consequences for their actions."

The wind picked up, spiralling through my hair. *They are precious to you.*

"Yes." I struggled to stay steady as my body swayed with the gusts.

The foreign mage interfered when I razed the shrine.

"He did it to save my family. As soon as they were safe, he let it burn."

I saw. I knew. Three thousand years I have watched humans. Children of kinaru only bring precious foreigners to their shrines. So I spared him.

"You . . . let him live . . . for me?"

For a Rin who has not forgotten. Long ago, the children of kinaru turned from my kind and built shrines to their human dead. You sacrificed one such shrine. For me. Mist curled around me, soaking through Parr's coat and my dress to my kinaru tattoo. *I agree to your request.*

I bent low, letting my hair brush the rocky ground. Parr bowed to Suriel and got to his feet. I stumbled after him back to the lake. Fog blurred my vision. My mind felt disconnected from my body, drifting among the glaciers. I unfolded my hands to see blood where my nails dug in. I waded into the shallows and washed them in the freezing water.

Parr put two fingers to his mouth and whistled. The piercing sound echoed off the crags. A kinaru glided across the lake toward us. Parr helped me onto its back and climbed up behind me. I slumped against him, too drained to care. The kinaru beat its vast wings, skidded across the surface with an upward rush of water, and launched into the air.

✻

Dark clouds had gathered over the ocean, their underside glowing red and orange like coals burning under ash. The kinaru deposited

314

us on the terrace at Parr Manor. I watched it vanish into the inky sky and didn't notice Parr looking at me until he spoke.

"Did Suriel answer your questions?"

"Yes. But I'm not allowed to tell anyone." I realized I was still wearing his coat. I held it out.

Parr draped it over his arm. "You did well, Kateiko."

I kicked at the flagstone. "We're still alive."

He looked west. "You should get home before this storm strikes."

"It won't matter much," I said without thinking.

"What do you mean?"

I floundered for an explanation, but nothing came to mind except the truth. "I . . . uh . . . live outdoors. My tent leaks."

"Goodness. You will catch your death." His voice was gentler than I expected. "You are welcome to spend the night here."

My eyes widened. "Councillor, I couldn't—"

"I insist. I could not rest knowing you are outside in a storm." He kissed my hand, avoiding the raw cuts. "Please. It would be my honour."

There was no reason to decline. Walking to Airedain's wasn't safe at the best of times, let alone when I hadn't slept in two days. I gave him a shy smile. "Thank you, sir."

❋

Parr lit candles and excused himself to the kitchen. I wandered the room in awe of everything. A brocade couch and chairs by a marble fireplace, paintings of battle scenes and ships in roiling waves, dark carved wood panelling over pale sandstone walls. The windows were murky, but the last trace of sunlight glimmered on a cluster of crystals that spilled from the high ceiling like a fountain.

It all seemed too beautiful to be real. Even the floor was ornate, with a woven rug laid over glossy squares of reddish wood. I recognized the pattern from the southern Yula-jouyen, the best weavers in our confederacy. I'd wiped the mud off my boots before coming inside, but I was so dusty from flying I was scared to touch anything.

"I am afraid this is all I have," Parr said when he returned with a wooden tray of bread rolls, fruit, and crumbling cheese. He set it on a low polished table by the fireplace. "How do you feel about wine with dinner?"

"I'm not sure. I haven't tried much. Just cranberry wine, and spiced wine once." Airedain and I had spent an evening in the Knox Arms trying Ferish drinks we couldn't pronounce, but brännvin was cheaper and stronger, even if it was like swallowing a headache.

Parr took a bottle from a cabinet and poured two glasses of deep red liquid. "See what you think of this. It is from southern Eremur. Many people insist imported wine from Ferland is better, but," he lowered his voice, "between you and me, my palate is not refined enough to tell the difference."

I took a sip. It was sweet and tart, like it couldn't decide what it wanted to be. "It's nice. Thank you, Councillor."

"Please, no need for formality here. I sometimes forget I have a first name, but you may call me Antoch outside the Colonnium."

"I'm not sure I can." I twisted my fingers around the stem of my glass.

"Whatever you are comfortable with." Parr settled at one end of the couch. He began slicing a melon with rough honey-coloured skin. A crisp scent like liquid summer burst from the orange flesh. "Sit wherever you like. I apologize for the dust. I spend far too much time at the Colonnium."

I hesitantly sat on a chair, sinking into the padding. "If you don't mind me asking . . . how did you know about Tiernan's research? It sounds like you knew before a Corvittai came to you."

"Heilind and I were good friends once. He took his first contract with the military the same year I became a captain. We fought the Rúonbattai together. I was grateful to have a mage, a way to use their power against them. It seems odd for a Sverbian national to fight his own kind, but he saw what their warmongering had done to us all."

"You said once you were away fighting the Rúonbattai when your wife died."

Parr nodded. "I was gone much of my son Nerio's childhood too, quelling conflicts across the province. Heilind was a great help — he mentored Nerio when they were assigned to the same company. Anyway, soon after I was elected to the Council, the mage registry became a major political issue. Heilind was a vocal proponent of eradicating it. We spent many long evenings discussing his work on rift magic over the course of that trial."

I pictured Tiernan in Council Hall, caught between rows of black-robed figures. It was a good thing marble didn't burn. "What happened? I mean, he . . . really doesn't like you now."

"The Dúnravn inquiry. I . . . admittedly erred by not defending Heilind's claim that Suriel was a spirit. It contradicted everything I was raised to believe. He took deep offence in the wake of his friend Jorumgard Tømasind's death." Parr realized he was cutting progressively smaller slices and set down the knife. "I fear what Heilind may have told you about me. Grief changes a man, twists his perceptions."

"He hasn't told me much. He never does."

"I appreciate your trust more than you know, Kateiko." Parr clinked our glasses. "I could not have persuaded the Council to defend our border from Suriel if you had not pushed for the Iyo nation to speak at the inquiry. Coaxing action from the government is like moving Council Hall one stone at a time."

I picked up a roll, smiling behind my curtain of tangled brown hair. "I have a secret. On the first day of the inquiry, Iann — um, Pelennus and I watched from the archer ledges. I heard you tell the entire Council off. That's why I came to you."

"Is that so?" He studied me over the rim of his glass. "I would not expect someone your age to take interest in politics."

"I did back home, but no one listened to me there." I bit into the soft roll and clapped my hand to my mouth. "Oh!" It was filled with deep red berry jam.

Parr chuckled. "*Pérossetto* bread. I recalled you had not tried it."

Grey sheets of rain began to fall as we talked, rattling the windowpanes. I winced the first time lightning shattered the darkness. Branches scraped the brick walls. Even in summer it felt like the aeldu were out there, shaking the willows and calling to me.

A draft chilled the room. Parr undid his collar and rolled up his sleeves to light a crackling fire. I stood next to him, soaking in heat from the flames. My body was exhausted, but my mind was wide awake, riding the stress of the last few days. I twisted a lock of matted hair behind my back. I looked awful. I was windswept and dusty, my dress grey from passing through Ashtown that morning. My hands shook. Maybe the lack of sleep was getting to me.

Parr looked just as bad. His hair was tangled below the ribbon tying it back. There were shadows under his eyes and dark stubble on his jaw. Up close, I could see his silk waistcoat had been mended with tiny stitches. He still had his slender knife on his belt. I felt a pang of familiarity — to live through war was to never feel safe.

"You don't have to stay up with me," I said. "I'm sure you must be busy tomorrow."

He finished stoking the logs and set the poker in an iron rack. "It is rare I am blessed with company, particularly that of such a spirited young lady."

I felt warm all of a sudden but didn't step back from the fire. "It must be lonely living here. I see why you spend so much time at the Colonnium."

"It must be lonely living outside." Parr looked at me. His lips parted slightly, but he said nothing else.

Thunder rolled, a long, low peal that resonated deep in my bones. "Antoch—" My tongue flicked through the unfamiliar sounds. I placed my hand on his chest, curling my fingers into his waistcoat, and pressed my lips to his.

He stiffened, not pushing me away, not returning the gesture.

I reeled back and clamped a hand to my mouth. "I'm sorry, I shouldn't have — I'm so sorry—"

"Kateiko." He pulled my hand down, an odd look on his face.

Then he was kissing me hard. He cupped the back of my head and nestled his other hand against my spine. My back arched as he gripped my hair. I inhaled the warm scent of his cologne and hooked my fingers over his collar, feeling his pulse in his throat—

But he was the first to pull away. He caressed my jaw with his thumb. "Darling girl," he murmured. "I cannot do this to you."

I traced my fingertips over his collarbone. "I want this, Antoch."

His expression twisted as if it hurt to touch me. "So do I. But not like this."

"What's wrong?" I blinked back sudden tears.

"You have been through so much today. You need rest." Parr released me and took a step back. "I am sorry, Kateiko."

※

I woke to blinding sunlight and a blanket tangled around my body. I was curled on the edge of a soft bed. I'd never been the type to forget where I was after waking, but it was disquieting to not remember falling asleep. After Parr showed me in here, everything faded into haze.

All the furniture in the white-painted room was made of glossy dark wood, from the bed to a chest of drawers to a table with a framed mirror, and everything was covered in a thick layer of dust. There was nothing to indicate who might've slept here before. Just a ceramic vase of dried flowers.

I sat up, twisting my bodice back into shape, and saw a paper on the carpet by the door. I scrambled out of bed and hurried across the room. A note with Parr's signature. I chewed my lip as I sorted letters into words, words into sentences. Parr had left for the Colonnium. I could eat whatever I wanted, and to please lock the door. Hopefully the sentence I didn't understand wasn't important.

I padded down the hall barefoot, passing portraits of the Parr family. One caught my eye. A boy with cropped dark hair and a smooth face, wearing a black coat with the elk sigil on the sleeve and braided red cord on the shoulders. The engraved plaque on the frame said *Nerio R. Parr*. Antoch's son. Even if he enlisted as young as possible, he'd be past twenty by now. Parr must've been younger than me when he had Nerio.

The hall doors were all shut, but I found the kitchen at the far end and spent a few minutes marvelling at it. Compared to the rest of the manor it was rough, with dull floorboards and soot stains in the brick fireplace, but everywhere I looked there were copper pots, glazed ceramic dishes, and iron tools I didn't know the name nor use of. Yet it took some searching to find actual food. I finally discovered *pérossetto* rolls and slices of dried apple in a cabinet. I filled a pewter mug with water and stared out the murky window at the overgrown lawn while I ate.

The sheets and blankets were filthy from all the dirt worn into me. I scrubbed them in the kitchen, wincing from the cuts my fingernails had made on my palms at Se Ji Ainu. I was nearly done drying the sheets when I remembered it was Iannah's day off. She expected me in Caladheå at noon. I peered outside and swore. Already late morning.

I left the unfolded bedding in the white room and hurried out a side door. The road was littered with willow leaves and broken twigs — not far off how my head felt. I braided my hair while I ran. It was shaping up to be a hot day, humid even on the Roannveldt.

Iannah was leaning on a tree at the bottom of Colonnium Hill. "You look like hell," she said.

"I'm aware, thanks." I doubled over panting, rested my palms on my knees, and flinched.

She took hold of my wrists and inspected the wounds. "What happened?"

"Doesn't matter. Look, I can't stay long. I have to go see Marijka."

"Why?"

"I can't tell you."

"Koehl." Iannah gave me a look. "Last week Parr sent me looking for you. This week you're late for the first time. What's going on?"

I sighed. She'd kept my secret about being Rin, at least, when any other soldier would've seen my kinaru tattoo as a link to Suriel. "Let's go somewhere quiet."

We stopped at Natzo's, bought cold noodles in hollowed-out wheat buns, and took our lunch to our favourite park in Bronnoi Ridge. Iannah said it was harder for people to eavesdrop in plain sight. We settled in the shade of a sprawling alder. Her perfectly flat Antler expression tightened as I told her about the past week and the planned meeting, leaving out only what I swore to Suriel I'd keep secret.

"You're walking a dangerous path," she said when I finished.

"It's our best chance. I have to try."

Iannah sat back against the alder, rubbing her bare arms. The heat had driven her to discard her coat on the grass. "What was Suriel like?"

I twirled a leaf. "Confusing. Not angry like everyone thinks. He . . . let Tiernan live after the shrine fire. For me."

"Huh." She looked up into the rustling branches. "His army's plenty willing to kill people."

My hand stilled. "Actually — maybe you can help me there."

"Killing people?"

"Nei, listen. I think Parr's source is the Corvittai captain. Suriel wouldn't let anyone else negotiate for him. It must be someone Parr trusts, maybe someone he fought the Rúonbattai with, who knows he and Tiernan were friends."

"Parr knows a lot of people, soldiers especially. The military is his entire life. Everyone says the war with the Rúonbattai never left him."

"Still, could you look into it? I want to know who it is and how they earned Suriel's trust. There's no point asking Parr again. I'm not sure I want to see him again anyway."

Iannah frowned as she picked up her waterskin. "Did he do something to you?"

"Nei!" I rolled onto my front so my face was muffled by grass. "I . . . uh . . . kissed him."

She spat water over her breeches. "*Why?*"

I tore up a clump of grass and threw it at her. "Isn't it obvious?"

"He's thirty-eight, Koehl. He's twice your age."

"Tiernan's thirty-two and you never said that was a problem."

Iannah held up her hands. "Do what you want with whoever you want. But if I was negotiating with Suriel, I wouldn't want any distractions."

"What, you don't think I can handle it?"

"You can't handle some little cuts." Her lips quirked up at the corners.

"Ai, just you watch." I tackled her. She flipped me onto my back and we rolled across the grass until she pinned me down, one hand on my arm and the other on my ribs, my skirt tangled around my legs. A Ferish woman with dark curly hair shot us a dirty look and pulled her son close.

With sunshine warming my skin and grass tickling my neck, Se Ji Ainu felt a world away. If this was to be the last time I saw Iannah, I wanted to remember her like this, the way her hair glowed red and she only ever smiled with her lips pressed together as if she had a secret.

26.

SILENCE & STILLNESS

I tracked down Airedain at Segowa's stall, saying only that I didn't know when I'd be back. He jabbed my ribs and gave me a tight hug. I clung to his skinny frame, hoping he wouldn't hear news about me like he had about Nokohin. Then I braced myself and headed north on the hike to Marijka's home.

Her yard was empty. "Hello?" I called.

"Over here," Marijka's voice drifted from down the creek.

She was on the shady bank braiding reeds picked from the shallows. Vivid green ropes sprawled across the grass. I sat next to her and dangled my feet in cool water, a relief from the muggy air.

"It's hard to be inside," she said. "A few months ago I didn't think my house was lonely, but when I know what I'm missing . . ."

The knot in my stomach tightened. "Tiernan's still gone?"

"Yes. Though three days is nothing. He disappeared for months after I refused his first marriage proposal."

I hugged her. It didn't feel like the right time to tell her about my trip to Se Ji Ainu, but we only had a day. I couldn't help checking over my shoulder as I talked.

"You can choose not to meet Suriel tomorrow," I said. "He doesn't know who you are or where you live. But I don't know if he'll give us another chance."

"Do you think he'll keep his word about not retaliating?"

"Maybe. You were at Crieknaast's military hospital last week, healing the soldiers opposing him. If he didn't kill you for that, I don't see why he would now."

She sighed, twisting reeds with deft motions. "I understand why you can't tell me his secret. Breaking an oath to a spirit is never a good idea. So if you believe he has good reason for wanting to reach the void, I believe you. But it's more complicated than just figuring out how to open a rift."

"What else is there?"

"When Tiernan and I . . . had our fight, I asked if he had burned his research for any reason besides marrying me. He admitted he doesn't know how to *close* a rift. He didn't want people crossing back and forth between shoirdrygen. That gets complicated fast."

"But if you opened one to the void — there's nothing there, right? It's between worlds."

"Which also means it might touch every shoirdryge. Then if every version of Suriel gets a mage to open a rift, the void would become a network between worlds, like the tunnels through the mountains. Millions of years from now, all these rifts could still be open. There's no saying how other shoirdrygen might develop over time or what might come through to our world."

I sucked in a breath. It seemed obvious spoken aloud. "Maybe Suriel has a way around that. Maybe he can seal a rift, just not open it. Saidu are meant to repair things."

"Perhaps. We don't know enough." Marijka set down another reed braid. "So . . . I suppose we ask Suriel tomorrow."

✳

We met the next morning outside her house. Marijka just shook her head. Tiernan wasn't back.

"I can ask Suriel to come again later—" I began.

"No," she said. "Every day we lose is another body I have to patch up in Crieknaast. Or one I can't fix."

She didn't talk much on the way. My attention stayed northeast, listening for the rustle of leaves. All I heard was the squelch of Anwea and Gwmniwyr's hooves on the muddy creek bank. Mist steamed away as sunlight heated the rainforest.

"Hang on," I said hours later at the first glimpse of rotten stumps. I slid off Anwea and passed the reins to Marijka. "Careful with her. I don't think horses will like this."

I'd never shown Marijka my attuned form, but of all itherans, I didn't mind her knowing. I closed my eyes and sank into my other body. Paws, bushy tail, silver fur — and a wolf's sharp senses. Anwea's startled *whuff* of breath felt like it was right next to my ears. A fresh scent burst from the ferns she trampled.

I pushed away the part of my mind aware of Marijka's gaze and focused on the valley ahead. Running water, scampering rodents, singing wrens two leagues away. I smelled the hot blood of rabbits deep in their burrows, but not of other horses or humans. So Suriel hadn't brought any Corvittai. I shifted back before Anwea got any more disturbed.

"It's beautiful," Marijka said. "Your wolf form."

I half-smiled. It was a lot of things to me, but *beautiful* wasn't one of them.

We rode into the valley, pushing into a mat of fireweed speckled with purple buds. The few alder saplings looked sickly, their leaves bruised, their bark weeping pitch. A ring of blackened stumps marked Tiernan's wall of fire that protected us from Suriel's rune last winter.

The place still felt wrong. Now I realized why. The loggers had fled during spring in the Storm Year. Fireweed quickly took over, helping the valley recover as it always did after disasters, usually forest fires. In late summer, near the end of the storms, the edim-saidu that managed the region's plants had died. The rainforest cycle got stuck in recovery. Stumps stayed half-rotten, woodchips underfoot stayed intact, trees couldn't grow.

All that moved was the creek, carrying leaves that whirled and dipped in the current. The clear sky curved down to the horizon like a blue bowl laid upside down over the world. Anywhere else, the mild, still heat would've been perfect. Here, the motionless saplings looked like watching ghosts.

I dismounted and peered at the sun high overhead. "It's noon. Suriel's meant to be here."

Marijka reached out, feeling the air. "I don't sense any magic. If this is a trap, it's well hidden."

"Suriel!" I called. "I've brought the mage!"

Silence. Stillness. I approached the loggers' buildings on the bank. My hand thrummed tense as snare wire as I touched a sun-bleached plank door. Nothing happened. Tiernan must've done something special to trigger Suriel's rune. Or it didn't work anymore.

Inside the dim room, cool, damp air filled my lungs. Mildew-stained bunks lined the walls. Old bootprints crossed the dirty floor. I checked the other plank buildings — a kitchen with a square of soot where an oven once sat, a shed with pegs to hang tools, another shed of empty crates. Everything must've been looted. I found only a few black threads snagged on splintered wood, then gave up and headed back outside.

Marijka held out a handful of soggy alder leaves. "These must've fallen into the creek recently. They're still intact."

I looked upstream. The logged area continued on beyond a bend of the creek. I swung onto Anwea. "Let's go see."

We rode along the reedy bank until the forest edge came into view. Between us and the wall of healthy trees, wind-thrown saplings crossed the ground. One lay with its crown in the water. Its leaves were torn off, roots scoured clean of dirt, bark drenched like water had been flung up from the creek.

I shivered. "It looks like Suriel came this far and stopped. But I've got no idea *why*."

"Maybe something happened back in the mountains?"

"Maybe." I gazed over the treetops at the eastern range, stark against the blue sky. If we left, we might not get another chance to talk with Suriel. And if he found another mage, that person might not care about closing the rift.

"What do you think?" Marijka said. "Do we wait for Suriel to return?"

I shook my head. "Something's gone wrong. I want to know what before we do anything else."

*

I accompanied Marijka home, then rode on toward Caladheå alone. Asking Iannah if she'd heard anything from Crieknaast seemed like the safest way to start. If needed, I could pry Parr for info. Slowly, I was fitting iron links into a chain that made sense, but so many pieces were missing.

At the edge of North Iyun Bel, overlooking Caladheå, I realized what I'd missed. Suriel could only be stopped by one thing. Other saidu.

I'd assumed every saidu in this part of the rainforest was dead. But the creek kept going, from mountains to sea, unlike the dried-up river through the wasteland. Snow and rain fell, fog came and went, the well Tiernan dug worked as intended. I'd never had a vision into another world the whole time I lived at his cabin. A water spirit lived here somewhere, repairing the barrier so I couldn't see through it.

I swung Anwea around. It was a solid hour to the nearest stretch of creek, but I had to be sure. She cantered back up the path, veered off through the underbrush, and plowed into the cold water. It churned around her, splashing against my calves.

How could I talk to a spirit that had no interest in humans? I called out, not surprised when nothing responded. I lifted an arc of water. Nothing. I tossed my weapons and purse on a high shelf of the bank, slid off Anwea, and plunged underwater. Minnows skittered through the murk. I kicked off the bottom, stirring up silt.

Maybe the anta-saidu would pay attention if I didn't go away. I stood waist-deep in the creek and waited. And waited. Anwea wandered downstream out of sight. A duck swam past, probably wondering what I was doing. My legs ached with cold.

I climbed dripping onto the grass. Wotelem had said an Iyo elder could sense saidu. I sat cross-legged and tried to meditate. Heat shifted across my head as the sun moved through the sky. A thrill of trepidation shot through me when I sensed motion in the water — but it was just Anwea returning.

If the anta-saidu did nothing except its duty, I'd have to interfere. I braced myself against a cottonwood, lowered my mind into the creek, and pushed against the current, forming an invisible wall. Slowly I spread it wider. The immense weight felt like it was crushing my skull. Sweat ran down my back. I imagined Isu, my mother, and Emehein all watching. Waiting to see if my antayul training paid off.

My wall reached both banks. Water flooded sideways into the forest, leaving the rocky creek bed bare. Anwea snuffled at empty air around her. Rivulets ran past her hooves.

Then, like a punctured waterskin, my wall ruptured. Anwea galloped onto the bank as the creek rushed down its bed toward her. A twisting column of water rose from the surface. I gasped. For once, I was sure I hadn't called it by accident.

"Do you . . . understand me?" I asked, but the column just kept twisting.

There had to be a way to ask it about Suriel. I called a flat plane of water, like a floating tabletop, over the soaked bulrushes. Matching it to my memory of Tiernan's maps, I formed spires for the eastern mountains and bumps for the lower slopes across North Iyun. I blew on the map, sending ripples through the mountains around Se Ji Ainu.

Something nudged my mind, pressing inwards. It felt different than sharing control with other antayul. This was deeper, slower, stronger. The ripples continued west across the watery slopes. Halfway along the map, a miniature column rose from the creek. The ripples struck it, then receded. So I was right — the anta-saidu didn't let Suriel enter its territory.

"But Suriel's come here before—" I began before remembering speech was pointless. Maybe he snuck in to set the rune on the loggers' building. It didn't really matter.

As I wondered how to ask *why* the anta-saidu didn't want Suriel around, it began showing me something else on the map. It raised another miniature column in the foothills near Crieknaast. A second water spirit in the creek, one west and one east.

The map warped, starting in the eastern range and radiating out. It sizzled and steamed. Mist coalesced and rained flecks of ice. The Storm Year — earthquakes, volcanoes, snowstorms. Then, abruptly, the east column disintegrated. That anta-saidu must've died in the storms. Suriel had been able to move freely around Crieknaast because the saidu there was dead.

Before I could ask anything else, my map dissolved. The pressure in my head eased. The saidu retreated, fading into waves. I felt a stir underwater as it glided upstream. Odd. Maybe I'd always sense its presence now, just like my mind learned how to see the shoirdryge.

I retrieved Anwea and spurred her into a canter along the bank. Suriel might not have gone back to Se Ji Ainu. Maybe Marijka and I could track him down.

Then I rounded a bend. Anwea pulled up suddenly, her glossy brown hide foamy with sweat. Tiernan stood on the bank ahead, hand on his sword hilt, staring at us. Twigs stuck in his tangled hair like he'd been sleeping on the ground.

In the distance, slivers of white light shone through the foliage. He didn't seem to have noticed. Maybe my crashing through the forest had just woken him.

"Leave," he said.

"Tiernan—"

"You knew what would happen if you told Maika about Suriel."

"I didn't know you'd storm off and leave her alone for four days! Where have you been?"

He edged Hafelús from its sheath. "I said leave."

"*Nei.* Shut up and listen." I fought to hold Anwea still. She snorted, annoyed at her run being cut short. "Maika doesn't want to do this without you. So you're going back there with me right now to apologize to her. We've got bigger issues than your marital problems."

"Just because Parr chose you as messenger does not mean you have a right to get involved. This is between my wife and me—"

"Then go *talk* to her instead of being such an aeldu-cursed coward!"

We faced each other down, leaf shadows playing across us. If it came to a fight, I had the advantage with the creek, but I'd never truly tested my water-calling against his fire.

Splashes and thudding hooves broke the silence. Gwmniwyr galloped down the shallows toward us. The gelding never spooked at anything.

"*Hjalag!*" Tiernan stepped into the creek. Gwmniwyr careened aside into deep water and slowed, tossing his mane. Tiernan grabbed his halter, speaking a rapid stream of foreign words.

Waves crashed up the banks. It looked like wind cleaving the surface, but I felt the anta-saidu streak toward us and wheel just past Gwmniwyr. It'd driven the horse here on purpose.

I peered northeast at the white light. "Oh, kaid."

Tiernan followed my gaze. He swung onto Gwmniwyr and rode off at a gallop. I urged Anwea after them, clinging to her neck as she crashed through the underbrush, swerving trees and jumping logs.

Only a human could set off Tiernan's warning runes, otherwise they'd light up every time there was a storm. I kept my sight fixed on Tiernan as we streaked along the bank. If he came face to face with a Corvittai in his home—

Anwea flinched as we passed through blinding light into Marijka's yard. The paddock fence was splintered. I slid to the ground, the reins slithering out of my hand. Colourful spots danced across my vision. I squinted at the house through runes seared onto my eyes. The door hung wide open.

"Maika!" Tiernan sprinted up the dirt path.

I barrelled into him in the doorway. A sweet burnt smell filled my nose. Something crunched underfoot. I looked down and saw dried herbs ground into dust.

"No. No." Tiernan's voice was hollow. I peered past him into the kitchen.

Marijka was sprawled on the floor in a pool of blood, the front of her bodice stained dark. She stared wide-eyed at the wall.

Tiernan fell to his knees, collapsing on her body. The sound of his quiet sobbing filled me with an ache greater than I'd ever known.

I backed out of the house and ran. The white light faded. All I could hear was my ragged breath, feet thudding on moss and dirt, weapons clanking on my belt. I ran as far from the creek as possible. When my lungs felt clogged and pain shot through my sides, I grabbed a branch and swung up. I climbed higher and higher until I broke the canopy.

"Where are you, Suriel?" I shouted. A flock of birds rose shrieking into the air. "Come face me! The anta-saidu can't stop you here!"

Silence. Stillness.

"You promised to take me instead! It's not her fault! She didn't do anything wrong!" I leaned into the sky, swaying on a branch. "Is this your way out? You promised *you* wouldn't hurt her, so you sent a human? You fucking liar! Cheat!"

I screamed until my throat was raw and my voice grated into silence. Then I pulled together as much water as I could muster. Dark clouds churned into a seething mass. Rain poured down, drenching my clothes through to my skin, battering leaves until they tore.

No reply. Suriel was gone.

27.

WHITE WOMAN

I dragged myself back hours later. Tiernan lay next to Marijka, his fingers knotted into her pale hair. Evening light bathed them in a warm glow. Glass shards glittered around them like stars. The burnt scent lingered from a pot hung over glowing coals, twisting my stomach into nausea. I gestured as if beckoning the fire down. Water splashed onto it and hissed away into steam.

All I found near the house was a reddish smear on the grass. I sliced the turf and flipped it over, leaving a scar of dirt. I groomed the horses without being aware of the motions. I couldn't figure out how to extinguish the runes, so I resigned myself to the glaring light that radiated into the sky like a beacon.

As darkness fell over Iyun Bel, I sat against the stable with my head on my arms. I couldn't cry. Even the shoirdryge looked more real in those brief glimpses than Marijka's lifeless figure. After they carried my parents back from the battlefield it'd been days before I cried.

Eventually the practical side of the situation sank in. I didn't know Sverbian funeral rites. I didn't even know where to dig a grave. But I couldn't bring myself to rouse Tiernan.

"Kateiko."

My head snapped up. Rhonos stepped out from the trees, longbow in hand.

I sagged against the wall. "Aeldu save me. Stop doing that."

"I saw the light from the plain. What happened?"

I pointed at the house. In hindsight I should've said there was no danger, because he pulled a dagger from under his cloak and crept up the path. He stopped in the doorway, lowered his blade, and slumped against the doorframe.

Rhonos was the best person who could've come. He knelt next to Tiernan and spoke in a low voice, coaxing him to get up. Then he lifted Marijka with all the gentleness of a father carrying a child, set her in the bedroom, and asked me to bring a sheet to cover her.

"Her wedding ring is gone," was all Tiernan said.

Rhonos gripped Tiernan's shoulders. "We will have to send her off without it."

I watched with confusion as Rhonos found leftover boards and nailed them together. He explained it was a raft to put Marijka on. Rin buried our dead, but I trusted him to know what Tiernan wanted.

He told me to get some rest, but between the hammering and harsh runelight, sleep was impossible. Instead, I lay in the garden between rows of curling beanstalks, damp soil chilling my bones, and cottonwood fluff tickling my skin. I stared into the sky until the sun rose.

We carried Marijka to the creek and laid her on the raft, her pale hands folded over the silver bodice of her wedding gown. I whispered the Rin death rites and scattered white petals over her body. Tiernan built a pyre of rioden branches above her, set them alight, and pushed the raft into the current. He sang a haunting Sverbian elegy as she drifted toward the ocean. His voice hung in the air long after he finished.

*

The runelight faded by mid-afternoon. Rhonos told me not to go off alone, even to gather food, so we picked vegetables from the garden. I couldn't eat without thinking how they'd grown under Marijka's gentle care.

I set to cleaning the kitchen. Her decorative plates with pictures of Nyhemur lay shattered. Mangled leaves covered the floor, mixed with dirt, broken glass, and dried herbs. As I swept, I found sparkling grey fragments by the fireplace. Tiernan's stone wolf makiri.

No matter how hard I scrubbed, the dark stain wouldn't wash out of the floorboards. I finally slammed my flail into it, tore up the splintered wood until my hands bled, and burned the fragments outside. Marijka deserved the peace of having her blood return to the earth.

Rhonos repaired the paddock fence and tended to Anwea and Gwmniwyr. He didn't have Tiernan's natural ease with horses, but he had a quiet confidence that made them listen to him. I went back to washing vegetables after he noticed me watching. By evening, we ran out of chores and wound up on the grass in front of the house. Long shadows fell across the yard. Clouds of mosquitoes came out, their drone filling the warm air. I swatted at them a few times before giving up.

Rhonos was the first to speak. "I found tracks. One person heading east on foot. The trail stops at a pond a quarter of a league into the forest."

"I didn't see any tracks."

"Then you did not search hard enough."

"We're not all as skilled as you," I muttered, and shrank back as he gave me a look that could wilt a rioden.

No doubt the tracks ended because the Corvittai left on a kinaru. That'd be why the anta-saidu bothered to get our attention. It didn't care about humans entering its territory, but knew a kinaru meant Suriel.

Rhonos laced his fingers together. "Tiernan told me you asked Marijka to help Suriel. What happened while he was away?"

"I don't know." My voice sounded hollow.

"Maika must have contacted Suriel, then changed her mind." Tiernan appeared behind us. His gaze was fixed far away as if he was looking through the surface of the world. "That is why the Corvittai took her wedding ring. A message of what will happen to me if I refuse again."

"Hardly anyone knows you were married." Rhonos eyed me. "Only those who were at the wedding."

"One other person knew." Tiernan crumpled onto the grass. "You were right, Rhonos. Someone threw me under the cart."

"Who?" Rhonos shook his shoulder. "Tiernan. Who was it?"

"Antoch Parr."

I clamped a hand over my mouth. I suddenly felt like throwing up.

Rhonos was silent for a long moment. "Are you sure?"

Tiernan jerked his head at me. "*She* told him about our marriage. Parr must have told Suriel to take the ring."

"He wouldn't do that," I said before I could stop myself.

Rhonos raised an eyebrow. "What would you know about Councillor Parr?"

My cheeks grew hot. "Nothing. But Suriel wouldn't take orders from anyone."

"Suriel has never shown any trace of love, loyalty, or emotion," Tiernan said. "I am not sure saidu can even comprehend what motivates humans."

He didn't know Suriel spared his life solely because I loved him. He'd never know. I stumbled to the creek, stepped into knee-deep water and threw up, silently apologizing to the anta-saidu.

※

I lay by the creek that night, listening to the burble of water and chirp of crickets. A few days ago, I hadn't been sure I'd ever return here, yet now my words seemed more important than ever. *I'll always come back. I promise.*

For once I heard Rhonos's soft footfalls. He settled next to me and gazed at the creek glittering in the moonlight. The cottonwood branches were a roof sheltering us from the night. Rhonos was far from my first choice of confidant, but he was all I had right now.

"I have to tell you something." I kept my eyes fixed on the branches so I didn't see his disapproving look. "I arranged the meeting with Suriel."

After I explained, Rhonos said, "Give me one good reason not to put an arrow in your heart."

"I didn't mean for this to happen—"

"Yet it did, and you went behind Tiernan's back."

"He wasn't here! How long were we supposed to wait? Months, while a war goes on around us?"

"You could have gotten help," he snapped. "Marijka did trust other people."

I glared at him. "Like you? Where have you been since their wedding?"

"Not getting our mutual friends killed through adolescent stupidity."

"You're barely older than me!"

"Far less naïve though."

"Aeldu save me — you're so fucking—" I tore up a handful of grass. "Look, I messed up. I admit that. But I'm asking for your help now, so *help* me. We need to figure all this out. Tiernan could be in danger."

Rhonos drew an arrow from his quiver and notched it with his dagger. "This is marked for you. Consider your death on standby."

"Fine. Whatever." I edged away. "Do you think Tiernan's right? It's a message?"

"No. I think Corvittai came to fetch Marijka and she resisted, simple as that."

"Why bother taking her wedding ring?"

"Petty theft. They are mercenaries, not paid well enough for war. The real question is how they knew she was the mage you told Suriel about. Did anyone see you at the logging camp?"

"Nei. No one was there."

"No one in human form."

I threw grass at him. "Don't start. I've heard the military reports — not a single viirelei has been found among the Corvittai."

Rhonos shrugged.

"What if they checked Eremur's mage registry and narrowed it down to Maika?"

"The registry is restricted. Only government officials can access it."

My stomach twisted again, though there was nothing left in it. "You don't think Parr . . ."

"No. He and Tiernan have had their disagreements, but everyone has limits. Parr never got over his own wife's death. He would not risk putting a close friend through the same grief."

"Then you have to convince Tiernan. Before he goes after Parr for revenge."

"Tiernan is not easily convinced." Rhonos lay back, his long dark hair splaying across the grass, and folded his hands over his chest. "He never forgets I am a decade younger than him. He trusted Jorumgard far more."

"He asked you to be his *stjolvind* at his wedding."

"Marijka asked you to be her *stjolvehl*. Yet we failed them both."

I dug my fingernails into the dirt. The evil spirits we were meant to protect them from didn't feel like a myth anymore.

Rhonos looked over at me. His anger seemed to have burned through. "I want to look into Marijka's death. It will be easier for me than you to get near the Corvittai. You must keep Tiernan here where Suriel cannot reach him."

"Tiernan won't listen to me. He'll fire that arrow himself once he knows I dealt with Suriel."

"Do not tell him yet. Only that the creek spirit will keep Suriel away."

"You just lectured me for hiding things—"

"That was when Marijka was alive. You *must* stay with Tiernan now. No one else has a way of communicating with the creek spirit. Do you understand? I will help you confess when I return."

"Fine." I rolled over, curling into a ball so my head was near Rhonos's chest. My skull felt too full of mush to care what he thought. I just wanted to be near someone. "I'm so fucking tired."

"Here." Rhonos unfolded a bundle and draped a blanket over me.

"Thank you," I murmured. My eyes watered. I could barely keep them open. The last thing I said before giving into darkness was, "When will you be back?"

"As soon as possible."

✳

Rhonos left the next morning. Too late I realized I should've suggested he track down Iannah. Not that it probably mattered — if she figured out who the Corvittai captain was, she could send Airedain to look for me.

I stood in the bedroom doorway, holding a folded cloth full of vegetables. Tiernan was slumped against the wall as if he'd given up on making it into bed. "Tiernan. You need to eat." I knelt and touched his arm. "Tiernan."

No response. No indication he knew I was there.

He was like a person asleep. Like his spirit walked in another world. It occurred to me maybe our bodies didn't have to die for our spirits to cross over. Maybe death was a place in our minds we sometimes found before our bodies were ready.

After a day of cooking in Marijka's kitchen, with a hole in the floorboards and dried herbs ground into every corner, I decided it wasn't necessary to stay in her house. We just had to be in the anta-saidu's territory. I felt it drift through the rainforest sometimes, maintaining ponds and brooks around the creek. I tacked a note to the door for Rhonos, built a stone cairn pointing north just in case, packed supplies onto the horses, and half-led, half-dragged Tiernan to his old cabin.

Days slid past. I slept in the clearing, huddled with my fir blanket, too worn out to be afraid. Nhys brought rye bread and salted goat from the Blackened Oak, saying Rhonos sent him. The Sverbian cleric who officiated Tiernan and Marijka's wedding came by and read from a book labelled with the nine-branched tree. Friends of theirs stayed a night or two and helped with the chores. Tiernan barely noticed them. I visited the spot where we sent Marijka down the creek and found fresh yellow flowers bundled with thread.

Still I didn't cry. I wondered if there was something wrong with me. Maybe my spirit had detached from my body, leaving me stuck repeating the same motions day after day. I wondered if that was better or worse than ending up like Tiernan.

I passed time between chores by reading my folklore book. When I knew the short stories by heart, I moved on to longer ones. The pages creased with use. I was reading by firelight in the clearing when I found a story I'd started in winter and given up on. I squinted at the pages, determined to finish.

A wise woman knew the ways of healing, so people came from all over begging her to mend their wounds and cure their sicknesses. She healed everyone who asked, but when she fell ill no one knew how to cure her. After death, her spirit walked the earth and helped those who spoke her name. People said she always appeared in the moonlight clad in a white dress.

I shut the book. I threw water on the fire and searched the sky until I found the constellation of Orebo, breaker of moon and maker of stars. Was Marijka up there, a fragment of the moon where she belonged? Would she return to this world if I called her? Would I be able to face her if she did?

There was no happy ending to Marijka's story. No constellations named after her. But I had to believe she was out there somewhere. If not on earth or in the sky, if not across the ocean in Thaerijmur or just out of reach in Aeldu-yan, her spirit would live on in my mind. I'd tell stories about the wise woman who helped everyone she met, whose blood I put in the ground.

Finally, finally, I cried.

28.

TO LOVE A SOLDIER

I smelled a storm one day and put the horses in the stable while dark clouds rolled over. I stood in the cabin doorway watching rain thrash the clearing and lightning streak the sky. Gusts spattered drops on my bare legs. It was a normal midsummer storm, the kind that shows up in late afternoon long enough to cool the air.

"Is Suriel coming?" Tiernan was on the floor by the fireplace, resting his head on his hands.

"Nei. He can't get past the creek spirit, remember."

He was silent so long I thought that was the end of it. Then he said, "Maika would still be alive if she had not married me."

"She knew what she was getting into." That was my only comfort. Marijka had gone into our plan willingly, as brave as any warrior.

Tiernan raised his head. His beard had grown out, not quite hiding the hollowness under his cheekbones. His tan had faded.

"She was the one bright spot in my life. When everyone else gave up on me, she was still there."

"Not everyone." I stepped inside, my fingers trailing along the doorframe.

"I feel old beyond my years. My path has ended." He rubbed the scar on his nose. "There will never be anyone like her. It is not an easy thing to love a soldier."

"I know." My voice didn't waver. No thunder drowned out my words. But he didn't look at me.

Tiernan tilted his head as if listening to the rain. "If Suriel cannot come here, I must go to him."

"Why?"

"He sent me a message. I have a response."

"You—" My breath caught. "We've been over this. Even Rhonos said no one knows how to kill a saidu."

"Everything that lives can die."

I knelt and took his cold hands in mine. He'd been spared once for my sake, but nothing would save him if he was trying to kill Suriel outright. "The wind dies a thousand deaths. You only get one."

"Maika is not the first person I led into Suriel's path. Jorum stayed at Dúnravn because I asked." Tiernan stood, pulling away from me, and took his scabbard from a nail by the door. Hafelús rang as he drew it. He flipped the blade over, studying the edge. "I must make amends to those who have gone to Thaerijmur before me."

"This isn't about being noble, or — whatever you think it is! It's suicide!"

"I am a soldier. When I die, it will be in battle."

Something inside me cracked. I couldn't let him do this. Nor could I wait any longer for Rhonos to return.

"Tiernan . . ." I gripped the stone mantlepiece, drawing on its steadiness. "Maika's death wasn't a message."

He stilled. Lightning glinted off his sword.

My words came out in a rush. "I'm the one who told Suriel she might be willing to open a rift. Maika and I went to meet him in the valley of stumps, but the creek spirit had driven him off. He must've sent Corvittai to get her instead. I never mentioned her name or where she lived — but somehow he found out. I'm so, so sorry."

Whenever I'd thought about confessing, I imagined the heat of his rage. The cabin burning, rainforest steaming, ash filling my lungs like the shrine fire. But there was nothing. Just cool rain striking the doorstep.

"I let you into my home," he said slowly. "Into my life. I thought asking Maika to help Suriel was the most you would dare betray me. Instead you went straight to him."

"We would've told you if you were here. You wouldn't even discuss it with us!"

Tiernan knocked the table over with a crash and forced me against the mantelpiece, his calloused hand on my throat. "After all my warnings—"

I choked out a laugh. "You going to kill me? My life for Maika's?"

He seized a fistful of my shirt and threw me clear over the fallen table. "Get out. Before I change my mind."

Wincing, I scrambled up. "Tiernan, I'm *sorry*—"

He crossed the small room and slammed me into the log wall. "Get. Out."

I coughed, clutching my chest. "You don't know anything! I offered to die for you and Maika. I tried to protect her. You *weren't here!*"

Tiernan pressed Hafelús against my neck, its edge stinging like hot iron, a single point of fire. Blood trickled down my skin. The realization slithered over me, cold and wet. *He might really kill me.*

I grabbed his wrist. Ice crackled across Hafelús. He let go in shock, the blade clanging to the floor. Crystal shards exploded across us. I raised my other hand to strike him, but he pinned it to the wall.

"Tiernan," I breathed. "Look at me. Please."

He trembled, staring at a point somewhere over my shoulder.

Tears broke free and streamed down my face. "Aeldu curse it, I'm right here! Just fucking look at me!"

Tiernan shoved me toward the door. He wrestled me halfway through before I got ahold of the frame, digging my nails into the wood. I planted my feet into the floorboards, my body wedged against his, our ribs pressed together. Sheets of rain blew into us.

"Why?" he asked hoarsely. "Why won't you go?"

"I can't let you die too." I cupped his jaw with my free hand and pulled his face toward me. His beard was rough under my palm. "I don't want to lose you, Tiernan. If I mean anything to you — please—"

I kissed him, twining my fingers into his dark hair like I'd dreamt of for so long. His lips were cracked and dry. Raindrops slid down his face. I loosed my nails from the doorframe and slid my arm around him, but there was no warmth left. My burning man had gone out.

His eyes met mine. In that moment I knew. I was one of his ghosts. No matter how much I pleaded or how loud I screamed, my voice could no longer drown out the voices in the wind, because mine was one of them now.

I fished the fragments of the wolf makiri from my purse, pressed them into Tiernan's palm, and folded his fingers over the cold stone. My lips formed words, but made no sound.

I love you.

And I stepped into the rain.

*

The Blackened Oak bustled with people and chatter. I leaned over the bar and managed to get Nhys's attention while he filled a row of mugs. "I'm looking for Rhonos Arquiere. Have you seen him?"

Nhys glanced up and down the bar. He passed out the mugs and beckoned me into a quiet corner. "I don't normally give out info about patrons, but he should be back tonight. How's Tiernan holding up?"

"Not well. That's why I need Rhonos."

Nhys grimaced and clapped a hand on my shoulder. "Dinner be on the house if you want to wait around."

I curled up on a log bench and picked at baked cod and rutabaga. I was still wearing Rin summer clothes, but my cloak covered my tattoos and bare skin — and the bruises from the fight. People trickled upstairs to their rooms as the evening waned. I was nodding off when I heard my name.

Rhonos stood next to me, longbow strapped to his back. His hood concealed his face, but I recognized his moss-green cloak and leather wristguard. "Come. Let us talk outside."

We went behind the pub, away from pools of light spilling out the windows. Flies buzzed around barrels reeking of offal. Horses shuffled and nickered in the stable. I made sure we were alone, then said, "Tiernan's decided to challenge Suriel. He's going to get himself killed."

Rhonos muttered something that was probably a Ferish curse. "Where is he now?"

"Hopefully still at his cabin. I told the creek spirit not to let him leave, or he and Suriel would burn Iyun Bel to its roots. I'm not sure it understood though."

"You promised to stay with him."

"He tried to kill me!" I jabbed at the red line across my neck. "I can't stop him leaving if my blood's in the ground!"

Rhonos closed his eyes. "You told him."

"I had to do something. *You* promised to come back. I've been taking care of him for half a month—"

"I apologize. I got held up."

Only then did I notice the rips in his cloak and a faded gash on his hand. "Where?"

"Crieknaast. Apparently Marijka magically healed soldiers in their military hospital, and plenty of townsfolk knew she often travelled there with Tiernan. That could be enough for Suriel to piece together that she was the mage you offered."

"But those soldiers wouldn't have sold her out to Suriel. Not after she saved their lives."

"Gossip spreads, especially in cramped barracks." Rhonos pulled a crumpled paper from his pocket. "I found this on the body of a soldier wearing the elk sigil."

I took it, pinching the corner between my thumb and fingertip. "You were searching dead bodies? Gross."

He gave me that withering look he was so good at. "It contains map coordinates to a site near Crieknaast. I found a Corvittai camp there. Either the soldier was aiding them, or he was a Corvittai in disguise. There is not much difference in the end."

My eyes flickered to his wounded hand. "Was he dead when you found him?"

"The point is, there may be far more at stake. I returned to Caladheå to find out how high up the military the traitors run."

I studied the paper. All it had other than numbers was a single word. "What's this mean? 'Nonil?'"

"A navigational aid, most likely." Rhonos tucked the paper back into his pocket. "We should find Tiernan. He may be more for-giving if he learns it was not entirely your fault."

"Did you miss the part where he tried to kill me?"

"You are giving up on him."

"I'm not! Just—" I looked down at the cobblestones, still wet from rain. "I messed up today. Give me time to sort myself out."

"What did you do?"

I squirmed. "Kissed Tiernan."

Rhonos gave me a long look. Finally, he said, "I see. Perhaps in another world . . . things worked out how we wanted them to."

❋

Hours later, I stood on the cliffs south of Caladheå listening to waves strike the rocks far below. The sky was clouded over with only a faint glow where the moon was. Cool wind rustled my hair. I took a swig of brånnvin and barely spluttered.

"Stop looking at me like that," I said.

Anwea snorted and flicked her tail.

I swished the flask around. "This was only half-full when I started."

A seagull cried. I glanced up and the horizon pitched. I dropped to my knees and rolled onto my back. Sharp rocks pressed into my skin. "Fuckin' spirits. Suriel *promised* not to hurt her. Aeldu-cursed, lying, cheating tel-saidu . . . bet he's never cared about anyone in all his three-bloody-thousand years . . ."

I waved the flask at the sky. Liquor sloshed onto the ground. "You hear that, Suriel? Fuck you! I hope Tiernan kills you! I hope he burns you so bad the sky turns black! I hope no one ever hears your name again!" I screamed every Coast Trader curse I knew, moved onto an extensive list of insults to the aeldu, and only stopped after

I'd gone through Sverbian. I wished I'd asked Iannah to teach me to swear in Ferish.

The only breeze was from the water. Some other tel-saidu far away, one that probably never came inland. Faintly, rising from the swell of waves, voices slid up the cliffs. I couldn't tell if one was Marijka's. The dead were hard to hear in summer.

"I'm sorry, Maika." My throat scratched. "For bringing you into this, trusting Suriel, leaving you alone . . . I thought you'd be safe at home. S'posed to be me out there and you here with Tiernan. He needs you. I can never . . ."

I wondered how far the dead could see over the ocean from Thaerijmur, if they watched the living world like spirits did from Aeldu-yan. "Sorry for kissing your husband," I mumbled.

The sky was brightening by the time nausea kicked in. I threw up behind a boulder and collapsed onto scrubby grass. My ribs ached. Airedain always distracted me through this part, cracking jokes and tapping out music with his hands. I pulled a blanket over my head and passed out.

When I woke it felt like my skull had split in half to let out some angry, clawing creature. I swallowed a vial of willowcloak tincture, thanking the nearest anta-saidu for the fog that filtered the sunlight into something bearable. Once the throbbing subsided, I tethered Anwea in a patch of grass and headed for the cliffs.

Airedain had shown me a route down, though we'd never gone hours after getting drunk. I went slowly, trusting the feel of footholds instead of my questionable vision. Sea spray battered my back and turned my hair crunchy with salt. In a cave near the bottom, I tucked my clothes on a rock shelf and dove into the sea.

Iren kohal. Rivers keep flowing, from mountain to ocean.

The cold knocked the breath out of me. I kicked off from the cliffs, straining every muscle against a current that threatened to dash me into the rock wall. The salt burned where Hafelús cut my neck. I swam into open water and plunged my head under.

I will go where your fire cannot touch me.

Everything was murky in the clouded light. A school of fish skittered below me. I dove at them and they shot out in every direction like splintering glass. I stayed down until my lungs begged, then kicked my way up, flipping my hair back as I broke the surface.

I am not a ghost. I am still of this world.

I shut my eyes and went under again. The ocean enveloped my naked body, rinsing away the feel of Tiernan's lips and the scent of woodsmoke. I drifted, not in stillness, but rocking with the tide as my hair floated around me.

I will not give into the wind. I will not drown in their voices.

My body cocooned itself with waves. When I stretched out, silver fur rippled across my skin. I spluttered and held my snout to the sky. Seven years and I'd never taken my wolf body into the water.

I must leave the dead behind so I can live.

29.

AWAKENING

Back on the clifftops that evening, I scrubbed the salt away until my skin was smooth as dew. My bodice felt too tight after wearing Rin clothes for weeks. I brushed my hair, braided it, and rubbed in a few drops of lilac oil to mask the smell of seaweed.

Airedain was nowhere to be found in the Knox Arms. I nabbed Emílie, the brawny pub owner, but she said she hadn't seen him all day. I glanced at the shelves of liquor bottles and thought better of it.

The stairwell door was locked at Airedain's flat. I stood on the sidewalk and threw chunks of ice at his window. I was about to give up when the shutter banged open.

Airedain's cousin Jonalin stuck his head out, rubbing his eyes. "Oh, it's you." He was bare-chested. His cropped hair stuck out in every direction.

"Is Airedain there?"

"Nei, he came by with some itheran girl and left again."

"Britte? The tall blonde one?"

He paused. "Nei. Brown hair, pale skin. Viviwen, I think."

"Oh." The ice in my hand melted and dripped onto the cobblestone. "Sorry for waking you."

"S'okay." Jonalin's head vanished. The shutter banged closed.

A muddy paper tumbled down the darkening street. I put my hands on top of my head and then slammed them into my thighs. "Kaid!" An Iyo man several buildings away looked up, but just unlocked his door and went inside.

I wandered Ashtown, going nowhere in particular. The streets were clean from rain. I was passing down a narrow lane, feeling tiny next to the red-brick buildings, when a group of itherans emerged from a pub. Their loud voices filled the lane.

One called out, too cheerful. "Hey, *tovakka*! Hey, come here!"

I stopped. "What did you call me?"

"Ain't you ever seen a *tovakka*?" he said as his friends laughed. "It's a flower. Grows through cracks in the road where it don't belong."

"Nah, *tovakkan* are actually pretty," another boy said.

I clamped my hands on my elbows to resist hurling ice at their heads. There was no one around to back me in a fight. I went back the way I came, laughter drifting after me.

In an alley drowned with puddles, I leaned against the brick and slid to the ground, wishing I was short enough to blend into a crowd, wishing I could pin my hair as neatly as Marijka. *Should've worn my cloak. Idiot.* But deep down, I knew my Ashtown wandering was just delaying what I had to do.

The southeast road out of the city was quiet. I recognized the draping willows even in the dark. I followed the sheltered lane to Parr Manor, almost hoping he wasn't there, but light spilled from the windows. I stepped into the covered entrance, took a deep breath, and knocked.

Several moments passed before a door swung open. Parr stood with a candle in hand, hair loose over his shoulders, collar unbuttoned above his waistcoat. His brow creased when he noticed the cut Tiernan left on my neck. "Miss Kateiko. Is everything all right?"

"I need to talk to you." I stared at him, too aware of the rise and fall of my chest.

He took me into the room where we'd had dinner. Candles flickered on the hearth. An open book lay on the low table by the couch. I refused his invitation to sit, lingering in the centre of the room with my hands knotted behind my back.

My throat felt dry. I swallowed and forced the words out. "Marijka Riekkanehl is dead."

Parr bowed his head. He folded his hands in front of his face and sighed. "I am sorry to hear that. Heilind must be devastated."

"I need to know the truth. Did you tell Suriel or the Corvittai anything about her?"

"Goodness. Of course not. I would not put her at such risk."

"And you're not helping them? Politically, or through your military connections—"

"Do you think so little of me?" He took a step closer, looking pained.

I lifted my chin. "Look me in the eye and answer the question."

Parr fixed his dark eyes on mine. "I have not helped Suriel nor the Corvittai beyond what we discussed about opening a rift. You saw yourself that I pressed the Council to declare war on Suriel. I promised to guard the identity of my source to keep negotiations open, that is all. I regret terribly if my actions had anything to do with Marijka Riekkanehl's death."

I held his gaze. Unlike Tiernan, it felt like he actually saw me. Suddenly I was tired of thinking. Of trying to see all the things that lay below the surface.

"Do you want to tell me what happened?" he asked.

"Nei. I don't even want to think about it."

"As you wish." He gave a slight bow. "I am glad you came. I was worried when I did not hear from you for so long."

I looked down at the woven rug. "I didn't think you wanted to."

"Whatever gave you that idea?"

"You just . . . left. In the morning. Without waking me or anything."

His eyes crinkled with a frown. "I thought my letter made my feelings clear."

I remembered the sentence I hadn't understood and wished I'd taken the paper with me. Iannah could've read it. Not that I wanted her to know whatever it said.

He settled into a chair near the fireplace. "I am sorry for leaving, Kateiko. Council business begins early. Given the choice between you and a building full of bickering old men, I would much prefer to be with you."

"Are you busy now?"

"Not in the slightest." He placed a ribbon in his book and shut the cover. "Please, stay. Your company would make a welcome respite from this drudgery."

I perched on the edge of the couch, glad I was clean this time. "What are you reading?"

"A treatise on immigration law. It can wait one more day."

The candles burned low as we talked, but I felt more awake than ever. Parr seemed amused when I asked if it was okay to take off my boots. I curled up in a corner of the couch, rubbing my bare feet over the textured brocade. There was so much in that room I wanted to explore.

When I admitted I hadn't read much beyond folk tales, he read me Ferish poetry from a leather-bound book. His accent flowed like music. My thoughts began to settle, not quieting, just falling into order like tracks in the soil. One after the other, moving forward instead of in circles.

"There's something else I wanted to ask," I said when he rose to relight a candle. I drifted after him to the hearth. "Why did you . . . turn me down last time?"

"Oh, my darling." The flame trembled as it caught on the wick. "You were too exhausted to know what you were doing. I could not let you do something you'd regret."

"That's all? Not because you think I'm — weird, or unattractive, or — or a freak—"

"Is that what you thought?" He set the candle down. "I apologize for offending you. That was far from my intent."

"It's what everyone else thinks."

Parr gave me a long, searching look. "Then they do not see what I see."

Warmth rippled across my skin. I moved closer and slid my palms up his chest. The spice of his cologne wreathed around me. "I don't regret it."

"Kateiko, Kateiko." He held my shoulders. "It is late. Perhaps we should let things rest for tonight."

"Do you want me to leave?" I brushed my lips against his cheek.

He drew a deep breath. "That is not what I said."

"Then let me stay." I tugged the ribbon free from my braid and ran my fingers through the plaits. "Trust me, Antoch. This is what I want."

Parr closed his eyes for just a moment, his jaw clenched — then he kissed me. He wrapped one arm around my waist, pushed me against the hearth, and knotted his other hand into my hair. A shock went from my scalp down my spine, setting my nerves on fire.

"Wait—" My breath hitched. Hafelús's mark burned on my

throat. Parr tensed when I lifted his waistcoat hem, but he let me take his slender knife. I'd never seen it outside the sheath before. The blade was curved, the polished wood handle set with bronze. I unbuckled my belt and tossed our weapons out of reach.

Parr made no move to stop me as I fumbled open the silver buttons on his waistcoat and shirt. He only intervened to undo the ones I didn't see on his cuffs. I pushed his clothes back and let them fall to the floor. He was still as I ran my fingers over the muscles on his arms, his broad shoulders, the dark hair on his chest. He was far from pale, but my tanned skin still stood out against him. It was strange to think his scars might be as old as me.

"May I—" he said haltingly. His hand went to my back. I nodded.

He turned me around and draped my hair over my shoulder. His hands shook as he undid the lacing and tugged my bodice over my head. He traced the line of my ear up, then seized me by the hips and pulled me against him, kissing my exposed neck. "Kateiko," he murmured. "Are you sure?"

I tipped my head back onto his shoulder. "Yes. Yes. Keep going."

Parr cupped my breasts through my thin dress. I arched my back and he made a low sound deep in his throat. He slid my dress off, the fabric pooling around my ankles. I hugged my ribs as he turned me back to face him. I'd been nearly naked in front of Fendul and Airedain when we went swimming, but that was different. Rin women always swam topless.

His fingers passed over my bruises and hovered above my kinaru tattoo. Panic blossomed inside me. As far as he knew I was Iyo. Now he had proof I'd lied the whole time I knew him. A councillor would recognize it as a jouyen crest, not mistake it for allegiance to Suriel like the newspaper had.

He said nothing. Maybe he'd figured it out months ago. His hand moved to the antayul tattoo that fanned across my chest, skirting the black lines, tracing my collarbone with rough fingertips. Wrapped up in all those marks was everything I had to hide — who I was, where I came from, how I grew up, and what I sacrificed to live here. I felt lighter, floating on his acceptance.

Parr's rings glittered with firelight. I wanted to ask if they meant something like my tattoos did, but my attention went elsewhere as soon as he kissed me again. Every part of me felt alive. Awake. I dug my nails into his back and felt his muscles tense.

"It's been so long." His voice was strained. "Beautiful girl. How am I so blessed to have you?"

A smile tugged at my lips. "No one's ever said that about me."

"Then I will say it again and again."

I kissed him hard. Suddenly I wanted all of him. I slid my hand between his legs and he gave a sharp gasp.

"Kateiko." He pulled away. "I have to ask. Is this your first time?"

"Yes — sort of." A flush spread across my body. Leifar the goat-herd and I had messed around in the Vunfjel pastures every summer starting when I was fifteen, but he'd refused to go all the way unless we married. "Is that okay?"

"It is up to you."

"I want you, Antoch." I pressed close to him. "I know how to . . . protect myself. I'll go to the herbalist in the morning."

"Be sure you do. I could never forgive myself if I . . ." Parr took a shuddering breath.

"I will. I promise."

"Here. Lie down." He eased me onto the couch and unlaced his breeches. I stretched out my legs as he pulled off my underclothes. He climbed on top of me, settling his weight onto my body.

I reached out with my mind and doused the candles. In the dim moonlight, something else nudged at the edge of my awareness. I felt all the water nearby, in the air and wood and dirt outside, but there was something new. I sensed the blood coursing through my body, through his body, pulsing in our veins.

"I do not want to hurt you, Kateiko."

"I'll be fine." I sought out his mouth with mine and weaved my fingers into his long hair. "Please, Antoch."

He pushed into me. I cried out — not a word, not part of any language that separated us — just raw sound that matched his low moan.

❋

I woke to Parr disentangling himself from me. I opened my eyes and saw him silhouetted in the soft blue light of dawn. My arms tingled with numbness, but I pulled his warm body back onto mine. "Not yet," I mumbled.

He brushed my hair out of my face and gave me a deep, lingering kiss. "I have to go, my darling."

I wrapped my legs around him. "Nei. You have to stay here with me."

His chest shook with silent laughter. He pressed his lips to the corner of my jawbone just under my ear. I gave a muffled giggle.

Cool air washed over my skin when he finally pulled away. "I am sorry, Kateiko."

The room was a haze of dark shapes that folded in on one another. My eyelids fell and rose like a slow tide as I watched Parr cross to the window and stretch his arms over his head. His outline blurred into trees across the courtyard. A wren trilled outside.

When I woke again, Parr was nudging my shoulder. The room had brightened, and he was fully dressed. "I have to leave for the Colonnium now," he said.

I blinked away the weight of sleep. "When can I see you again?"

"Any night you want." He traced his fingers down my arm. "You are even more beautiful in daylight, darling girl. You have no idea how hard it is to leave you."

I pulled him down into one last kiss. He was smiling when I let go.

"Remember your promise," he said.

The first thing I did in Caladheå was visit the Iyo herbalist, a terse woman who didn't ask questions. I tried not to think that it should've been Marijka who I went to. I headed up the shoreline to an empty stretch of beach before opening the cottonspun bag of dark green tablets made from dried leaves. I choked one down and drank water from my cupped hands until the taste of decaying moss was gone.

Five years before, Isu caught me kissing a Rin canoe carver's apprentice in the huckleberry bushes at Aeti Ginu. I'd listened in mortified silence that night as she explained how to use bloodweed. It was poisonous, but would induce my bloodflow early and protect me. It turned out not to matter then — I fought with the boy over something stupid — and I never got far enough with Leifar to need it, but in Caladheå five summers later I was grateful for Isu's lesson.

The morning was cloudy and warm, so I wandered west collecting seashells. I was sore between the legs, but I'd dealt with worse. The throb of the ocean distracted me. I walked along driftwood with my arms spread wide and hummed to myself.

My stomach began to turn inside out when I was halfway back to the city. I ignored it as long as possible, but the pain pulled me toward the earth until my spine bent and cold sweat ran down my neck. I finally lay on the rocky beach, the tide lapping at my boots. I had no idea how much time had passed when I heard Iannah's voice.

"Hey, Koehl."

I tilted my head to look at her. Sword. No spear. "Shit. I forgot it's your day off."

"Airedain said his cousin saw you in town. I've been looking for you all day. You need a postal box."

"A what?" I sat up and groaned as the world spun.

She peered at me. "Are you hungover?"

I rubbed sweat off my forehead. "Nei. I just — feel weird."

Iannah crouched, held two fingers to my neck, then rolled up my sleeves. A bright rash speckled the inside of my elbows. "Oh. Bloodweed. You slept with someone." She sat back on the rocks. "Who? Airedain?"

"I haven't seen him in weeks! Why does everyone think I'm sleeping with him?"

"Who was it then?"

I glared at her. "Not that it's any of your business, but Antoch Parr."

"Bloody hell." Iannah stood up and turned away, then twisted back with a look of disgust. "You had *sex* with Parr? How'd he convince you to do that?"

"He didn't have to. I wanted to."

"Why? What's wrong with people your own age?"

I threw a rock at her. "Did it occur to you I might actually like him? Parr's a good man. He listens to me, and he's nice to me."

She rolled her eyes. "He's nice to everyone. That's how he got elected to the Council."

"That's not a bad thing."

"Koehl, this won't go anywhere." Iannah ran a hand over her hair, stopping on her bun. "People would throw a fit if a councillor courted an eighteen-year-old viirelei. He can't marry you. He can't even go out in public with you."

"I know, Ia." I put my head in my hands. "I don't expect any-thing. It just — happened."

"See. I knew you'd get distracted. One night with a man and you forget what day it is. You've been gone three weeks and didn't think to tell me you were alive."

"Look, I'm sorry." I got to my feet, pitched forward, and grabbed her arm. "Everything went wrong with Suriel. I just lost track—"

She yanked out of my grip. "No. You always do this. Latch onto men because you can't figure out your own damned life."

"That's not true!"

"You left Caladheå to go back to Tiernan. Then he got married and Airedain turned you into a deadbeat alcoholic. Did he reject you, too? Is Parr just the first one who said yes?"

"Shut up! Like you've got it all figured out! I know you're miserable. You hate every day you're at the Colonnium. You're just too scared to leave!"

"We can't all be homeless drunks." Iannah spat on the ground. "You know what happens if I get caught taking bloodweed? I get kicked out of the military. But I gave that up to do something with my life. I made a commitment."

I laughed. "Ai, you're accusing me of letting men control my life? At least I decide where I sleep and who I fuck."

She punched me.

I crumpled to the ground. Pain shot through my stomach and I retched. I dragged myself back to my feet, holding a hand to my cheek.

"Don't try. I can knock you down even when you don't have bloodweed poisoning." She lifted her chin. "And don't throw up. You'll have to take another one. God knows you'll need the rest if you sleep with everyone who's nice to you."

I gave her my best two-hand salute. "Fuck you."

30.

TRUST

It felt like all of Caladheå was watching me.

People's glances caught on my uncovered, unbraided hair. I stared back, daring them to speak. Part of me wanted to yell out right there. *Yeah, I was with Councillor Parr. Yeah, a filthy wood witch fucked one of the people running your province.* If I was going to stand out, it may as well be for something I'd done, but it wasn't only my reputation at stake.

I gave an Iyo baker three pann for my flatbread, took two steps down the lane toward Segowa's embroidery stall, and turned around. Airedain would ask why I wasn't with Iannah. I ignored a prickle of guilt as I left Caladheå. At least Jonalin had told him I was alive.

Anwea had wandered away from the cliffs. I followed her hoof-prints inland and found her in an overgrown pasture with a collapsed fence. The sun had come out and she was resting in the shade of a broad alder. She ignored both my apology and a lump of sugar.

I picked burrs from her tail and lay in the grass to wait out the blood-weed poisoning.

As sunshine warmed my face, I daydreamed about what life could be like with Parr. Long discussions about Council decisions, going home to someone other than a sulking horse, waking up in that beautiful manor. My lips twitched into a smile, remembering the weight of his body. He wouldn't have much time for me, but maybe I could help at the Colonnium. Maybe we could fix things. Change some of the stupid laws.

I knew it was delusional. The rest of the Council barely listened to Parr, and Iannah was right. He'd probably get thrown out just for courting a viirelei, let alone one twenty years his junior. I stabbed my throwing dagger Nurivel into the dirt, rolled over, and put my face in the grass.

A flock of crows passed over, their caws piercing the quiet fabric of afternoon. "Shut up," I muttered. "Aeldu curse it, you're worse than seagulls." Anwea pawed at the ground, but it wasn't until she snorted and stamped her foot that I looked up.

A crow perched on a fencepost, staring at me. I scowled back. "Go away. It's bad enough having a horse judge me." I closed my eyes and tried to return to my daydream. I heard a rush of wings and figured the crow had left.

Then I heard a caw. My head snapped up. The crow had come several fenceposts closer.

"Fuck off!" I whipped Nurivel at the post. The knifepoint sank quivering into the wood. The crow launched into the air in a blur of black feathers.

Anwea skittered away. I heaved myself off the ground and was halfway to her when my eyes widened. "Nei. That's not—" I whirled.

Fendul stood by the fence holding Nurivel.

Even though nearly a year had passed, he looked the same as always. His soot-coloured hair was short, the tattooed lines on his arm unfinished. Still unmarried, still okoreni. All of a sudden everything I was holding deep inside spilled over. I burst into tears.

"Kako." Fendul strode forward and pulled me into his arms. "Kako, it's all right."

"Mudskull! Why did you—"

He touched the cropped strands over my forehead, the first time ever. "You cut your hair. I wasn't sure it was you. Not until you threw a knife at me."

I clung to his narrow ribs, my laughter muffled by his shoulder. "Sorry, Fen. You know I wasn't trying to hit you."

"I know." He slid Nurivel into the sheath at my back.

Everything about him was familiar. The timbre of his voice, the graceful curve of his crow amulet, the way my skin blended perfectly with his. It was like being back at our favourite swimming hole where I knew every current and fallen log and sharp rock.

I drew back. "What in Aeldu-yan are you doing here?"

Fendul wiped my eyes. "We're all here. The whole Rin-jouyen is camped near Toel Ginu."

"Wait, what? How did — *why?*"

"We've been trying to persuade Behadul to rebuild ties with the Iyo since you left last year. After the spring equinox, the Okoreni-Iyo came to Aeti Ginu and invited us south. He said you helped them when their shrine burned down. I suppose you changed their minds about the Rin."

"Wotelem went to . . . but none of the Iyo ever mentioned it!"

He shrugged. "Tokoda probably kept it quiet. Not all Iyo are happy about us being here, but we told Behadul it'd only get worse with time."

"Who's 'we'?"

"Nili and her family, a few elders, anyone with relatives in the Iyo."

"How did you get here? The eastern mountains aren't safe—"

"I know. Wotelem told us about Suriel. We came by sea. I asked the Tamu-jouyen to help us carve canoes that could make the trip." Fendul rubbed the black lines around his arm. "That's why it took so long. We had to build an entire new fleet."

I choked with laughter through my tears. "Fen, have I ever told you you're amazing?"

He frowned as if giving that serious consideration. "No. In eighteen years, I don't think you've ever said that."

"Don't get used to it." I took a shuddering breath. "How did you find me?"

"Luck, to be honest. We're just scouting. Dunehein said you were living with an itheran man and then left." There was an odd strain to his voice. "Nili wanted to look for you as soon as we landed, but—"

"Nei!" My voice rose. "She can't go back there. Tiernan—" A fresh wave of sobs overcame me. I flung my arms around Fendul again.

"What's wrong? What happened?"

"Everything. Everything's gone wrong. I did something awful, and he'll never forgive me, and — and I don't have anyone else left—"

"You know I love you no matter what, Kako," Fendul said quietly.

"Fennel . . ." I hadn't called him that in years. "Not this time. This is too much."

"It's all right. Tell me when you're ready." He kissed my cropped hair, sending a tremor down my spine. "Come back for a few days. You still have a home with the Rin."

I tilted my face up to him. "Nothing's like it used to be, Fen. I'm not the same person I was when I left."

"Neither are we." He looked at me steadily. It reminded me of his crow form, although I no longer felt the urge to throw sharp things at him. "I wouldn't ask you to come back if nothing had changed."

The thought of being somewhere I belonged was like a gentle thread pulling me forward. I glanced at Anwea, who eyed Fendul with her ears back. "I'd have to bring my horse."

"You can bring as many horses as you want if it'll get you to come home."

I laughed and wiped my eyes. "Fine. Just for a few days."

✳

I pried Fendul for news on the way, but he kept to simple things. Good hunts, bad storms. One birth in the Rin, two deaths, three attunings. Someone had married a Tamu canoe carver and stayed in their settlement at Tamun Dael. Fendul's attention seemed to be everywhere at once — the sky, the sea, the dark smudge that was South Iyun Bel in the distance.

We stopped along the cliffs so I could gather my things and change clothes. I was relieved the rash on my arms had faded. As I stuffed the empty brånnvin flask into my carryframe, hoping Fendul didn't notice, a thought occurred to me. "When did you land?"

"Yesterday afternoon."

The boats must've passed while I slept off my hangover. If I'd gone swimming a few hours earlier, found the Rin sooner — I pushed that out of my head. That kind of thinking would take me down the same path as wondering about shoirdrygen.

The jouyen was camped two hours north of Toel Ginu where mountains smoothed into a plateau. I saw people before I could hear them, gathered between stands of blue-green salt spruce and twisted shore pine. A heavy storm hit the area some months ago, leaving the bluff criss-crossed with rotting logs. I tethered Anwea in the shade of a thicket and promised I'd be back.

My eyes watered as we approached, maybe from the smell of cooking fish as much as the smoke. No matter where the Rin went, the campsite always looked the same. Canvas tents roped to branches, woven bark mats, carryframes stowed in neat rows. I never wanted that to change.

But walking through Caladheä was nothing compared to the campsite. People looked up to greet Fendul and did double takes when they saw me. Some welcomed me back and some just stared. I remembered Airedain's words like a thorn in my ribs. *It's easier to deal with strangers thinking you're a freak than your own family.*

The upside was only about half the people were Rin, and the others ignored me. I peered at their tattoos as we passed. Mostly Iyo dolphins, some Tamu sharks, a few Kae herons. "Why are so many jouyen here?"

"We landed at the Tamu docks just down the coast," Fendul said. "The Kae traders were already in Toel Ginu. I don't think they believed we still existed." He looked slightly annoyed.

I didn't need to ask where we were going. Nili's brother, Yironem, was stacking kindling near a firepit. He didn't have his tattoos yet, but he'd grown a palm-height and was clearly still getting used to it. He tripped over a log when he saw me and went sprawling. His best friend, Umeril, smirked.

Yironem scrambled up, wiping dirt off his breeches. "Kateiko! You came back!"

"Ai, Yiro. Good to see you." I grinned and hugged him. "Do you know where Nili is?"

He chewed his lip. "Our tema sent her to hunt dinner, so she's probably still here. I mean—" He glanced at Fendul and his eyes widened. "I'll go find her."

"Nei, you don't have to—" I began, but he'd already scampered off, vaulting a mossy log.

"You should not be here," said a rasping voice.

I turned to see the eldest elder, Ohijo, leaning on a cane, more hunched than ever. I was surprised she wasn't one of the Rin who died.

"Nisali told us what you did." She pointed a gnarled finger at me. "Calling water in that accursed wasteland. Defying the anta-saidu. You disgrace antayul and the Rin."

Suddenly everyone around us was staring, regardless of jouyen. My hands tightened into fists. "We would've died if I hadn't."

Ohijo's lips pulled back. Her mouth was a dark gash in her wrinkled face. "Then you would have got what you deserve."

Fendul put his hand on my shoulder. "Kateiko has every right to be here."

"Just you wait, Okoreni." Ohijo's shaking hand moved to point at him. "Those girls will bring the wrath of the saidu on us."

"If the saidu come, we will meet them with courage," Fendul said, raising his voice for everyone to hear. "Kateiko and Nisali crossed the wasteland to reach out to the Iyo-jouyen while we allowed history to keep us apart. Let them be an example to us all. Anyone who has an issue with them will have to deal with me."

I was too stunned to speak. A ball of warmth coalesced in my stomach and spread through my body.

Ohijo glared at me. "Just you wait." She stumped away.

"She did the same thing when Nili came back," Fendul said under his breath. "I think Nili was just excited one of the elders remembered her name."

Yironem appeared at my side panting. "I found her, Kateiko!" He grabbed my hand and dragged me around firepits, under gnarled pine branches, over low dirt shelves and crushed rock.

Nili stood amid a group of boys, twirling an arrow and chattering like a wren. They could probably only understand half her words, but none seemed to care. Taworen, a Rin drummer and her admirer from last year, was among them. I stopped for a moment just to grin and watch Nili. The droplet necklace I'd given her at the autumn equinox glittered above her shirt. Her dark brown tail of hair swung as she talked.

The moment didn't last long. "KAKO!" Nili dropped the arrow and shoved past the boys. She hit me with the force of a boulder hurtling down a mountain. We spun, laughing and stumbling on the uneven ground. "I'm so glad you're okay! Did the Iyo find you? Dunehein said you wouldn't be at Tiernan's—"

"Later," I interrupted.

Nili switched tack mid-sentence. "Isu and Behadul are at Toel Ginu. They'll be back this evening. Are you staying that long? Of course you are—" She hooked her arm around Yironem's neck and rumpled his hair. He tried to duck out of her grasp, but his protests waned at the same time Nili cut off talking.

I followed their gazes. Falwen, Officer of the Viirelei, strode toward us alongside two men with shark tattoos.

"Okoreni-Rin, a moment please," Falwen called. He glanced past Fendul at me. "The vagrant returned. How nice."

I wasn't surprised when he showed up anymore. What surprised me was that when he and Fendul started speaking the Tamu dialect with the others, I realized he'd spoken Fendul's title with a perfect Rin accent.

"You know him?" Nili whispered to me.

"Not really. He just knows everything about everyone. It's creepy."

She shrugged. "I admire a man who can talk faster than me." I smacked her arm.

Fendul turned back to us. "I'm sorry, Kako. I have to go meet the scouts." He squeezed my hand. "We'll talk later, I promise."

"Oh!" Nili said as the men left. "I'm supposed to be hunting. D'ya want to come, Kako? Yiro, go find Tema and tell her Kako's back, ai?"

Yironem lifted his chin. "You can't boss me around. I'm bigger than you now. I want to come hunting."

"Yes I can, and nei you can't." She nudged him. "Go on. We'll be back soon."

South Iyun was quiet after the bustle of camp. The trees muffled the wind and the cries of seagulls. I could pick out the hum of rainforest life — rustling leaves, running water, croaking frogs, moss squishing under our boots. The air was hazy with moisture. Nili kept up a steady stream of whispers as we crept to a pond half-hidden by bulrushes. Their tall stems bent under the weight of their fuzzy brown heads. Tealhead ducks drifted across the cloudy green water, swirling through tangles of floating weeds.

"Are we allowed to hunt here?" I asked.

"The Iyo said it was okay. Haven't seen itherans down this way."

I watched Nili pull an arrow from her quiver. She moved with a fluidity that was missing last time I saw her use a bow, not long after killing the Corvittai archer in North Iyun. Her eyes followed the path of the ducks, an easy smile on her face, fingers tapping the bow.

"I was worried you'd never get it back," I said.

Her gaze flicked to me. "I didn't for a long time. I couldn't hunt all winter."

"What changed?"

"I dunno. That's like asking how seasons change." She lowered her bow. "Fendul helped a lot. He was . . . really good after I got home."

"You should've heard him defend us to Ohijo. Never thought I'd see the day." I held up Nurivel and gauged my sightline to the pond. "Last year I thought he permanently had itchbine stuck somewhere unpleasant."

Instead of laughing, she frowned. "Y'okay? Your hands are shaking."

I bit my lip. "Bloodweed poisoning."

"Ooooooh!" Her face split into a grin. "Who was it? I want to know everything!"

"Shh! Not now, for aeldu's sake. It's no one you know, anyway."

"Fine, but let me do it. You'll screw up and lose your dagger." Nili nocked the arrow and took aim. Her bowstring twanged. All but one duck rose screeching into the air. She fired again, and another duck tumbled into the rushes with a splash.

"So is this ongoing?" she asked as we waded in, slimy water lapping at our boots.

"Nei. Last night was the first time." I paused. "*My* first time. Look, I'll tell you about it later. I can't think straight yet."

"At least tell me this. Was it an itheran?"

"Yeah."

She thrust her fist into the air. "Yes! You owe me ten pann!"

"Aeldu save you, Nili." I pulled aside handfuls of bulrushes until I found a floating duck with an arrow in its chest. "Don't tell anyone, ai? People already hate me enough."

"They don't hate you. Everyone's just on edge. No one knows

how to deal with being here." She shook water off the other bird. "You should talk to Fendul though. I mean it."

I kicked at the pond mud. "He has other things to worry about."

Nili rolled her eyes. "Kako, he's Okoreni-Rin. Looking after the jouyen is his job."

"I'll think about it," I said, and she let it rest at that.

We didn't get a chance to talk alone in camp, but I was happy having dinner with Nili's family. Her mother, Hiyua, hugged me as tight as a knotted rope and plied me with halibut drenched in smelt oil. Fendul walked among the crowd seeming to talk to everyone but us. Aliko, a twenty-year-old Rin weaver, saw him coming and tugged down her shirt to show off the curves of her chest. Fendul's cheeks flushed, and he veered off in another direction. I clamped a hand to my mouth as I giggled.

In the evening, Yironem and Umeril pulled Nili and me into a game of leatherball — Rin and Tamu against Iyo and Kae. It was a nice change to run without weapons at my side. I and a few other antayul pelted people with flecks of ice until we got kicked out. I was watching from behind the logs that marked the sidelines when someone called my name.

Dunehein, his wife Rikuja, and Isu walked across the camp. Rikuja held a bundle in a sling over her shoulder. I broke into a grin that couldn't be darkened by all the clouds in the world.

"Kako!" Dunehein lifted me off the ground, almost crushing my ribs.

"Congratulations!" I gasped once I could breathe. "When did it happen? What name did you choose?"

"Nine days ago. Her name is Sihaja." Rikuja pulled the fabric back. The baby had thin dark hair, flushed cheeks, and tiny hands that latched onto my finger. "She came earlier than expected, but we're all fine."

"You look exhausted."

Rikuja laughed. She and Dunehein had new tattoos, a square cross on their forearms that would be repeated for every child. Their skin peeled over the black lines.

"We asked Fendul to keep it a secret until we got here." Dunehein put his arm around my shoulders and kissed my hair. "I'm so glad you came."

The shrine fire had left its mark. The skin on his left arm was twisted from his shoulder past his elbow, mottled reddish-purple and pitted like leather. His kinaru tattoo was faded and warped as if under clouded glass. The tiger lilies had almost disappeared.

I smiled up at him, a lump in my throat. "Your crest will live on through her."

I stepped back to give them space as people began to recognize Dunehein. Once I was away from them, I couldn't put it off any longer. I turned to Isu.

She was silent. I couldn't work out her expression.

I took a deep breath. "I'm sorry, Isu. I shouldn't have said those things or left the way I did. It wasn't fair to you, and I . . . I'm just sorry."

"Oh, Kateiko." Isu drew me into an embrace. "I'm the one who needs to apologize."

"You're — not mad?"

"Not anymore." Her chest shook. She was crying. "I've never seen Dunehein so happy. I'd do anything for Emehein to have had the same chance. You understood even when I didn't. Nothing, not even protecting our home or our aeldu, was worth losing one of my children."

I didn't know what to say. I just hugged her back.

"I should've come south with you. When the aeldu took my son, they blessed me with you instead, my sister's only child. Then I let you leave alone." Isu stroked my hair. "There are so many things I should've done better. I never would've had a daughter but for you—"

"Isu—" I could barely get anything out because suddenly I was sobbing. "I wouldn't have made it here without you. You taught me everything I needed — you did everything a mother is supposed to—"

She gripped my shoulders. "I want you to have a good life, wherever and with whomever that is. If that's home at Aeti Ginu, here with the Iyo, or somewhere else, know that I love you whether I'm with you or not."

❋

The other jouyen trickled off, the Iyo and Kae heading to Toel Ginu, Tamu to their camp down the coast. Rikuja and Sihaja fell asleep in Isu's tent. Dunehein stayed up and gave me a rundown of events. Behadul and Tokoda had come to a tentative agreement, the Rin were invited to a feast tomorrow, and a new shrine was being built well away from the island that housed the charred one.

After Dunehein went to sleep, I slipped off with the excuse of checking on Anwea. She stuck her nose in my palm until I found some sugar. "I didn't forget you," I murmured.

My tent was still buried in my carryframe from when I left Tiernan. I sat with my back to a spruce and looked at the stars instead, tossing my bag of bloodweed tablets from hand to hand.

"Ai, Kako." Nili bounded around the edge of the copse. I fumbled and tossed the bag too far. She scooped it up. "Is this—"

"Yeah."

She dropped it into my outstretched palm. "Thinking of going to see him again?"

It took a second to realize she meant Parr. "Nei. Not tonight, anyway."

She put her hands on her hips and beamed. "Fendul and I are going swimming at the Tamu docks. Wanna come?"

Cold water sounded appealing. The humidity had persisted past sunset, and Anwea seemed to be asleep. As Nili and I looped around the camp, I asked, "What about you? I guess you and Orelein didn't get back together."

"Nei." Her smile faded. "Two years of sharing a bed and canoe, and then . . . he didn't even look at me after I got home. He didn't expect me to stay. I wasn't sure I would. But then the Okoreni-Iyo came, and I knew I had to persuade Behadul to change things so no matter where you and I wound up, we could visit our families.

"Stupid how things turn out. I split up with Ore last spring because he didn't want to leave home. Then this spring, he came to Tamun Dael with the other Rin woodcarvers to build new canoes. Pretty sure he hooked up with a Haka trader there. I dunno. We don't really talk."

"You seem okay without him."

Her grin snapped back into place. "Yeah, I've been tapping Taworen instead."

I snorted. "Really? I didn't think brawny ones were your type."

"Not many options in a small jouyen. Taworen's fun, he's tall enough, and he's really good with his—"

"Please stop talking."

Nili burst into giggles.

Fendul met us on the way carrying a lit torch. Narrow wooden steps zigzagged down the steep cliffs. I went slowly, glad the blood-weed had worn off. A breeze carried the tang of salt and seaweed. The heat faded as we neared the bottom.

I stepped onto a floating wharf anchored to the cliff. Docks faded into darkness on either side. Boats rocked around us, each one a hollowed-out rioden log with a steep bow and stern. A few had prows carved into shark heads, the curving teeth as long and sharp as daggers. All others were plain.

There was a splash followed by Nili swearing. She clung to a canoe, the water up to her chin. "Yan taku! Can't you do something about the temperature, antayul?"

"Yeah, I'll get right on warming the entire ocean for you." I dropped my belt on the dock, undid the knotted straps of my shirt, kicked off my boots, and slid into the water. "Oh, kaid. That is cold."

"Blame Fendul. This was his idea."

I rolled onto my back and kicked off from the dock. The stars looked brighter away from the campfires. Fendul set the torch in a bracket, stripped to his breeches, and dove in.

My body slowly got used to the cold until the water felt like a blanket. We swam further and further out, competing to see who would turn back last. In the past I usually won, and Fendul would call Nili and me idiots for not giving up sooner. This time he pushed past us, long arms making graceful strokes through the waves.

Nili and I looked at each other. "Ai, Fendul!" she yelled. I flipped water over his head and heard him curse in the distance. Nili and I erupted in laughter, spluttering as seawater rushed into our mouths.

The torch guided us back to shore, a tiny beacon in all the darkness of the world. Only the taste of salt and sound of breaking waves reminded me this wasn't home. As I drifted toward the docks, something settled into place in my head. I trusted the water to hold me up. I knew without a doubt my friends would do the same.

We pulled ourselves onto a dock, skin dripping, teeth chattering. I dried us off and we lay side by side, gazing at constellations as familiar as each other's names. Planks creaked, boats rubbed against lichen padding, wharves rocked back and forth on the endless tide.

I told them everything. About shoidrygen, the war as I saw it with Iannah and Airedain, my plan with Marijka and how it went so terribly wrong. I admitted I was in love with Tiernan, yet I'd slept with Parr. I even told them that Suriel wanted to reach the void because other saidu didn't want him here. After he broke his promise not to hurt Marijka, he didn't deserve to have secrets.

Nili couldn't resist commenting on it all. Fendul stayed silent, but when my shaky voice trailed off, he finally spoke. "I understand."

"What?"

"I don't agree with all the choices you made. But I understand why you made them."

Nili took my hand. "I'm not gonna say I understand, because all that stuff about other worlds kinda confuses me. But I still love you, Kako."

I let out a deep breath. My heart felt a hundred times lighter.

"It took me awhile to figure things out," Fendul said. "If you were both giving up everything just to leave the Rin, I was doing something horribly wrong as okoreni. I left you at the wasteland because I had to choose between helping you or the jouyen. You'd go forward without me. The Rin wouldn't."

He sighed. "I know what regret feels like. I regretted not going with you, and all the years I spent following my father's lead. So don't think you're alone with your guilt, Kako. But all that brought us back together. At least that's one good thing."

"You brought us together, Fendul," Nili said. "You're the only one Behadul listens to."

I poked Fendul's ribs. "That's why I was mad at you."

He shifted next to me, and I knew he was holding his tattoo. "I'm sorry I left without saying anything. I'm not very good at admitting I'm wrong."

"There's something I never told you, Kako." Nili's voice wavered. "I almost killed that third rider because I was furious. Maika's blood is in the ground because you were trying to end a war. That's a lot more noble than killing someone because you're mad."

"I never wanted to be noble. I just wanted people to stop dying."

"That's never been an option," Fendul said. "We lived through a war with roots far older than us. Now we're on the edge of another and, honestly, I'm not sure we can avoid it. But I'm determined to make things right."

We fell silent. Then Nili's giggling drowned out distant seagulls. "I want to see this Parr. He must be something to look at."

I went to push her off the dock, but Fendul leaned over me and got to her first.

31.

WINGS

The next morning, Nili and I went to a stream and came back with baskets of trout. We sat on a wind-thrown log, its dirt-caked roots resting sideways on the ground like the antlers of a toppled elk. Fendul got away from his duties long enough to help Nili gut the fish. Soon they were both up to their wrists in blood, the bucket of innards reeking in the sun. I rinsed the shimmering pink-banded fish and packed them in ice to carry to Toel Ginu for the feast.

The air felt sticky. Even the breeze off the ocean was warm. My hair clung to me in tendrils, and mist washed over us from a willow. Nili and Fendul kept stealing ice chips to rub on their necks.

"I love summer," Nili said with a dreamy sigh. She gazed across the bluff, a half-gutted fish in her hands. A group of boys crossed the rocky ground from the north, their laughter loud and carefree. Iyo had been trickling in from Caladheå since late morning. The boys were bare-chested, tanned, gleaming with humidity.

"Me, too," I said. We dissolved into giggles.

"Someone's coming." She craned her neck. "Ooh, he's lush. And tall."

"Everyone's taller than you," Fendul said without looking up.

I dropped a handful of ice chips. "Nei. *Nei*." I jabbed Nili's ribs. "Hands off. He's a sleaze."

She burst into laughter. "That must be Airedain!"

"Ai, Rin-girl," he called. He stopped in front of us, thumbs hanging off his belt. The scar on his ribs where he got stabbed at Skaarnaht had faded slightly, but there was still a jagged line above his dolphin tattoo from when he fought Elkhounds after Nokohin's death. "Okoreni-Rin. Other Rin-girl. Wondered when you'd show up."

Nili waved the bloody fish at him. "I'm Nisali. I've heard about you."

"Hopefully good things." He winked.

I thrust out my hand. "*See*? That's exactly what I mean."

Airedain rubbed the cropped hair above his neck. "Guess I can't call you Rin-girl now, Kateiko. You ain't the only one anymore."

"You'll always be Iyo-boy to me." I flicked icy droplets at his chest.

He twisted away and laughed, but it seemed strained. "I was getting worried. Your Antler friend came by my tema's shop looking for you yesterday."

"She found me eventually." Better not to mention that Iannah and I fought. I didn't want to explain it'd been about Parr — and partly about Airedain. "Ai, is Segowa coming to the feast tonight?"

"Yeah, she just has to close up the shop." He glanced away as Jonalin called his name. "I gotta go. Jona wants me to meet some Rin he knew way back. We'll catch up later, okay?"

"Sure."

Airedain leaned forward to whisper in my ear. I smelled pine resin in his hair, spiked into its usual fin shape. "Don't worry. You'll always be my favourite Rin-girl."

He flashed a brilliant grin and walked off, swinging his long legs over a fallen spruce. A shark in a sea of people. He moved like nothing mattered, shoulders thrown back, ignoring everyone around him. Nili stared at me.

I pushed an ice chip against her nose. "Stop that. It doesn't mean anything. He flirts with anyone whose name ends in a vowel."

She held up her bloodstained hands. "You said it, not me."

I turned to Fendul. "Isn't this when you say you hate his hair or something?"

But Fendul, his hunting knife halfway up a trout, stared after Airedain. "He must be the one."

"What one?"

"The one who suggested the Iyo contact us. Tokoda said Segowa's son came to her after the spring equinox. Apparently he threatened to go north himself if Tokoda didn't send someone."

"Wait. *What?* That was Airedain's idea?"

I ran through the last four months in my head. All the time I spent with him in Caladheå, the night I confessed over a bottle of brånnvin how much I missed everyone but was too scared to go home, he'd kept it a secret. Probably so I wasn't disappointed if they didn't come.

Fendul's knife slid the rest of the way through the fish. "I do hate his hair, though."

✳

"I can't believe you kept that archer's horse," Nili said later that afternoon, hesitantly stroking Anwea's smooth brown neck.

Most Iyo had gone to Toel Ginu to prepare for the feast. Rikuja had taken Sihaja home to rest. Dunehein, Airedain, and a few other Iyo remained, still catching up with family or friends in the Rin. Heat hung over the bluff like a blanket. I was about to saddle Anwea when I heard distant footsteps. Through the edge of the thicket, I saw people approach, one figure holding the arm of another, a third carrying a longbow and leading a black horse.

"Scouts must've caught an itheran," I said. Several Rin strode across the bluff toward them. Nili and I met both groups by a cluster of boulders spotted with lichen. Anwea's lead rope slid from my hands. "*Rhonos?*"

He didn't seem surprised to see me. His wrists were bound behind his back, forehead beaded with sweat. There was a purplish bruise on his cheek, stubble on his jaw, dark half-moons under his eyes. He looked smaller without his longbow on his back.

"Found him riding in from the plain," said a Rin scout with an ugly scar on her shoulder. Her grip was tight around Rhonos's elbow. "Said he needs to talk to the Okorebai-Rin."

Behadul stepped forward, his grey braid plunging down his spine, the wrinkles etched on his face like bark. He looked Rhonos over before turning to me. "You know this man?"

"Yes. He — I trust him." I hoped Tokoda had followed through on her promise to defend me to Behadul.

Behadul's hand stayed on his sword pommel. "Release him. Speak, itheran."

The scout undid the rope. Rhonos rubbed his wrists. "My name is Rhonos Arquiere. I am a ranger in service of Eremur. I captured a Corvittai scout three leagues northeast who said a hundred soldiers ride to battle. Thirty archers and seventy spearmen. They will be here before the afternoon is out."

Behadul and Fendul exchanged a look, only for a second, but it was enough. Fear gripped my insides with icy fingers.

"We have no part in this war," Behadul said. "Suriel should not even know we are here. He cannot see so far from the eastern mountains. Our boats are unmarked, we fly no flag, and we have not seen a Corvittai scout within a day's walk."

"Then I found the one you missed. He mentioned the Rin nation by name, sounding furious over some past conflict. He died before explaining."

"Something's not right." I glanced at the vivid blue sky, at rotting logs covered in moss, undisturbed for months. "There's no warning storm. There hasn't been wind from the east in days. Where's Suriel?"

"We should take the boats and go," said the second Rin scout, a middle-aged man holding Rhonos's horse.

Fendul shook his head. "They attacked Rutnaast by sea. They'll find us eventually."

"Suriel spared the Iyo," the female scout said. "Maybe we can negotiate."

"That was different," I said. "Suriel came to Toel Ginu to raze the shrine, not to butcher people. This . . . I don't know what this is."

"I warned you," a voice rasped. "You girls called the wrath of the saidu on us."

I turned to see Ohijo pointing her cane at me. More people had gathered. Isu and Dunehein were nearby, but everywhere else I looked, angry eyes fixed on Nili and me. Anwea snorted and drew her ears back.

Isu moved to stand beside us. "Suriel does not live by the same laws as other saidu."

"Itheran," Behadul said. "You are sure these are Suriel's soldiers?"

Rhonos pulled a square of black cloth from his jerkin pocket. The edges were frayed as if it'd been ripped, and the white outline of Suriel's sigil was stained with blood. "The scout wore this under his armour. Do the Corvittai still take orders from Suriel? I could not say."

"Meaning?"

"They are mercenaries, desperate and run ragged, fed up with serving an erratic spirit. If you have no reason to believe Suriel would attack your nation, consider the possibility that they have mutinied. They are led by a man called Nonil. The scout spoke of him with great respect."

I sucked in a breath. "Nonil — that was written on the note you found pointing to a Corvittai camp. He must be the captain they've been following all this time."

Rhonos nodded. "My advice is to press your advantage in combat. They will ride through the forest to avoid Caladheà, but they do not know the terrain and their horses will be hindered."

"We don't have the numbers," said the Rin scout with Rhonos's horse. "We never should've left Anwen Bel." Muttered agreement rippled around us.

"It was the okoreni's idea to leave," someone else said. "Let him answer for it."

Behadul's voice rumbled like a flood. "This has been many years coming. It is the fault of me and every okorebai since my grandfather's grandmother who led the Rin into the First Elken War. Do not blame our youth for old mistakes."

Fendul was right. Things had changed.

Behadul surveyed the crowd. "Dunehein, you are not Rin for me to command anymore, but I bid you ask Tokoda to send her warriors. We must hope the Iyo will reforge our alliance."

"My place is in battle." Dunehein folded a hand over his scarred kinaru tattoo. "Put a weapon in my hands, Okorebai. I owe that to the Rin."

"We should send two people, anyway," Fendul said. "The Corvittai might be watching Toel Ginu. We need the message to get through."

"I'll go." Airedain slipped forward. "I'm no warrior, but I'm fast."

Jonalin followed. "I'll go, too."

Behadul pointed his sword at them. "Why should I entrust my jouyen's diplomacy to those who live among itherans?"

Airedain's hands clenched. "We live in Caladheå 'cause it's Iyo land. I know too many people killed by itherans. I'll make Tokoda listen."

"It's all right. Send them." Fendul laid a hand on his father's shoulder.

Behadul cast him a brief look. "Very well. Ask any Tamu you see on the way to join us. Everyone else, back to camp."

I stood still with Anwea as people dispersed. Nili went straight to find her family. I hadn't even been back a day and everything was getting ripped away, as if the cliffs themselves were eroding, sending me plummeting toward the ocean.

"Ai, Rin-girl." Airedain ran a hand over his hair, took a step toward me, and stopped.

I gave him a bleak smile. "Don't get stabbed this time, Iyo-boy."

His expression broke. "I'm sorry. This wasn't supposed to — I never told you—"

"Fendul told me what you did." I drew him into a tight hug. "The Rin came knowing this might happen. I'm just glad I got to see them first."

For the first time ever, he pressed his hands to my hair. I traced the arrowhead leaves tattooed on his arm, remembering the morning after Skaarnaht. *Lucky.* The aeldu weren't looking out for us then, and I wasn't sure our luck would hold out much longer.

Airedain pulled away. "See you on the other side."

A second later, a lean coyote stood in front of me, its greyish fur flecked with cinnamon. It twitched its long ears and bounded south. Coyotes rarely crossed the mountains. I wondered if he'd attuned far from home. Jonalin shifted into an osprey, rose into the sky, and soared after him.

Rhonos watched them with his mouth half-open, then shook it off, seeming to recall where he was. The Rin scouts returned his longbow and horse, and allowed me to lead him aside to speak privately, but kept watch with their weapons ready.

"Where's Tiernan?" I demanded. "You told *me* off for leaving him."

"Nhys is with him at the cabin. I had business in Caladheå. Do not complain — it led me here."

I folded my arms. "You didn't learn anything else about Nonil?"

"No. I do not even think that is his real name." Rhonos slid his bow into a sling on the saddle. "He may not be who you expect, given how long he has managed to hide his identity, but look for him in battle. Killing him will be the worst blow you can deal the Corvittai."

"Wait — won't you be here?"

"This is not my fight."

"You came all this way and—" I stuttered to a stop. "You lecture everyone about duty, but always leave when people need you. Aren't you a soldier, too?"

"I apologize. I have done what I can."

Ice crackled in my palm. "You still blame my people. You think we deserve this."

His mouth pressed into a thin line. "Nobody deserves what is coming. I am sorry, but I cannot be here when the Corvittai arrive. You could not imagine what they would do to me for siding with you."

My ice melted onto the ground, pooling on damp soil and evergreen needles. "I'm sorry. Thank you for warning us. I just — don't know what any of this means."

"You are right to be upset, just not at me." He swung onto his horse.

"Rhonos." I squinted against the harsh sun. "If I don't survive this . . . take care of Tiernan."

"Always." He bowed. "Goodbye, Kateiko."

His horse took off north at a canter, jumping fallen logs until they were lost among soaring spruce and twisted pine. It felt like parts of me were splintering off in every direction, but I had one more goodbye to make.

I rubbed the white patch between Anwea's eyes. "I promised to take you away from battle. This is it, Anwea. You have to go now."

She nuzzled me, tickling my neck. I took a slightly crushed lump of sugar from my purse. She inhaled it and gave a soft nicker.

"You have to go." I untied the lead rope and tugged on the halter to steer her into the depths of South Iyun Bel. "Go. Run far away. Go! I don't want you here when they come!"

Anwea tossed her head, black mane flying. The last I saw was her tail streaming out before she disappeared into the rainforest.

※

I found Nili and her family at the firepits. All around us, people sharpened blades, strung bows, rubbed poison onto arrowheads, tinted their skin with mud or lichen. Nili unpacked arrows from a roll of leather, checking the duck-feather fletching. She and Hiyua wore leather archery guards on their chests and wrists.

Yironem's knuckles were white around his bow. "I'm not leaving."

"It's our law." Hiyua's face was drawn tight. "You haven't attuned."

"I'm a better archer than any Rin my age—"

Nili swatted him with a handful of arrows. "Fendul didn't fight in the Dona war. He was fourteen then, too. Y'think you're allowed to do something the Okoreni-Rin wasn't?"

"I'm not a child! Umeril's fifteen and he's fighting!"

Nili turned to me in exasperation. "Talk some sense into him, will you? Behadul's sending all the kids to Toel on the boats, but he refuses to go."

"Yiro. Listen." I pushed his bow down. "The Corvittai might be waiting at the docks. We need people to protect the kids. Just because you're not fighting here doesn't mean you're not fighting. Okay?"

His mouth twisted, but he slung his bow over his shoulder. "Okay," he muttered.

"Thanks," Nili said as I pulled her aside. "He won't listen to me or our tema anymore. Brat."

I dropped my voice. "Nili — do you think I brought this on? I promised I wouldn't tell anyone why Suriel wants to reach the void—"

"*Nei.*" She pointed the arrows at me. "Don't get that in your head. All that matters right now is survival. And if you have some bludge-headed idea about — luring the Corvittai away or whatever — piss on that. We started this together and we're finishing it together."

I backed away from the stone points aimed at my chest. "All right. I got it. The Rin are right though. We have maybe sixty people old enough to fight, some too old to wield a weapon."

"And we're the only ones from our generation who have killed someone," Fendul said as he passed, a lumber axe in hand.

I tilted my head. "Fen, when did you . . ."

He kept walking. My brows knit together. There was so much he never told me. So much rested on his shoulders. I wondered if I'd been too hard on him.

"Rin-jouyen." Behadul's voice rumbled over the bluff. He stood by the ashes of a firepit, Fendul next to him.

I moved closer. As people clustered around, I saw Dunehein holding the double-edged steel axe that had belonged to his father and then to Emehein. Isu must've brought it from Aeti Ginu. She stood next to Dunehein, the top of her head barely reaching his shoulder.

"Ever since itherans arrived at our borders, we have defended ourselves," Behadul began. "The Rin swore to always stand with the Aikoto Confederacy. We bled and died through two Elken Wars. Yet seven years ago, the fallout of those wars caused conflict with the Dona-jouyen. I led you to war with our blood relatives in the name of protecting all we ever fought for.

"Of all the choices I have made as okorebai, I regret that the most. I do not ask forgiveness, only understanding. The Rin have suffered for generations. We stand here because of choices made in desperation. Now, as we stand on the brink of making amends, an army of itherans rides to destroy us. I do not know if Suriel accompanies them.

"I will not command anyone to fight. The Okorebai-Iyo agreed to harbour refugees if the need arose. You may go with your children to Toel Ginu or leave Aikoto lands entirely. I do not begrudge anyone who makes that choice. To those who stay, I say this. We are far from home. We fight not for land, honour, or the aeldu. We fight to keep soldiers from reaching Toel Ginu so our children have safe refuge. So they will outlive us.

"This is only the beginning of the war for the Rin. Many of us will not see the end. But in my twenty-eight years as Okoreni-Rin and thirteen as Okorebai-Rin, you have all done me proud." Behadul had been looking across the crowd as he spoke, but his gaze settled on me. "You have survived everything and risen stronger. Today we rise again."

Fendul lifted his sword over his head. Sunlight glinted off the steel, winking like a star. "Rin-jouyen. Today we fly. Will you fly with us?"

Isu raised her spear at the same time Dunehein raised his axe. Hiyua and Nili were right after, their bows like ribbons against the blue sky. Umeril, Nili's old lover Orelein, and her new lover, Taworen, lifted their weapons. Across the bluff, steel and wood and iron met the sky.

"*Kujinna kobairen*," the chant began, louder and louder, spreading like running sap. The Rin battle cry, as old as the rainforest and the flowing rivers and the legend of the kinaru that birthed our jouyen from a great egg on the shore of Kotula Huin.

I raised Nurivel above my head. I would fly with my people.

32.

CORVITTAI

The rainforest had never been so full of noise. Water dripped into a pond, leaves shivered as birds alighted on twigs, a squirrel darted up the red bark of a rioden. In truth, it was quieter than usual, but as I strained my ears for the thud of hooves, everything else seemed impossibly loud.

A dirt road ran from Caladheå to Toel Ginu like an artery through South Iyun Bel. Countless half-forgotten paths splintered off toward the coast. An Iyo woman named Mereku said only two paths were wide enough for riders. The Rin-jouyen split in half and barricaded each one. We felled a hemlock over the southern path, its bristling needles jutting like fingers, and took up posts along it. Sunlight dappled everything in misty green.

I nestled in the crook of a cottonwood, looking down on the path. My skin was smeared with mud, my hair braided with vines.

My grey clothes matched the dull, fissured bark. The kinaru on my arm was blacked out by charcoal.

Fendul led our detachment. He stood below me, perfectly still in a stand of fir, his skin painted grey to blend with the mottled silvery bark. Nili stood behind a curtain of red lichen the same shade as her clothes. A tealhead duck and grey-winged kingfisher dipped in and out of the canopy to keep watch. A wolf, larger and darker than my form, sat listening with its tail curled around its paws.

Dunehein was with Isu in the other detachment. Ours had Mereku, three other Iyo who'd been at our camp, and nine Tamu that Airedain and Jonalin had sent our way. No one had come from Toel Ginu.

Sweat ran down my neck. My hair stuck to my forehead. The Corvittai would be worse off, used to an alpine climate, but that wasn't much of an edge. I rubbed damp palms on my cropped leggings. One thing we had in common with Antlers — we fought without armour.

I wondered who would hear about my death. Maybe Rhonos would tell Tiernan I left the province. Airedain might track down Iannah, but I wasn't sure she'd tell Parr. I closed my eyes, remembering the warmth of Parr's lips, the caress of his voice in the dawn light. *Darling girl.* I wished I could see him once more. Tell him if I didn't come back, it wasn't because I regretted being with him.

My hands trembled. I was scared, there was no question about it. I'd never had time to be properly scared before. This time, I knew. I was on the other side now, going to war instead of waiting for people to return. Yironem, Dunehein's daughter Sihaja, Airedain's nephew — they'd be safe in Toel Ginu if we could hold the Corvittai back. *If we die, let it be to protect the people we love.*

In the end, it wasn't horses or people I heard. It was the low, rippling call of the Rin horn from the north.

I streaked through the forest, paws slamming the dirt, branches snagging my fur. My wolf body *knew* how to run. I'd never gone so fast in my life, but I knew exactly where to put my feet, how to make four legs coil and spring in perfect timing. From the moment I attuned, I heard shouting, clanging metal, whistling arrows, shrieking horses. The smell of blood followed — hot, metallic, mixed with the sweetness of sap and decay.

A horse with an empty saddle dashed past me. I rose into my human body, stumbling over a gnarled root. The charcoal fox keeping pace with me shifted into Nili. Birds swooped down, changed in midair and hit the ground running.

The Corvittai hadn't fled the north barricade. A column of riders writhed along the path like a snake with a hundred heads. Spearmen and archers in leather armour, a few in steel plate, wooden shields painted with black kinaru. Spears cut the air, sending out sprays of blood.

We crashed into them like a wave. I hurled balls of ice at the soldiers, calling new ones as they left my hand. A rider fell from the saddle and met Fendul's blade with his throat. Arrows hurtled past. Bodies littered the path in a tangle of crushed leaves and churned soil.

"*Ainu-méleres! A len sulos!*" shouted a deep voice.

The nearest Corvittai spurred their horses toward us. I grabbed a branch, swung up and into a tree. I kicked a spearman in the teeth as he charged under me. Pain sliced across my leg. Warm liquid spilled down my skin.

He tried to turn, but his mount got tangled in dense bushes. I dropped from the tree and seized the rider. We tumbled off the horse and landed on a pile of ferns with a *fwump*. I slit his throat before he could retrieve his spear. Blood sprayed across me.

Two, I thought. Two lives I'd taken now.

His horse skittered, trampling the body, thrashing the under-brush. I dove aside and rolled. My head smacked against something. Dizzy, I saw a flurry of hooves—

"*A len ouelos!*" the deep voice called. Every rider in sight veered west — except a spearman and an archer who galloped the other way.

Don't let any escape. That was the last thing Fendul told us.

"Nili!" I yelled, hoping she was near. I caught the reins of the dead rider's horse, leapt into the saddle, and chased the two who'd gone east.

Steel and black horsehair flashed ahead as I raced along the twisting path. Even if Nili caught up, neither of us could get a shot in. I gritted my teeth, focusing on the ground in front of the two riders. *Ice. Need ice.*

A flood erupted across the path, freezing as soon as it formed, spar-kling green from the moss. Their horses slid and fell with a *crack* that shattered the ice. The Corvittai archer's arrows flew from his quiver and spun across the glassy surface. His horse writhed on the ground. Its knee was bent the wrong way, bone jutting through bloody hide.

My horse pulled at the reins just as I threw Nurivel. The dagger flew past the archer. He stumbled up, grabbed a spilled arrow, and fired. Feathers brushed my ear as it whistled past.

I melted the ice and rode at the archer, knocking him down. I slashed with my hunting knife and caught him across the face — then flung an arm around my horse as it reared. My braid whipped through the air like loose rigging on a ship.

By the time I got control of the horse, the archer was firing down the path, ignoring me. An arrow sprouted from his stomach. He staggered and fired again. Someone cried out. I snapped around — but it wasn't Nili.

Yironem stood in a tangle of bushes, his face pale as fir bark.

Blood ran from a gash on his arm. He was already nocking another arrow.

"Why the *fuck* are you here?" I shouted.

Yironem's next arrow thudded into the Corvittai archer's chest. A third, a fourth, and the man went down twitching.

The second soldier, the spearman, pulled himself back into a saddle. I threw my hunting knife, but it clanged off his breastplate. Yironem's arrow pinged off his helmet and ricocheted into the trees. The next two arrows thudded into his wooden shield.

The spearman took off east. I sent another wave of ice crackling down the path. His horse jumped and hit dirt on the far side. It took an arrow in the flank and kept galloping. I swore.

I slid to the ground, grabbed my knife, found Nurivel in the crook of some mossy roots. Yironem ran up. I thrust a handful of spilled arrows at him, swung onto my horse, and pulled him up after me. He was light, just a scrawny boy.

We raced after the spearman, ducking branches and cascades of grey-green witch's hair. Yironem's arm was tight around my waist. The forest slid past in a brilliant green blur. I pulled up at a crossroad, saw a glint of metal, and swung left.

The main road. Just as I wondered where we were going, Yironem yelled, "There!"

We veered off the path and crashed through the underbrush. Ahead, the mounted spearman plowed into a lake, sending water cascading over bulrushes. His armour flashed in the sunlight. He raised his spear, pointing toward the coast.

I pulled back on the reins. My horse jerked to a stop, squelching in thick mud at the edge of the trees. I blinked in the sudden glare. "Yan taku."

Kinaru circled over the glittering blue lake — twenty birds, thirty, I couldn't tell. Huge wings beat the air, long necks straight as spears, undersides pale against the sky. Every one carried a rider. Yironem drew a sharp breath.

"Get ready," I whispered. Yironem slid down from my horse and nocked an arrow. I raised Nurivel. "Ai!"

The spearman turned, flinging up his shield — a second after an arrow sank into his throat. Another thudded into his shoulder, foot, knee. He fell from his horse and splashed into the water.

I looked down. Yironem's arrow was still on the bowstring.

Nili ran up behind us, panting. "Yiro — you fucking mudskull—"

He scowled. "I said I wasn't leaving!"

"How'd you find us?" I demanded.

"Attuned. Followed the smell of idiot." Nili smacked Yironem's arm. "What in Aeldu-yan were you *thinking*—"

"Lecture him later. Yiro? Now's a good time to tell you kinaru are real. And they're on Suriel's side." I squinted at the cloudless sky. We were too late. The kinaru banked, following the spearman's direction toward the battle. "We have to get back—"

I fell silent. Two birds swooped low over the lake, wings spread like sails.

"What do we—" Yironem's voice was strangled. "We're Rin! We can't kill kinaru!"

A memory ruptured into my mind. Last autumn, the snowcat at Aeti Ginu that didn't attack. "Don't shoot the birds. Save your arrows for the riders."

We waited, hidden among leafy cottonwood. I tried to form a ball of ice, but all I got was warm water that ran between my fingers. Rivulets of sweat ran down my back. Then I heard it.

Crackling, popping, wood exploding. Black smoke curled into the sky from down the shore. Southwest, where we came from.

"How can it — we haven't had a forest fire since the Storm Year!" Nili cried.

My breath caught. "Jinra-saidu."

The two kinaru landed with a torrential spray of water. Two archers leapt off and waded toward the dead spearman, surrounded by a patch of red water. I spent a moment in desperate indecision. Fighting them risked getting caught in the fire. Running would attract their attention. Either way, we were cut off from the Rin.

My horse buckled. I went down with it and slammed into the mud. It screamed, a high, wretched sound that sent goosebumps across my skin. Blood trickled from an arrow in its chest. I rolled aside in horror as it died next to me.

Arrows whistled past. One pierced Nili's calf and came out the other side, spraying blood into the bushes. She fired back, hands a blur.

I scrabbled through slippery mud that smelled like rot. My hand closed on Nurivel where it'd fallen. I ducked behind a tree. A Corvittai toppled into the water, riddled with arrows. Firelight flickered on the rippling surface.

Nili dropped to the ground. "I'm all out. Yiro, give me some arrows—"

I took a deep breath. One chance. It had to be perfect.

I swung around the tree and flung Nurivel. It whipped through the air and stuck in another archer's neck. He went down, splashing into the shallows.

Three lives.

The kinaru swung their heads around to look. They skittered across the lake, water rising in long trails behind them, and flapped into the air.

"Where's Yiro?" Nili's voice was oddly flat.

I whirled, looking up and down the shore. Yironem's bow and quiver lay in the muck. Bloody water swirled around the bulrushes. A rush of air almost knocked me over. Suriel—

But it wasn't the wind. A kinaru thrashed in the bushes, wings beating furiously. A stand of cottonwood saplings went down, snapping under webbed feet. White and black feathers fluttered through the air.

"*Yiro!*" Nili flung herself against the bird, her hair dark against its snow-white breast. "*Wala, wala.* Yiro, *dayomi*—"

My skin went cold. No one had attuned to a kinaru in Rin memory. It took me ages to calm down after I first attuned, but we didn't have time. Glowing embers drifted toward us. I smelled smoke. Down the shore, blazing trees crashed into the bulrushes.

The kinaru swung its head, shrieking. Blood stained its wings where branches tore into it. Nili clung to its sleek feathers. "You're still in there, Yiro. It's just a different body, it's still you—"

He curved his neck down, peering at her with a huge red eye, clacking his bill. For a second I thought he was calming — until his wings thrashed again, taking out a small alder. Leaves spun past me onto the water.

I split my focus in half. I pulled a wave from the lake and threw it at the burning forest. "Nili!" I tossed Yironem's muddy bow to her and slung his quiver over my shoulder. "We have to go!"

I fixed my gaze on Yironem's eye even as I flung wave after wave onto the flames. "Yiro! We need your help. Fendul could fly the first time he attuned. Trust your wings. Trust us. We've been through this."

"Kako's right," Nili soothed. "You'll be fine. We trust you."

His wings stilled. I leapt onto a fallen tree and vaulted onto Yironem's back. Nili ducked under a wing and I hauled her up after me. She sucked in a breath, swearing at the arrow in her leg.

"Come on, Yiro," she said. "Come on, little brother. Today we fly."

He lunged forward. Water erupted around us. We shot across

the lake, black wings beating, bulrushes streaming past. The spearman's horse lurched out of the way—

—and we soared up through smoke into clear air. The sky blossomed above us, such a thick blue I could almost touch it.

"West!" I shouted over the rush of wind.

We pitched to one side. I clung to Yironem's neck, Nili's grip tight around my ribs. We dropped suddenly. The world rushed up toward us. My insides wrenched — but Yironem caught himself on a billow of hot air, steadied, and glided toward the ocean.

I felt a stab of guilt for leaving the horses. The one in the lake might survive, but the one back on the path couldn't escape the fire with a broken leg. I should've given it a quick death.

Clearly visible from above, a black burning crescent glowed among the deep green of South Iyun. The crescent reached to the coast, enclosing a bluff where tiny figures darted among copses of spruce. Endless blue ocean sparkled beyond.

Riderless kinaru circled the bluff like wolves around prey. The soldiers we ambushed must've forced the battle to the open coast where kinaru could drop off the Corvittai rearguard. The fire kept our side from retreating. I cursed.

The kinaru themselves didn't attack. They swooped through the haze, their trembling calls like cloth snapping in the wind. Then I saw the orange glow. One bird carried a white-masked rider. The air shimmered around them.

Not a jinra-saidu. A jinrayul.

There had to be fire-callers other than Tiernan. Ingdanrad was full of mages. Aeldu knew why one might side with the Corvittai, but it *couldn't* be Tiernan. I ignored the creeping doubt of why Rhonos refused to fight.

My mind raced. Yironem couldn't attack another kinaru — the

taboo seemed far worse now that he *was* one. Nili couldn't use her bow without falling. And I didn't dare, not until I knew—

"Hold on tight!" I yelled. "Yiro! Take out that glowing person on the kinaru!"

He wheeled, flapping hard. Cool air streamed past as we rose. The world dropped away. He banked again, soared toward the other kinaru, and dove. By the time the bird saw us coming it was too late.

Yironem slammed into the rider. We spun away, the horizon vaulting. Arrows slid from the quiver on my back and fell toward earth. Nili's hand caught my shirt, the fabric yanking against my chest.

The other kinaru rolled, plummeted, and caught the falling jin-rayul in its bill. We streaked after them. The bird dumped the jinrayul on the ground and took off. My guess was right. The kinaru were torn without Suriel here to command them. They'd carry Corvittai into battle but refused to fight Rin.

Yironem spread his wings, soared over a thicket, and landed with a *whump*. I hit the dirt, my breath bursting from my lungs. The world spun. Nili gave shallow gasps nearby, holding her calf.

I pushed myself to my feet and dropped Yironem's empty quiver. "Look out for each other." I ran back toward the jinrayul, ducking behind boulders and splintered stumps. Salt spruce burned like bright flowers in the distance, forming a flickering red and gold wall straight to the cliffs. Heat washed over me.

Shouts and clangs echoed from the north. I stumbled on something and reeled back. A Rin woman sprawled in a pool of blood, her stomach torn open. A Corvittai lay beside her. His arm was three paces away.

I crouched behind a jumble of mossy rocks. The jinrayul grabbed at the reins of a rearing black horse. His mask had come off in the fall. He had a similar build to Tiernan, a scabbard at his waist — but through the hazy glow I saw darker skin and short black hair. I sagged against a boulder.

I reached for Nurivel and found an empty sheath. "Kaid," I muttered. It was back in the lake, buried in an archer's neck. I drew my hunting knife instead—

—and someone grabbed my braid. I screamed.

I twisted around and plunged the blade into something soft. It came out bloody. I stabbed again and again, writhing, kicking. The soldier let go of my hair, struck me in the face, and threw me on the ground. My knife flew from my hand. He put his boot on my chest, crushing me into the earth, and raised his spear.

So this is how I die. The sky spread out behind him, perfect deep blue woven with smoke. The drifting birds looked like white petals. I wondered if there were kinaru in Aeldu-yan.

The man's head jerked aside. Something huge and brown plowed into him.

I rolled the other way and scrambled up, scraping my palms. The world tipped like I was still flying. I spun back toward the soldier. He'd landed on the rocks. Blood flowed from his head, dripping down mossy stones like a waterfall.

A sleek horse cantered back around, thudding on the hard soil. It stopped in front of me and tossed its black mane.

"*Anwea!*"

She whuffed air from her huge nostrils. The fire must've driven her back here. I grabbed my knife, leapt onto a boulder, and swung onto her sweat-lathered back. Her spine dug into me. Good thing I learned to ride without a saddle.

The jinrayul sat astride the black horse watching me. He was young, maybe early twenties. Grey smoke drifted between us. I gripped the rawhide cord on my knife handle. It wasn't weighted as well as Nurivel. I couldn't count on a good throw.

Only then did I notice how ragged he was. His shoulders slumped and sweat shone on his skin. The orange light flickered. He wavered in the saddle.

"Are you Nonil? The captain?" I called.

"Yes." His voice was flat, with a slight Ferish accent.

This was it. A missing iron link in the chain. For three years, Suriel had been killing people to keep them away from Dúnravn Pass. In three years there'd been no reports of a fire mage — because Nonil hadn't helped guard the pass. He was *being* guarded. Suriel couldn't die, but the mage serving him could.

"You helped Suriel raze the Toel Ginu shrine."

"Yes."

"And it didn't work, so Suriel wanted Tiernan Heilind instead. A proper rift mage."

"Yes."

"Why are you here? Doesn't Suriel need you still?"

Silence.

"Why do you want the Rin dead?"

"It is safer than letting you live." He drew his sword, but it seemed heavy in his hand.

I spat blood. "You should've killed me in Toel."

I threw my blade. It sliced his arm as it sailed past. His sword thumped to the ground. The second the knife left my grip, I drew my flail and dug my heels into Anwea.

We were on him before he could dodge. The flail's iron spikes bit through leather, spraying out blood. I heard his ribs shatter. Nausea rose into my throat.

I whirled Anwea back around, my flail rattling on its chain. The black horse bolted. Nonil lay broken. His hand twitched and went still.

Four lives.

The glow faded like a sunset. The wall of flames dimmed. The crackling quietened.

Horses still galloped across the bluff to the north. Screams shattered the air. I had to keep going, keep fighting, but all I wanted to do was throw up.

A hawk screeched. My head jerked up. Ospreys, ravens, geese, and owls shot overhead like winged arrows, all heading for the battle. Anwea shied.

I whipped around to look south. Frothing waves rose over the cliffs and slammed onto the burning forest. Steam billowed into the sky like a cloud bursting to life. Deer bounded over scorched logs, foxes darted around blackened bushes, a grizzly bear plowed through blazing grass. A coyote tumbled over a ridge and veered toward me.

Airedain shifted back to human, stumbling from the momentum. His eyes skimmed the blood dripping from my flail, Nonil's crushed ribcage, Anwea tossing her head. "Kateiko—"

My flail thudded into the dirt. I slid from Anwea and crumpled against Airedain.

"It's okay. We're here now." He brushed damp hair from my face and wrapped an arm around me as animals thundered past.

He stood with me, keeping watch over the bluff. Water flowed over the cliffs in clear ribbons, following Iyo antayul into the depths of South Iyun Bel. The only Corvittai who fled our way fell with an Iyo woman's javelin in his back. The sounds of battle faded. Horses ran past. The water ribbons cut off and slithered back into the sea.

"The healers will be here soon," Airedain said. "You should get those wounds cleaned."

"Not yet. My family . . . I have to find . . ."

"Come on then." He picked up my flail and slid his hand into mine. He led me north, weaving between spruce and twisted pines. Anwea trailed behind us.

The dead lay everywhere. I saw Taworen with an arrow in his eye. A Tamu woman crushed by a horse. Yironem's friend Umeril riddled with arrows. A seventeen-year-old Rin drummer I grew up with, sprawled across a Corvittai with her dagger in his stomach. The canoe carver I was caught kissing long ago, now too torn apart to tell what killed him. I vomited in a thicket after that.

I forced myself to look at them all, even the Corvittai. I wanted to see the faces of the people who did this to us. But there were no answers in their staring eyes or mangled bodies. Nonil's words scratched at my mind. How could letting us live be worse than this?

A huddle of people had formed near a tangle of rotting logs. I pulled away from Airedain and forced my way through. Fendul knelt in the dirt. Relief washed over me — until I saw him cradling his father's head in his lap.

Behadul stared up at the blue sky. His body was a mess of arrows and wounds, as much blood as skin. My chest suddenly felt too tight.

"Fen," I whispered. I was supposed to call him Okorebai, but in that moment, he was just my friend. My family.

He looked up, his eyes hollow as the logs around us. I knelt and put my hand on his arm. The crowd trickled away. I heard voices, footsteps, wailing kinaru, but ignored it all until I heard Dunehein shouting.

"Go," Fendul said. "I'll be all right."

I kissed his hair. "I'm sorry, Fen."

I followed Dunehein's voice until I found him on the far side of a copse. A broken spear jutted from his thigh. He towered like a bear, huge hands balled into fists.

"I have to go back!" he yelled at Mereku, the Iyo woman who'd helped us plan the ambush. "You don't know for sure!"

"I *saw* her. And you can't go like this. Not while the fire's still burning—"

"Fuck the fire! That just means I have to get her out!" He curled his fists toward his chest like it took all his strength not to hit something.

"Dunehein—" Mereku reached out.

He twisted out of reach. "I just got her back! Nine years and I just got my mother back!"

My stomach wrenched. As he spoke, two women carried a body from the forest. A grey-streaked braid trailed in the dirt. I recognized Isu's reddish-brown clothing. Everything else blurred into smudges of colour.

"Dune."

He turned to me, then to where I pointed. His voice scraped like broken glass. "Nei. She can't be — she *can't!*"

I didn't remember walking to him, only crumpling against him. I knotted my fingers into his long hair, unable to stop my shaking. The whole world was just the two of us clinging to each other.

"Kako." He rested his chin on my head. Droplets landed on my hair. "It's not fair. We just got her back—"

"I know." The air clouded with mist, but I felt dry inside.

She was gone. Like losing my mother all over again. Isu had comforted me after the Dona war, kept me safe during the Storm Year, held me when I woke as a wolf. She suffered, too, but she locked away her grief and helped me carry mine.

I still heard her voice, the way she drew out my full name. I saw her smile as she spun warm summer rain into soaring birds. But I'd never hug her on my wedding day or hear her laugh as she played with my children's tiny fingers. She gave her life so I'd have the chance Emehein never had — but she wouldn't be there to share it with me.

Tears streamed down my cheeks when her words came back to me. *I love you whether I'm with you or not.*

33.

BLOOD & WATER

I had no idea how much time had passed when someone pulled me from Dunehein. I felt like a submerged log, buffeted by the ebb of footsteps and voices. A terrible weight kept me under. There was light somewhere, but I didn't have the energy to reach for it.

It wasn't until fire stabbed my leg that I broke the surface.

I clenched my teeth to stop from crying out. I was sitting on the ground against a boulder. A grey-braided man cleaned a palm-length wound on my thigh. He had a dolphin tattoo on his arm and a fan-shaped antayul mark on his chest.

Blood had painted flaking tracks through my mud camouflage. The healer ran a stream of water over my thigh, nudging it deep into the gash. Fresh blood began to flow. I held out until he started to remove bits of leaves and bark with a bone needle, and then a gasp escaped my teeth.

"I have tulanta, if you need something for the pain," the man said.

"Nei." My throat grated. "I don't want the visions."

Airedain took my hand and offered a lopsided smile. "You helped me at Skaarnaht. My turn now."

I focused on his warm, calloused fingers. He hummed some familiar tune. Everything felt muted — the sticky air, the rock pressing into my spine, the crunch of evergreen needles as someone passed.

To stanch the bleeding, the healer packed a gauze bag of bog-moss into the gash. It smelled like seaweed and damp wood. He bound it with cottonspun bandages, and then repeated the process on a deep cut on my arm that I didn't remember getting, shouldered his wicker carryframe, and moved on.

"Oh. Forgot about this." Airedain stretched past me and took my flail down from a ledge on the boulders. "I cleaned it for ya."

Sunlight gleamed on the iron spikes. I slid the flail into its leather sheath, but its weight on my belt was no longer a comfort. I already knew what to name it in memory of the first life it took. *Antalei* — waterfall, destroyer of fire.

Airedain sat back on his heels. "They're still pulling people out of the forest. I should help, but if you need me to stay . . ."

"Go ahead. But can you . . . do one thing for me?"

"Yeah. Anything."

I drew a shuddering breath. "There's . . . three dead Corvittai in the lake, just off the main road. By a dead horse and kinaru feathers on shore. They don't deserve to be left there."

His mouth twisted, but he nodded. "I'll get Jonalin to help me."

"My dagger's there too. It . . . it was my temal's before he died."

He nodded again and brushed dirt off his breeches. "Hang in there, Rin-girl."

Once he had left, I glanced around. Twenty or so people rested on sun-browned conifer needles — a patchwork of purpling bruises, white and red bandages, auburn bark splints. The hastily-made camp was a triangle bordered by bluish salt spruce, rocks speckled with rust-orange lichen, and a wind-thrown cottonwood with green moss on the underside. Smoke turned it all into a haze of smeared colour.

Fendul leaned against a stump, talking to Tokoda. She sat cross-legged so they could see eye-to-eye. A gash ran from his left shoulder to his bottom right rib, sealed with gobs of sticky pine resin. The clear golden layer was rippled with red. Mereku and an Iyo man held Dunehein down while a woman worked the spear from his leg. He might've been cursing, but other people's groans drowned him out. Hiyua's arm was a bloody mess. She'd never fire a bow the same way. Orelein had bandages across his stomach.

Rin, Iyo, Tamu alike refilled waterskins, shared woven baskets of berries, passed around ice to numb wounds. A sombre excuse for a reunion feast. I knew who'd taken tulanta by their flickering eyes and trembling hands. An axe sang as a man cut saplings for stretchers. In the distance were rows of bodies, the Corvittai set apart from ours. I shuddered at how many there were. Flies buzzed past, lured by the stench of death.

I rested my head on the boulder and closed my eyes. Even the sun felt faint on my skin. I was sinking again, my lungs filling with water, the current threatening to pull me under. *Should've taken the tulanta. Should've asked Airedain to stay. Should've died back in the forest.*

The patchwork of bodies grew. I could tell without looking. The acrid reek of burnt hair and flesh overtook the mouldering smell of bogmoss. I heard hacking coughs, moans, a flurry of wings as scouts landed. And all the while, only the faintest of breezes nudged my skin.

Kinaru still circled overhead. They were leaderless, Nonil dead,

Suriel absent. Their calls wove a pattern — not quick, rippling alarm cries now, but low and drawn out like wolf howls. I wondered which side they mourned. *The wind dies a thousand deaths.*

"Kako."

My eyes fluttered open. I dragged myself to the surface. Fendul stood in front of me, a hand on his sword hilt. I got to my feet, ignoring the throb in my leg.

"The fire's mostly out," he said. "It burned such a narrow area that none of the bodies were touched. I don't know why a jinra-saidu would care, but I don't like the idea of one interfering in our battles."

"It wasn't a saidu." I kicked a pine cone. "Nonil was a jinrayul. Like Tiernan."

His brow furrowed. "No human should be able to burn rain-forest like that."

"It's . . . possible. Tiernan found ways to strengthen fire with runes. Nonil must've done something similar to the Iyo shrine, enhancing his magic while Suriel stoked the flames. But it's hard. He almost killed himself causing this forest fire."

Fendul pinched his temples. "I get the feeling you have some-thing to tell me."

He listened silently as I recounted the battle. His lips pressed into a thin line when I mentioned Yironem showing up, thinner when I got to him attuning to a kinaru, like a mountain wearing down bit by bit. He turned aside and swore when I repeated what Nonil said.

"The Corvittai know everything about us, but we don't even know if they still follow Suriel." He scraped a hand through his damp hair. "No time to dwell on it. Some of these people won't sur-vive a night outside. We're moving everyone to Toel Ginu."

I looked out at the ocean, which was gentler than I'd ever seen it. "Did our boats with the kids make it through?"

He nodded. "Wotelem met them. I hate to ask more of you, but if your horse can carry some people to the Tamu docks . . ."

Most of the Corvittai horses had fled. I found Anwea in a gap between two copses. She jerked sideways, backed up, turned again like she couldn't get away from something. I approached slowly. "*Wala, wala*, Anwea. *Dayomi.*"

She skittered away, tossing her mane. I grabbed her halter — and as I heard kinaru crying, something clicked.

"You've seen them before." I glanced up at them wheeling. "That's why you spook every time you meet a flock of birds — the crows on the Roannveldt, the squalling birds in North Iyun, the Iyo who just came. You've seen kinaru in battle."

Anwea stilled. She gazed at me with huge brown eyes.

"They won't hurt you. I won't let anyone hurt you." I stroked her neck. "You saved my life, but I need your help again. Can you do that for me?"

She nudged her whiskery nose into my shoulder. I smiled.

I got ropeweed cord from the stretcher builders and knotted it onto her halter for reins. Once I'd mounted, a healer settled a Tamu woman in front of me. The bandage around the woman's foot glistened with blood. Her pupils were wide and her face was pale, but she was aware enough to pull her hair forward so it didn't rub against me.

Fendul and I headed south in a small convoy. Scars of over-turned dirt marked where people's blood met the earth. I skirted well around the rocks where Anwea had knocked a Corvittai to his death. Soft grey ash rustled under her hooves as she stepped past blackened stumps. I doused a few smouldering fires. The swath of scorched trees wasn't much deeper than a dozen canoes end to end. I was astonished how precise Nonil's control had been.

I recognized our tents from a distance. We passed the wooden box of trout Nili and I had caught for the feast, the ice long melted into cloudy water. That morning felt like a lifetime ago.

"Shark waters," the Tamu woman mumbled, grasping at air.

Healers hurried over as we neared the docks. I wasn't sure how they'd get people down the winding steps until I saw the pulley system used to haul goods up the cliffs. They nestled the woman into a canvas sling and lowered her with a creak of wood and rope.

"Kako! Over here!"

I spun. Nili sat among the roots of a spruce, her leg wrapped with cottonspun. Yironem stood nearby clutching their bows. He looked unscathed other than angry red scratches across his arms and chest.

I dismounted and led Anwea over to them. "Thank the aeldu you're okay."

Nili grimaced. "'Okay' is pushing it. I left so much blood on the ground when they pulled out the arrow, you may as well dig my grave there. Have you seen our tema?"

"Hiyua's all right. She'll be here soon. What happened after I left?"

"A Corvittai saw us land." The bows trembled in Yironem's hands. "He attacked right as I changed back."

"You shoulda seen the man's face." Nili gave a shaky laugh. "Bet he started wondering if all kinaru are viirelei. He got us right up against the cliffs, but an Iyo warrior took him out. What about you?"

"Turns out Nonil was a jinrayul. The fire's out now. So." I shrugged.

Nili reached toward her throat and fumbled at nothing. Her brow creased. "My necklace. The one you gave me last year, right before we separated—"

"Maybe someone will find it." I tried to smile.

"Kako." She looked at me closely. "Who did we lose?"

"Too many." I fiddled with the ropeweed reins. "Isu. Umeril. Taworen. And we have a new Okorebai-Rin."

Yironem crumpled. Nili pulled him close, stroking his hair. When she bit her lip, I could tell she was trying not to cry. She never cried in front of Yironem, not even when they'd seen their father's and sister's bodies in the Dona war.

I couldn't bear to look at their faces. I gazed out at the ocean, deep blue sprinkled with shards of light. Dolphins surfaced among the waves.

"Oh no," Yironem said faintly.

Hiyua approached, two paces ahead of Fendul. She held her mangled arm close to her body. Her tail of hair spilled down her back, dark as a stormy sky. She stopped in front of us, looming over Yironem. "You have a lot to explain, *akesidal*."

He ducked his head. "I'm sorry, Tema, Okorebai. I . . ." His voice wavered.

"Don't be too hard on Yiro," I whispered to Fendul. "He saved Nili and me. And I just told him about Umeril."

Fendul rubbed his temples. His lichen camouflage was almost gone. "The law is the law."

"*Fen*," I said desperately.

He beckoned to Yironem. "Come here."

Yironem stepped forward, pale as his kinaru feathers.

Fendul put his hands on the boy's shoulders. "Kateiko told me what happened. Attuning the first time is never easy. Rin have died in combat because people couldn't get it under control. You put others in danger by staying today. Do you understand?"

He nodded, staring at Fendul's feet.

"I'm obligated to sentence anyone who breaks the law." Fendul's voice was steady. "But I think the sentence has been fulfilled. You saved two lives today. You also took one and lost one. Remember what war costs, and that'll be the best lesson you can take from this."

Yironem's eyes widened. "I'll remember. I promise."

Fendul stepped back. "You should get to Toel Ginu. Hiyua, I'm putting you in charge until I get there. Look after the jouyen for me."

"I will." Hiyua embraced her son with her good arm.

"Okorebai . . ." Yironem scuffed his boot in the dirt. "What do you think it means? Kinaru aren't even supposed to exist."

Fendul gave him a thoughtful look. "I think you saw something in a kinaru that held a certain truth for you. Maybe the truths we once lived by have to change, too." He touched my elbow. "Kako, we should get back."

I pulled Nili to her feet. "Can you walk?"

She nodded. Her silence carried more weight than words. We hugged for a long moment before I helped her limp to the pulleys. I peered over the cliffs and watched people far below settle her in a canoe, rocking in the tide.

Our numbers dwindled. Only a trace of smoke lingered when I passed through the burnt area with a young Rin girl who was cloudier than the Tamu woman. By the time I got Dunehein onto Anwea, the kinaru had left.

"That's everyone," Fendul said when I returned. The triangular camp was empty except for a man packing supplies into a carry-frame. Shadows stretched across the uneven ground. "They're just bringing the dead out from the forest now."

I gazed at the bodies laid out like notches in wood. The rows curved around stumps and rocks, broken up by saplings. Flies buzzed past in black clouds. Anwea pulled at the reins until I let her back away. Tokoda and another woman carried Ohijo's limp body on a stretcher. Seventy-five, walking with a cane, and Ohijo had still joined us at the ambush with a bow and poisoned arrows. We'd have a new eldest elder now.

"How many lost?" I asked Fendul.

"Forty-four Rin, ten Tamu, seventeen Iyo. Eighty-two Corvittai and counting."

"Sixty-two Rin left in the entire world." The number felt hollow. So small it was meaningless. The Rin had been the most powerful jouyen in the Aikoto Confederacy once.

Fendul rubbed the interlocking lines on his arm. "We need help, and soon. For all I know, Suriel could send more Corvittai tomorrow. Aeldu willing, we can reforge the Aikoto alliance from the Elken Wars."

I looked up at his weary face. Until then I'd been treading water, barely staying afloat. Fendul pulled me the rest of the way from my haze. This had all been thrust on him at once, but he was still fighting the current. *Rivers keep flowing. We're not out of the rapids yet.*

"Falwen has contacts in every jouyen," I said. "I can ride to Caladheå tonight. Iannah said he's at the Colonnium until sunset almost every day."

Fendul was quiet for a moment, thinking. "I should go myself. Normally the okoreni acts as envoy, but until we get one . . ."

"Can you even get into Caladheå? You have to be registered—"

"I am." He took a card from his breeches pocket and held it up between two fingers. "Since birth."

"Then let's go together. I know my way around the city. You can't waste time getting lost."

He hesitated, glancing at the fiery light on the ocean. "How soon can we make it there?"

"An hour, maybe. If you can keep up."

Fendul raised an eyebrow. "Don't insult your okorebai."

Anwea streaked across the rocky ground, sweat lathering on her smooth coat. South Iyun Bel faded behind us as we curved inland to join the road to Caladheå. A crow flapped tirelessly overhead, a shadow against the sky. Fendul drifted away a few times to scout the area. Anwea folded her ears back whenever he returned, but kept galloping.

Rough, tumbling hills splintered by brooks flattened into the low plain of the Roannveldt. A breeze carried whispers of the dead through the cooling evening. The sun kissed the horizon as we passed through a flax field, the ground littered with thousands of pale blue flowers. Fendul swooped down, shifted in midair, and landed on the road panting.

I pulled up on the reins. "You okay?"

He touched his chest. The golden resin glowed like fire, streaked with fresh blood. "It looks worse than it is. The guardhouse is up ahead, that's all."

"Ride with me." I pulled him up behind me, draping my braid over my shoulder so it didn't stick to the resin.

I'd reapplied charcoal over my kinaru tattoo so I could pass as Iyo. Fendul refused to cover his, saying he wouldn't spend his first hours as okorebai hiding who he was. I didn't press it. Not so soon after his father's blood met the ground.

He let me do the talking at the guardhouse. Elkhounds with spears and grey armour squinted at our identification in the fading light. Lying about the battle was pointless with our injuries, so I told the blunt truth and for once they let us pass without trouble. Itherans stared as we rode through the quiet streets of Ashtown — whether due to our bare skin, fresh wounds, or flaking camouflage, I wasn't sure.

The trees along the Colonnium avenue were thick with foliage. I'd only been on the hill at dusk once, during the vigil for Baliad Iyo. How different it looked then, full of viirelei and itherans shivering together in the icy wind.

"No viirelei permitted until further notice," said a black-bearded Antler at the iron gates.

"We need to speak with the Officer of the Viirelei," I said. "We've just been attacked by Corvittai near Toel Ginu."

His expression didn't change. "No viirelei."

Fendul slid down to the cobblestone. He gave his identification to the guard and showed him the black lines on his arm. "I'm the new okorebai of the Rin-jouyen. Our last okorebai was just killed in combat."

The guards exchanged looks. "I've never heard of the Rin nation," said a man with a deep scar across his cheek.

"How?" I said incredulously. "They fought in two Elken Wars on this very spot. I thought Colonnium guards were better informed than other itherans."

"A hundred Corvittai were just outside your city." Fendul spoke levelly, but his hand was tight around his sword hilt. "The Council should be concerned."

"We have our orders," the bearded guard said.

I dug around in my purse and held out the card from Parr. "Councillor Parr gave me this. He won't be pleased to learn I or the Okorebai-Rin was refused entry."

The scarred Antler skimmed the card and handed it back. "You can enter. Not him."

Fendul's eyes met mine. His lips pressed into a thin line.

"I'll be back." I stressed the last word slightly. He nodded.

The guards opened the gates with a loud wrench. I passed under the rearing stone elk, their hooves forming a bridge far overhead, and skirted around the Colonnium. The deep green grass was soft as a pillow under my boots. Crickets chirped. Warm light spilled from windows in the north pavilion. Most of the building was dark. Only the top sliver of its domed towers glowed orange with sunlight.

I tied Anwea to a hitching post on the back lawn. Guards gazed down from the covered loggia. I climbed the steps and hurried down the walkway past thick stone pillars, peering in each set of glass doors. Whenever I glanced over my shoulder, an Antler was watching me.

Falwen was in his office shuffling through a drawer. His sleeves were rolled up, waistcoat tightly buttoned over his starched shirt. Thin white candles glowed on his desk. I rapped on the glass.

His head jerked up. He shut the drawer and pulled the door open. "Sohikoehl. What is it?"

"They wouldn't let him in," I whispered. A crow landed on the stone railing with a flurry of wings.

Falwen's eyes flickered up and down the loggia. He spoke loudly, his words falling hard and fast like arrows. "You are late. I needed this two hours ago. Good god, did you fall down a mineshaft on the way? The Okorebai-Iyo could not have assigned me a more hopeless aide." When the guards turned back toward the lawn, he whispered, "In. Hurry."

Fendul flew in after me and perched on a cabinet, talons clacking on the wood. The door clicked shut.

Falwen pulled heavy drapes over the panes. "Sohikoehl, watch the door."

I gazed through a gap in the fabric, hearing a rustle of feathers and a faint thump. The loggia was entirely in shadow. Stone arches framed orange peaks on the horizon. A pigeon pecked at the auburn tiles.

"Night visits from an okoreni are never good," Falwen said.

"Okorebai now," Fendul said.

Falwen swore. It sounded even stranger from him than it did from Fendul. "Sit. Speak."

Exhaustion crept over me as they talked. My thigh pulsed. Every muscle ached. I leaned my forehead on the cool glass, gazing at the barracks where Iannah was probably asleep. I felt a burst of anger, remembering our fight on the shore.

"Do you know anything about this itheran Nonil?" Fendul asked.

"He had a vendetta against the Rin. But you figured that out." A quill scratched rapidly. "I would tell you more if I could, Okorebai. All I know is you are in danger in Caladheå."

I glanced back into the cramped office. "From who?"

Falwen jerked his quill toward the city. "The hundred thousand itherans that live here. Would you like their names?"

"We're going back to Toel Ginu," Fendul said. "The Rin are staying there for now."

"Good." Falwen stopped scribbling long enough to dip the quill in an inkpot. "I will contact you when I hear from the other jouyen."

"Thank you." Fendul rose with a wince. "We should go, Kako."

"Falwen," I said hesitantly. "Do you know if Councillor Parr is here?"

"You just missed him," he said without looking up. "Council was not in session today. He came by his office and left."

"Oh." I tried not to let my disappointment show. I unlatched the door and stepped back as Fendul flew past me into the cool night. He was gone before the guards noticed light spilling onto the tiles.

"Sohikoehl."

I turned. The candles sputtered in the breeze. An owl hooted.

"I just remembered." Falwen pulled something from his breast pocket and dropped it into my palm. "Parr wanted an antayul to look at this."

I untangled a delicate chain and held up a silver pendant of snare wire twisted into a leaf. Three clear orbs shimmered with fire-light. I gasped. "Where did he get this?"

"I do not know. He was merely curious about its craftsmanship. He is a great admirer of such things. No doubt you noticed."

He knows about Parr and me, I thought, but at the same time, *why did Antoch have it* — "It belongs to my best friend. I made it."

Falwen arched a pale eyebrow. "Can you prove that?"

I held it near the candles so he could see. The water orbs stretched into thin ropes and wrapped around the wire. A second later, they turned into mist — and reformed into perfect orbs where they started.

Falwen gazed at me for a long moment before turning back to his writing. "Go. Return it to its owner. I have a long night ahead."

"But—"

"Go. *Now.*"

34.

LIKE MOTHS TO LIGHT

I hurried down Colonnium Hill. Caladheå was dark, lit only by tiny points of light like scattered stars. Black silhouettes of ships rocked against the violet horizon. A crow passed overhead like a ghost and followed me into a grove.

"What's wrong?" Fendul said when he saw my face.

I held out the necklace. "Falwen said this came from Parr."

Fendul's eyes widened. "How did he—"

"Nili lost it during the battle." I closed my hand around the chain. "Maybe an Iyo found it and came to Caladheå, but . . . I don't know. I need to go talk to Parr."

His mouth twisted. "You shouldn't go alone."

"Fen, if he wanted to hurt me he could've two days ago. You should be with the Rin."

"Kako." Fendul gripped my arms. "I let you and Nili come south alone and look what happened. I can't lose another Rin today. And if Parr's involved, I should know about it."

I looked up into his dark eyes. "All right. Just . . . promise you'll let me talk to him."

He nodded. "I promise."

I barely noticed the brick buildings slide past, or when the cobblestone streets changed to dirt as we left the city. A torch glowed at the southeast guardhouse, but the rest of the Roannveldt was as dark and soft as otter fur. Shadowy fields rippled around us. The willows along the lane to Parr Manor rustled in the breeze.

The outlines of the sloping roofs were like mountains against the inky sky. No light came from the windows. Leaves whispered around our feet in the half-moon courtyard. I tethered Anwea by a dead garden bed, crossed to the covered entrance, and knocked.

Fendul came up beside me, looking around at brick pillars wreathed with trailing vines. "Maybe he's asleep."

I knocked again harder, then crossed to the windows of the room where I spent the night with Parr. The square panes set in an iron grid rose twice as high as my head. I pressed my face to the glass and squinted in. Deep in the shadows, I saw movement. "Someone's in there."

"Parr?"

"I don't know who else it'd be." I banged on the window. "Antoch! It's Kateiko!"

The door rattled. "Locked," Fendul said.

I circled behind the manor, trying doors set into niches in the brick. The grounds were quiet except for droning mosquitoes. Worry grew in me like catching flame. Parr had been so sweet and gentle I couldn't believe he'd avoid me.

"I have to get inside." I stepped back into tall grass and eyed the windows, remembering my torn nails after breaking into Criek-naast's town hall.

Fendul rubbed his forehead. "Unless you have a battering ram hidden somewhere . . ."

"There." I pointed at an open window on the second floor. A dense mat of blazebine covered the wall around it.

Leaves scratched my hands as I fumbled in the foliage. I grasped a woody vine, scraped my boot against brick until I found a foot-hold, and pulled myself up. My sore muscles protested every move. Fendul muttered something and started up after me.

As I neared the second storey, my foot slipped. A branch jabbed my thigh wound. I cried out and lost my grip, hanging off the building by one hand.

"Kako!" Fendul caught my leg and supported me until I grabbed a vine. "Don't die here. I can't carry you all the way to Toel."

"Shut up or I'll fall on you." I climbed until I hung next to the open window, then swung one leg over the sill and toppled inside. Pain jolted through my thigh.

I touched shapeless white objects in the gloom. Fabric draped over furniture, maybe a cabinet. The long, low object was probably a bed. Rectangles on the wall might've been paintings. I edged forward on creaking floorboards.

Fendul slid through the window. He unlatched a wooden case hanging from his belt and took out his irumoi, the thin rod covered with glowing mushrooms. Faint blue light pushed back the shadows and made our skin look translucent.

The only uncovered furniture was a desk with finely carved legs. I squinted at a dark shape on top. The sickly sweet scent of moth-balls filled the air. "Ai, bring the irumoi here."

Fendul drew closer. The shape was a polished wooden box, its lid askew. I dug through crinkling paper and pulled out a heavy wool coat. The elk sigil on the black sleeve was unadorned. Parr's uniform would've had a red band for a captain.

My stomach twisted. "Parr's son was a soldier. Maybe this was his bedroom."

"You didn't mention he had a son."

"Because it's weird." I folded the scratchy fabric and set it back in the box. "His name's Nerio. Tiernan mentored him in the military, but Parr said he's been gone for half a decade . . . ohhhh. Oh, fuck."

"What?"

"Nonil. A young Ferish soldier whose magic is almost identical to Tiernan's. Parr trusted someone in the Corvittai—"

Fendul frowned. He pushed the box away.

I followed him into a corridor. Moonlight filtered through a smudged window at one end. I opened a door and found an empty room. No furniture, nothing on the walls. I backed away, disconcerted.

"Antoch?" I called.

Dust muffled our footsteps. Every door we passed was closed. Fendul checked one side of the corridor and I checked the other, but it was more of the same. A few pieces of furniture draped with white cloth, a few empty rooms. The air tasted like dead flowers.

When I found an open door, I stepped inside. Fendul stayed in the doorway, holding up the irumoi. The room was a mosaic of texture — panelled walls, filigree mouldings around soaring windows, a damask blanket on a wrought-iron bed. A candle stump and a thick book sat atop a table by a padded chair. The blue tinge made it look like we were underwater.

"We shouldn't be in here," I murmured.

"Is this Parr's bedroom?"

"I think so." I wandered further in, sinking into an embroidered rug. Guilt poked sharp needles into me, but when I saw trinkets scattered atop a lacquered cabinet, curiosity won out.

It looked like Parr had set them here while undressing. Goat-horn cufflinks, a black ribbon, his silver elk pin and green silk pocket square. I lowered my face to a crystal vial and breathed the spice of his cologne. Only then did I notice hoop earrings in a glass-topped wooden case.

I undid the latch. Three shelves unfolded like steps, separated into grids of shallow squares. I poked through the contents. A bracelet of glass beads, a brooch in the shape of a bird with a sweeping tail, a pendant set with a gem that looked viridian in the watery light. On the bottom shelf, I found a delicate gold ring.

I dropped it when I saw the etched knotwork. It clinked off the cabinet and bounced onto the carpet. Fendul strode forward and plucked it from the ground.

"What is it?" He held his palm flat, the ring balanced on his fingertips.

"Maika's wedding ring."

Fendul recoiled from his own hand. At the same moment, I heard footsteps.

I grabbed the ring and the irumoi. "Stay out of sight," I hissed. The only answer was a rustle of black feathers.

"Kateiko." Parr stood in the doorway, his dark hair tousled on his shoulders. He wore a loose white shirt, the collar unbuttoned. "What in god's name are you doing?"

I thrust out the ring. "What are *you* doing with this?"

His expression changed so quickly I couldn't read it. "Kateiko—"

"The truth, Antoch." I brandished the irumoi like a club.

"You will have it, I promise. Come downstairs." Parr held out a hand. "Please."

I felt sick at the sight of his rings, knowing they'd been all over my body, but it'd give Fendul a chance to get out from wherever he was. I jerked my chin at the door. "You first."

He backed into the corridor. I slipped the ring into my purse and followed him down a spiral staircase, the iron balustrades casting warped shadows like bony fingers. Parr led me to the room with the brocade furniture and crystals hanging from the ceiling. He shut the door and lit a row of white candles on the hearth. I blinked as warm light washed out the blue glow. A bottle and glass of red wine sat on the polished table by the couch, reflecting rays that danced across the wall.

When he turned, I realized how worn he looked. There was a shadow of stubble on his jaw, a rip in his sleeve, mud on his boots past the ankles. His shoulders slumped. "Would you like to sit down?" he asked.

"Nei." I stood on squares of glossy auburn wood, gripping the irumoi. "Talk."

Parr picked up his glass and twisted the stem between his fingers. "The day after we flew to Se Ji Ainu, my Corvittai source told me you offered Suriel another mage. I checked the provincial mage registry, found Marijka Riekkanehl's name, and guessed she might be familiar with Heilind's work. I said nothing to the Corvittai. I hoped to discuss it with you and offer my help.

"The next day, my source asked me to locate you, and by extension, the anonymous mage. Apparently Suriel had tried to meet you and was unable. The city guard last recorded you heading north, so I, assuming you were at Riekkanehl's home, went to warn you that the Corvittai were searching for you both. She said you had just left."

"*You* set off the runelight," I breathed. "Why didn't you tell me when I asked about this?"

"Riekkanehl and I . . . argued about several things. My past with Heilind, my interest in you, and my association with the Corvittai. She demanded to know who my source was. I refused to say." He set down the glass. "A good many angry words were exchanged. I was a soldier for eighteen years. Some reactions are ingrained for life."

I reeled back. "But — two days ago you said—"

"I said I regretted if my actions had anything to do with her death." His dark eyes fixed on me. "That will be one of the greatest regrets I carry to my grave. Riekkanehl was a good woman, a respected medic."

Horror prickled my skin. "You *murdered* my *friend*!"

"I acted on instinct. I did not mean to kill her."

The slender knife at his waist. I'd tossed it aside during our night together, never knowing what it had done. "Then why take her wedding ring? Is that — something you *do*? Steal from people you kill? Does everything in that jewellery case belong to dead people?"

He looked appalled. "Goodness. No. I knew Heilind would see it as a sign from Suriel. I hoped to return the ring one day, so I hid it among my wife's jewellery." A trace of annoyance crept into his voice. "Why were you looking through her belongings?"

"Trying to figure out why you had this." I clamped the irumoi between my teeth, taking sick pleasure in how the glow must distort my features, and fished Nili's necklace from my purse. The droplets sparkled like tiny oceans.

Parr's jaw clenched. "Falwen asked you to look at it."

"Yes. And I know where it came from, so be honest, Antoch."

"I was at the battle today, observing only. One eye on your enemies and one on your friends, remember. I found three Corvittai dead in a lake. I carried their bodies to land — as one soldier to another — and found the necklace among a great deal of blood and kinaru feathers. I asked Falwen if it was of viirelei origin. Curiosity, nothing more."

I pressed my lips together. "Do *you* know why the Corvittai attacked?"

"That is somewhat more complicated." He twisted one of his rings. "Please sit, Kateiko. Your leg must hurt."

I glanced at the trickle of dried blood on my thigh. It stung more than I wanted to admit. I put the necklace back in my purse and slowly sat on the edge of the couch, digging my nails into the brocade.

Parr took another glass from a cabinet and filled it with wine. When I refused, he set it on the table and sank into a chair. "What do you know of the Sverbian Rúonbattai?"

"Not much."

"They were the most radical of several militant groups that sprung up around the Second Elken War." He sipped his wine. "They blamed Ferish immigrants, ordinary people fleeing famine, for the crimes of a few warmongers."

"They wanted to drive the Ferish out of Eremur, right?"

He nodded. "The Rúonbattai were worse than anything we had ever suffered. Murder, torture, entire villages razed, immigrant ships sunk, bodies thrown in the harbour. Two decades ago, during the flu epidemic that took my wife and thousands more, rogue Ferish took advantage of the weakened military and held a coup. It was a minor scuffle, but the Rúonbattai's retaliation caused the Third Elken War."

I picked up my glass and swirled the liquid around just to occupy my hand. The scent of pepper and cranberry wafted out. "I know about that. The Okorebai-Iyo's children died in that war."

"A new figure rose to prominence in the Rúonbattai shortly after. Liet was . . . almost a cult leader. He planned to wake the elemental spirits in hopes of turning them on my people, and recruited mages from Ingdanrad to help. Suriel, however, believed other spirits would interfere with his attempt to access the void. He resolved to stop Liet at any cost."

My head snapped back up. "Suriel told me he wants to reach the void because other saidu don't want him here. You're saying he started trying *before* they woke?"

Parr raised his eyebrows. "I suppose that is why he swore you to secrecy. So nobody realized he was lying."

"Fucking saidu," I muttered.

"According to my source, eight years ago Suriel recruited Ferish mercenaries and destroyed the Rúonbattai in a single stroke. Those mercenaries later became the first Corvittai. It seems plausible. I was heavily involved in fighting the Rúonbattai and never knew why they simply vanished."

"But the saidu woke anyway. Seven years ago, in the Storm Year."

"The military long suspected a viirelei nation was assisting the Rúonbattai. It seems they succeeded where Liet did not. I only just learned which nation it was."

"Who?"

"The Rin."

I jerked to my feet. The glass slid from my hand, splashing wine on the woven rug. The irumoi rolled under the table. Its blue glow made the stain look like blood. "You're wrong."

Parr didn't move. "I am not surprised they kept it a secret from your nation."

"Wh—" I stared at him. "You still think I'm Iyo?"

He set down his glass. "You are listed as Iyo in the birth records," he said slowly. "You asked me to call on the Iyo nation for the inquiry. You delivered a plea for Baliad Iyo's release. You spoke of your family in Toel Ginu."

"I'm Rin! You saw this!" I wiped charcoal off my kinaru tattoo. "Falwen recorded me as Iyo so I could get past the city guard!"

He was silent.

The realization hit me like a crashing wave. "You didn't know it's the Rin crest. You're a councillor and you never bothered to learn—"

"I knew it is common in the north, where you said you grew up. I do not know the nuances of viirelei tattoos."

"You could've asked!" I turned aside, knotting my fingers into my hair. "You don't know who I *am*! You don't care!"

"That is not true." Parr rose and came around the table. "I care about you quite a lot. I did not want to make you uncomfortable by prying into your life."

I looked into his eyes. The peppery scent of wine rolled off him, but underneath there was something familiar — pine resin, sea spray. Up close, I saw dirt rubbed into his skin.

"Darling girl." He reached for me, hesitated. "I am sorry I have upset you. Where you came from has no impact on my desire to see you happy and safe. You have . . . no idea how much you've affected me."

"Tell me then." My voice was quiet in the cavernous room.

His hands shook almost as much as his voice. "You bring light and life to this house in a way I have not felt in many years. I found joy somewhere I never expected." He stepped closer. "My marriage was arranged. I was fifteen when I wed, seventeen when my wife passed. I was not in love with her, but her memory was all I had. Until you, my dear."

Parr ran his thumb across my lips. "There is a brightness to you that rises above the grief and futility of our world. As I came to know you, I thought, 'Perhaps I am not so alone.' I have rarely felt so blessed as two days ago. I . . . do not know if this is love, but I would like to find out."

He kissed me, gently at first, then with sudden fierceness. He tasted like wine, spicy and bitter at once. My lip stung where the Corvittai split it. For a moment, I was still.

When he reached toward my hair, I stumbled back, squishing on the wet carpet. "Nei. Don't touch me."

His hands fell to his sides. "Kateiko—"

"Is that why the Corvittai attacked us? Revenge for waking the saidu?"

He looked pained. "You really did not know any of this?"

"Nei. Until last winter, I thought the saidu were still dormant."

"The Corvittai are primarily Ferish. They suffered greatly at the hands of the Rúonbattai. In their minds, eradicating the Rin is a safeguard against the rebirth of a dangerous militia — particularly given the Rin are reuniting with the most powerful viirelei nation in Eremur."

It is safer than letting you live. "So Suriel didn't send them."

"No. Suriel has withdrawn from overseeing their actions. The Corvittai fought under their own leadership today."

"Under Nonil." My hands curled into fists. "Is he your son?"

Parr's expression turned to surprise. "Goodness. What gave you that idea?"

"You're protecting your Corvittai source. Or you would've told Marijka who it is instead of killing her."

"Nonil, my source, and my son are three different people. I had never met Nonil until recently. My son has nothing to do with the Corvittai."

"So you don't care that I killed Nonil?"

He didn't flinch. "I consider it a blessing. Too many people have died because of him."

My nails dug into my palms. "Why should I believe you?"

"I have never lied to you, Kateiko."

"You left out some pretty fucking important truth."

Without looking away, I took stock of my surroundings. Couch on my right, table on my left, chairs beyond it. Fireplace behind me. I picked up Parr's glass and took a sip, letting my lips linger on the edge. The spice burned my throat. I set the wine on the table and backed toward the fireplace. Heat radiated from candles on the mantelpiece above my head.

"Tell me one thing," I said. "You know I don't care about the law, or — what anyone else thinks. I just want the truth."

He drew forward, a slow step at a time. "Ask, my darling."

I knotted my fingers into his shirt, feeling the strained rise and fall of his chest. Firelight flickered on his face. Branches scraped at a window like rattling bones. His knife was within reach, but I'd never get it before him.

My voice trembled. "How'd you know the Corvittai's plans? Your source trusts you that much?"

His hand hesitated by my side. "Please understand—"

"The *truth*, Antoch. Or you'll never see me again, I swear to the aeldu."

Parr closed his eyes. His breath was shallow, his jaw tight. When he opened his eyes, he looked oddly calm. "I sent the Corvittai."

I stared at him for just a second. Then I shoved him as hard as I could.

He toppled onto the table with an explosion of shattering glass. I vaulted over the couch, braid snapping through the air. A cry tore out of me when I landed on my wounded leg.

The door burst open. Fendul dashed in, sword drawn. Parr seized an iron poker and met the attack. He drew the slender knife with his other hand. Metal clanged on metal, echoing into the depths of the room. The knife spun to the floor and slid under a cabinet.

I reached for Nurivel and swore. Airedain hadn't made it back in time.

Fendul pushed Parr toward the fireplace. Blood splattered across the floor. Parr's face twisted and he smashed the poker into Fendul's wrist. The fight shifted like a river reversing course. Steel flashed with firelight as Parr pressed Fendul into the open. I couldn't even track their blows — then Fendul went sprawling.

I leapt forward. My flail slammed into Parr's arm. The poker clattered to the floorboards. He wrenched the flail from my grip and flung it across the room. It smashed into something that fell like a toppling tree. I hit him in the mouth and choked as his elbow rammed my chest.

"Idiot!" Fendul snapped.

Distance. He knew my strengths.

I darted toward the far wall. Parr struck Fendul's shoulder with a *crack*. The sword clanged to the floor, Fendul's arm dangling limp. Parr shoved him back and seized the sword.

I snatched a marble figurine and threw it at a window. Glass rained out into the courtyard. In the second Parr looked aside, a crow shot toward the ceiling. It lurched and vanished into the shadows. I heard a thud and cringed.

Parr spun toward me, shoulders shaking, his sleeve shredded and bloody.

"Stay there." I drew my hunting knife. The space between us yawned like a gorge. Cool air swirled through the broken window. The buzz of mosquitoes filled the air.

He spat blood. "You brought another viirelei to kill me?"

"How long?" I demanded. "How long have you been on their side?"

"I am not on the Corvittai's side. We just have a mutual goal." Parr watched me levelly. "See it from my eyes, Kateiko. I devoted my life to stopping the Rúonbattai. They kept me from everything precious — my wife's last weeks on this earth, years of my son's childhood. I held my comrades as they died. I pulled burnt bodies from farmhouses and drowned children from the sea. The Rin nation helped cause those things. I cannot allow history to repeat itself."

"You're saying this was to *save* people?"

"My goal has always been to protect the citizens of Eremur. Today I set two violent groups against each other. I have been working to destroy the Corvittai since last autumn, well before this war started."

"Crieknaast didn't know Suriel brought the Corvittai back until winter."

"My family owns the abandoned logging camp on Tømmbrind Creek. I received word that poachers were using it for storage. I investigated and found a Corvittai supply cache."

Images flashed through my mind. Suriel's blinding sigil in the valley of stumps, the looted loggers' buildings, riders wearing elk-sigil armour on a stormy autumn night — I inhaled sharply. "Give me the sword."

Parr didn't move.

"I trust my aim more than my patience." I drew back my arm.

He still didn't move.

I jerked my chin at the shadows behind him. "If you say you love me, you won't hurt him."

A muscle twitched by his mouth. Finally, he bent down and spun the sword across the gleaming floor. It skidded to a stop near my feet.

"Now take off your shirt."

Parr's brows drew together. "What—"

"Do it! I've killed four people! I can make it five!"

He unbuttoned his shirt and tossed it aside. His skin gleamed with sweat, his chest marked with scars under dark hair. Only one mattered — the jagged line under his collarbone. I'd seen it, touched it, not giving it a second thought.

The room suddenly felt too small. I couldn't be far enough away from him. I balanced on the edge of a windswept cliff, a heartbeat from falling into an abyss.

"We've fought before." I pointed at the scar with my blade. "In North Iyun Bel last year. Your horse broke my leg. I threw this knife at you."

Realization swept across his face like wind through dry leaves.

Out of nowhere, the words of Airedain's friend Nokohin came to me. *I'm not afraid of the spirits out there. I'm afraid of the people right here.* I choked with laughter. "All this time I've been worried about Suriel. We should be afraid of each other."

Parr touched the scar. "I never told my men to harm you."

"You didn't tell them *not* to." My revulsion twisted, hardened, froze into cold fury. "You talk about protecting people, but — we weren't *people* to you — just stupid wood witches no one would miss—"

He stepped closer. "Darling girl—"

I thrust the knife forward. "I said stay there. And don't ever call me that again."

"Kateiko, please listen. I made mistakes—"

"It wasn't a fucking mistake! That had nothing to do with the Rúonbattai — you just didn't care! And the worst part — aeldu save me, the *worst* part is I defended you. I believed you were better than Montès and all the rest, but the whole time—" I spat on the floor. "When did you decide you might love me? Before or after I let you fuck me?"

Finally, finally, his expression broke — a second before Fendul put his hunting knife to Parr's throat.

"Your choice, Kako."

A trickle of blood ran past Parr's collarbone. The words burned on my tongue. *Kill him. Make him bleed into the ground. Kill him.*

Parr twisted. Before I knew what was happening, Fendul was

face-down on the floor with Parr's knee on his back and the knife at his neck.

I bit back a scream. Fendul lay perfectly still even as Parr gripped his hair.

My pulse beat against the bogmoss in my right arm. The wound wasn't as bad as my leg, but the bandage felt too tight. *One clean throw.* I shifted my knife to my left hand.

Parr's eyes flickered from my blade to my face. "Kateiko." My name was dead ash in his mouth. Wind stirred his hair around his shoulders. "Before. I loved you before."

The knife trembled at Fendul's neck. Parr couldn't do it. Not in front of me. But if he ever got ahold of the Okorebai-Rin again — I remembered his words the day Baliad Iyo was sentenced to death. *I will be dead before I give up.*

"I believe you," I said.

I threw my hunting knife. It spun through the void between us.

Parr flung himself sideways. The blade sailed past and crashed into something across the room. Fendul rolled, scrambling out of the way.

In the same moment, water froze into a spike in my right hand. *One clean throw.*

The ice thudded into Parr's chest. Fendul's knife clattered to the floor. Parr looked down and wiped away a trickle of blood as if in a dream. His eyes met mine just before he crumpled.

I leaned forward and fell into the abyss. I sank fast as a stone and drifted light as snow, arms spread like wings. The walls of the gorge rushed past, blurring, fading into greyness. Nothing else. No air, no light, no voices. Just endless space below.

We are falling, all of us falling one by one.

35.

INK & IRON

"Kako."

A star winked in the abyss. I reached toward the icy light as I fell. It split into a thousand threads, weaving up my arm, cool and gentle as water.

"It's okay, Kako. We're okay."

I stopped plummeting. Like a bird pulling up from a dive, I began to rise. The walls of the gorge fell away. The sky opened blue and infinite.

Fendul's arms were around me. I was shaking. I slumped against him as dry sobs racked my chest. *I won't cry. I won't cry for you.*

He held me tight, but soon pulled back and gripped my shoulder. "I'm sorry, Kako, but we need to go."

My eyes wandered the room. It was speckled with lights — the blue irumoi in Fendul's hand, sputtering orange candle flames, white moonlight dappled with shadows. A moth bobbed near the shattered window. The spike in Parr's chest had melted. He stared at the ceiling, black hair fanned out around his shoulders, a dark pool staining the floor.

I looked away, fighting back the urge to throw up. "How badly did he hurt you?"

Fendul grimaced. "Dislocated my shoulder. Couldn't fly properly, but I popped it back in place. Listen — can anything in this place be traced back to you?"

"I . . . I don't . . . A note. He left me a note."

"Go look for it. I'll find your weapons. Take these for now." He pressed his hunting knife and the irumoi into my hands.

I crept through the manor. The corridors were suffocating tunnels. Candle brackets emerged from the gloom like bats clinging to the walls. I leapt into a doorway when the ceiling groaned, but nothing else made a sound.

The faces in the portrait hall looked pale as corpses, washed out by the glowing mushrooms. Sombre eyes watched me pass. I tried not to look, but the painting of the boy in the black elk-sigil coat snagged me. He felt the slightest bit familiar, but I couldn't work out if he looked like Nonil. Maybe there was just something of Parr in his face. I wondered where he was, when he'd learn about his father's death, if he'd return to this sepulchre of a home.

"I'm sorry," I whispered.

I blinked fast and hurried to the white room. The bed had been remade, its sheets and blankets neatly tucked, but the note was on the table where I left it. I stuffed it into my purse, avoiding my reflection in the framed mirror.

Outside, wisps of cloud drifted in front of the moon, diluting the light into a dull glaze. Broken glass glittered on the flagstone. Anwea whinnied when I approached. My hands shook too hard to untether her, so I gave up and dropped the reins. "I can't," I told Fendul. "I just — can't yet."

I stumbled away to the willows and pushed aside curtains of leaves. The wind called my name, insistent. I emerged into waves of rippling grass, crumpled to my knees, and screamed. I screamed until my throat was raw and a flock of birds rose screeching. There was nowhere to hide here, no walls, no cocoons nurturing secrets. Just aching, bruising truth.

Fendul found me on my back with stalks dancing at the edge of my vision. He slumped next to me. The kinaru constellation in the north seemed to be watching us.

"I wish I knew sooner," he said. "I wish I put my sword through his heart before he ever met you."

I drew a spiral of water in the air. "Sverbians name weapons after they take a life. How do you name a weapon that doesn't exist anymore?"

"You don't, I guess. You let the weapon go and keep the memory."

"What if I don't want the memory?"

"I don't think we get to choose." He tore up a rustling handful of grass.

"Tiernan said Ferish believe some spirits go into the sky and some into the ground." I split the spiral in the middle. Half drifted toward the clouds and turned into mist. The other half sank into the dirt. I rubbed my eyes with my wrists, the only part of my hands not covered in grime. "I told myself I wouldn't cry for him."

"Cry for you. Cry because it's your pain, your grief, your anger. Cry because no one else gets to decide how you mourn."

I rolled onto my side and drew my knees to my chest. Like a downpour you can taste coming, my tears broke free for the second time that day. Not the elegant tears of women in folk tales, but messy, wild tears that made my lungs burn and nose run and chest ache. Fendul stroked my hair until my sobbing faded into quiet gasps.

"I can't go back to Toel," I said when I could breathe. "Not tonight."

"We have to get away from here. The city guards saw us come this way."

"I know. Just not Toel. I . . . think I know somewhere we can go."

He nodded. "All right. We'll go back in the morning."

We cut across the Roannveldt to the south, avoiding farms and a sleeping village. Fendul walked and I rode, trying to ignore the stinging in my thigh. Anwea's head drooped and her tail swished slowly. I guessed at the direction, so it was a relief when a collapsed fence loomed out of the darkness. An alder rose like a rustling cairn above overgrown grass.

"This is where I found you," Fendul said with sudden recognition.

A dirt path led from the pasture to a timber farmhouse. Its door hung open, creaking in the wind. The garden was choked with weeds. A weasel darted under a bush as we approached.

Fendul climbed the porch steps and glanced inside, holding up the irumoi. "Looks like they're not coming back. Most of their things are gone."

"A lot of people moved away when the war came west." I rubbed Anwea's neck. "I'll be there soon. Yell if anyone comes."

Flies buzzed up when I entered the barn. It reeked of rotting hay and dung. I lit a rushlight I found by the door and searched through rusted tools until I found a brush. The familiar motions of cleaning Anwea's coat calmed me almost as much as her. I filled the water trough in the yard and tethered her away from the stench.

Orange light flickered from the farmhouse window. I crossed the porch and paused in the doorway. The place was an empty shell. Rough wooden furniture, a chipped clay bowl on a shelf, a mouldering onion in a bin. Dirt had drifted under the door and sunk into the floorboards. A candle stump guttered on the mantel, filling the air with the meaty smell of tallow.

I rested my head on the doorframe. Fendul leaned against the wall, staring out through a grimy window framed by faded curtains. With his back to the candle, I could barely see his face. The resin on his chest was almost black.

"I'm sorry," I said. "Tiernan warned me. Iannah, too. They knew not to trust Parr."

He shook his head. "I should be the one apologizing."

"What do you mean?" I stepped inside and shut the door.

Fendul pushed off the wall and paced across the room. "I knew about the Rúonbattai."

My breath caught. "It's true then."

"The Rin and Iyo both allied with them. I can't . . . deny what Parr said. They were brutal. So were the Ferish. We were desperate. The Bronnoi Ridge fire wasn't an accident, nor were our dug-up burial grounds, gutted wolves left on the Colonnium steps . . . it goes on."

"What about waking the saidu?"

He pinched his temples. "That's true, too. The Iyo pulled out of the alliance when Liet suggested it. We refused at first, but after Suriel used Ferish mercenaries to massacre the Rúonbattai, my father decided we had no choice. We figured out in a year what the Rúonbattai had been working on for fourteen. Suriel didn't try as hard to stop us. I suppose he didn't want to kill children of the kinaru."

I collapsed onto a chair, stretching out my aching legs. "What went wrong?"

"The saidu argued over whether to interfere in human affairs. Some said it was their job to protect us from outsiders. Others were afraid of turning out like Suriel, too involved with us. We think being dormant disoriented them. Normally when saidu fight, one surrenders, but this time one killed another, and . . ."

"A locust plague. That's how Wotelem described it. The first death set them off on a rampage." I picked at my unravelling bandages. "How *did* we wake—"

"That's the one thing my father never told me. He didn't want this to ever happen again."

"Why did no one ever talk about this — not even my parents—"

Fendul rubbed the ink lines on his arm. "Most Rin didn't know. We never fought for the Rúonbattai. Just gave them info, resources, passage through Anwen Bel. Same with the Iyo here in their territory."

"You have to tell the Rin-jouyen. They have to know why so many people died today."

"I know, Kako. But . . . we already had a schism once, and . . ."

"Fen." I stared at him. "What is it?"

Fendul stopped pacing. "The Dona-jouyen didn't come back to settle on our land. They found out we were continuing Liet's plan. I guess they thought going to war with us, their blood relatives, was better than interfering with nature."

"They—" I slumped onto the table. "Aeldu curse us all."

I'd been collecting iron links since I left home, but could never join them into anything that made sense. Now they melted, twisted, forged into a chain — the whole bloody history of the Rin-jouyen.

When I looked up, Fendul was on the floor with his back against the wall, head in his hands. "Fen. Are you okay?"

"I shouldn't talk about it now. You're hurting."

"So are you." I pushed off the chair and sat next to him.

He ran a hand over his face. "I know how Nili felt last year. I wanted to kill Parr. That kind of anger . . . terrifies me. But I should've done it so you didn't have to."

"I'm glad it was me." I gazed into shadows among the ceiling rafters. "If you killed him, I might've spent the rest of my life hating
you. Resenting you for deciding for me."

"You might hate me anyway before this war is out. This is my
life now. Dealing with our enemies and making impossible decisions.
I'm going to mess up sometime."

"No one expects you to be perfect."

He sighed. "I know today wasn't my fault. But I keep thinking
. . . I brought the Rin here. It was supposed to make things better.
Instead it made us an easy target."

I chewed my lip. "Nei. If the Corvittai attacked us in Anwen Bel,
Rhonos couldn't have warned us. The Iyo wouldn't have been there
to help. We'd *all* be dead."

"Everything leads back to death though. Ever since the fighting
that led up to the First Elken War. We've been stuck in a spiral for
a hundred years and I don't know how to stop it." Fendul stuck his
hunting knife into the floor. "Look how we grew up. The next generation will be just like us."

I picked his knife up and spun it around. "Who did you kill?
Before today."

"The Dona scout that got into Aeti Ginu. My uncle said he killed
her so no one could accuse my parents of involving me in the war."

"I remember that." I set the knife down. He'd been fourteen, just
like Yironem.

"I don't know what to do, Kako. We have to defend ourselves,
but it feels wrong putting a sword in a nine-year-old's hands. I'm
supposed to protect the Rin and I don't know how in Aeldu-yan to
do that." Fendul's shoulders shook. He rubbed the heels of his palms
into his eyes. "I thought I'd have my father longer than this—"

"Oh, Fen." I slid my arm around him. "You don't have to be
strong all the time."

He twisted around to bury his face into my shoulder, and then it was my turn to stroke his hair as he cried. I remembered finding him in our plank house after his mother was brought back to Aeti Ginu. I held his hand, and for three whole days we didn't argue.

When his tears ran dry, I kissed his hair and gently pulled away. "Stay there."

I got up with a wince, took the chipped bowl from the shelf, and held it upside down over the smoky candle, casting the room into darkness. Heat radiated over my hands. I tipped the bowl up to check as the smooth clay turned black.

"Kako," was all Fendul said.

The soot flaked into dust when I scraped my hunting knife through it. I washed my hands in a basin, scrubbing off all the grime and blood, then called a drop of water into the bowl and stirred it with my knife. I sat next to Fendul, washed his upper right arm, and unfolded the silk packet from my purse.

Somehow the bone needle had survived. If my parents were watching from Aeldu-yan, I didn't think they'd mind me using their wedding needle for this. I took a deep breath and dipped the point into the black ink.

Fendul sucked in a breath as I pierced his skin next to the interlocking lines. His muscles tensed, but he was silent as I filled in the pattern. Dip, jab, repeat. I wiped away the blood with the silk square. The okorebai tattoo was designed so it could be completed any time, by anyone. After the Okorebai-Rin died in the First Elken War, Fendul's great-great-grandmother had been tattooed on the battlefield with healing supplies.

The pale silk was mottled black when I finished. I rinsed the lines, tore a clean strip of cottonspun from the bandage on my thigh, and wrapped it around his raw skin. "I don't know what the words are."

"You don't have to say anything. This is enough."

I washed everything and dumped the water over the porch, pausing to close my eyes and breathe cool night air. Back inside, I stood and just looked at Fendul. He'd turned twenty-one in midwinter while we were apart. He'd grown into a man, but I'd never seen him that way until now. He'd always been the boy I grew up with.

He stared straight ahead, elbows on his knees. "I'm the youngest Okorebai-Rin in longer than I know. First time in six generations we haven't had an Okoreni-Rin."

"That's easy to fix." I twisted my braid. "Aliko's been trying to get your attention for years. Ai, she's even pretty."

"Aliko's as dumb as a rock."

I laughed. "Is that how you talk about me behind my back?"

"No. That's how I talk about you to your face."

I slid down the wall on his left so I didn't bump his tattoo. The candle sputtered and went out. Fendul fumbled at his side and pulled out the irumoi. The blue glow wrapped around us like a blanket. I undid my hair ribbon and untangled the vines from my braid.

"Did you love him?" he asked. "Parr, I mean."

"Nei." I rested my head against the wall. "I liked him. A lot. After Tiernan . . . it was nice to be wanted."

Fendul set the irumoi on the floor. His breathing quickened. He knelt in front of me and took my hands. His skin felt scratched and raw. "Marry me."

"*What?*"

"Marry me. Stay with the Rin."

I choked with laughter. "I betrayed the man I love — I killed the first man I slept with — and you want to *marry* me?"

"We might not love each other like that. But I do love you, in a way. We trust each other, and — you know I'll never leave. Or try to kill you."

"Oh, Fennel," I said softly.

"I need your help, Kako. I can't do this without you." His hands tightened around mine. "I need someone who's not afraid to tell me when I'm wrong. You never let me off just because I was okoreni. You pushed me to do better."

"I can't help you, Fen. When I left Aeti I thought I knew what to do, but I *don't*, not at all. Look at me — I've fucked up everything—"

"You did some stupid things. I won't lie. But we have to get out of this spiral. We have to stop tearing each other apart and build ties with anyone we can, even the Ferish. Especially them. You already did that. Parr betrayed you — but Rhonos and Iannah haven't." Fendul wove his fingers into mine. "We will mess up. It's bound to happen. But we have to do *something* different. Maybe you and I can figure it out together."

"I hope you're better at leading the jouyen than you are at romance."

He looked down and smiled. "I haven't had any practice with either."

I bit my lip. "Isu wanted me to marry you."

"I know. But that's not why I'm asking."

"Fennel." I pulled one hand free and tipped his chin up. My fingers wandered from his jaw to his crow amulet. The faint light of the irumoi made his skin seem to glow from inside out. I was curious — maybe because this would be my only chance.

I kissed him. He returned it hesitantly, reaching up to stroke my hair. His lips were warm and soft, and even this part of him I'd never touched felt familiar. Some part of me that was lonely and aching whispered *say yes*.

But another part was louder.

"I'm sorry, Fen. I can't marry you. Not now." I ran my thumb over the carved crow. "I love you, but I'm too much of a mess. I need time. I'm not . . . over Tiernan. Not really."

"Stay with the Rin, at least."

"I will for a while. Until we sort out . . . all this. But I'm not sure I can stay forever."

Fendul nodded. The strands of my hair fell from his fingers. He sat back against the wall, his arm brushing mine.

We lapsed into silence. I closed my eyes and listened to the ebb of the wind, the drone of a mosquito, Fendul's breathing slow and deep next to me. Rain beat down on the roof and faded again.

When I woke, my head was on Fendul's shoulder. I rubbed my stiff neck and stretched. The farmhouse was hazy blue, a muddle of light and shadow. Fendul didn't stir as I stood and cursed the pain in my thigh.

I wandered outside into cool, damp air. Anwea nickered and went on chomping grass. Fat drops of dew clung to the porch. I leaned on the railing and watched the sky turn pink. A wren warbled. The world sharpened, turning clear with the dawn.

The door creaked. Fendul came to stand beside me. He'd peeled the resin off his chest, leaving a deep gash flaking blood, and taken the bandage off his tattoo. "I'm so hungry I almost want to eat that rotting onion."

"Me too. Wish I could eat grass."

He rested his elbows on the railing. "How long do you think you'll stay?"

I pressed my fingers to my lips. "A month? I can promise that much."

He nodded slowly. "A month it is, then."

I looked up at his serious face. "Ai, let me see your identification." Fendul took the card from his pocket. I peered at the letters below the red elk sigil. "Your second name is listed as Rin."

"I don't know what you expected."

"I don't know either."

He slid his arm around my waist as light erupted over jagged peaks. Streaks of pink clouds radiated across the sky, glowing gold over the mountains. "What are you going to do after a month?"

"Settle things with Tiernan. Beyond that . . ." I ran a finger through the dew. "It feels like the whole world's spread out around me, and it's just . . . empty. The only thing is this storm beyond the horizon. I can't see it yet, and I don't know what will happen when it hits. But I have to be ready."

36.

TRUTHS

It was the smell of burning flesh I'd remember most of all. The Iyo had worked through the night cutting and drying wood. I'd heard of pyres being used in the Elken Wars, but never seen one. There were nine on the cliffs, massive structures of arrow-straight spruce in criss-crossing layers, with pine branches for kindling. The Corvittai were laid in rows on top.

"Ninety-seven, including the ones at the lake," Airedain said when he returned Nurivel. His eyes were bloodshot, his crest of hair tousled. "If there were more, they fled."

Tokoda ignited three pyres. The Tamu lit another three. After Fendul did two, he passed the torch to me. I ignited the pyre with Nonil's body. *Fire in life, fire in death.*

The Tamu were taking their dead back to Tamun Dael. A group of Iyo had dug graves for the Rin in South Iyun, each at the foot of an old rioden. The triangular site was near a junction between two streams. The third side was open — an invitation to expand the burial ground if needed. The Iyo had gathered crow feathers, too. They remembered.

Dunehein and I performed Isu's burial rites together. We each cut one of her palms and spoke the death rites. He couldn't climb into the grave with his wounded leg, so Rikuja helped me place Isu's body in the ground. I turned her palms skyward so she could receive the earth, then laid a crow feather on each side of her. I carved a kinaru in the rioden, and Dunehein carved Isu's tiger lily crest around it.

Hiyua finished guiding another burial at the same time for a Rin woman with no relatives. She came over to give me a hug. The smell of fish oil reminded me not just of my mother, but of Isu, too.

"I still remember the day we buried Aoreli," Hiyua said. "I thought I'd done something terribly wrong. Why else would the aeldu take my eldest daughter away? But they must've forgiven me, for it seems I have two daughters again — if you'll have me."

I couldn't speak around the lump in my throat. I just nodded.

Behadul was the last to be buried. Someone had brought kinaru feathers from the lake — pure black wing primaries, as long as a person's arm. Only five of us knew why Fendul asked Yironem to lay them in the grave. They looked like swords, the same colour that Behadul's grey braid once was.

One of the worst parts, I thought as I gazed at raw patches of soil in the underbrush, was viirelei and itherans didn't know each other's funeral rites. When jouyen went to war, they knew to burn anything stained with the blood of the dead. I wondered if the Corvittai would care if they knew. I wondered what we didn't know about them.

❋

Tokoda granted us use of the visitors' plank houses. There were fifty beds a house, but no one wanted to be apart, so we crammed in one and spread extra bedding on the floor. We shared food, tended the wounded, comforted children who had no surviving relatives. For every person old enough to have attuned, two more hadn't.

Fendul gathered the Rin by the hearth that evening. Not just current Rin, but everyone who married into the Iyo, plus their families. I stood next to him, our people seated on bark mats around us, as we explained everything. The arguing lasted well into the night, long after the children fell asleep and oil lanterns were lit. A few people demanded we elect a new okorebai. I said they might all be dead if Fendul hadn't made amends with the Iyo. One woman threatened to go with her son on the next boat leaving Toel Ginu. Hiyua said no jouyen outside the Aikoto Confederacy had any obligation to protect them. By sunrise, Fendul was still okorebai and we still had sixty-two Rin.

Elkhounds showed up soon after, demanding to speak with the viirelei seen leaving Caladheå to the southeast the night Parr was killed. Tokoda refused to let them enter Toel Ginu until they relinquished their spears. At the central firepit, surrounded by people, Fendul told them that we went straight from Falwen's office to the pyre site. Airedain and Jonalin confirmed we'd spent the rest of the night helping gather the dead. Tokoda, arms crossed, said that if the Elkhounds were more suspicious of two injured viirelei than a company of Corvittai, the Caladheå guard was more broken than their spears were about to be.

At my request, Airedain left to find Tiernan and tell him Parr admitted to killing Marijka. I hoped he could convince Tiernan not to go after Suriel. I hoped it wasn't already too late.

Five Rin died of their wounds. Five more burials. Three Rin

attuned. Counting Yironem, there'd be at least four initiations at the autumn equinox.

Mostly, I was too busy to think. Yironem helped me set snares and forage food. I made willowcloak and tulanta tinctures, dried wood for fires, gathered bogmoss for dressing wounds. Two young girls who'd been orphaned in the battle tagged along. Anwea tolerated them stroking her smooth coat, and only tried to eat the girls' hair once.

Nili sat outside, sun or rain, stitching cottonspun so people could burn their bloodstained clothes. I saw the pain in her face whenever she moved her injured leg. She supervised her own group of tag-alongs as they embroidered cloth scraps or wove bark, anything to keep them busy. Segowa spent a day with them before returning to Caladheå.

Only once did Nili cry, late at night when everyone was asleep. She showed me two pieces of black cloth that drummers wore around their wrists, half-embroidered with sprays of rioden needles. "I was making them for Taworen for the equinox. I don't know what to do with them now."

"You don't have to decide right away," I said. "But if he's in Aeldu-yan, he'll be happy if you finish them."

Envoys arrived from other Aikoto jouyen — the southern Yula and Kae okoreni first, Tamu next, northern Beru and Haka two days later, all accompanied by three or four other members of their jouyen. No doubt they'd attuned to travel so fast. A few fights broke out around firepits. There hadn't been a meeting of the entire confederacy since the Third Elken War, the year Fendul was born.

Fendul asked Hiyua and me to attend the summit. Tokoda promised us protection so we could speak freely. The Iyo outnumbered all other jouyen and no one seemed keen to challenge them on their land. Still, Tokoda forbade weapons in the gathering place where the summit was held and posted guards by the Rin plank house.

Even after seeing the Council inquiry, I couldn't have imagined how complicated it was to coordinate seven jouyen. The southern ones resented the northern ones for our absence from the Third Elken War. The Kae criticized our alliance with the Rúonbattai, saying Sverbians committed as many war crimes as Ferish, while the Yula criticized us for not bringing them into the alliance. The Beru defended our decision to wake the saidu, which angered the others more. The Haka made a less-than-subtle threat to move into Anwen Bel, prompting a threat of retaliation from the Tamu, who occupied its coast.

Fendul mainly just listened. Tokoda and Wotelem always referred to him as Okorebai-Rin, and by the end of the summit's first day everyone did the same. No one cared we had killed an itheran politician except to worry about the impact of viirelei being blamed. As the weather cycled through sun, rain, and hail that battered the roof so hard we could barely hear, the summit turned to practical issues — learning about the Corvittai, connecting with the Nuthalha and Kowichelk confederacies, keeping our own jouyen from killing each other.

Dealing with Suriel was more complicated. A Kae had flown over the mountains and felt traces of a tel-saidu, but didn't know exactly where, or if it was even Suriel. The eastern winds stayed mild. I spoke more during that part of the summit, explaining what I knew of shoirdrygen and the void. With no room for argument in his voice, Fendul said Tiernan was to be left alone. I suggested making contact with Ingdanrad's mages and to my surprise everyone agreed.

The envoys left the next morning. It was a blessing to be outside after so many days in dim light and still air. Dunehein and Rikuja came by the Rin plank house that evening while I was washing a basket of brassroot. They spoke to Fendul away from the firepits before sitting with me.

"We decided something," Dunehein said with a nervous smile at Rikuja. "We're gonna join the Rin. The Okorebai-Rin just agreed."

I dropped the roots in the dirt and flung my arms around him. He squeezed my ribs so tight I couldn't breathe. "That's never happened, has it?" I asked. "Coming back to a jouyen after marrying out of it?"

"Not in the Rin," he said. "But we want our daughter to know what she came from. Someone's gotta keep our traditions going."

Rikuja kissed Sihaja's thin hair. "Right now I can't think about anything except how much I want to sleep, but the Rin will need help raising these children."

By the time Airedain returned, half a month had passed. We talked by the ocean, watching waves throw fountains of spray against the stone pillars. He'd tracked Tiernan down and, with Rhonos's help, persuaded him to hold off looking for Suriel. I wanted to tell Airedain about my relationship with Parr, but something in me curled into a tight ball every time I tried.

"I changed my mind," he said as we headed back to the plank houses. "You Rin are weirder than the Haka if you thought waking some ancient fucking spirits was a good idea."

It wasn't even that funny, but it felt good to laugh.

✳

On the trip north, I stopped at the battle site. People had taken to calling it the Blackbird Battle, two opposing sides with kinaru as their crests. The pyres had burned to almost nothing, just swaths of blackened earth with bits of bone and crumbling wood. I stripped the branches from a wind-thrown sapling and strung up my Iyo flag. The soot was smudged, but the dolphin, outstretched like the Rin kinaru, was still visible as the pale linen snapped in the wind.

By the time I reached Caladheå, it was raining. I kept my hood up, my tattoos hidden. People flowed around me like fish dodging a shark. Airedain had warned me that itherans still suspected viirelei of murdering one of their most well-liked councillors.

The first place I went was the Blackened Oak. Nhys said last he'd heard, Tiernan was at his cabin with Rhonos. The second place was the bookstore in the square, to buy a book to pass the time on my upcoming journey. The third was Natzo's noodle shop.

For a moment I thought Iannah would punch me again. We went to the old Shawnaast docks and sat in an abandoned boat-house, dangling our bare feet in cold water cast greenish-black by the shadows. Rain drummed on salt-stained walls and bounced off tilted docks covered with barnacles.

"I got . . . inklings," she said. "I've been at the Colonnium longer than Parr and never learned any of his secrets. That's what made me suspicious."

I pulled his crumpled note from my purse. "What does this part at the end say?"

She smoothed it out on her breeches and skimmed his bold, narrow writing. "It's an old Ferish quote. From a poem. 'I know not where this light leads me, only that the sea will hold me up until I arrive.' It's . . . I think it's about finding love in unexpected places."

"In Sverbian myth, there's a torch on the ferry to the land of the dead. Tiernan named his sword after it." I tore up the paper and dropped the scraps into the water. "I guess we can speak the same language and still say different things."

Iannah tilted her head to look at me. "Airedain showed up at Natzo's a month ago."

"I asked him to find you. Tell you I was alive. But I wanted to apologize myself."

"I'm sorry for punching you." She fiddled with a rope tinted green by algae. "You were right. I hate it at the Colonnium. But I don't want people like Parr running it unchecked."

I kicked my feet through the water, watching weeds swirl in the murk. "You were right, too. I want to do better. Be better. I'm . . . leaving for a while."

"Where?"

"Ingdanrad. The Okoreni-Iyo is leading a delegation to figure out what to do about Suriel. He asked me to come since I met Suriel directly."

"There's something else you can look into there." She set down the rope. "I think I figured out who Nonil was. A Ferish soldier named Alesso Spariere resigned nine years ago, when he was seventeen. His former comrades said he was obsessed with mages. Envied their strength in battle. He was later spotted serving in Ingdanrad's militia, probably in exchange for studying magic. He might've found Tiernan's old work on rift magic and copied the methods."

"You think that's more likely than Nonil being Parr's son?"

"Officially, Nerio Parr left to serve in Ferland's military six years ago. Not sure if that's true. But if Nerio was at the Blackbird Battle, Parr would've done whatever it took to protect him."

I gazed out at white sails in the harbour, blurry through the rain. "There's still so much we don't know. But at least with Nonil dead and Suriel quiet, we might get a break."

"Maybe." Iannah leaned back on her hands. "The military's been finding empty camps in the mountains. I think Nonil pulled out most of the Corvittai to send against you. People will hear about the Rin-jouyen now."

"Ai, that reminds me." I took something from my purse and set it on the crumbling planks. "It's supposed to go on a mantelpiece to ward off spirits, but I got a Rin carver to make it small enough for you to wear."

Iannah picked up the thumbnail-sized kinaru, carved from the red wood of an alder, the same colour as her hair. Its wings were spread, a leather cord laced through its straight neck. She put the makiri over her head and tucked it under her coat. "When do you leave?"

"Tomorrow. I don't know when I'll be back in Caladheä. I should stay away for a while, in case anyone connects me to Parr."

She nodded. "You know where to find me."

✳

The rain faded as I rode into North Iyun. I found fireweed growing in a patch of sunlight, each stem as long as my arm. Tall and proud, the flower of warriors like in my tattoo. I gathered a handful of purple blossoms and scattered them on the creek where we sent Marijka off. The fireweed would be losing its flowers by the time I returned from Ingdanrad, the cottonwoods turning yellow, the first frost not long after that.

I made sure the clearing around Tiernan's cabin was empty before stepping out from the trees. There were bootprints in the mud and boards nailed over the workshop door. I lay in the wet grass, blades tickling my shoulders, and held up a hand. Afternoon sunlight bled through my skin. When I pressed my palms to my face, the burning man was seared inside my eyelids.

It was hard to drag myself up, but he could be back any time. I climbed the porch steps and pushed the door open. Dried mud crunched under my feet. The cabin was as sparse as always. Tiernan's and Rhonos's cloaks on nails, books on the shelves, a few pots on the wall. The shutters were closed, casting stripes of yellow light across the floor.

I placed a folded letter on the table. Iannah had guided my

spelling while I scrawled words in shaky handwriting and smudged ink. I set Marijka's wedding ring on the paper. The gold etching looked dull in the dim light.

Everything in the cabin spoke of Tiernan. I heard his voice in the still air. I ran my finger along the fireplace and came away with a smear of black soot, breathing the scent of woodsmoke and winter nights. Outside, I scraped at my carvings on the porch railing until the sun, wolf, and roof were gone, leaving just a dip in the wood. Sawdust drifted away and settled in the grass.

Anwea was grazing, brushing away flies with her tail. I put her in the stable and brushed the sweat and muck from her brown coat until it shone. "It really is goodbye this time, Anwea." I stood on my toes to kiss the white patch on her forehead. "Tiernan will look after you. This is the best place I can leave you."

She nickered and bumped her head against mine. I hoped that meant she understood.

I left as a wolf, darting between huge auburn pillars cloaked in brilliant moss and lichen, bounding off the carpet of scaly rioden needles. The sun was near the horizon by the time I made it to my old campsite. I'd stowed my book there with a cloth bundle, wanting a few hours alone before spending days in a canoe fleet with the Iyo.

I stripped off my clothes and wrapped my kinaru shawl around my body, curling my toes into the cool grass. The soft cottonspun felt like wings folding around me. I gazed at white sails silhouetted against orange sky. The sun sank until it kissed the ocean, never to truly meet.

Iren kohal. Rivers keep flowing. I'd travelled all the way from the mountains to the sea, but I'd just been drifting, caught in a current and barely keeping my head above water.

It was time to learn how to sail.

EPILOGUE

Tiernan,

I wanted to say this in person, but it's probably better this way.

It's true that Parr killed Marijka. He admitted it to my face. He came to warn us the Corvittai were looking for us, but he and Marijka argued instead, mostly because he wouldn't name his Corvittai source. He claimed he didn't mean to kill her.

I'm sorry for so many things. For causing your fight with Marijka, dealing with Suriel behind your back, and trusting Parr. I don't expect you to forgive me. I should've listened to you. Parr betrayed me, too, but I can't say anything else in case the wrong person reads this.

Don't be mad at Marijka. Wherever she is, she still loves you.

Please don't go after Suriel. I don't think he had anything to do with Marijka's death or the Blackbird Battle. I'm going to get help. Maybe there's a way out of all this. Take care of Anwea for me.

Thank you for everything. I wish I could explain how much our time together meant to me. I know you don't want to see me again, so I have to break my promise. I won't come back this time.

— *K*

GLOSSARY

etymology: A: Aikoto, F: Ferish, S: Sverbian

aeldu: spirits of the dead in Aikoto mythology

Aeldu-yan: land of the dead in Aikoto mythology

antayul: [A. *anta* water, *-yul* caller] viirelei who have learned to control water

attuning: shapeshifting into an animal; a rite of passage for viirelei adolescents

bloodweed: semi-poisonous leaves used as birth control by viirelei

bogmoss: moss used for dressing wounds; antiseptic and highly absorbent

Bøkkai: a god in the Sverbian pantheon who steals souls

Bøkkhem: [S. *Bøkkai, hem* flatlands] a barren land in Sverbian mythology

brännvin: [S. *bränn* burn, *vin* wine] several varieties of clear rye
   liquor, including vodka
Coast Trader: a pidgin trade language derived from Aikoto,
   Sverbian, Ferish, and others
Corvittai: [F. *corvide* blackbird, S. *vittai* ghost] Suriel's human
   soldiers
duck potato: underwater root of arrowhead plants; ground up
   for flour by viirelei
Elken Wars: a series of wars fought between Ferish colonists
   and a Sverbian-Aikoto alliance for control of the coast and its
   natural resources
Hafelús: [S. *hafe* ocean, *lús* light] Tiernan's sword, named after
   the mythical lantern on the ferry to the land of the dead
irumoi: a wooden rod covered with glowing blue mushrooms,
   used as a light source
itheran: [S. *ithera* "out there"] viirelei term for foreign colonists
Jinben: [A. *jin* sun, *benro* meet] Aikoto summer solstice festival
jinrayul: [A. *jinra* fire, *-yul* caller] mages who have learned to
   control fire
jouyen: viirelei tribe(s) typically belonging to a confederacy
kinaru: giant waterfowl sacred to tel-saidu and the Rin-jouyen
makiri: Aikoto charms carved in the shape of animals that protect
   a home from cruel spirits
needlemint: evergreen-scented leaves native to Sverba; used as
   numbing painkiller
Nurivel: [A. "shimmer of light on water"] Kateiko's throwing dagger
okorebai: political, spiritual, and military leader of a jouyen
okoreni: successor to an okorebai, typically passed from parent to
   child
pann: a denomination of the sovereign currency; 100 pann to
   1 sovereign

plank house: a large building and social unit of the Aikoto, housing up to ten families

rioden: massive auburn conifer trees used for dugout canoes, buildings, bark weaving, etc.

Rúonbattai: [S. *rúon* rain, *battai* guard] radical Sverbian militant group who swore to drive off the Ferish, but mysteriously vanished several years after the Third Elken War

saidu: spirits that control the weather and maintain balance in nature

ANTA-SAIDU (WATER), EDIM-SAIDU (EARTH AND PLANTS), JINRA-SAIDU (FIRE), TEL-SAIDU (AIR)

sancte: Ferish holy building

shoirdryge: [S. *shoird* shard, *ryge* realm] parallel world that splintered off from other worlds

Skaarnaht: [S. *skaar* red, *naht* night] Sverbian new year festival

sovereign: a form of currency introduced by the Sverbian monarchy

stavehall: Sverbian holy building

stjolvehl: [S. *stjolv* shield, *-ehl* female] Sverbian bride's guardian

stjolvind: [S. *stjolv* shield, *-ind* male] Sverbian groom's guardian

Thaerijmur: land of the dead in Sverbian mythology

tulanta: hallucinogenic painkiller made from tularem leaves; used by viirelei

viirelei: [A. *vii* they, *rel* of, *leiga* west] colonists' term for coastal indigenous people, including the Aikoto, Nuthalha, and Kowichelk confederaries

War of the Wind: war between Eremur's army and Suriel, fought for control of border lands

Yanben: [A. *yan* world, *benro* meet] Aikoto winter solstice festival when the worlds of the living and dead unite

PHRASES, SLANG, PROFANITY

akesida, akesidal: Aikoto terms for "young woman," "young man"

Antlers: slang for Colonnium guards

Elkhounds: slang for Caladheå city guards

hanekei: [A. "it is the first time we meet"] formal Aikoto greeting

hijke: casual Sverbian greeting

ikken naeja: [S. *ikken* enough, *naeja* lacking] protest slogan, lit.
  "not enough"

iren kohal: [A. *iren* river, *koro* flow] Kateiko's mantra, lit. "rivers
  keep flowing"

kaid: any insult to the aeldu, used as strong profanity by the Aikoto

kujinna kobairen: [A. *kujinna* today, *kii* we, *obairo* "to fly"] Rin
  battle cry, lit. "today we fly"

någva: [S. "to fuck"] highly versatile Sverbian profanity;
  adjective form is *någvakt*

pigeon: slur for itherans

rettai: shapeshifting spirits in Sverbian mythology; slur for viirelei

takuran: [A. *taku* shit] highly offensive slur alluding to Aikoto
  burial rites, referencing someone so foul they must be buried in
  shit because dirt rejects their blood

tema: Aikoto affectionate term for "mother"

temal: Aikoto affectionate term for "father"

wood witch: slur for viirelei, referencing their shapeshifting abilities

yan taku: [A. *yan* world, *taku* shit] profanity with religious
  connotations

CULTURES

Aikoto: [A. *ainu* mountain, *ko* flow, *toel* coast] A confederacy of
  seven (formerly eight) jouyen occupying a large region of
  coastal rainforest.

Ferish: Colonists from Ferland who landed on the west coast of the Aikoto's continent. Later, a mass exodus from Ferland of famine victims caused a population boom in Aikoto lands.

INDUSTRIES: wheat farming, manufacturing, naval trading.

RELIGION: monotheist.

Kowichelk: A confederacy of jouyen in the rainforest south of the Aikoto. Largely wiped out from disease brought by foreign colonists.

Nuthalha: A confederacy of jouyen in the tundra north of the Aikoto. Largely isolated.

Sverbians: Settlers from Sverba who landed on the east coast of the Aikoto's continent, migrated west, and later allied with the Aikoto against the Ferish.

INDUSTRIES: rye farming, goat herding, logging.

RELIGION: polytheist.

AIKOTO JOUYEN: NORTH

Beru-jouyen: "People of the sea." Live in Meira Dael on the coast of Nokun Bel.

CREST: grey whale.

INDUSTRIES: whaling, soapstone carving.

Dona-jouyen: "Nomad people." Lived in Anwen Bel. Formed when members of the Rin and Iyo split off. Wiped out in a recent war with the Rin.

CREST: white seagull.

INDUSTRIES: none.

Haka-jouyen: "People of the frost." Live inland in Nokun Bel.

CREST: brown grizzly bear.

INDUSTRIES: fur trapping, tanning.

Rin-jouyen: "People of the lakeshore." Live in Aeti Ginu in central Anwen Bel. Oldest jouyen in the Aikoto. Large in territory and influence, but small in population these days.

INDUSTRIES: woodcarving, embroidery, fur trapping.

Tamu-jouyen: "People of the peninsulas." Live in Tamun Dael on the coast of Anwen Bel.

CREST: orange shark.

INDUSTRIES: fishing, boatcraft.

AIKOTO JOUYEN: SOUTH

Iyo-jouyen: "People of the surrounds." Live in Toel Ginu and Caladheå on the coast of Iyun Bel. Largest and most powerful jouyen in the Aikoto. Historic allies with the Rin.

CREST: blue dolphin.

INDUSTRIES: stone carving, textiles.

Kae-jouyen: "People of the inlet." Live on the coast of Ukan Bel alongside Burren Inlet.

CREST: green heron.

INDUSTRIES: fishing.

Yula-jouyen: "People of the valley." Live inland in Ukan Bel in a network of river valleys.

CREST: copper fox.

INDUSTRIES: weaving.

A BRIEF HISTORY OF EREMUR
AND SURROUNDING LANDS

-70	The Iyo-jouyen constructs a shrine in Toel Ginu, one of the oldest surviving buildings in the Aikoto Confederacy.
-60	Sverbian sailors land on the east coast of the Aikoto's continent and begin migrating west.
1	The Sverbian monarchy introduces a new calendar, marking the birth of an empire.
428	Sverba founds the province of Nyhemur across the mountains from Aikoto lands. The two groups begin trading.
487	Ferish sailors land in Aikoto territory. They clash violently

with Aikoto and Sverbians over trade routes and natural resources.

513   Barros Sanguero, lord of the New Ferland Trading Company (NFTC), builds the Colonnium stronghold in Iyo territory. He quickly dominates regional trade.

❋

533   FIRST ELKEN WAR

Sverbians and Aikoto ally to drive out the Ferish. Fighting spans the entire Aikoto coast. Some Rin and Iyo refuse to go to war and instead split off to form the nomadic Dona-jouyen.

The Sverbian-Aikoto alliance kills Sanguero and repels the NFTC. Iyo, Rin, and Sverbian settlers build a fort around the captured Colonnium to ensure Ferish soldiers cannot retake it. They name the fort Caladheå.

❋

545   Sverba founds the province of Eremur in Aikoto territory, declares Caladheå the capital, and establishes a local military. The Aikoto Confederacy refuses to recognize these actions.

547   Famine hits Ferland. Thousands of Ferish immigrants flee overseas to Eremur and nearby lands. Caladheå blooms into an international trading port.

557-8 SECOND ELKEN WAR

A Ferish naval captain attempts to retake the Colonnium and claim land for new immigrants. The Sverbian-Aikoto alliance nearly defeats him — until his soldiers raze Bronnoi Ridge, the Aikoto district in Caladheå. The Rin-jouyen abandons the city and returns north.

Sverba agrees to share control of Eremur with Ferland via an elected Council. The Iyo surrender Bronnoi Ridge in exchange for land and housing in the Ashtown slums. Sverbian dissenters form the Rúonbattai, a radical militant group, and vow to drive out the Ferish.

604-5 THIRD ELKEN WAR

An influenza epidemic ravages Eremur, killing thousands. Ferish rebels, angry about treaties from the previous war, take advantage of the weakened military and hold a coup. The Rúonbattai have a resurgence of support and retaliate against the Ferish rebels.

The war-torn Rin and other northern jouyen refuse to come south and fight, breaking the Aikoto alliance. The Iyo temporarily abandon Caladheå. After great losses, the Council regains control of the city.

606   Several Sverbian mages, accused of helping the Rúonbattai massacre Ferish immigrants, are murdered in Council custody. The mage city Ingdanrad cuts diplomatic ties to Eremur.

618   The Rúonbattai vanish with no explanation.

619   The Dona-jouyen return to Rin territory. The Rin declare war and eradicate the Dona. Soon after, devastating storms hit Rin territory, known as the Storm Year.

623   A military expedition from Caladheå is massacred in Dúnravn Pass. A few survivors and the Iyo claim the air spirit Suriel was responsible.

625   A logging camp near Dúnravn Pass is massacred. Nearby townsfolk suspect Suriel's return.

ACKNOWLEDGEMENTS

My gratitude to the following:

Rob Masson, my husband in all but name, for your abiding love and support. My compass will always point to you.

Susan Renouf, my editor, for your wise insights (and patience while I realized you were right). David Caron for believing in this series. Everyone else at ECW who graced these pages with hard work and creativity.

Simon Carr, my cover illustrator, and Tiffany Munro, my cartographer, for your beautiful and attentive artwork. Robert Williams of the Haida for your thoughtful consultation.

Michael Knudson, Jessica Smith #453, and the rest of the Cythera crew. Roy Leon, fellow Metallist (THALL); Rochelle Jardine, my secret agent; and the rest of the Squid Squad. You guys are my *Canterbury Tales* companions.

Kathleen and Douglas, my parents, for helping me through

university where this project began. Florence and Nic, my siblings, for absurd science (conclusion: magically heating water would freeze the caster to death).

Dr. Rob Budde for showing me the breadth of CanLit. Dr. Dee Horne for invaluable advice on this book's first draft. Jackson 2bears of the Kanien'kehaka (Mohawk) and Luke Parnell of the Haida and Nisga'a for teaching me how to blend old and new culture.

The Lheidli T'enneh, in whose territory this novel was started; the Wurundjeri, in whose territory it was finished; and the nations of the Northwest Coast, in whose territory it's set.

The youth of today, because you're the leaders of tomorrow.